Toxic Obsession

A Whitmore Elite Standalone

J.A. Owenby

Download Your FREE BOOK!

Trigger Warning

Please click here to visit my website for TWs including mental TW or copy and paste https://authorjaowenby.com/about/toxic-obses sion/

Playlist

Bad Idea by Dove Cameron
Kings Never Die by Eminem and Gwen Stefani
Welcome to My Life by qwinn
Call it Love by Felix Jaehn and Ray Dalton
Oxytocin by Chandler Leighton
Drinking With Cupid by Voila
The Devil I Know by Allie X
You Should See Me in A Crown by Billie Eilish
Love on the Brain by Rihanna
Bury a Friend by Billie Eilish
Butterfingers by Oli Fox
Different Man by Kane Brown and Blake Shelton
Fangs by Neoni
The Art of Survival by Ramsey

Prologue

My bedroom door flew open, startling the shit out of me.

"Quinn, Brody needs your help," my twin sister Bellamy said, her cheeks flushed, most likely from her frantic race up the stairs to find me.

I tossed my chemistry book to the side before I jumped off my bed. "Where is he?"

"In the kitchen with Dad." Her voice climbed in pitch with each word. She motioned for me to hurry, then pulled on her long brown braid. Bell was scared as hell if she was tugging on her hair.

I grabbed her hand, nearly dragging her behind me as I hurried into the hall and down the stairs.

Brody's scream tore through the mansion and my heart clawed its way into my throat. "That motherfucker." I reached the main floor and took off running, my bare feet slapping against the white and black marble floors as I hauled ass toward the shriek.

Tearing around the corner, I screeched to a halt and silently walked into the kitchen. My fists clenched and unclenched, ready to deal with the bastard. Father seemed oblivious that I was in the room,

1

his cheeks red with rage as he held Brody by the front of his grey polo shirt and hit my younger brother in the face.

"You little punk. You're a pathetic excuse for a son," he growled.

Brody's lip split open and a trickle of blood ran down his chin. He thrashed about, trying to break free from Father's grasp.

"Get your hands off him." I took a menacing step toward him, my eyes blazing with rage. Father's grip on Brody slackened and he let him go.

Brody stumbled to the ground, and I hurried over to him, crouching and scanning for signs of injury other than to his mouth.

Without thinking, I rushed forward and barreled into Father with my shoulder. He hit the floor with a loud thud and floundered beneath me as I pinned him down. My fist connected with his nose, and his warm blood coated my knuckles. I pulled my hand back again, ready to pummel him into unconsciousness when I heard Bell call to me from across the room. "Quinn! Don't do it! He's not worth your future."

I struggled to get a hold of my anger and reminded myself that if my brother and sister witnessed me killing Father, it would scar them for life. But I kept my fist raised, urging him to challenge me just once more so I could finish him off for good.

From the corner of my eye, I spotted Bell watching us closely and ushering Brody behind her protectively. Blood bloomed from his lower lip, and I winced. I should have gotten to him sooner.

"Get him cleaned up." I returned my attention to the piece of shit father I shared a last name with. "Touch him again, Adam, and I'll fucking kill you." My voice was low, full of venom.

He hated it when I referred to him by his first name, but he didn't deserve to be called Dad or Father.

I seethed as I climbed off him, taking a step back in case he may still have a spark of energy left to battle me. A twisted part of me hoped he would find the courage to get up and fight so I could beat him to death, then spit on his lifeless body when they lowered his casket in the ground. Wiping my mouth with the back of my hand, I backed out of the kitchen. Adam had recently started in on Brody, and I wouldn't tolerate it. He'd beaten my ass until I was fourteen, so it was only a few years ago when I had finally put him in his place. I'd worked hard to develop my strength in order to be able to take him down and defend myself.

At least now I was a junior in high school, and I could get the hell out of the house as soon as I graduated. Fuck, I wasn't even planning on staying in Forest Dale, Washington. If I had my way, I'd be relocating to Oregon and attending Whitmore University, where they were known for their exceptional football program. I had every intention of being drafted and playing for the NFL, and Whitmore would provide me exposure to recruiters.

I headed back toward my room, wondering if Bell had taken my younger brother there to calm him down. I'd installed a lock on my door not long ago, so it was a safe place to hide when Adam was at his worst. My fists clenched so hard my knuckles turned white, and my chest tightened in anger. I was known for my temper at school, but it had all started with Adam. Fortunately, I was able to channel the rage through football, where I could tackle and hit motherfuckers without a second thought.

Hurrying down the hall, I passed both Brody's and Bell's rooms and reached mine. I attempted to turn the handle, but it didn't budge.

"Bell, it's Quinn. Let me in."

Seconds later, the lock clicked, and the door cracked open. One hazel eye peeked through the opening before Bell moved back and allowed me in.

Brody sat on my bed, tears streaming down his cheeks. His brown hair stuck up in every direction, and his red-rimmed eyes peered up at me.

"Hey, man." I sat next to him, the mattress creaking beneath my weight, and wrapped my arm around his scrawny shoulders. My little brother had just turned twelve, and even though he'd hit puberty, he wasn't strong enough to take Adam. I hoped like hell he would be able to soon. Once he beefed up, he would be able to stand up to

Adam, and I wouldn't feel like a piece of shit for leaving him behind when I left for college.

I placed my finger beneath his chin and tilted it up. "Your lip is pretty busted up, but it'll heal. I'll get you some ice and Tylenol in a minute. Did he hit you anywhere else?"

His hand shook. "No. I—" He hiccupped. "I got a B on a test," he explained, his voice trembling. "He said I was stupid."

"Fucking asshole," Bell said, pacing the carpeted floor. "Brody, you're one of the smartest kids I know." She hugged herself tight, as if trying to keep her emotions tucked inside.

Even though Bell and I were twins, her petite frame was five inches shorter than mine, and her features resembled my brother's more than my own. Bell's brown hair was behind her shoulder, and she fidgeted with the strings of her hoodie before pushing her hands deep into the pockets of her jeans.

"Quinn, you have to do something. We all realize he was building up to this. You and I *know* what he's capable of." Tears welled in her eyes until she shook her head and angrily swiped them away.

"Let's just hope the threats I just gave him work. But Brody, if at all possible, I don't want you around him alone. If Bell and I aren't home, try to stay in here as much as you can, and keep my door locked. Got it?" I pulled him in for a hug.

"Yeah." He clung to me, his thin frame shaking. "Thanks, Quinn."

Heartache gripped my chest. "Love ya, kiddo."

"Yup. You, too." He straightened and wiped the moisture from his cheeks.

"Got homework? If so, go get it. You can hang out with me tonight." I patted the side of my bed where my schoolbooks were piled.

His face lit up. "Okay!" He bolted out of the room.

Bell walked to the door and poked her head into the hall, keeping an eye on him. "I'm not sure how much more he can take, Quinn.

You were always the tough one, always have been ..." She glanced at me, fear etched into her expression.

"I know. I'll figure something out."

She smiled as Brody flew back past her and leapt onto my bed. I forced a laugh, not feeling the same excitement he did. Despite my efforts to be a good big brother, I had let him down more times than I could count.

"I'll leave you guys to study," Bell said, giving me a wistful look that made my heart skip a beat. "Thanks."

Our gazes locked briefly before she walked out of my room. Little did I know that it would be the last time I would ever see her again.

Chapter 1

Wynter

Five Years Later

"Take your clothes off." Dimitri winked at me, his Russian accent thick with lust.

I laughed, the sound echoing through the photography studio. "You're such a perv."

"It's why you like me." He ran his fingers through his dark hair, his blue-grey eyes flashing with eagerness. "You can start anywhere you're most comfortable." He motioned with his hand to the room that included a green screen, a bed, and a chair that looked like it came from an Ikea dining set. After the photoshoot was finished, Dimitri would add different backdrops to make the images appear more lifelike.

Dimitri had approached me one day when I was grocery shopping. He gave me his business card and promised me the money would be worth my time. I was intrigued to say the least, and the rest was history. I'd worked with Dimitri for a few years, and I'd grown to trust him, but I still got nervous at the beginning of a shoot.

I removed the bobby pins from the messy bun on the top of my head, letting my strawberry blonde hair cascade over my shoulders. Using my fingers, I fluffed the thick waves.

"Beautiful." Dimitri reached for a lock, twirling it around his hand before he let it go and draped it over my shoulder. "I changed my mind. Let's begin in the chair." He backed away, then collected a big, white shirt off the top of the cabinet that safely secured his cameras and lenses.

Dimitri was one of the best photographers in the business, which was intriguing in itself, but he was also gorgeous and dripped with sex appeal. So far, Dimitri had kept his word and never touched me, but I wouldn't have objected if he had. When we first started to work together, he said his job was to take the pictures, not play with the employees. I appreciated that I could trust his words.

"Change into this." He held the piece of clothing out to me.

"Thanks." I raised an eyebrow at him, then pulled off my baby-blue T-shirt and dropped it to the tan carpeted floor. "No use changing in the dressing room when you're going to see it all anyway."

He rubbed his lightly stubbled jaw and grinned as I removed my plain beige bra.

My heart skipped a beat, my body tingling with nerves as the cool air in the studio brushed across my nipples, making them harden in seconds. Kicking off my flip-flops, I slipped out of my shorts but left my thong in place for the time being. I took the oversized button-down shirt from him and put it on, leaving the front gaping open slightly to showcase my flat stomach and the swell of my breasts. I'd prepared for the photo sessions enough times that it was almost second nature.

"Perfect. Now straddle the chair and face me." He held his camera as he waited for me to settle in.

My bare feet padded across the small room, and I sat down, waiting for his next suggestion.

"Relax." Dimitri snapped a few pictures. "Are you ready?" The soft clicks of the shutter filled the room.

"Hell yes. I need some stress relief." I laughed, propping my elbow on the back of the chair. "Where's my music?"

Dimitri paused, then reached into his jeans pocket and removed his phone. "You pick." He handed it to me, snapping away as I searched through Spotify before landing on "I'm Not Sorry" by Neoni. It was the perfect song to start the session.

I threw my head back and hung onto the chair, my shirt falling open as I sang along, feeling the words flow through my veins. Pushing thoughts of my real life outside of the studio to the back burner, I focused on Dimitri.

I slipped the shirt off both shoulders and exposed my breasts for the photo shoot.

"You're a natural," Dimitri said.

I flashed him a wide smile. "I'm ready to have some fun."

Dimitri lowered his camera. "Nick!"

I glanced around the room, my focus landing on a tall, blonde, naked guy. His hazel eyes connected with mine. "Nice," Nick said, approaching.

"Wanna play?" My greedy stare slid across every toned dip and valley along his chest, pecs, and abs. "Holy hell," I whispered as I stared at his long dick.

"Oh yeah. This will be fun." Nick wrapped his hand around his cock, stroking it as his heated gaze traveled over my tits and down my belly.

My core clenched, suddenly soaked with anticipation. "I can help with that."

I rose from my chair, my tongue darting over my lower lip. Then a noise pulled my attention away from Nick.

"Ah. Anthony is also ready for you, Wynter." Dimitri flashed me a wicked grin as a nude and hot-as-hell Anthony strolled my way. Dimitri made the introductions, then rubbed his hands together. "Everyone on the bed," Dimitri ordered.

"This way," Anthony said, his British accent nearly melting me on the floor. He held out his hand, and I placed mine in his.

Nick crawled onto the queen-size bed, and I followed. Sitting in the middle of the mattress, I glanced at Anthony again. He was as delicious as Nick—muscular, gorgeous smile, big dick. Just how I liked them.

"Spread your legs," Dimitri ordered.

Nick got on his knees behind me and cupped my breasts as Anthony joined us. Nick nipped at my ear, then parted my legs father apart and ran his finger over the thin material of my thong.

I bit my lip, my body growing needy with each man's touch.

Anthony leaned over and kissed me gently as Dimitri resumed taking the pictures.

"Is that pussy nice and wet?" Dimitri asked. "Let me see, Wynter."

Nick slipped his arms beneath mine, supporting me as Anthony eased the thong over my hips and down my legs. Anthony pushed my knees to my chest while Nick grabbed the back of my thighs, holding them in place.

I moaned as Anthony spread me apart. "Damn, your cunt is glistening. So ready, aren't you, Wynter?"

"More than you know." Heat unfolded inside my lower belly, my core begging to be fucked. I gazed at Anthony's hard cock.

"I see you looking." Anthony chuckled. "I'll fuck you soon."

Nick dug his fingers into the back of my thighs as Anthony rubbed my clit.

"Oh, God." My hips wiggled on the mattress.

"Are you ready to suck my cock, Wynter? I can't wait to see those pretty little lips wrapped around me." Anthony winked, his dark hair falling onto his forehead.

"I've been ready," I responded, my voice breathy and needy.

Nick released my legs, and we all shifted on the bed. Nick turned me around and I settled on all fours, my ass facing the camera as he slid his body beneath me. Nick's tongue swept over my entrance and fucked me, his hips thrusting up from the mattress, forcing his dick near my lips. I trembled with desire while Dimitri moved closer to get the up close and personal shots.

My fingernails dug into the emerald-green comforter as Nick's skilled mouth sent ripples of heat through me.

Anthony situated himself in front of me, then rubbed his cock on my lower lip. "Open."

I did as I was told, taking him in inch by glorious inch. I sucked his smooth shaft as he palmed the back of my head, fucking my mouth as Nick licked my pussy. Every part of me hummed with expectation and desire, and I writhed and whimpered as the guys played with my body.

Anthony moved my hair out of the way, allowing Dimitri a full view of me sucking him. I increased the suction as Anthony slid in and out. My breathing became more labored as familiar tingles rippled through me, promising a mind-blowing orgasm soon. I grabbed Nick's hard dick and ran my hand up and down his shaft as he buried his face in my sensitive flesh. I would have moaned, but my mouth was full of Anthony's cock.

Nick spread my butt cheeks apart and slipped a finger into my ass. He pumped me until my entire body shook with an earth-shattering climax.

Anthony pulled out immediately and shuddered while he grinned. "Not sure who taught you to suck dick, but Jesus, that's good." He hopped off the bed and stood next to it. "Too good."

I wiped the saliva off the corners of my mouth as I crawled off Nick and looked at Anthony. "Hang on, baby. It gets better." Feeling confident, I winked at him.

The sound of condom wrappers reached my ears, and I watched as Anthony and Nick rolled the rubbers on.

"Bend over." He playfully swatted my butt.

Staring at Nick as he moved to the sidelines, I bent over, eagerly waiting for Anthony to fuck me. I sucked in a breath as Anthony lined up at my entrance, then forcefully thrust inside. My greedy core gripped him tightly as he grabbed my hips, digging his fingers into my skin. The flash of the camera filled the studio as Anthony continued hammering into me, the bed creaking with the rhythm as Nick watched us.

I peeked sideways at Dimitri, noticing the bulge in his dark-wash designer jeans.

Anthony grunted and shuddered as he came. He paused, remaining inside me for a moment before fully pulling out, then moved to let Nick position himself behind me.

Nick was gentler than Anthony was as he eased inside me. My moans filled the room as he took a different approach, taking time to hit my G-spot with every agonizing and sweet push. If I had the ability to take one of them home with me and use him whenever I wanted, it would definitely be Nick.

My chest heaved as the sensation began to build inside again. Nick stopped and pulled out, and I glanced over my shoulder to see Anthony hand him a tube of lubricant. I waited as Nick applied the slippery substance to my puckered hole. He pressed the head of his dick inside my asshole, testing the waters, but I was ready for him. I pushed against him, moaning and eager for more.

"That's a good girl," Nick said, his voice deep and sultry. Moving gently at first, he groaned, "So fucking tight."

"Fuck me. I won't break," I gasped.

Apparently, Nick was good at taking orders. He plowed into me, and my body jerked forward with his powerful thrusts.

Nick grabbed my long hair and wrapped it around his hand, roughly tugging my head back.

"You take it in the ass really good, my pretty little slut."

Oh, shit. Keep talking dirty to me, and I'll come for you like a good girl.

Nick pounded into me until I screamed, begging him to get me off. The scent of our arousal filled the room, and I peeked at Anthony as he watched his friend turn me into a hormonal puddle.

"Take it all in," Nick encouraged me.

I relaxed, enjoying every inch of him. His fingers slid between my legs, massaging my clit in slow circles.

"Come for me, Wynter. Come on my hand while I fuck your tight little ass."

I slammed my eyes closed, black dots exploding behind my eyelids as my release ripped through me and stole my breath.

Nick let go of my hair and ran his nails down my back, sending shivers through me as he growled and climaxed.

Sweaty and completely spent, I shook on all fours as I came down from the high of my orgasm. Nick eased out of me, and I collapsed on my stomach as Dimitri snapped a few more pictures.

"Excellent work, everyone. These will be amazing."

I slowly sat up, then crawled off the bed and strolled across the room to where I'd left my clothes. I dressed as I looked the guys over one more time, wondering if they ever made house calls because today had been one hell of a ride.

Then reality punched me once again, reminding me that I would no longer live in Washington by this time tomorrow. Fear and excitement welled inside me at the possibility that I would be able to create a new life for myself. New school, new friends ...

My fingers tightened into a fist when the guilt hit me, cold and solid as a brick on my chest at the thought of leaving my younger sister. The sound of Nick's voice pulled me out of my inner turmoil, forcing me to stay present. I looked over at him, plastering a wide smile on my face.

Nick's lips curled up with a cocky grin. "It was nice to meet you, Wynter."

I tilted my head as I smoothed my T-shirt. "Likewise. If you're ever in Oregon, look me up."

"I will." He gave me a little wave before he left the room.

My gaze was glued to his ass and long, muscular legs as he left.

"Wynter, I'll be in my office." Dimitri nodded in that direction, then strolled out behind Nick.

I turned to Anthony. "Thanks for the fun." He had no idea that showing up for work was the only fun I ever had. Once I left, it was back to the real world. At least here, I could leave the nightmare behind me and pretend to be someone else.

"You should come back," Anthony said, standing naked in front of me.

"I wish I could, but I'm off to start another boring year of college tomorrow." I hoped that wouldn't be the case. The reason I'd worked my ass off to attend Whitmore University was because it was a school for the smart kids that had the money to pay the tuition. Lucky for me, I'd managed to obtain a full scholarship for the next two years.

"Too bad. I would have been happy to spice up your boring existence." He winked at me. "Later." Anthony strolled out of the room, confidence in his stride.

I grinned, then walked in the direction of Dimitri's office. Rounding the corner, I came to an abrupt halt. Dimitri leaned against the wall with his eyes closed as another guy sucked his dick. Dimitri grabbed the back of the guy's head, and his mouth dropped open as his body shook.

I disappeared back around the corner, smiling. So that was how Dimitri managed to keep his hands to himself when he was working.

"Wynter, I know you're there. Come on, and I'll pay you."

"Sorry," I said, joining him as he secured his jeans.

The other guy had disappeared, but at least Dimitri had a good time.

"Will you be back for winter break?" he asked, placing his palm on my back and leading me down the hall to his office.

"Not if I can help it." I folded my arms across my chest, not wanting to dive into another conversation about my personal life.

"If you need some quick money, you know where I am." Dimitri handed me a roll of cash, and I clasped it in my hand like a lifeline.

"Thanks. I appreciate everything you've done for me."

A flicker of sadness graced Dimitri's brown eyes. "You're a good one, Wynter. I wish you nothing but the best. I think a fresh start will be perfect for you."

"Me too. I mean it can't get much worse, right?" I rounded his desk and threw my arms around his neck. "You've been a great friend. I won't forget you when I'm rich and famous," I joked.

His chuckle rumbled through the room. "I have no doubt that you'll be a success no matter what you choose to do."

Releasing him, I stepped away. "I gotta go. Grocery shopping awaits. Stay out of trouble." I flashed him a big smile before I left. As soon as I was out of his office, I shoved the roll of money in my bra to protect it. Even though messing around with hot guys and posing for a camera wasn't what I'd planned to do with my life, desperate people made desperate choices.

Chapter 2

Wynter

Balancing grocery bags along my arms, I nearly tripped up the steps of my house. It was almost six, and I was late for dinner.

With my keys clutched in one hand, I unlocked the front door and bumped it open with my hip. "I'm home!" I called out, my voice bouncing off the scuffed and worn wood floors. At one time they had been so well cared-for they gleamed. Not anymore.

"I'm coming," Janine called. My seventeen-year-old sister bounded down the stairs, her socks muffling her hurried steps. She rarely dressed in anything other than running shorts and an oversized hoodie, but she always had socks on her feet no matter what the weather was doing outside.

As if reading my mind, she said, "Yes, my socks have the grippers on them."

She joined me in the entryway and took some of the bags from me.

"Good. I can't have you breaking your neck when I'm gone. No one will be able to help you." I winked at her as we walked down the short hall and turned left into the kitchen. I was trying to pretend to be happy in front of her.

I wasn't.

I forced a smile while I unloaded the groceries onto the white counter, once again noticing the blackened grout between the tiles. I'd tried everything to scrub the stains away, but they never fully faded. It was all just a reminder of what had happened.

I removed the bread and placed it on top of the refrigerator. "Sorry I'm late. Apparently, everyone in town needed food tonight."

Janine shot me a worried look. "Are you sure you're doing the right thing? Leaving for college, I mean." She collected the gallon of milk and put it into the refrigerator.

I blew a strand of hair out of my face. "We've talked about this a hundred times. You're seventeen, and you'll be out of here soon. It's only for a year."

Janine's blue eyes filled with regret. "I know. And it's not that I want you to stay. I mean, I *do*, but I want you to live your life too. You've been taking care of Mom and me for the last five years."

"And I've completed as many classes as I can at the community college. I have to transfer somewhere. With Mr. Odgen's help, I have a full ride to Whitmore University. It's one of the best schools in the country." I continued to unload the groceries as we talked.

Janine threw her hands up in the air as tears slipped down her cheeks. "But it's hours away from here. What if something happens?" she choked out.

I set the lettuce down and grabbed her to give her a tight hug. "I have money saved in case of an emergency, and you know I'm only a phone call away." I smoothed her light brown hair and again wished I wasn't leaving my sister behind.

What I hadn't told her was that getting out of here was the only way I could move on. Staying in this town was destroying me from the inside out.

I kissed the top of her head. "I've given you all the knowledge you need. You know how to access the bank account, pay all of the bills, and keep track of our finances. Plus, you take excellent care of the house." I broke our hug before I tipped her chin up to wipe away her tears with the pad of my thumb. "You've got this."

"Okay." She took a deep breath. "I'm starving, let's make this a damn good dinner." In a few strides, Janine crossed the kitchen. She gave me a sad smile as she opened the cabinet over the dishwasher and removed a few white stick candles. "We're gonna be fancy and eat by candlelight."

"Oh, that's ..." I frowned. "I paid the power bill, right?" I asked myself more than her.

Janine laughed. "Yeah, the new one just came in. Just thought it would be fun."

"Nothing better than Hamburger Helper with candles." My heart ached as I stared into her eyes, wishing again that I could stay with her forever. But as much as I wanted to, I knew I had to leave. The pain in my chest was agonizing, and it felt like my whole world was crashing down around me.

After dinner, Janine and I tackled the stack of dishes in the sink, the sound of clanking metal a sorrowful reminder of how things used to be. I silently reminisced about our family-race nights; Dad had brought a dull evening to life by creating a makeshift race track down the stairs using pieces of cardboard boxes. He had pretended to be a commentator, his booming voice making outlandish predictions of who would win. We'd laugh so hard our stomachs hurt, while Mom sat in her chair watching us with a glowing smile.

I paused at the foot of the stairs as a pang of sadness pierced my soul—those happy days were now just memories. In an instant, our lives changed from ones full of love and laughter to ones with oppressive darkness. I clenched my jaw as I remembered how Dad had just up and left without a word, not even bothering to stay in touch. Moisture welled in my eyes, making my sight blur. Only Janine and I were left of our family as far as I was concerned. Although we occasionally talked about Dad, we never spoke about *him*.

Briefly gritting my teeth, I mentally screamed as the dark thoughts rushed in. I refused to allow them to rip through me. I was leaving the next day, searching for a better life.

I clutched the rickety banister and pushed myself forward. One thing Dad had been able to do was put away money for college, but Mom blew through it pretty fast when the entire community turned against us and she lost her job. I couldn't blame them, but the fact that we never moved from Forest Dale, Washington, was beyond me. Why stay and put us through hell?

Hatred swirled in my heart for my mother, for the way she had abandoned Janine and me the day our lives turned to shit, and again when Dad left. She had chosen to hide away in her bedroom rather than act like an adult and find a job. I worked whenever I could while trying to be there for my sister and keep up with schoolwork, but it wasn't enough. Desperately needing a solution, Dimitri's offer provided a lifeline. The increased salary allowed me to pay the bills and make ends meet, plus the shorter hours offered me more time with Janine and my studies. Even if it meant doing something morally questionable, I'd do whatever it took to provide for myself and my sister until I was able to make it on my own at Whitmore.

My legs felt like they were filled with lead as I slowly walked down the hallway, passing Janine's room. I paused at the door between ours and all the memories flooded back. The guilt and shame overwhelmed me, and I desperately tried to take a deep breath.

I placed my forehead against the wall and whispered, "Goodbye."

I made my way down the rest of the hall to Mom's bedroom, my pulse spiking against my wrist. Quietly, I pushed the door open. The room was dark, but I knew she was there by the stench of whiskey and dirty clothes.

"Mom, are you awake?" I asked, wondering if she would even make an appearance on my last night at home.

Only silence greeted me, so I flipped on the light.

Mom groaned and jerked the brown comforter over her head. "Go away."

Disgust threaded through me. "Do you need anything? Other than a shower, I mean."

After debating on whether to remind her that I would be leaving bright and early in the morning, I decided not to. If I'd been important to her, she would have gotten out of her bed years ago and been a real mother. Instead, she had alcohol delivered and drank herself into a stupor every day. Dad had only been gone a week before she checked out on her kids, and we had no other choice than to fend for ourselves. Now, Janine would fill my shoes with a full-time job while she finished high school, paying the bills and fending for herself. I was probably a piece of shit sister for leaving her, but it was the only hope I had to be able to make a better life for us. Once I did, I would move Janine in with me.

"Sleep, Wynter. I need fucking sleep. Turn off the light, you're killing me."

"Well, you're killing me too, so I guess we're even. Maybe the apple doesn't fall far from the tree, huh? Maybe I'm just like *him*." I nearly gagged on my words as I folded my arms across my chest, waiting for her reaction.

Mom shot up in the bed, her blonde hair matted to the side of her head. "It wasn't my fault!"

"But it was. It really was." I flinched as the memories rushed at me, stealing my breath. Mom had been a fun, loving, nurturing parent at one time, which made her words sting even more.

"Don't you dare speak to me, you ungrateful little bitch." Her hatred for me clouded the space like a thick, heavy fog.

"Yup, that's me. Paying the bills, taking care of your other kid, running the errands, cooking ... I'm pretty sure most of that's supposed to be your job, not mine." I smirked. I was ready for a final fight with her before I left for college. Taking a deep breath, I throttled my anger and disgust with her down to a dull roar. If I wasn't careful, she would take it out on Janine, and I wouldn't be around to run interference.

"Get out!" Mom raised a skinny arm and pointed to the door.

I raised my hands in surrender. "I am." I'd had enough of her anyway. My tolerance for a deadbeat parent was zero, and lucky me, I had two of them. It was time that I carved out a future for myself and my sister. The only reason I'd stuck around this long was because of Janine.

Hurrying out of Mom's room and into the hall, I slammed the door closed behind me. Mom's shrill screams hurt my ears, but not nearly as much as it hurt my soul when she'd dismissed my pleas for help.

An ache that had become too familiar spread through my body, a physical reminder of all that had been lost. My head bowed, allowing my hair to cloak my face and hide the tears pricking my eyes. "Good-bye, Mom," I whispered.

"She sounds pissed," Janine said, climbing the stairs.

"Yeah, I might have had something to do with it." The corner of my mouth kicked up in an ornery grin. "Wanna help me pack? Mrs. Ogden will be here at six in the morning, so I need to be ready to load the car when she pulls up."

"I'm glad she's driving you. I feel better that you're with someone you know instead of a stranger driving an Uber." Janine walked into my room and opened my closet.

"Me too." I followed her in, then went to my bookshelf to grab my most important books. I didn't have a lot to move, so packing wouldn't take too long.

"You'll have to let me know how Oregon is. I'm guessing not much different than here except for the scenery, and I don't mean the trees and buildings."

I made my way to my sister, then slid my arm around her shoulder and grinned. "I think a lot of things will be different. I'm not too concerned about any guys, though." *Except to get laid. Turn 'em and burn 'em.* I flipped on the light in my bedroom before I released a heavy sigh. Glancing at my sister, I said, "You can't save her, Janine. Don't try. It's not your responsibility to save your parent. It was our parents' job to save ..." I couldn't finish my sentence and instead leaned my head against hers. "It's easier if you don't rely on anyone except yourself. That way the only person you have to blame when life goes to shit is you. Don't forget that."

Chapter 3

Quinn

"What do you think?" I asked Anderson and Kane, my best friends and fellow teammates on the Whitmore football team.

"It's amazing what a new coat of paint will do," Anderson said, looking around the newly painted office I was taking over. After some negotiating, Kane had agreed that the Viper Secret Society, a secret sex club, could keep the same location as last year. Since he owned the house, we were all aware it was his decision. Once we had all settled on some ground rules, repainting the office was really the only change needed to the building. The playrooms were already set up, the locks on all the doors were thumbprint entry, and all the toys, whips, and equipment we wanted to fulfill any fantasy were at our fingertips.

"Just remember that you guys are responsible for paying any damages." Kane shoved one hand through his light brown hair, his brown-eyed gaze serious.

I tipped my chin up. "We've got you, bro. Don't sweat it," I said, reassuring him that his gift was appreciated.

"I know you didn't have to keep this place for the society, but man, that was cool as shit. You could have sold it or rented it out." Anderson grinned at Kane.

"What he said." I slapped Kane on the back as I looked at our hard work.

Not only had the guys and I painted the office, but we also bought better furniture for our meetings. Sneaking around and discussing details in an empty classroom at college would eventually land us in hot water. We had flirted with disaster for way too long and at some point, Lady Luck would slap us on the ass and say good riddance. Someone was bound to overhear us talking about sex kinks and the girls we had taken in the middle of the night to fuck senseless. Kane and I were gunning to get drafted and play pro, and we couldn't afford any scandals. I'd lived through enough bullshit already.

"You're welcome. I figure it's better to hold onto the house as a financial investment for the time being. Might as well have some fun with it." He cracked a grin, the tension melting off him. "Brie and I want to use the playrooms too, so it works out."

"Damn, you got lucky with her. She's fucking hot and super sweet too," Anderson said.

My brow quirked, waiting to see if Anderson had just entered dangerous territory. The last time a society brother stepped out of line concerning Brie it hadn't ended well.

"She is. And she's all mine." The corner of Kane's mouth curled up.

It appeared like it was an opportune time to change topics. "Well, I gotta get the hell out of here," I said to the guys. "Thanks for your help. Anderson, I'll meet you later to review the new applicants."

"Eight o'clock?" he asked.

"Sounds good." I looked at Kane. "I'll catch ya later. Thanks again."

We bumped fists before we left, and I locked up behind us. The gravel crunched beneath my Nikes as I walked to my silver Mercedes AMG GT coupe.

Adam was always trying to buy my loyalty, which would never work, but I got a great set of wheels from his latest lame-ass attempt. I climbed in and started the engine, then waved to Anderson and Kane as they hopped into their vehicles as well. Removing my phone from my back jeans pocket, I pulled up Spotify and tapped my favorite playlist. "Kings Never Die" by Eminem and Gwen Stefani thumped through my speakers. I bobbed my head to the beat as I shifted into drive and left the society's house in my rearview mirror.

It was past five in the evening and Adam was expecting me for dinner. Despite my resentment and anger towards him, living at home allowed me to keep tabs on Brody. As far as I was concerned, I had no choice but to continue living with a man who had done so much to hurt us, even though it became more like a prison each day. On one hand, I wanted to move on and begin a new life, but at the same time I couldn't bear the thought of leaving Brody alone with Adam. I couldn't leave my little brother with a monster and keep a clear conscience.

Hopefully, Kane and I would both be drafted and off to the pros next season. By that time, Brody would be eighteen and able to fend for himself. Hell, I'd been training him, and if Adam crossed a line again, I had no doubt that Brody could handle it, but I had to be sure before I left. One loss had fucked me up enough, and I couldn't do it again.

Life without my twin had left me a shell of the person I'd been. Not even football could fill the hole left from her absence.

Blinking my tears away at the thought of Bell, the drive became a blur, my brain kicking into autopilot while I mentally reviewed the late afternoon practice. We had several new players, and Coach had busted the upperclassmen's balls the entire time. I wasn't sure if he hadn't gotten laid in a while or what, but he was focused on perfection and making our lives hell.

Fifteen minutes later, I drove into the windy driveway of my house. Maybe Adam had to travel for work again and wanted to talk to me before he left. I always made sure I was home with Brody at night when Adam was gone. He traveled often, which left the big-ass mansion to us. I was cool with hanging with my brother, and it gave me time to throw an occasional party and have friends over. On those nights, I sent Brody to his friend's since he was a minor. Besides, he was in high school, and he had no business trying to hook up with the college girls. Adam had said that as long as there wasn't any damage to the structure or furnishings, it was all good. Shit, the mansion was big enough to hold a hundred people comfortably. Probably even more, but I hadn't ever pushed it.

A ball of anxiety landed in the pit of my stomach, making me nauseous. "It's good, man. Stop being a fucking pussy." I sucked in a deep breath in an attempt to clear my mind and rid myself of the tension snaking through my shoulders and neck. After all the shit Adam had pulled with me, I occasionally still got sick when I had to spend time with him. Old beatings died hard, I guess.

Pausing long enough to punch in the code to the front door, I let myself in. After securing the locks and resetting the alarm, I leaned against the white pillar in the marble entryway and took off my tennis shoes before strolling into the kitchen to see if Adam was there. Even though I hoped he'd changed his mind about wanting to talk to me, I doubted that I would get that lucky.

"Hey, Lena. Have you seen my father?" I asked our chef and housekeeper. She'd been with us since I was a kid, and at times Lena had been like a mother substitute.

When Adam had bought the house, he remodeled parts of it and built the kitchen the way Lena had asked—state-of-the-art stainless steel appliances, cream-colored granite counters, an island with a sink, and all the space she could dream of. It wasn't like Adam was that nice of a guy, but when I was younger, Lena had taken us kids off his hands, so I guess that was worth whatever money he could throw at her to keep her around.

I often wondered if she really knew what went down. Adam was an expert at hiding the fact that he beat his sons from the rest of the world. He was a master manipulator when it served him.

"Hi, hon. He's in his office waiting for you." She wiped her hands on the navy apron tied around her ample waist.

I tipped my nose up to sniff the air and grinned at her. "What's for dinner?"

"I made a turkey breast with roasted vegetables, mashed potatoes, and rolls." She opened the oven a crack and peeked in. "It's almost done, so go chat with your father, then you can eat if you want. Brody should be here in about thirty minutes."

"Sweet." I rubbed my hands together like a kid in a candy store.

Lena's cooking was mouth-wateringly amazing. She'd spoiled me with her skills. Hell, she'd been so good to me that if I went pro, I was going to buy her a home of her own. She was nearing sixty and I wanted to set her up financially so she could get the hell away from my father. A while ago Lena had admitted to me that Brody and I were the reason she'd stuck around, but I'd be long gone in another year.

I kissed her on the cheek, then ran out of the kitchen and into the marble hallway, sliding the last bit in my socked feet. Adam hated when I did that, so a quick jab behind his back made me feel a little better. "Adam?" I called before I reached his office.

"Come in," he said, not looking up from his computer. "And shut the door."

Shit. This was serious.

Quietly, I did as ordered, swallowing over the dryness in my throat. I settled into the brown leather chair in front of his executive desk, scanning the framed images on his floor-to-ceiling built-in bookshelves—a professional family photo and another of Mom laughing and smiling with four-year-old me on one hip and Bell on the other. That picture had been taken before Brody was born, when we were on vacation in Hawaii. Then the pictures stopped a few months after Brody arrived. Bell and I were five. I'll never forget the moment that the cops knocked on the door. Mom had run to the grocery store while Lena kept an eye on us. She never made it home. Some drunk fucker ran a stop sign and hit her at fifty miles an hour. Adam turned into a different man that day.

I folded my hands in my lap, attempting to appear calm even though the memories made my heart pound so hard against my chest I thought it might make an attempt to leap out and run away without me.

A heavy silence filled the room as I waited for him to finish what he was doing and clue me in on what he wanted. Finally, he shut his laptop and grabbed a file.

"It's come to my attention that there's a new student at Whitmore." He smoothed a hand over his brown hair before he looked at me.

What does this have to do with me? I kept my mouth closed, careful to keep my snarky comment to myself.

"Wynter Baldwin. You might recognize that name."

I searched my mind and could only think of one person whose last name matched. Hatred burned inside me, and a flood of recollections came to the surface. "Baldwin is common, so what's your point?"

Adam tapped his fingers against the top of the desk, his expression growing cold and calculating.

The hair on the back of my neck stood on end as I waited to see if he was going to fuck up and lunge at me. My body tensed, ready to defend myself if he crossed that line with me again. I put him in his place every time, but he didn't seem to understand that his sons were younger and stronger and not putting up with his bullshit anymore.

He rose slowly, his gaze narrowed as he sneered at me.

"That day ... she was there. She could have stopped it all. It was her fault."

Astonished, I blinked several times, trying to clear my head of the words he'd just gutted me with. I stood, closing the gap between us, my earlier anxiety dissipating.

"What do you mean it was her fault?" I growled, my short fuse getting the best of me.

Adam squared his shoulders and scooped up a file from his desk. "I have all the details here. That should clear it up for you."

I snarled at him, not liking his tone. I definitely got my temper from him, but instead of beating the hell out of innocent people, I took it out on the football field.

Fire flashed in his brown eyes. "The important thing is that Wynter didn't do anything to stop ..." He swallowed.

Huh, the motherfucker had feelings.

"She chose to stay silent. Do whatever you have to but get rid of her. If that doesn't work, you have my permission to ruin the little bitch." Venom dripped from his words.

I stepped backward, and the weight of the situation settled on my chest like an elephant.

"Are you sure?" I had to make sure Adam had the facts straight before I went after someone.

Without another word, he slid the file to me. "See for yourself. Like I said, it's all in there."

I felt the color drain from my face as shame washed over me, twisting me into a million brittle pieces. Shit shouldn't have gone down the way it had.

"This contains all the information you need to know about Wynter, but the most important thing is that she's responsible for what happened." He sat back down in his chair, appearing older than he was for a moment.

I stared at the plain folder before I picked it up. "Why did you wait until now to tell me?" My voice trembled. "We've been in school for a few weeks."

"Because her attendance just came to my attention." He sighed. "But even though Wynter was the cause, I never want you to forget your part in it."

I tore my gaze away from him as the pain from his words sliced through me. "Don't worry, Pops." I popped the first *p* in disgust. I wasn't sure if me calling him Pops or Adam pissed him off more, so I used both to make sure I got under his skin. "I'll never forget. I'll live with that guilt the rest of my life."

Chapter 4

Quinn

Even though Lena expected me for dinner, I hurried to my room to have some privacy.

When I closed my bedroom door behind me, I said, "Alexa, lamp on." The light came to life, highlighting a poster of one of my all-time favorite NFL players, Michael Irvin. He was inducted into the Pro Football Hall of Fame and had played for the Dallas Cowboys as a wide receiver when I was little. Even as a kid, I was glued to the television when he was on the field. He was magic, and I wanted what he had. He was my inspiration to work my ass off and give my father a big *fuck you* as I left him in the dust.

I tossed the file on top of my bed, then grabbed the back of my neck and rubbed, hoping the tension would ease up. In order to focus, I needed to take a piss before I sat down and looked through it all.

My mind whirled as I made my way to the bathroom. Was Adam lying, or was this Wynter Baldwin actually responsible? When that cold, heartless asshole wanted something, he would go to any extreme to get it, and piling on the manipulation was just the first step for him. My throat tightened as I blew out a sigh.

I crawled onto my bed, wrinkling the dark blue and red

comforter. I scooped up the manila file and wondered what horror I was about to witness. What I wanted more than anything was to have proof that what Adam had said was true. That this girl was the one responsible.

Sweat beaded on my forehead, and I forced myself to look inside. My breath stuttered as I stared at a gorgeous girl about my age. Her long strawberry blonde hair flattered her face, but her blue gaze at the camera was dull.

Good. I hope she suffers as much as I do.

A deep-rooted hate reared its head and targeted Wynter, but I couldn't deny that she was hot as hell.

My attention traveled to her photos and my cock jumped to life when my eyes caught sight of her full, slightly parted lips. I forced myself to momentarily forget what she'd done and instead studied her, drinking in every beautiful detail of her full tits, flat stomach, and toned legs. Her pink T-shirt accentuated the natural tint to her cheeks.

"Jesus," I muttered, not wanting to believe anything bad about this chick. She was stunning.

I gritted my teeth, forcing myself to look at the next page in the file.

"Holy fucking shit." Wynter was naked with two dudes, one licking her pussy while she sucked the other guy's dick. I barked out a laugh, appreciating my luck.

Then it dawned on me that Adam had also seen her exposed. Suddenly, I wanted to rip his eyes out of their sockets for looking at her. I shook my head, clearing my lust-filled thoughts. *She's the enemy, asshole.* A plan began to brew about how to work my way into her life. It would probably be pretty easy to get her into the society if she was down with having her picture taken. If these photos were anything to go on, the girl was a freak in the sheets, and I couldn't wait to sink my cock into her cunt before I destroyed her life piece by piece.

Flipping the sheet, I stared at several more pictures of her with different guys, my dick paying as much attention as my eyes were.

"Yup, bud, we're going to come all over those gorgeous tits. Just have to get her an invite to the society first."

Suddenly Adam's words rang through my mind. *Ruin her.* That might be what Adam wanted me to do, but no way in hell would I seek revenge unless I knew for a fact that she was involved in that day.

After flipping through more images of her—at college, with her younger sister, walking into her house—I realized the file I was seeing was most likely from a PI. Maybe Adam was as invested in revenge as I was. Even when he was a piece of shit to Brody and me, he'd always been good to Bell. The piece of paper listed Wynter's current school and the names of the people she had used to live with ... one sister and her mom. She was five feet four and a hundred and five pounds. Tiny. Hell, I bench-pressed more than she weighed. It should be easy to fucking toss her in my trunk at some point.

Then the blood gelled in my veins. She'd attended Timber Creek High School in Forest Dale, Washington. Copies of school pictures were next. In most of them, she smiled and laughed with friends. Another page listed Wynter's accomplishments while there: basketball cheerleader, track team, drama club, class president. All during her sophomore year. After that, nothing. At the bottom of the sheet was a note that she'd homeschooled until she graduated.

"I bet you did, bitch." I snarled, racking my brain to remember if we'd had classes together, but it didn't matter. After confirmation that we'd attended the same high school, I knew exactly who she was.

My enemy.

A liar and a coward.

Shock coursed through me as I picked up a newspaper article. Her arms were protectively folded across her chest and her eyes were rimmed with red. I held my breath, flipping through the next several pages. With each additional word and image I saw, a knife twisted in my gut.

"Fuck!" Adam wasn't bullshitting me. She'd been involved. There was no way I could deny it, the proof was right in front of me. Pictures, witnesses, newspaper articles ... everything. Adam might be a mean son of a bitch, but at least this time he wasn't a liar.

My hands shook and my breathing came fast as I slammed the file shut, my heart pounding furiously against my sternum. Tears blurred my vision as I stood from my bed and began to pace. She knew. She fucking knew every detail of the day that ripped my world to shreds. Adam's words echoed in my head, but I wasn't about to try and send her running away from Whitmore.

No, I was going to do something much more satisfying. I was going to destroy her.

Chapter 5

Wynter

"Do you miss me?" I fought against my tears as I looked at Janine on FaceTime.

She rolled her eyes. "Ego much?" She snickered. "I see a few weeks away from home has done nothing to change you."

I laughed and fluffed a pillow on my bed before I tossed it behind me and leaned against the headboard. "It's different," I confided. "But it's also good because no one knows who I really am." I slammed my mouth closed, unwilling to speak the rest out loud.

Her face fell and sadness flickered in her gaze. "You need a fresh start."

"How's Mom been?" I honestly didn't give a shit, but I did care about my sister and how much Mom was derailing her.

Janine gave me a half-shrug. "I'm not sure she knows you're gone."

Her words stabbed me in the heart. I swallowed over the pain, reminding myself that Mom would never change.

"Is she being halfway decent to you?" My forehead creased, my brain running rampant with horrible scenarios of Mom throwing empty alcohol bottles at her and knocking Janine out. I stared at the rubber band on my wrist. Propping my iPhone on my lap, I popped the rubber band and welcomed the sharp sting. Maybe I was a selfish piece of shit just like Mom. After all, I'd left my sister to fend for herself in order to focus on my life.

"Stop, Wynter." Janine's voice pulled me out of my quick descent to hell.

"Stop what?" I feigned ignorance.

"Remember when you found out that you got a full ride to Whitmore?"

"Of course, I do. I was fucking stoked." I released the rubber band against my skin again, wishing it would hurt more.

"Yeah. The happiest I've seen you in a long-ass time. And remember the conversation we had that same day?" Janine crossed her arms over her chest and narrowed her gaze.

"You're about to get bossy with me." I pointed at her. "Don't."

"Wyn, you might be older than I am, but I'm not your average seventeen-year-old kid. When you were accepted to Whitmore, I willingly stepped up to the plate. It's only for a year. Once I graduate, we'll find a place to live and be roomies. We'll be together again soon enough, but without a sorry excuse of a mom holding us back. I need this too, sis. I need that fresh start like you do. Living here is hell and not just because of Mom."

She didn't have to explain. I understood all too well.

"I need to know that we can still dream and build a new life. I'm in this with you a hundred percent. Let me handle Mom for a change."

I bit my lip, studying her. "When did you grow up on me?"

Janine wiped the moisture from her eyes. "We can do this, Wyn. The year will fly by."

I wondered if she was trying to convince me or herself. Heaving a big sigh, I reminded myself to relax. Janine had teachers who adored her and a boyfriend that loved her. We only had a few more months to get through before everything changed for the better.

"You're right. I just struggle with my choice sometimes." I tucked my hair behind my ear.

"It's not your decision. It's ours. Don't forget that. I need you to do this too."

I nodded. "I love you, and I miss you so bad."

"Miss you too, brat." She flashed me a smile, her cue to change the topic. "Are there some gorgeous guys on campus? How are your roomies?"

"The roomies are really nice so far. Everlee is hilarious and full of energy. Leighton keeps to herself when I'm around, so I'm not sure what to think about her. Gabby is super sweet, and I've talked with her the most. They're all cheerleaders, so I have the place to myself at times. It's kind of nice, actually. The house is cute, and they take good care of it. It was pure luck that they needed a roomie this year."

"Destiny." Janine laughed as she gave me the jazz hands.

I rolled my eyes. I didn't believe in destiny. If there was such a thing, I always got fucked by it and not in a fun way. I pulled my thoughts back to my sister, grateful for the time we'd had to catch up. "There's a party Saturday after the football game, so I'm thinking maybe I'll go. The girls invited me, so I'll know a few people there at least."

Janine clapped her hands. "Yes! Go have fun. That's an order."

I gave her a salute. "Yes, ma'am."

Our hoots and hollers filled the room as we continued to tease each other.

I glanced at the clock on my phone. "Ah, shit. I needed that, sis." I blew her a kiss.

"Me too, but studying calls. If I want a full scholarship to college, too, I have to maintain my GPA."

"Same. I'll let you know how the party goes this weekend."

"Only a few days away," Janine said in a sing-song voice.

"Two, but who's counting?" I waved goodbye and disconnected the call.

As a wave of guilt swept over me, I busied myself by getting off my bed and heading to my closet. Janine had been the one who had pushed me to take this chance and move states, and I wanted to make her proud.

Staring into my wardrobe, I was grateful that I'd used some of the money I'd saved to buy some new clothes for school—a drastic change from the hand-me-downs that I'd had to wear in order to pay rent and buy groceries for my family.

A knock interrupted me.

"Yeah?"

The door cracked open. "Wynter? Can I come in?"

"Hey, Gabby." I motioned for her to join me. "I'd love your thoughts on what to wear to the party."

She rubbed her hands together, clearly excited. "Oh, I love picking out clothes."

I waved her over to the closet. "Have at it." I sat back on the bed. "I thought you would be at cheer practice."

Gabby rifled through my wardrobe, then glanced at me over her shoulder. "It's already over. Coach got sick, so we all hightailed it out of there. We can't afford for the entire team to feel like shit and miss the game." She winced as though the idea had punched her in the stomach.

"Yeah, probably wouldn't look so great."

She pursed her lips before she returned to the closet. "So, you got a guy back home?"

"Like a hookup or a boyfriend?"

"Either." She removed a pair of skinny jeans from my closet and tossed them on the bed. "Can I see these on you?"

"Sure." I stood and pulled my grey yoga pants off, then answered her as I stepped into the jeans. "No to both. I didn't have time to date." Nor did anyone want to be around me after shit went seriously south. *But I had a lot of sex at my job. Good sex.* I wondered if the college guys could match the experience the men who worked for Dimitri had. Maybe it was time to find out.

"I see."

My brows furrowed. "What about you?"

She faced me, her gaze traveling up and down my body as she tapped her finger against her lower lip, clearly thinking.

"Nah. I haven't found anyone I would want to settle down with. Two of my best friends have, though. Teagan and Brie. They met their guys at Whitmore, so maybe I'll have some luck this year."

I nodded. "Well, it's encouraging that Whitmore has some good guys around, right?" But no one for me. I couldn't take the chance of someone getting too close to me. It would be too easy for them to find out who I was; then my life would turn to shit again.

Gabby's emerald-green eyes sparkled as she practically skipped to my bedroom door. "Be right back."

Curious to where she was going, I poked my head out of my room and down the hall.

"What are you doing?" I giggled.

"This!" She jogged toward me again, holding up a shirt in her hand, a see-through gold top with black flowers covering the breasts. She shoved it into my arms. "Try it on. I think we're close to the same size, and I'm guessing the color will look phenomenal on you."

"This is gorgeous. Are you sure?"

"Yes! It's not even the best color on me. Try it on." She impatiently tapped her foot against the wood floor.

I tugged off my sweatshirt and tossed it onto my bed, then carefully put on Gabby's shirt. Something poked me in the side, and I fumbled around before I spotted the price tag still attached. "Um, this is expensive, Gabby, I can't wear this. What if I accidently spilled food on it?"

She held up a finger. "Shh, no talking." Gabby helped me pull the top into place, smiling. "It's perfect and reveals just enough of your boobs and tummy to look sexy and not slutty."

I glanced down at the fabric hugging my breasts and showcasing my stomach and belly button piercing. At one time, Dad had his ear pierced, and the small diamond had been his before he disappeared. When I realized he'd left it behind, I used it for the piercing. It reminded me that there had been good times before he'd left us without a word.

Gabby placed her hands on her slender hips. "That shirt does me no justice at all. My aunt was trying to be nice, but it makes me look pale. It's all yours."

I stammered like an idiot before I finally found my words. "It's too much."

"It's not. We're friends. Besides, you're helping me out."

My throat tightened with her words. I hadn't had friends since I was a sophomore in high school. "How?" I wasn't sure how she figured that.

Gabby winked at me. "Because I just made room in my closet to buy something new."

I laughed. Although I owned name brand clothes now, I'd purchased them at Ross and Nordstrom Rack. I'd justified spending the money by reminding myself that until I was financially comfortable, I could fake it until I made it.

"You look stunning, dahling." Gabby gave me a thousand-watt smile. "Every guy will be looking at you the moment you walk through the door."

"Thanks, but really, I can pay you for the shirt."

"Wynter Baldwin, no. If it bothers you that much, think of it as a welcome to Whitmore gift. Besides, we could have gotten stuck with a bitch for a roomie. You're not one, so that's payment enough."

She had no idea how her words were healing my shattered heart. Maybe there was hope for me after all. As quickly as I thought it, though, the truth snuffed it out. I would never be whole again.

It was clear that there was no changing Gabby's mind once she had decided something. I would have to be sneaky about how I repaid her.

"So, it's settled. You'll meet us at the party."

My stomach flip-flopped. "I don't have a way to get there."

Gabby briefly frowned. "No biggie. I'll swing by and pick you up on the way. Leighton and Everlee will ride together, so it will be perfect."

"Are you su—"

Gabby held up her hand, halting me midsentence. "Wynter, I'm happy to or else I wouldn't have offered. Seriously, you have no idea how much we all really like you. You're a perfect fit for our house and group. Like I said, some crazy-ass bitch could have moved in. I mean, I have *stories*. Whether you know it or not, you saved us." Gabby placed her palm over her heart, her words filled with sincerity.

"Thanks. I like you guys too."

Don't get attached! If they ever find out, you can kiss these friends goodbye, too.

"I've gotta hit the books, but bring your shit downstairs and join me for a beer. We can study on the couch." Gabby spun on her heel, her brown hair lifting off her slender shoulders as she disappeared from my room.

I stepped up to the mirror, admiring how I looked. Maybe Gabby was right, and I would attract some fun attention at the party. God knew I was ready to get laid.

Carefully removing the shirt, I hung it up and grabbed my sweatshirt to pull over my head. I collected my backpack and my laptop from the desk that had come with my room and made my way downstairs.

What if I really can start over? Maybe this really was the beginning of a new life— something different, good.

Unfortunately, life was definitely about to change, but not the way I'd hoped.

Chapter 6

Quinn

"Keep your shit together on the field, guys. I'm not sure where your heads were yesterday in practice, but I hope like hell I see everyone dialed in and working as a team." Coach rubbed his stubbled jawline while he paced the locker room. He looked tense.

"Yes, sir!" the team yelled in unison.

I tugged on my shoulder pads and shot both Kane Cooper, our quarterback, and Jagger Whitlock, our running back, a look and smirked. We were ready to play ball.

"Let's go!" Coach motioned for us to hurry.

The sound of our cleats smacking the cement floor echoed through the room as we filed out. As soon as I was in the tunnel leading to the field, I took a deep breath. I was ready to tear some ass up and win the game.

"You doing good, man?" I asked Kane.

"Yup. I'm just focused as hell. A couple of scouts are in the stands, so I want to make sure we're all playing top-notch." Kane's gaze briefly narrowed.

I cracked a grin. I suspected his brain was definitely running full speed ahead. "I'm there with you. I can't afford to fuck up my chances of being drafted."

"You know I'm in," Jagger said from my left side.

"And after we win, we're gonna party." I chuckled as we all bumped fists and jogged down to the field.

I hadn't mentioned Wynter to the guys, but I was hoping that she would show up later. From what I'd heard, she was sharing a house with Gabby, Everlee, and Leighton. If they liked her, they would make sure she was at the after party, and I would be waiting for her.

Anger laced with bitterness pumped in my veins as my hatred of Wynter Baldwin shot through me at the mere thought of her. The sooner I dealt with her, the better. I had a life to live, and if she were around, she'd get in my head. My plans to get out from under Adam's thumb and go pro were my top priorities, and I wasn't about to lose my shot at the NFL.

After thinking it through, I'd decided the best way to ruin Wynter was to make her fall for me. Make her believe I was the perfect guy for her, then destroy her. In the meantime, I certainly wasn't opposed to playing with my prey first. While the party was in full swing, I would introduce myself. It would be a great opportunity to get close and slip her an invitation to the society too. Then the real games would begin.

Adam had left for another business trip a few days before, so I'd offered to throw the party at my place after the game. After winning with a fourteen-point lead, I was ready to blow off some steam.

More than that, I was ready to find Wynter.

The vibrations of the music thundered through the walls and rumbled through my chest as I surveyed the wild scene. Near the kitchen, I propped myself against the wall and watched the chaos.

Guys clustered near a small wooden end table were arm wrestling, each boasting and laughing with a bravado that only came with alcohol. By the front entrance and living room, a group of girls shed their inhibitions and spun around the white columns as if they were stripper poles. Loud laughter accompanied the teetering stilettos and spilled drinks.

Last year, one girl attempted to swing around the column and face-planted into the floor. Apparently, she was too drunk to feel any pain. I got her the hell out of my house as fast as I could. Adam would rip me a new one if someone sued him.

To cover our asses, the football team decided we would all pitch in and monitor the pole activity. The society members weren't worried about trying to get laid, so we chilled and made sure something insane didn't happen.

"Dude, you look so serious. It's a fucking party." Zeke, a sophomore teammate, handed me a red Solo cup nearly filled to the rim with a brown liquid.

My eyebrows shot up. "What is it?"

"Rum and Coke. Drink up and chill." Zeke slapped me on the back before he joined a group dancing in the middle of the living room. The crowd jumped up and down to the beat of "Welcome to My Life" by qwinn while I kept an eye out for the one and only Wynter Baldwin. The details of Wynter's life bombarded my mind, causing a toxic hatred for a girl I hadn't met to churn inside me.

But she's gorgeous.

I reminded myself to get her an invite to the society, but then thought maybe I should just kidnap her. *Fuck, I sound like Adam.* Disgusted with myself, I focused on looking for her again.

"Don't do it," Kane said, easing up next to me. "Whatever is going through that thick skull of yours, just don't do it." He took a drink from the blue Solo cup in his hand, then nodded at his girlfriend, Brie, who was dancing with the other girls on the cheer squad.

I smirked. "Night out, huh?"

"Yeah, Brie was excited to spend time with her friends. Our lives have changed so much." Kane grinned at me as though he'd won the lottery *and* already been signed to play pro ball.

"No shit." My breath hitched in my throat as a tall dude moved to the side and I finally spotted Wynter.

She was dancing with Gabby and Everlee, her hair flying around her face as she threw her hands up in the air and shook her ass. My dick hardened on the spot, her pictures with the other guys moving front and center into my mind.

"Does Brie know the new girl that's living with Gabby, Everlee, and Leighton?" I stared straight ahead, not wanting Kane to witness my expression in case I slipped up and he realized that I was interested in Wynter. The longer I glowered at her the more pissed off I became. Kane would check my shit, and I wasn't in the mood. He had no idea what she'd done. What had happened. I would never tell him why, either.

"She has her in a class, I think, and she also knows her through Gabby. Brie said she's nice but a bit standoffish." Kane drained his cup, then eyed me. "Since being able to both get out at the same time has been rare lately, we've decided to make the most of tonight. We'll grab an Uber and head to the Viper Secret Society, then Uber home later."

"Drink up and get buzzed then, motherfucker." I laughed and slapped the back of my hand on his chest.

"Oh, I am." Kane tossed his empty cup in one of the many trashcans placed around the house. "So, what's up with you and Wynter? Need an intro or something?"

I pursed my lips together, then spotted my opening. "Nah, I think I got what I need." I pushed off the wall and elbowed my way through the crowd and to the coffee table.

Wynter had hopped up on it and was lip syncing to "Call it Love" by Felix Jaehn and Ray Dalton. The guys around her moved back to give her more room and watched while she busted out some serious dance moves without missing a word.

My cock strained against my jeans as I took in the denim shorts grazing her ass cheeks and a mostly see-through top clinging to her like a second skin. Fucking stunning. So much for standoffish. Apparently, if she got a little alcohol in her, she was ready to go.

Reaching the table, I glanced up at her and gave her a panty-dropping smile. Her eyes widened as she spotted me, then Wynter stumbled over her words. I reached out and she tucked her long hair behind her ear, took my hand, and assisted me up.

I stood next to her and threw my arms wide, joining in the lip syncing.

She licked her lips, staring at the obvious bulge in my jeans as I continued to move my hips in a slow, seductive circle. The girls cheered for more as I motioned for Wynter to join in.

Wynter sank her teeth into her plump lower lip, then strutted over to me and eased her leg between mine. I took her cue, slipping my arm around her waist and pulling her close.

"You're new to Whitmore." My hand trailed down to her ass cheek, giving it a little squeeze.

"I am. It's been a busy first few weeks, but I'm ready to have some fun tonight." She winked at me, full of confidence.

"I can definitely help you with that. I'm Quinn by the way."

"I'm Wynter, and I'll think about it." Wynter laughed as she threw her arms up, riding my leg as we danced. Shit, she was hot. For just a few minutes, I forgot my plan to ruin her and just enjoyed her body writhing against mine.

The song ended, and I flashed Wynter a lazy smile. "Want a drink first, or ...?"

Her gaze traveled from my football jersey down to my crotch. "Fuck first. We can drink during intermission."

There was a slight slur to her words, and I wondered if she was drunk or just buzzed. Maybe she could hold her liquor well. I couldn't help but chuckle. I liked the way her mind worked. "Follow me." Taking her hand, I helped her off the table, then led her through the crowd and up the set of stairs to the bedrooms.

"Is this your house?" she asked, trailing behind me.

"Yeah. My younger brother and I live here. When the parental unit is gone, I throw parties. He's an investment banker and travels a lot." I pushed open my bedroom door. "After you, gorgeous." My plan was working out perfectly. I'd fuck her so good she wouldn't be able to stay away from me. Over the next few weeks, I would walk her to class, take her out, and pretend to fall for her. Hopefully by then she would reciprocate. Then, I would strike.

She stepped inside, her mouth gaping as she looked around at the king-size bed, a flat-screen television over the gas fireplace, the sitting area, and an open door that led into a walk-in closet.

"Your room is nearly as big as my home back in Washington," she murmured.

"Washington, huh?" I was ready to fuck her, but it might be the best time to get some information out of her first. "What's in Washington, other than a lot of rain?" I knew about her mom and sister from the PI report, of course, but I was more curious in finding out whether there was a boyfriend that would miss her if she fucking disappeared.

Sicko! I sound just like Adam.

"My sister, Janine, and a pathetic excuse of a mother."

Interesting.

"Wanna play a little game?" I sat on the edge of the bed and flipped open the button on my jeans. Her gaze followed my movements as I slipped my hand into my boxer briefs and freed my throbbing cock.

A small gasp escaped from her as I stroked my shaft and raised a brow.

"What type of game?" Wynter licked her lower lip, her attention never left my dick as I continued.

"I would never want to leave a chick feeling as though I wasn't attentive, so why don't you tell me about yourself? Then I'll reward you for each comment. But"—I held up my free hand—"you have to tell me the good shit if you want me to fuck you. Telling me your hair is reddish blonde isn't enough."

She tapped her finger against her chin, considering my offer. "What if I just like to watch you jerk off? Maybe I don't want to share a lot about myself."

Smart girl. I changed tactics quickly. "Okay, then tell me what you like and what you're willing to do."

Her light brows furrowed together.

"You mean in bed?" She took a step toward me, smiling. "I like a big thick cock in my mouth and another one in my pussy at the same time."

"I like that answer." I stood and slowly looked up and down her body. "Get on your knees."

Without hesitation, she knelt and flicked her tongue across the tip of my dick.

"What if I handcuffed you to my bed and brought in one of my buddies, then we took turns fucking you?"

She peeked up at me as she slid my shaft between her lips slowly.

I grunted as she ran her tongue along the sensitive head and sucked, stopping only long enough to answer, "I'm in." Then she shoved me back into her mouth, lightly raking my skin with her teeth.

"Shit," I muttered, threading my fingers through her hair and roughly jerking her neck back. Thrusting in and out, I hit the back of her throat, cutting off her air. Her pretty face turned red as she stared up at me, meeting my gaze. No fear, no pleading, just holding her ground. I stroked her cheek with my thumb. "You like it, don't you?"

I pulled out a little bit, allowing her to breathe. Wynter grabbed my shaft, stroking as she continued to suck.

"That's it, pretty girl. Take it all in before I shove it in your cunt and fuck you until you're screaming my name." Heat zipped up my spine, and I abruptly stopped her. "As much as I want you to swallow, I have other plans for tonight."

A loud kick against my door startled me. "Fuck off!" I glanced down at Wynter still on her knees, her lips red and swollen from sucking my dick. She didn't know that this was just the beginning, that I was trying to find her weak spot. Was it my fault I got to get off while I figured out what would hurt her?

My door burst open, and I looked over my shoulder to see who the hell had the audacity to barge into my room.

"What the fuck are you doing?"

I froze, terror coursing through my veins.

Chapter 7

Wynter

Quinn didn't have to ask me to leave. I wasn't sure who the older guy was, but he and Quinn looked enough alike that I could make a guess. Horrified that anyone had caught me on my knees with Quinn's dick in my mouth, I ran out of the room and down the stairs, elbowing my way through the crowded kitchen and out the back door.

The night air chilled my clammy skin as I huddled against the side of the house, trying to catch my breath. How was I going to get out of here without telling Gabby what had just happened?

Nausea rolled in my stomach as dark thoughts slammed into me fast and hard. Screams filled my mind, and I grabbed the sides of my head, hoping no one would find me until the flashbacks were over.

"Breathe," I said softly. Forcing myself to look around, I rattled off what I saw as the flashback continued to gut me. "A pool, shed, lawn chairs, an outdoor kitchen, a privacy fence." I repeated it several more times until my heart rate calmed down and I could understand where I was. How the fuck had seeing the man who was possibly Quinn's father send me into a full-on panic attack?

The creak of the door opening caught my attention. "There you are. I thought I saw you come outside. Are you sick?" Gabby strolled toward me, concern in her pretty face.

"Yeah." I gulped, hating my lie, but under no circumstances could I go back inside and see Quinn or that man again.

"Oh, hon. Did you drink too much?" Gabby put her arm around my shoulders and led me to one of the lawn chairs. It was still relatively clear for a northwest fall, but it was still cool outside. At least it wasn't raining. I shivered and rubbed my arms.

"I think I need to go home. I'll call an Uber, though. I don't want to mess up your evening."

Gabby grinned at me. "No way, I'll take you. Hell, I even have a barf bag in my car. I'm prepared for this. Everlee wanted to leave early, too, so let me grab her. Stay put." She hurried back into the mansion, and I leaned my head against the red bricks of the house.

Confusion swept over me as I recalled Quinn's door slamming open and an outraged man bursting in. I had to find out more about who he was, but more than that, why he'd triggered me so badly.

A few minutes later, Gabby, Leighton, and Everlee appeared back on the patio.

"Girl, it's good we're leaving. Quinn's father came home, so everyone has to clear out. He looked pissed as hell, yelling at everyone to leave," Gabby said.

"He's usually cool with the parties, but something definitely tickled his asshole tonight." Everlee clucked her tongue. "We're out, bitches. Let's continue the drinks at the house."

"What does his dad look like? I saw an older guy but had no idea who he was." I twisted a lock of hair around my finger, trying to not seem too eager to learn who the man was.

"A lot like Quinn, except older, of course. He's a little shorter than Quinn, too. As I said, I'm not sure what was going on tonight, but Mr. Astor didn't look happy," Leighton explained.

Shit. I'm right. Quinn's dad walked in while I had his son's dick in my mouth. *Son of a bitch.* "I think I saw him." I attempted a smile, feeling the color drain from my face as the full realization hammered my alcohol-muddled brain.

Everlee finally took a good look at me. "Oh shit, you're pale. Are you all right?" Everlee came closer and slipped her arm through mine. "You still seem a bit wasted, if you ask me, but I can't tell for sure. Have either of you been so drunk you thought everyone else was drunk, too?" Her giggle bounced off the cement patio.

"Don't worry. I'm sober since I'm driving." Gabby took my other arm and looped hers through it. "I'll drink when we're safe and sound at home."

Safe and sound wasn't something I'd had in several years. It sounded heavenly. Everlee chatted nonstop as we located Gabby's blue Audi R8. To my surprise, Everlee crawled in the back seat and laid her head in Leighton's lap.

"Oh, I don't feel so good, Gabby."

Gabby peeked at Leighton and Everlee. "Buckle up, babe. I can't have you bouncing around like a soccer ball on steroids if I have to stop suddenly."

Leighton patted her back, then Everlee groaned but sat up and fastened her seat belt.

Fifteen minutes later, Gabby pulled into our driveway. Even though I was feeling a ton better, I didn't want any more to drink. When I drank too much, I got loose lipped, and I was afraid of what I would tell the girls. I was just beginning to have friends, and even if I refused to get attached, it was nice not to be the outcast for a little while.

Once we were safely inside the house and the door was locked, Everlee flung herself face-down on the couch. "I need water."

I couldn't help but laugh. She was even more dramatic when she was drunk.

"Got it." Gabby disappeared into the kitchen and returned a few minutes later with two bottled waters and a rum and Coke she had made for herself. She doled out the drinks, then sat in the recliner.

Everlee sat up, twisted off the cap of her bottle in one motion, then guzzled the water. I gawked at her.

"Won't that make you sick?"

She wiped off her mouth with the back of her hand. "Nah. Keeps me from having a massive hangover."

"I taught her that important trick." Leighton laughed.

Everlee grinned and leaned against the couch, turning her attention to me. "So, Wynter Baldwin." My heart stopped beating for a moment.

She knows.

I fought the urge to run to my room and lock the door. It would be easy enough to pack and move when the girls were asleep.

"I saw you dancing with Quinn Astor, amazing wide receiver, and according to the rumors, a total sex god. But you, my darling, were dancing with him on the coffee table. Bitch, you've been holding out on us. You've got some moves." Everlee laughed.

Tension eased from my neck and shoulders with Everlee's words.

"So does Quinn, holy hell." Gabby fanned herself.

"I'd take a piece of that for damned sure," Leighton chimed in.

I gave them a sheepish grin. "I, uh, tend to let loose a bit when I'm tipsy."

"No kidding. I mean you've been our roomie for a few weeks, but I don't really feel like I know a lot about you." Everlee flipped her brown hair behind her shoulder and focused on me. "Dish. I want all the deets. Every last one of them."

I froze as Gabby, Leighton, and Everlee stared at me, waiting for me to say something. *Be careful and don't fuck this up.*

"Is Quinn dating anyone?" Maybe keeping him as the center of everyone's attention would work. For some reason he was still the center of my thoughts as well. I'd been with enough guys working for Dimitri that I didn't get attached easily, but there was something about Quinn that seemed familiar. I just couldn't put my finger on it. Not to mention that he was sexy as hell and his long, thick cock had almost made me drool.

Irritated that we'd been interrupted, I reminded myself that if he knew who I was, he would never want to be with me. A relationship with anyone was off-limits. Inwardly, I sighed and focused on my roomies.

Gabby snorted. "Quinn is a player. He's never dated anyone longer than a night, and he's attended Whitmore for four years. So have we." Gabby tilted her head in Everlee's direction.

"Interesting." I wasn't about to tell the girls that I'd sucked his dick earlier. It was something I wanted to keep to myself, just like my job and my past. Attempting to clear my brain from the lingering effects of the alcohol, I remembered my plan.

"He is, for sure, but are you? I mean, are you interested in Quinn?" Leighton asked.

"I have no idea. I only met him tonight." I raised my hand. "New girl here, remember? I don't know anyone other than you guys."

"Stalk him on Instagram or TikTok. You'll see a lot of the football players there," Everlee said.

I fidgeted in my seat. "I don't use social media. It got in the way of my studies, and I needed a scholarship, so I deleted my accounts. Even when I looked at Whitmore online, I didn't look at the sororities or sports teams. Mostly, I tend to keep to myself." *I hope they buy that reason.*

"Hey, social media can be bad for your mental health sometimes. I'm glad you walked away from it. Besides, there are plenty of parties, so I'm sure you'll meet some guys soon." Gabby took a sip of her drink. "Where did you learn to dance and lip sync at the same time like that?"

I grinned. It had been the most fun I'd had all night until Quinn and I had been interrupted. Chills traveled down my spine as I recalled the hate and anger in the older man's face.

"Dance team in middle and high school."

"Wait, dance team as in the dance team for the cheerleaders?" Gabby asked.

"Yup. I was a basketball cheerleader through my sophomore year." *Here it comes. The million dollar question.*

"Why'd you quit? You looked badass tonight." Everlee played with her bottle cap as she waited for me to reply.

"Life. I started taking AP classes, and I'm sure you two know how cutthroat and catty some cheerleaders can be when their competitive nature kicks in."

"Girl!" Everlee placed the back of her hand against her forehead. "So much drama."

"Yeah, I just didn't want to put up with it anymore."

Liar! They didn't bully you until after shit went down.

"One of our friends quit for the same reason. It can get brutal. Thankfully, I have Everlee and Leighton on the team with me. Otherwise, I probably would have quit too. Sometimes you have to make a good mental health decision, ya know?"

I know all too well. "Yeah, it got bad. I actually homeschooled my last two years of high school."

"Damn, then got into Whitmore? You must be super smart. I'm not that smart." She giggled. "Okay, more please. Do you have brothers? Sisters? What do your mom and dad do for a living?"

Everlee's questions were like rapid torpedoes firing at me. I wanted to duck behind the chair, but I took a breath, reminding myself that Janine and I had gone over every question and answer possible in order to protect me. Protect us.

"My dad took off a few years ago. I haven't talked to him since then. Mom is a ... a sorry excuse for a parent. She'd rather drink herself into a stupor and ignore the fact that she has two daughters to take care of." I waited for their responses, but they remained silent. "I've been taking care of my younger sister for a while. She's seventeen, so it was a good time for me to finish my degree."

"Well, fuck!" Everlee said. "That's some shit, girl. You have to be strong to deal with all of that."

"Do you think your mom suffers from depression?" Gabby gently asked. "We have a friend that had a difficult relationship with her mom. Come to find out she was mentally ill and needed treatment."

My world tilted on its side, black dots dancing before my eyes, and my pulse spiked. "It runs in the family." I stared at my feet, trying to get a hold of myself for the second time that night.

"Hey, are you okay?" Gabby jumped out of her chair and crossed the room.

"Yeah, I think I drank too much at the party. It hits me in waves." I wasn't lying. I just wasn't telling her that a conversation about mental illness wasn't on the table. "I'm going to get some more water and go to bed."

"Okay. I hope you feel better," Everlee said.

"Thanks. Me too." I wish sleep were my friend and would help me feel better, but half the time when I tried, the nightmares plagued me. Maybe thinking about Quinn would give me something else to focus on.

Chapter 8

Quinn

As soon as Wynter was gone, Adam slammed the door closed. I put myself back in my jeans, which meant I took my eyes off Adam for a moment too long. He bolted across the room, punching my jaw hard enough to knock me backward the minute I glanced at him.

I hit the floor with a thud, and pain shot through my tail bone. I hauled myself up, then launched my fist into his gut and laughed as he doubled over.

"Forgot your place for a minute, old man." I might have been drunk, but I was clearheaded enough to inflict some damage.

"You're going to mess it all up like you always do." Adam groaned as he held the end of my bed and pulled himself off the floor.

"Mess what up? Wynter Baldwin? If you hadn't noticed, I had her exactly where I wanted her. On her knees, bowing to me." I shoved my fingers through my short hair. "I can't destroy her if I don't know what makes her tick." I glared at Adam. "Keep your enemies closer, right? That's what you've taught me my entire life. Oh, and take what you want, no matter who it will hurt." Disgust with Adam's teachings churned in my gut.

"So your plan is to get in her pants and make her fall in love with you?" Adam chuckled, shaking his head. "If she can love someone like you, then I'd keep her instead of fucking her over." His smile faltered, then he leered at me. "I mean, once she knows the truth about you, she'll take off just like everyone else."

My body shook with anger. "Stay out of my fucking way so I can handle the bitch." Spittle flew from my mouth.

Adam tossed up his hands in surrender. "Just don't fuck it up. You've got one chance to finish her off. Maybe she'll kill herself and rid the world of another pathetic Baldwin."

I flinched at the coldness in his words. Even though I hated Wynter, that was too far. "Get out, and don't come in without knocking again." I pointed at the door, ready to get rid of him.

"Clean up the fucking mess you and your friends made." Adam left. The beat of the music floated through the air, but the rest of the house was quiet except for laughter that I recognized came from Kane and Sterling.

I gave Adam a head start before rushing out of my room and closing the door behind me. Hurrying down the stairs, I found my teammates cleaning up already.

"Sorry, guys. Dad had a bad day." They had no idea how badly it ended up being. I rubbed my swelling jaw, the ache spreading through my entire head.

The guys suspiciously eyed me but didn't say a word. "We've got it, man. Still was a good party." Anderson dumped one of the trashcans into a large, heavy-duty trash bag that Kane held open for him.

"Look at it this way. A few more hours in and we would've probably been cleaning up some puke," Sterling added, picking up the beer bottles that were scattered across the living room.

"True." I walked to the kitchen, then down the hall to the bathroom, but I didn't see Adam anywhere. I joined the guys again. "Who's sober enough to drive?"

"Me," Zeke said. "You need a ride?"

I nodded. "Yeah, as soon as this shit is cleaned up, I want to deliver an invitation."

"Hell yeah. It's about time, Q." Kane laughed as his brow lifted in my direction.

"Wynter Baldwin? The way you two were going at it tonight, my money's on her." Anderson shot me a cheesy grin. He clearly wasn't sober.

"Has anyone else dropped her an invite?" That should have been my first question.

We all stared at each other, waiting to see if anyone had.

"Excellent. If I get tired of fucking her, I'll let you all know. She made it clear she's pretty much up for anything."

From the pictures of her with the guys, she was down with more than one person and couldn't care less if she got passed around a few times.

"Here?" Zeke asked, turning the headlights off as he inched down the road in front of Gabby, Everlee, and Wynter's house.

"Yeah. Good thing your parents bought you a Tesla for graduation. This bitch is super quiet."

"She's pretty sweet." Zeke grinned at me, then slowed a few addresses down from the target. "I don't see anyone around, do you?"

I searched through the darkness but didn't see anyone. It was three in the morning, so of course the homes were dark, and people were asleep. Thank fuck she had a mailbox with a slot in the front, so I wouldn't be breaking the law by opening it and popping in the invite. These days everyone had a door camera that would record any activity around the neighborhood. At least I'd thought ahead.

Tugging my skull mask over my head, I noticed Zeke did the same, just in case. The masks for the Viper Secret Society came in handy for more than hiding our identities while fucking some chicks.

I quietly opened the car door, then crouched and ran to Wynter's mailbox. After I dropped it in, I hurried to the Tesla, remaining as hidden as possible.

Once I was safe and secure in the passenger's seat again, Zeke pulled a U-turn and drove away.

Zeke slowed to a stop and tugged off his mask, tossing it in the back floorboard. "Hopefully we didn't set off anyone's security camera." He smoothed his short blonde hair, then grinned.

I removed my mask as well but kept it in my lap. "Thanks for the ride."

"Ain't a thing. I was disappointed your dad came home, but there's another party next weekend. You think you'll ask Wynter or just meet her at the society?"

"Probably both." I fisted my hand, hoping like hell Wynter would find the invite and fill out the online form. My dick grew hard thinking about her pretty little lips wrapped around my shaft. I would have fucked her if Adam hadn't shown up. That son of a bitch always ruined everything, but not anymore. As soon as I graduated and was drafted, I was cutting him out of my life. The only reason I had anything to do with him now was because of Brody.

My phone pinged with a text, and I fished it out of the back pocket of my jeans. Adam's name popped up, and I debated opening it at all. Finally, I tapped the message. A picture of Wynter getting royally fucked by some dude I hadn't seen before.

Use this to jerk off to and stay focused on dealing with her.

What a fucking asshole. I pushed the side button, making my screen go black before Zeke could see the image.

Why was Wynter having her picture taken when she was fucking guys? Did she like it? Was she getting paid?

Zeke parked in front of my house, and I grabbed my mask in my other hand. "Thanks, man. I'll catch ya tomorrow."

"Have a good one."

I climbed out and hurried up the walk to my front door. The guys had all cleared out before I went to Wynter's place, so I didn't have to talk to anyone as I made a beeline across the mansion and to my room.

This time, I locked myself in before opening the dresser drawer and locating the key to my desk. Unlocking it, I snatched up the file Adam had given me on Wynter. I sat down in the chair and opened it. After shuffling through a few pieces of paper, I finally spotted her personal details with her address, sibling's name, and last employer.

Dimitri Gusev, photographer.

My forehead creased and I collected my MacBook from my desk and walked to my bed. Seconds later, I leaned against my headboard before I typed his information into Google. I clicked on his website and images of threesomes and foursomes popped up on the screen, but the faces were all blurred out. I scrolled through the photos, then located my phone and opened the picture Adam had sent me.

There. Wynter had a light birthmark on her back, directly above her right ass cheek.

Over the next ten minutes, I looked at every image on Dimitri's site. Wynter was in a lot of them, but the only way I could tell it was her was from the birthmark. So where the hell was Adam getting these images from? I dug into the website a little farther, then realized it was a paid website. But why would Adam want these? Blackmail? Horny fuckers all over the world would pay to see these pictures, and I assumed Wynter knew that when she posed for Dimitri.

While mentally running through a hundred different possibilities, I had another idea. After looking through the fifteen images again, I finally found what I was searching for—a tiny copyright and date in the lower left-hand corner. My eyes narrowed as I did the math.

Son of a fucking bitch.

"Checkmate, Adam."

Chapter 9

Quinn

I read through Wynter's society application for the tenth time. Finally needing to stretch, I stood from my desk in the office and placed her information in the top drawer before I locked it. Then I pushed up the sleeves of my burgundy long-sleeved T-shirt and flexed my fingers.

Wynter had taken several days to reply to the Viper Secret Society invitation and complete the questionnaire on the website.

Wynter had filled out the section of her fantasies, likes, and dislikes in great detail. I didn't give a shit about her dislikes. I was in this for revenge and to get laid. Hate sex had never looked so damn good, and I planned on taking everything I wanted from her.

Adam's voice rang in my head. *If she won't fuck you, slip her a roofie and take what you want. You don't have to ask permission, you're an Astor.*

My skin prickled as I remembered the time when I was eleven, and Adam first started teaching me his twisted views on sex. For years I listened to his warped opinions, believed his every word. I even suggested that one of the guys in the society drug a girl and fuck her. When the other guys stared at me like I'd lost my fucking mind, it finally hit me that these teachings were completely warped and wrong. My hatred for Adam only grew as I thought of all the ways he had manipulated me growing up, and I vowed not to turn out like him. I squared my shoulders and with newfound motivation, I mustered up my courage, determined to never let him hurt me again.

The alarm on my watch beeped, and I removed it and placed it on the stack of rejected applications. It was crazy how many invitations we'd sent out this school year. Crossing the room, I opened the closet door and grabbed the black shirt and slacks I kept there. It was time to see what Wynter Baldwin was made of.

My phone vibrated against the desk with an incoming text. I quickly changed my clothes and tossed my jeans and T-shirt into a chair before I read the message from Anderson.

Wynter is here and in the blue room waiting for you.

My fingers danced across the screen with my reply.

Perfect.

Before I joined her, I rolled my long shirt sleeves to my forearms and reminded myself of who she was and what she was capable of. Being with her wasn't about the sex. It was about cold-hearted vengeance. She had destroyed me several years ago, and now it was my turn to repay the favor.

Chapter 10

Wynter

My insides quivered with giddiness when I circled the room to take in the small space. A single chair and table were tucked away in one corner, and I hurriedly pursed my lips to hold back a nervous laugh. Shadows loomed on the walls, and a shiver ran down my spine. It was eerily quiet, as if I were alone in a secret lair, waiting for the king to arrive. I tried to shake it off, reminding myself why I was here—hot, yummy sex.

The Viper Secret Society invitation had mentioned to leave my bra and panties off, making me hopeful that I would finally get laid. It had been a few weeks since my last job with Dimitri, but it seemed longer. I'd decided to wear a short denim miniskirt and lilac top with buttons down the front. My outfit provided easy access for sure.

My attention drifted to Dimitri and the good times we'd had working together. I wondered if whoever had invited me to the society would be as much fun as Dimitri's guys, or if the men back home could teach him a few things. My mind danced with dirty thoughts and quickly shifted to Quinn.

"Stop thinking about him," I muttered to myself. "He's a player."

The creak of the door opening caused me to jump, and I spun

around to see a tall person dressed in black. His hands were large with long fingers—definitely man hands.

"Hello, Wynter Baldwin," he said, and I realized his voice was disguised with a modifier beneath the white skull mask that covered his neck and hid his face.

"Hi." I chewed on the inside of my cheek, eager to get to the fun part. I had no idea who he was, but the mystery was intriguing as hell. As long as he knew what he was doing in bed, then I really didn't care.

"Do you know why you received an invitation to the Viper Secret Society?"

I clasped my hands in front of me. "No clue. I didn't even know there was a secret society."

He walked forward slowly, staring at me. "If you did, it wouldn't be a secret now, would it?" He circled me, the powerful hunter about to devour his prey. "You're beautiful."

That was unexpected. My pulse stuttered from the compliment. "Thank you."

The masked man closed the gap between us and threaded his fingers through my long hair, wrapping it around his fist. I took advantage of the moment and assessed him. His biceps bulged in his shirt sleeves, and his broad shoulders stretched the fabric of his black button-down shirt. I squinted and leaned into him, his leather and sandalwood scent intoxicating me. My gaze latched onto the red stitching on his dark collar. A dragon?

"Bow."

I hesitated, and my body tensed as his words drew me to the present again. Even with a voice disguiser, his tone was clipped and harsh. He jerked my hair, forcing my head back, and pain shot through my scalp as he pushed me to my knees.

"Let's make something clear, Wynter. You're here to serve *me*. Do you understand?"

I stared up at him. "Yes." My thighs clenched with longing. I was totally down with fucking a stranger, and the excitement of not knowing who was beneath the skull mask intensified the situation even more. I still wanted to know who the Red Dragon was and why he was ready to set the world on fire, but my hormones were in the driver's seat and kicked my curiosity to the curb.

He released my hair, then walked behind me, my gaze watching his every move until he was out of my sight. The sound of a drawer opening and closing caught my attention and my pulse ticked up a notch as I anticipated his next step. Seconds later he tied a silk scarf over my eyes and restrained my wrists in front of me. A whirlwind of fear and excitement pumped through me as he jerked me to a standing position by my arm.

I stepped closer, hearing the sound of a chair scraping across the cement floor. My skirt was yanked up my hips, and a chill caressed my thighs.

Strong hands forced me forward until I was bent over what I assumed was his lap.

"Do you know what will happen if you disobey me?" He squeezed my butt.

I presumed I was about to find out. "No."

A loud smack filled the room, and my ass cheek began to sting. I inhaled sharply, welcoming the pain as I was spanked until tears flowed down my face.

He parted my legs and ran his fingers over my sex. "You're wet for me, Wynter. Do you like pain? Is that what makes you come?" He sounded intrigued.

I stiffened in reaction to his interest. I hadn't told anyone that I loved the endorphin rush of pain and sex. It had always been my secret. "Sometimes." I squeaked and prepared for him to smack my butt some more. Instead of hitting me, he roughly shoved a finger inside me.

"Such a tight little cunt. I can't wait to sink my cock into you."

I squirmed on his lap, chills shooting through my body as the anticipation of the unknown flickered through my mind. Unable to see what the stranger was doing took the sensations to a whole new level.

The sound of the door opening again filled the room, and I listened as footsteps came closer. Maybe my first time at the Viper Secret Society would be with two guys. I'd submitted a long list of fantasies, but I didn't mention that I'd lived most of them. What they didn't know was that they had competition, and I was grading their performances.

A hand roughly gripped my arm and forced me to my knees on the floor. The sound of a zipper made me tense while I waited to see what would happen next.

Once again, I was pulled to my feet and turned around.

"Straddle him," someone said beside me.

I stepped backward and hands tugged on my hips, forcing my back against the seated man's chest. In position, he pulled me down and lined up his dick at my entrance.

Whimpering as he shoved himself inside me, I sucked in a sharp breath. A strong arm slipped around my stomach and pushed my knees against my breasts while he thrust.

"Fuck, that pussy looks good enough to eat."

There had to be at least two guys in the room with me. Even though the voices were disguised, one was gentler than the other.

I bounced up and down, moaning. God, it felt like forever since I'd been fucked senseless, but it had only been three weeks since my last day working for Dimitri.

Another set of hands grabbed my thighs, forcing my legs back even farther. I gasped as something flicked across my clit, sending delicious shivers through me.

"Oh, God," I said as I realized that one guy was licking me while the other was inside me. Holy shit, that was hot as hell. One wrong move and the guys would be touching. I would totally be down watching two men. Hell, if they liked two chicks together, then I was an equal oppor- tunist all the way around. As long as they took care of me, I was game.

My core throbbed and tingles traveled through me as I bucked against his mouth, still full of the other guy's dick.

My head jerked back. "Are you ready to come?" he asked.

"Yes." My answer was short and breathy, and I was teetering on the edge of oblivion.

Hands cupped my breasts through my shirt, pinching my nipples through the thin fabric. My lips parted, and I groaned as my world exploded, my orgasm ripping through me at mach speed.

Panting, I collapsed back against the guy's chest. Shuffling filled the small space, and I imagined the guy who had been licking me stood.

My legs were pushed closed, and I was jerked to my feet, my core immediately feeling the loss of body heat. A hand dug into my flesh, pain shooting through me as the first guy forced me to bend at the waist against a hard surface, then rammed his cock into me so hard, I stumbled forward. Jerking my head back, I cried out. His grunts and our bodies slapping together were the only sounds left in the room. But I hadn't heard the other person leave. Was he watching?

Fingers teased my asshole, then he applied a slippery liquid. He pulled out and forcefully shoved into my ass, and a soft cry escaped me. I gasped as he thrust deep inside me again, my body quivering. Scraping my nails against what I suspected was a table beneath me, I slammed my eyes closed as he continued to move. Waves of intense pleasure swirled low in my belly, radiating through me with each movement, and I gave in to the sensation, allowing it to wash over me.

"Do you like being fucked in the ass, Wynter? Do you beg the guys back home to fuck both holes at the same time?"

Behind the blindfold, my gaze narrowed, and a flicker of irritation overtook my desire. "I don't have to beg."

He adjusted, driving deeper into me. "Oh, but you do."

He grunted, then he trembled against me. Remaining still, I waited for him to pull out.

"Why do you have to beg for it? Because you're evil ... that's what you are. I just fucked the devil herself."

What is happening right now?

The warmth of his body left mine.

"I'm not evil." My voice betrayed me, shaking to the rhythm of my heart thudding in my ears.

Hot breath fanned across my face.

"Rumor has it that you attended Timber Creek High. Did you really think you could run from your past? Girls like you need to be punished, reminded of who they are. Fucking. Worthless. Trash."

Chapter 11

Wynter

By the time I got home, the urge to puke was so strong, I ran up the stairs to the hall bathroom. With trembling hands, I pushed the door open and scrambled to the toilet. I sank to my knees in front of the porcelain throne just in time as my lunch bubbled up from my stomach and noisily landed in the commode. Sweat slickened my forehead as I clung to the seat, hoping like hell that my body had finished revolting.

I sat on the floor and pressed my back against the teal-painted wall, my brain in overdrive. A cry clogged my throat. If my wrists hadn't been restrained, I would have ripped off the motherfucker's mask and beat the shit out of him with it. But by the time I got the silk scarf off, he'd left the room.

Someone fucking knew who I was. Tears stung my cheeks as they fell fast and hard. I slammed my eyes closed and images of fists and kicks to my body shot me into a panic. I struggled to breathe, the flashbacks overpowering reality. Hiding my face in my arm, I sobbed uncontrollably.

Goddammit. How? I'd been painstakingly careful when I'd applied to attend Whitmore that my past was fabricated. The vicious words whispered through my mind, *girls like you need to be punished and reminded of who they are. Fucking. Worthless. Trash.* That motherfucker was right, and even though his words hurt, I'd heard worse—much worse.

"Wynter?" a soft voice broke through the horror I was reliving.

I sucked in a shaky breath and peeked through my fingers. For some reason I thought the roomies were out for the night, and I had a safe space to fall apart.

"Hey." Everlee sank to the floor and gently squeezed my forearm. "Are you okay? I mean, that's a stupid question. You're clearly not. How can I help?"

The kindness in her tone gutted me. If I told Everlee what had happened, she would turn on me just like everyone else. Then I realized it was only a matter of time before the entire campus found out. My name would spew from every mouth at Whitmore University, and their comments would be full of bitterness and hate.

I leaned my head against the wall, willing my tears to dry up. Wiping the moisture from my cheeks, I glanced at Everlee. "I have flashbacks sometimes." Shame and fear clung to my tone, my voice cracking with my confession.

Everlee grabbed my hand. "Did something bad happen today or did it just come out of the blue?"

I snorted, my brain attempting to find humor in the fucked-up situation. I couldn't admit to Everlee that I'd been in an incredible threesome, then the hateful words came at me followed by the horrible flashbacks.

"I was triggered by someone." I brought my knees to my chin, wishing I could disappear from the world.

When I learned I'd been accepted at Whitmore, I'd foolishly thought my past wouldn't follow me. I licked my lips, digging deep inside myself to find the courage to share even a bit with Everlee. If I tested the waters, then maybe someday I could tell her everything. Surely, I could take little steps at a time. I was strong, I'd lived through hell and back. But the desire to be loved and accepted was driving me hard and forcing me to take chances again. Other than Janine, I didn't trust anyone, no matter how much I wanted to.

My chest heaved, and I tucked my hair behind my ear. "You know when I said I quit cheer due to the drama?"

Everlee rolled her eyes. "Girl, I feel you. The world's hard enough on us. Women should support each other, share each other's wins, not tear each other down and be catty bitches."

I picked at a hangnail, needing something to do with my hands. "Yeah, isn't it all supposed to get better at some point?"

Everlee nodded enthusiastically. "I know we've only been roomies for three weeks, but I swear I'm here for you."

"I appreciate it. You've been really sweet."

"I'm all ears but remember, sometimes the anticipation of a person's reaction is worse than reality." She squeezed my arm in reassurance.

Not in my case. "I was on the cheer team, and it was my sophomore year in high school." I swallowed down the panic that was threatening to rip me apart from the inside out.

To my surprise, Everlee didn't fire a million questions at me, she just waited for me to continue.

"Some rumors started to spread, and my friends ... I found out they weren't my friends after all. The team staged a fake meeting one night. When I showed up at the school gym, they jumped me before I could even go into the building."

Everlee gasped. "All of them? That seems like an unfair fight to me." Her brown eyes narrowed as anger rolled off her in waves.

I pursed my lips together and nodded. "I was in the hospital for a week with a fractured rib, and broken jaw, wrist, and knee."

"Jesus fucking Christ! Why would people do that to you? To anyone? Please tell me they were arrested."

My shoulders slumped, the weight of the memories too heavy to bear. "No. The girls had shit figured out and avoided any cameras that would have caught it all. The rumors weren't even true." I stared at the floor. "So, I appreciate that you want to be friends, but know that it will take some time for me to trust anyone again."

"Oh, babe, of course! I just want you to feel safe. Rumors can be so horrible. It's like no one cares that they're hurting a human being with feelings. It's pretty disgusting if you ask me."

I snorted. "No shit. It's insane how lies can spread like a fire in the wind. After that, I homeschooled." I peeked at Everlee. I wanted to trust her. Her bubbly personality had grown on me. "Wanna know what else is insane?"

Her brown brow rose. "Lay it on me."

"After being beaten, I started to like really rough sex. It's one of the few times I feel alive. Talk shit to me, hurt me, fuck me until I scream … I love it." There, seed planted to see how she reacted and if my words would travel from her mouth to everyone's ears. I didn't give a shit who found out I liked it rough, so it was a good thing to share.

"Your secret is safe with me." She twisted her lips, appearing deep in thought. "That makes a lot of sense. I mean, what destroyed you is what makes you feel alive."

I tilted my head, wondering how in the hell she put that together. Hell, *I* hadn't even put that together.

"How do you get that?"

Everlee's grin brightened the entire day. "I'm majoring in social work and minoring in psychology. I love to see patterns in people's lives. It's something that's natural for me." Her forehead creased. "But if my parents found out, they would be absolutely livid."

"What? They don't know? How?"

"Girl, have you met the internet? You can fake anything if you know the right people and have enough money, including class schedules, grades, everything." She grinned like she'd just won the lottery. "My parents think I'm getting a degree in business. I don't plan on telling them until I've graduated."

"Why? I mean would they not pay for your college, or…?" Her

revelation puzzled me until I realized she was giving me one of her secrets as well. Trust went both ways.

"Wynter, we all have our secrets. Some more serious than others, but like you, I have reasons to keep my mouth closed." She patted my leg. "I know it will take you time to see that I'm genuine. If you piss me off, I'll talk to you about it. If you have a fucked-up day, I'll cry with you. What you see is what you get."

"A WYSIWYG." I cracked a grin. "My dad used to say that."

"What the hell is a wizzy-wuh?"

I couldn't help but laugh. "It stands for what you see is what you get."

"Oh." She tapped her chin. "I like it. And yes, that's what I am." Everlee jumped up from the bathroom floor. "Are you in for the night?"

"Yeah."

She offered a palm to me. "I have a stash of Ben and Jerry's ice cream. Wanna share with me? We can watch a chick flick."

My heart warmed. It had been a while since I'd hung out with anyone other than my sister. "Yeah. That sounds nice."

I took her hand and wondered if she would treat me the same when she learned what had really happened. Since someone in the society knew my secret, it would only be a matter of time before my entire world imploded once more.

Only this time, it would destroy me in the process.

Chapter 12

Quinn

"What the hell was that?" Kane asked me as I trudged off the football field after a long practice. "The defense was on you like a dog in heat. You definitely had your head up your ass. My question is why." Kane, removed his helmet, glaring at me. "Look, man, I get that life happens, and you can talk to me, but you *cannot* show up to play like that on Saturday."

"Yeah, fuck you too." I was pissed at myself for allowing Wynter to get in my head and at Kane for acting like an asshole. "If I remember correctly, you had some fucked-up days last year, not to mention your panties were all twisted over Brie. And who helped get you through that shit?" I slapped my chest.

Kane sighed, his stern expression falling. "It's a girl, then?" His words were nicer this time, which was good because at this rate I wouldn't mind clocking one of my best friends in the fucking nose.

My jaw clenched, sending pain ricocheting through my face, but it was better than the reminders of what Wynter had done. What she'd stolen from my family. "It's complicated, but yeah."

"Wynter has my man rattled, huh? Everyone at the party saw the way you two were dancing on top of the table the other night." Kane patted me on the shoulder. "Let's shower, then get the hell out of here. Brie won't be home until late, so we're going to drink and figure out how to get your head in the game again."

"I could use a drink or two." I massaged the back of my neck as Kane opened the locker room door and we walked into air that smelled like a mixture of soap and sweat.

"Good. Meet me at my place. If we get shitfaced, you can crash there."

"Cool. See ya in thirty." It never took me long to shower and dress in clean clothes, and Kane and Brie only lived fifteen minutes off campus. Slipping off my shoulder pads and jersey, I tossed them on the floor in front of my locker. If I was going to tell Kane the shit that was going down, I needed to swing by my house first. I reminded myself to take some of the pages out of the file since I hadn't read it all yet. How much I would share with him, I wasn't sure, but maybe enough to get that bitch out of my head.

She was definitely fucking up my mojo, and recruiters would be at the game Saturday. I had to take her down before I ruined a chance at my dream.

Kane swung open the mahogany front door and waved me in. "Took ya long enough." He gave me a lopsided grin. He'd changed into faded jeans and a black sweatshirt and looked more comfortable than I felt. Just the idea of showing up and telling him about Wynter made my stomach churn.

"Yeah, I had to stop by my place longer than anticipated. I wanted to see how Brody was doing and let him know where I was in case he needed anything." I held the file tightly as I toed off my Nikes in the entry way and followed Kane down the hall. His and Brie's home had a warmer feel than Adam's did. Maybe it was who someone was that made a house feel inviting and comfortable.

"The wood floors look good. When did you get them refinished?"

We entered the kitchen, and I took a seat at the table. Kane opened the tallest cabinet above the stainless-steel refrigerator and removed a full bottle of Jim Beam. He poured us a few shots, then joined me.

"New counters and cabinets in here, too." I lifted my glass to my mouth and tossed it back.

"Yeah, we've had a lot of remodeling done. I wanted Brie to put her touch on the house, too." Kane stretched his legs in front of him, then took a sip.

"So, what gives?" He tapped his fingers against the whiskey tumbler and stared a hole through me.

I slapped the file on the table and placed my hand on top of it. "This." I slid it across the wooden surface to him. "My father gave it to me. I haven't looked through all of it yet, but I have through those pages."

Kane's expression flickered with curiosity. He opened the folder and his eyes nearly popped out of his head as he gawked at the pictures of Wynter with the guys.

A flash of jealousy ripped through me. I didn't like that Kane was looking at her, friend or not. "I was with her at the society last night." My dick sprang to life, recalling how it felt inside her. I needed her sweet little pussy again, but it wasn't just her body that was addictive. When I'd told her I knew who she was, her fear was palatable, and I craved the taste of it again. Rubbing my jaw, I decided hate sex with Wynter was my new hobby. An idea began to form, but it would have to wait until I had time to think it all the way through. For starters, I needed to find her on campus and ask her out.

"I can see why." Kane flipped through the rest of the images, then to the information about her school, family, and other details.

I remained quiet as he read. The picture of her talking to the cops was next. Kane frowned and glanced up at me, baffled.

"Keep reading." I folded my arms across my chest, waiting.

Kane returned to the newspaper article, silence filling the room. He turned the page and released a low whistle as he looked at Bell's obituary. I clutched my T-shirt as a suffocating feeling flipped to full-blown agony.

Kane leaned back, his intense gaze on me as he shoved his fingers through his dark hair. "No fucking way, Q. No fucking way." Kane shot up from the table and paced the floor. "I had no idea you even had a sister, not to mention a twin. You've not said a word. That's had to fuck you up in the head. I don't understand why the cops questioned Wynter, but I'm guessing it's in the file."

I pursed my lips, my brain foggy with the horrific memories. "We went to the same high school together. I didn't personally know her, and I don't have any idea if Bell knew Wynter or not. We ran in different crowds, but I always watched out for my sister. Then, things started to change. Bell pulled away and instead of confiding in me, she shut me out. I tried to get her to talk but ... After we moved out of Washington, I thought it would be over, and I never had to speak about it again, but then Wynter showed up. It's brought up a lot of shit."

Kane collected our glasses. "This calls for another drink, and I know I don't have all the pieces yet, but holy fuck. If I saw someone that reminded me of my twin, I would be fucked up too, bro."

I shifted in my seat, weighing the pros and cons of telling Kane everything I knew about Wynter but decided against it. "There's more, but I don't know how much I can talk about it."

Kane refilled our drinks, then set mine in front of me.

"I'm trying to wrap my brain around the fact that you and Bell went to the same high school as Wynter. Not that I should ask"—Kane hesitated—"but what happened to Bell?"

I wiped my sweaty hand on my jeans and looked away as Kane leaned against the countertop. "I can't tell you how it went down, but Wynter was involved. Maybe it was indirectly, but she was responsible for Bell dying." Choking on the words, I forced myself to breathe through the pain. "I haven't told anyone before."

"Your dad and Brody clearly know." Kane gave me a sheepish smile. "Yeah, that was a stupid thing to say. And now that I think about it, like I know some shit about you, but you've been pretty quiet about life before Whitmore."

"We've all got our secrets, man." I leaned across the table and retrieved the folder. "I'll have to keep looking at the details about Wynter to see how deep the information in the file goes."

"Keep me posted. And Q, you understand that none of this ever leaves the room. Whatever you need, I've got your back."

I nodded. "I need to get my head into the game."

I took another drink, wishing the whiskey would flood my system faster, but I knew I should pace myself. "One good thing has come out of this shit so far."

"What's that?" Kane sat at the table with me again.

"Those pictures of Wynter with the dudes are from a website. When I searched it, I found the year some of the photos were taken. She wasn't eighteen yet."

Kane gave me a half-shrug. "We all know that half the time chicks look older than they really are. I mean whoever took them should have checked her ID." He chuckled. "I take that back, hell I had a fake ID when I was seventeen, so I'm sure she did."

"Yeah, I get that, but the information has her date of birth, so I know for a fact that she was underage." I raised my glass, then slammed the amber liquid down.

"What are you getting at?"

My gaze narrowed as I gave him a wolfish grin. "Adam gave me everything you see, which means he's been doing a lot of research on her. I get it. I want revenge for Bell, too. But dude, I'm guessing he found that website, paid for access, and printed off the pictures."

Kane's brown eyes widened. "Holy shit. If you find the history on his laptop ..."

"Yeah, I've got the motherfucker on child porn. I've got him right where I want him."

Kane's laugh filled the room. "Just make sure if you take him down that you don't go with him. You're in custody of the pictures now, so I'd burn them or whatever you gotta do. Make sure your search history is scrubbed for real, not that delete history bullshit."

"Yeah, I thought of that too. I'm going to see if it's on his computer and grab any proof I can." I blew out a sigh. "And if the evidence is there, he won't ever lay a hand on Brody again. I'll report him in a New York minute."

"Let me know what you need. I'd love to take the fucker down for what he's done to your bro—"

I looked away from him, realizing that he was putting two and two together. Adam hadn't touched me since before we moved to Oregon, so none of my friends at Whitmore ever knew. Hell, none of my friends in Washington did either. I'd become a pro at hiding my secrets. At least it was Kane and no one else. I trusted him with my life.

"Q?" Kane's voice was soft. "Did he beat you too?"

My pulse pounded in my neck as I glanced at him. "It was a long time ago. Bell was the only one who didn't receive the wrath of the devil himself."

A thick silence filled the space between us.

"Before I was adopted by Coach and Mom, I was nearly beaten to death several times. It sucks because you think when it's over the bruises will heal, and they do." He tapped his temple. "The sons of bitches don't even have to touch you anymore. Those memories and flashbacks don't leave overnight. I've been there. Again, you let me know if we need to set the son of a bitch up and make sure Brody is safe."

"All right. It's why I still live at home. For Brody." Dark thoughts rolled into my head, clouding my vision. Seeing Bell's obituary again had torn me to fucking shreds. I wondered if it would ever get any easier, but not only was she my sister, she was my twin. When I'd lost her, I'd lost myself too. The friends I had on the football team and in the Viper Secret Society were the only reason I was sane.

I fiddled with the edge of the file, then shoved it across the table in a fit of anger and watched as the papers went whirling everywhere.

"Goddammit." I stormed out of my chair, sending it flying backward and clattering against the tile floor. Feeling like an ass for allowing my grief to stoke my temper, I scrambled to reassemble the file. As I locked everything back inside, a white envelope caught the corner of my eye. I scooped it off the floor and stared at the messy handwriting. Where the hell had it come from? Maybe it had been stuck between the pages, and I'd missed it altogether.

"What is it?" Kane knelt next to me.

I flipped it over, but the envelope was sealed. Without a second thought, I ripped it open, then removed a letter. I unfolded it and immediately searched for who had written it. My hand trembled and heat climbed up the front of my neck. "Son of a fucking bitch." I read it several more times, then stood.

"Dude, I hate to cut our evening short, but there's some shit I gotta do."

Kane briefly frowned at me, surprised at my sudden need to leave. "Let me know if I can do anything."

I held the letter up. "I've got everything I need right here, but thanks."

Chapter 13

Wynter

I was a glutton for punishment, and I knew it. Maybe after everything that had happened in my past, I thought I deserved it.

Four days had passed since my time at the Viper Secret Society, and I was eager to return. Not just for the sex, but I had to figure out who knew the truth about me. His disguised voice had haunted my dreams. Each night I woke up with my pajamas clinging to my sweat-slickened skin and my heart banging relentlessly against my chest.

The rain blew sideways, and my long strands of hair clung to my face as I ran from the comfort of the house to our mailbox near the street. Typically, Everlee checked it, but she hadn't been home all weekend. None of the girls had. The football game had been away, which left me alone with my thoughts. It was dangerous territory.

My teeth chattered as the rain soaked my skin and I gathered the mail in the box from yesterday. Hauling ass to the porch, I ran back inside and locked the door behind me. The girls would be home later that afternoon, but I was a stickler about ensuring all of the locks were secure, especially after our house in Washington had been broken into. Mom had been passed out drunk in her bedroom, and

Janine and I had gone out that evening to run errands together. By the time we'd arrived home, the entire place had been ransacked. The larger valuables had been left alone, but the cookie jar where I kept some cash had been raided, and so had Mom's jewelry.

Shivering in my long-sleeved navy T-shirt and yoga pants, I shuffled through the mail, my eyes widening as I stared at the legal-sized white envelope with my name and address on it.

I never received letters. Janine and I texted or used FaceTime, so it wasn't from her. Since I wasn't working for Dimitri any longer it wouldn't be him either. I glanced in the upper left corner, but there wasn't a return address. Quickly glancing through the rest of the stack, I spotted the black envelope with my name on it as well. That one made me smile. I carefully opened it and removed the white card. Frowning, I read the message.

Be ready.

I flipped it over, but those were the only words, and a small Red Dragon adorned the lower corner. *What the hell does that mean?* I huffed and stomped to the kitchen, angry that whoever was beneath the mask was fucking with my head instead of my body.

I set the rest of the stack on the dining table before I sank into the chair and remembered that I had more mail. Snatching the other letter from the top, I ripped it open. I pulled out a white sheet of paper with blue lines and unfolded it. I stood, frozen, and listened to my pulse roar in my ears while I stared at the handwriting. I pressed my fingers against my temples for a moment, trying to catch my breath. It couldn't be, but I would recognize the messy cursive anywhere—thin and scrawly.

Dear Wyn,

I hope this letter finds its way to you and not in anyone else's hands. When all of this goes down, I want you to know that I love you and you had nothing to do with what is about to happen. You are my safe space, but there were things I couldn't tell you.

. . .

My legs trembled, and I collapsed into the chair as I continued reading.

There's a girl, and no I'm not in love with her, but she's a close friend. She's in a horrible situation, and I don't know how to help her. I would tell you her name, but she made me swear not to reveal her identity. I think if you two became friends it would make a difference in her life, but maybe not. I'm trying to protect her the best I can, but it's calling for drastic measures now. I have to figure out what to do.

Not even you could stop what's been happening. Even though society has progressed, there's still so much hate. Maybe in another letter I can tell you what happened ... who broke me. It wasn't as if one day I just snapped, it was months and months of brutality. I've confided in an adult, but nothing has changed. The darkness is closing in.

Keep your chin up. You're strong and beautiful and I have so much love and respect for you.

Love,
  Ky
  P.S. There's more information. Find it. You need to know the truth.

My soul shattered as I dropped the letter and watched as it fluttered to the floor before I shot out of my chair and ran to the sink. My lunch from earlier in the day splattered against the stainless steel. My shoulders shook with my sobs, the past ripping my fucking heart out then steamrolling it with shards of glass.

I struggled to pull myself together and wiped the string of snot from my nose as I straightened. Turning on the water, I rinsed and cleaned the sink before I washed my face. Numb and unfocused, I somehow managed to grab the society mail and the letter from the floor before I made my way up the stairs and to the bathroom. I scrubbed my teeth as if it would remove the stains from my soul, my senses reeling from the brutal blow. But Kyler said there was more, so how could I track it all down?

After I rinsed my mouth, I stared at the letters in my other hand and my eyes narrowed. The Red Dragon. The secret society. His words bounced around in my head.

Whoever was under that mask knew the truth. I just didn't understand how he would have found the letter. Maybe it was from my father and not someone else. Dad had packed a few things of my brother's and closed Kyler's bedroom door before he left. From that moment on, we never spoke about Kyler again.

My body shuddered, a chill tiptoeing down my spine.

I glared at myself in the mirror and took a deep breath. "Wynter, you have two choices. Run or find out who is fucking with you and make them pay. It's your choice. How strong are you?"

Emotions I had shoved into the recesses of my heart sprouted to life, rage overtaking every inch of self-pity and fear. Rage at the adult who hadn't helped him, at my parents for ditching us and not paying attention when I screamed at them that something was wrong. And at Kyler, for leaving his family and not talking to me.

My nostrils flared. It had been almost five years, and now I had a goal. I had to learn who the man beneath the skull mask was.

I squared my shoulders, a new resolve pumping through my veins. It was time the world knew the truth and I stopped hiding.

"Ky," I whispered, "I love and miss you. I'll do everything I can to find the truth."

A chuckle slipped from me and filled the bathroom. I never thought that I would be chasing down letters from my dead brother.

Chapter 14

Quinn

The grass turf squished beneath my practice cleats as I tucked the football under my arm and hauled ass across the field. I had barely slept the night before, overwhelmed by the sheer amount of proof the case file had on Wynter. Despite my exhaustion, a potent mix of adrenaline and fury drove me to investigate even more on my own. So far, everything Adam had given me matched what I'd found online. Every detail uncovered about Bell's passing fucking sliced me deeper, and I swore to avenge Bell's death one way or another.

I stepped into the end zone and looked over my shoulder, grinning like I'd just won the game for the team.

"Dude, that was a sick play," said our running back, Jagger Whitlock, as he slapped me on the back. "Do that on Saturday and there's no way we can lose."

Coach blew the whistle, gaining everyone's attention. "Save the show-off shit for the game, Astor!"

"Fuck. Man, he's been on my jock worse than a fucking itch." I removed my helmet, pissed that Coach hadn't acknowledged that I was on point.

"What does he say? He rides us hard because he sees our potential and knows several team members are hoping to go pro. Shrug it off." Jagger punched me in the arm and nodded before he jogged toward the rest of the players and Coach in the middle of the field.

I hurried to join them, not wanting Coach to have another reason to give me shit.

My thoughts wandered back to Wynter's file. Even though I had proof on paper, I had to hear her confess her part in my sister's death. I wanted to watch her cry and beg for forgiveness—beg for mercy. I would bring her to her knees, wrecking her the way she had me and my family. Then, I would destroy her. A twisted excitement bloomed in my chest. I would enjoy every second of watching it all unfold. After everything she'd done, I deserved to take pleasure in her pain.

You're a sick fuck just like Adam.

The thought punched me in the gut, leaving me breathless. I gritted my teeth. I was nothing like that son of a bitch. I didn't hurt innocent people, only the ones who deserved it.

"Get your mind on the game, men. It's early in the season, so just because we're undefeated doesn't mean we can afford to get cocky. Get some rest, and I'll see you bright and early in the morning," Coach said.

"Yes, sir!" we all answered in unison before dispersing.

Kane strolled over to me and took off his helmet. "You seem to be holding up pretty well after we talked last night."

"Yeah, I wish I could say I got some sleep, but I looked at more of the file." I ran my hand over my short hair, flinging sweat in every direction.

"Q, man, don't get pissed, but I have to ask." The muscle in Kane's jaw twitched.

I braced myself, unsure of what he had to say.

"You said Adam put the folder together, right?" He glanced over at me, then continued to stare straight ahead as we walked toward the locker room.

"Yeah. He gave it to me with all the information in it."

Kane looked at me dead in the eye. "And you trust him?"

My pulse stuttered against my wrist. "Hell no. He's a piece of shit, but he wants to avenge Bell. That I'm sure of."

"I get why you want to think that, but Adam isn't on the up and up. I just wonder if there's more to it than what is in the file. And how do you know some of it's not fabricated in order to make you hate Wynter?"

Anger rushed through me, and I stopped walking. "Yo, man. I didn't share with you to bust my balls. I wanted you to understand why my head wasn't in the game. I didn't realize you'd turn on me."

Kane shot me a hard frown. "You've got it all wrong, Q. I'm not turning on you. I just have this feeling that there's more to it. I don't trust Adam and neither do you, so why would you swallow everything he fed you? Think about it, Q. You're smart as hell, and I'd hate to see you get played and shit go south. We've got to stay focused on the draft."

I rubbed the sweat from my face and looked at Kane. Somewhere inside myself, I wondered if he was right. "I get it. It's why I've been doing my own research too. Everything that Adam gave me is straight up legit."

"Q, I'm not saying there's false information. What I am saying is that there's a lot more to it than the shit I saw. You can read people and situations pretty well, but this one seems to be really catching you off guard. So just think about what I'm saying. That's all."

I hung my head, overwhelmed by memories of my twin. "It's everything with Bell," I admitted while I started walking again. "I want so badly to understand what happened. Maybe it makes me a gullible target." I glanced at Kane then back at the ground, tears pricking my eyes.

"I get it, but I've gotta call bullshit on Adam. I don't have any proof, and it's just a gut feeling, but Quinn, keep digging and don't take Adam's word for anything. Talk to Wynter and see what she has to say."

There were only a few people that I trusted with my life and one of them was Kane. He'd never steered me wrong and last year when he was going through hell, I was there for him and I would be again, whenever he needed it. Remembering that, my overzealous emotions chilled out, and I was able to calm down.

"I appreciate it. I'll see what else I can find out, but no way in hell am I talking to Wynter about Bell right now. Maybe someday, but not now."

"Let me know if I can help. I've gotta shower and get home to Brie. We're meeting our families for dinner."

A twinge of jealousy stabbed me in the chest. I wish I had a family. Other than Brody, I had no one. "Have a good night."

I watched as Kane jogged off and left me alone with my thoughts. Wrestling with the idea of trusting Adam or digging into Wynter's past on my own, I decided not to make a decision just yet. There was something I had to do first.

Being king had its perks. I pulled the skull mask into place and tested the voice disguiser, then adjusted the collar of my black shirt, hiding the Red Dragon from view. I turned away from the mirror in my office, ready to play with my prey.

A knock sounded at the door, and when it cracked open, Anderson's head poked in. "Ready?"

"Yeah."

"Have fun." He shot me a grin before he disappeared.

I shoved my hands in my slacks pockets and adjusted my hard-on. The anticipation made my pulse skip a beat, and I strolled into the hall, closing and locking the door behind me. My black dress shoes slapped against the concrete floor as I walked to the room where Wynter waited for me.

I placed my thumb against the fingerprint reader until the sound of the lock popping open echoed through the corridor. Quietly, I entered. It took a moment for my eyes to adjust to the dim light, but there she was.

Her naked body trembled as she huddled in the corner of the cage blindfolded, her wrists bound with rope. She was completely helpless and dependent on ... me. The twisted reality made my cock throb.

"Wynter."

Her head popped up as her teeth chattered. I'd been a real asshole and turned on the air conditioner.

She shuddered. "Who are you?"

I walked to the front of the container and reached through the bars. "The Red Dragon."

Her shoulders visibly slumped. Relaxing was her first mistake.

"Try to get comfortable. You're going to be here for a while." My chuckle filled the room— I loved the fact that I was messing with her mind. I cupped her breast and roughly pinched her hard nipple. "Did you miss me?"

"Y-yes."

"Have you been good for me, Wynter? Have you been with anyone else? Girls or guys?" I had no idea if she was bisexual or not, but she needed to understand who she served.

She licked her lips. "Only you."

I sat on the chair and leaned forward, studying her. From what I understood, she hadn't realized the Viper Secret Society was behind it when my guys kidnapped her and brought her here. She had probably been fucking terrified. I smiled beneath my mask. Excellent. She needed to feel what Bell had.

Terror and pain.

The room grew silent. My heart beat loudly in my ears as I mentally sifted through the information in the file. After thinking it over, I understood what Kane had said, but I didn't think Adam would pull any shit with me about Wynter. Why would he? We had both lost Bell. The loss had made him even meaner, but he had no reason to lie to me about her.

I reached for the key to the cage near the chair leg, then stood. Unlocking the door, I tugged her out by her arm and onto the floor. I dug my fingers into her bicep until she whimpered.

"You've been holding out on me, Wynter. I saw the pictures of you online."

I watched as the color drained from her pretty face.

"Tell me why. Did you like being a little slut getting fucked for the camera?" I touched her and trailed my fingertips down her soft cheek.

She squirmed, and I tightened my grip. "Yeah, but I needed the money too."

Her answer caught me unprepared, and I frowned beneath the mask.

"Money for college?"

"No. I have a full scholarship." She pursed her lips.

I cupped her chin and forced her to look up to me. Granted, she couldn't see shit with the blindfold on, but maybe she should. I ripped the purple scarf from her eyes.

"Then why?"

Her gaze dropped to the floor, but she remained silent for a moment.

I knelt and wrapped my fingers around her throat, cutting off her air. "Tell me your secrets or I will rip them from you one by one."

Her blue eyes widened with fear as she struggled to breathe. I loosened my hold on her and she sucked in a deep breath, then pinned me with a hateful glare. "Then you'll have to rip them from me. When you do, I hope they cut you to shreds and leave you bleeding on the floor just like they have me."

I tipped my head back and laughed. "We'll see how feisty you are after I'm finished with you." I parted her legs and gently spread her apart, then massaged her swollen clit. "Does that feel good?"

Her breasts heaved with her longing. I rose and unzipped my jeans, then grabbed my dick and freed myself. She focused on my movements, her expression filling with hunger.

I positioned myself in front of her, jerking her hair so hard she yelped as I shoved my cock into her mouth. Her red lips wrapped around my shaft as I slid in and out, her attention trained on me. Wynter definitely knew how to suck dick, I would give her that. Images of her with other guys flashed through my mind, and a quick jab of jealousy speared me. At the same time, I wanted to watch as she got fucked.

I moved in and out of her mouth, then thrust as far as she could take me. Her cheeks turned red as I once again cut off her air. She struggled against the restraints that bound her wrists, and for a fleeting moment I finally saw what I'd hoped for.

Submission.

I pulled out and wrapped my fingers around my cock to stroke myself. My body jerked as thick ropes of my come landed on her face and tits. When I finished, I tucked her hair behind her ear. "Do you think you deserve to come?"

Her silence spoke volumes. Did she hate herself for what had happened? Was there an ounce of humanity inside her?

I shook away the thoughts, but Kane's words boomeranged through my head. Even with proof that the file was true, he thought Adam was playing me. My hands fisted at the idea that I would allow Adam to fuck with me anymore.

Pissed that Kane had gotten to me, I pushed her away before I tucked myself in my pants and stormed out of the room.

Chapter 15

Wynter

I shivered on the cement floor. My body was numb from the cold, and I wasn't sure how long the Red Dragon had left me there, but I guessed about an hour.

I'd wrestled with the ropes, managing to loosen them. If he was going to play dirty, then I would give it right back to him, I just had no idea how yet. It seemed that his ego was fragile if he got all pissy about me working for Dimitri. I could use that. When Ky was still alive, we'd said some mean shit to each other, so I had plenty of practice. Whoever the Red Dragon was, fuck him. He didn't know my life and the choices I'd had to make.

Not to mention the bastard walked out of the room without getting me off. Wasn't that what the society was about? Orgasms for everyone?

The door flew open, and two guys entered with their hands behind their backs.

"About time you came back to finish the job." I smirked. "Guess that blowjob was too much for you to handle." I rolled my eyes. "I wondered if a bunch of boys could really hold up to the men that have been fucking me for that website."

Even though I couldn't see behind the masks, I did catch one of them flex their fingers. I'd hit a nerve. I looked for any sign that he was the Red Dragon and saw a peek of red on his collar.

The guys strolled over to me as if a naked and bound girl on the floor was an everyday occurrence for them. Each grabbed one of my arms and they hauled me to my feet.

"I took a nap while you were gone. Figured I had nothing better to do. I was a little disappointed that, after you bothered to kidnap me and toss me in a cage, all you could deal with was your dick getting sucked. I expected more from you." I was bound and determined to piss the Red Dragon off, and it felt damn good. I was sick and tired of hiding and shoving all the anger down. It was almost ironic that an asshole in a secret society would be the person that finally pushed me over the edge, and I finally gave myself permission to hate the fucking world.

One of the guys sat down, then the Red Dragon forced me to bend over his lap. My attention remained on the guy still standing as he walked to a corner and popped open a hidden compartment in the wall. Okay, that shit was kind of cool. I stilled as I saw what was in his hands ... a paddle and an object I couldn't make out.

I struggled to get off the dude's lap, but he held me down. The first swing caught me off guard, and I lurched forward. No wonder he was holding me in place.

Another sharp sting landed on my bare ass, then another and another until I was screaming for him to stop. When he finally did, my body went as limp as a dishrag tossed on the kitchen counter with no more purpose.

I lifted my head. "If you think you can break me, good fucking luck. It might hurt, but you have to have a soul left in order to be broken. I lost mine a long time ago."

I was suddenly set on my feet. I'd be lucky if I could sit down for a week.

Without a word, the Red Dragon took my arm and led me to a table.

"Lay down on your back," he ordered.

I did as he asked in hopes it would go a little better, and I could get what I came for. A good fuck and some fun.

He produced a knife with a red dragon that matched the one on his collar carved into the pearl handle. He dragged the tip of it between my breasts. I stilled, scared to move.

"Excellent. Keep your eyes on me."

I gulped and nodded slightly. Footsteps sounded through the room, then my legs were parted. Forgetting my order, I attempted to glance down. The cold blade of the knife landed against my neck. If I looked down again, I would most likely get nicked.

The ropes on my wrists rubbed my skin, but there was nothing I could do about it.

A rough touch grazed my sensitive core. I was pretty sure the second guy's tongue was working my pussy like a bow on a violin. Pleasure flowed through me as I attempted to relax. He shoved a finger inside me as he licked and nipped at my clit. I tried to control the rise and fall of my chest, still very aware of the knife being held to my throat.

A moan escaped me as heat swirled low in my belly. I hated to admit it, but the combination of feeling in danger along with having a guy eat me out was exhilarating. I hadn't had an experience like it, and I was teetering on the edge of losing my mind. Apparently, I was just as sick and twisted as the Red Dragon.

I sucked in a breath. The second I did, the bastard between my legs stopped.

"Seriously?" I gritted my teeth as the knife scraped my skin.

"Silence."

I peeked while the Red Dragon held the weapon out to the other guy, and they switched places.

The sound of a zipper filled the room as the blade was pressed against my breast. I listened as a condom wrapper opened and nearly collapsed with relief. I hoped like hell I was about to get fucked.

My core throbbed as the Red Dragon lined up at my entrance,

then slammed inside me. My raw ass cheeks grated across the table, sending pain and pleasure coursing through me at the same time. I sank my teeth into my lip in order not to scream.

He filled me with his thick cock, thrusting in and out, once again bringing me to the brink of an orgasm.

Oh. God.

His hips moved in a circle, then pumped into me, hitting that sweet spot deep inside. I rocked my body against his, greedy for my release.

The knife trailed away and a hand plumped my breast before the second guy pinched and played with my nipple.

My mind blinked offline as my body took over and I lost control. I trembled from my intense orgasm as my tormentor slid inside me one more time, then shuddered with his release.

Panting, I relaxed against the table.

Instead of pulling out and leaving, the Red Dragon hovered above me, his creepy skull mask looking right at me. Power rolled off him in waves and overwhelmed me. He leaned closer to my ear, then said, "Tell Kyler I said hello. Oh, wait, you can't ... he's dead."

Chapter 16

Quinn

The second Sterling and I were out of the room, I pulled off my mask.

"What the fuck was that, man?" Sterling tugged off his mask, his features twisting with shock.

"Not your concern." I stormed down the hall. "Get her dressed and take her home." My jaw clenched before I entered the office, irritated with Wynter and her smart mouth. Closing the door behind me, I balled my hands into fists. I wasn't sure if I was more pissed that she stood up to me or that it turned me on.

I sank into my desk chair. The look of shock and panic on her face when I'd mentioned Kyler should have given me more pleasure than the orgasm I'd just had, but instead it threw me off my game.

I'd felt the exact same emotions that were in Wynter's expression minutes ago. When Adam received the call about Bell, my gut had clenched at the news. First there was a wave of disbelief, but the pained look in Adam's eyes spoke volumes. Then the grief and horror overwhelmed me, and I was brought to my knees, sobbing so hard it stole my breath.

I never cried like that again. I wouldn't allow myself to feel that deeply. When Bell had died, so had I.

I stretched my legs in front of me, leaned back, and wondered why hurting and scaring Wynter hadn't given me the satisfaction I'd craved. *Fuck!* Kane had gotten in my damn head. Even though I was bound and determined to inflict pain on Wynter, Kane's mistrust of Adam had stuck with me. Maybe I was in too deep and my need for revenge had clouded my judgment. I tapped my fingers against the desk, trying to clear my muddled brain. Adam wouldn't have fabricated the police report, plus I remembered that day as if it were yesterday. The screams and crying ...

From my online research, the details had been accurate and had even filled in some holes I'd been missing.

I stood, shoving my fingers through my short hair. Maybe I didn't have the entire story, but I had most of the facts in front of me. If Kane was right, what would be the point of Adam feeding me shit? *You would be able to take revenge on Wynter when he couldn't.* I shook my head, unwilling to listen to the voice tapping on my skull.

Anxiety pricked my skin as a horrible thought formed in a corner of my mind.

What if Adam was having me do his dirty work, then would use it against me and destroy my career? *No fucking way. Why the hell would he do that?* Adam was a fucking prick, but he wouldn't intentionally ruin my football dreams. What would he have to gain?

"Facts," I said to myself, mentally reviewing the file. "Wynter worked for a porn site, check. The police report matched the events, check." I'd already Googled her address in Forest Dale, Washington, and found the rundown home with the blinds closed, the people inside hiding from the rest of the world. I could get on TikTok and Instagram and search if her sister, Janine, had an account, see what I could find out from her posts.

I located my car keys and phone. If I had to decide right now, Kane was just watching my back, which I appreciated. But something was fucking with me ... everything else in the file was true. *Then why had the letters from Kyler to Wynter been sealed?*

I blew out a breath, pissed that I hadn't thought this through and asked Adam more questions. Hatred for both Wynter and Adam rushed over me along with a renewed purpose to make her pay. I shook off Kane's words and recommitted to getting revenge for Bell. At least I'd messed with Wynter's head pretty badly when I mentioned Kyler. I hoped she was up all night, shaking and planning to run. The little bitch had it coming. I'd lost Bell because of her.

I left the society's house and walked up the road to where we members hid our cars when we had the chicks around.

A laugh escaped me as I climbed into my Mercedes. I'd fucking hit gold when I'd found additional letters between the file pages from Kyler to Wynter. I'd read the first two, then made copies before I had to go to football practice. Wynter had only seen the first one, and I wanted to send more, but the timing had to be right. I wished like hell I'd been a fly on the wall and watched her as she realized who the letter was from.

As I started to drive home, a thought hit me. Where had Adam gotten all the information on Wynter? Some of it was public, but not the website, and certainly not the notes from Kyler. Hell, I wasn't even sure a top-notch PI couldn't have managed that. I massaged the back of my neck, trying to figure out what I was missing.

I white-knuckled the steering wheel, my thoughts whirling faster than a tornado on a warm spring day. Something was wrong.

"Dammit! Dammit! Dammit!" I yelled. I hated the fact that I was questioning Adam. He was my father for Christ's sake, but even if I had wanted him to act like one, he never had. I reminded myself that nothing had changed. But once Kane planted a seed of doubt in my mind, I couldn't seem to dig it up and throw it away.

Glancing at the car's clock, I realized that Adam would most likely be asleep, which might be exactly what I needed.

I sped up, eager to get there.

Silence filled the house as I slipped in through the kitchen door. The light over the stove was on, and I crept through the room, searching for Adam, but he wasn't there. I hurried to the other side to make sure Brody was asleep. Since he was a teenager, he kept some odd hours. I didn't need him to look over my shoulder and ask a million questions that I didn't have answers to.

After checking in on Brody, who was sprawled out on his bed and snoring softly, I backed out and into the hallway. Then I headed to my room as I remembered that I needed some help with my mission.

Quietly hurrying back down the stairs, I rushed to Adam's room. He normally kept his bedroom door locked, so I wasn't positive he was asleep, but it would have to work. To the best of my knowledge, Adam was tucked away for the night.

A few minutes later, my pulse kicked up a notch as I reached his office. I tested the handle, but it was locked. Retrieving the lockpicks I'd grabbed from my nightstand, I started to work my magic. There was rarely a lock I couldn't open.

A soft click told me I was successful, and I snuck in. Afraid to turn the overhead light on, I shoved the tool into my back pocket and peered through the darkness. If anyone saw the way I waved my hands in front of me, they'd probably laugh their asses off. Finally locating the floor lamp, I turned it on and blinked a few times as I adjusted.

I glanced around the room, then spotted his laptop on his desk. "Bingo." Once I settled into the chair, I opened Adam's MacBook. The message for his password or fingerprint flickered to life, and I typed in Bell's and my birthdate along with our last name. His desktop appeared, and I stifled a laugh. The bastard hadn't changed his password in years.

"Let's see what you've got, old man."

I searched his folders until I found the one for Wynter. Hesitating briefly, I swallowed, my throat dry and my heart pounding in my ears. Years of Adam conditioning me to be afraid of him jumped to the front and center of my being. "Don't be a pussy. What are you scared of?" I muttered to myself.

I clicked the mouse, my attention landing on the documents that Adam had printed off and given me. He also had the porn website bookmarked. The thought of him jerking off to pictures of Wynter infuriated me.

"How many times have you visited that site, Adam?"

A sick excitement sprang to life inside my gut. If I had the ability to take Adam down for possession of porn with underaged girls, then that proof would protect me from whatever shit he had in mind.

If he's planning anything at all.

Next, I checked Adam's search history, expecting it to be cleared out, but I was in luck. Multiple websites popped up, and I started clicking on each of them. Not only were there several with Wynter, but the rest of them were all underaged sites.

"Jesus," I muttered. My father had a sick fetish. Bile rushed up my throat as it sank into my brain that some of the bookmarked pages were of girls in their early teens. My mind reeled as I began taking pictures of his laptop and websites with my phone.

Adam Astor was a perverted shit. Not once had I fucked an underaged chick or checked out porn sites of girls that had barely reached puberty. If I rubbed one out to a video or picture of someone under eighteen, it wasn't on purpose. Hell, I hadn't even watched porn since the Viper Secret Society had been formed. I had everything I wanted at my fingertips there. I didn't need to pay for images and videos when I had the real thing.

Once I finished collecting proof, including the details of Adam's computer that would show he visited the sites, I continued searching the information Adam had on Wynter. An image of Adam with another man who looked similar to Wynter caught my eye. Was he related to her? If so, how did Adam know him?

The more I stared at the pictures, the more questions I had. I clicked on another file, then my mouth gaped. "What the actual hell?"

Chapter 17

Quinn

I'd tossed and turned the rest of the night after snooping on Adam's laptop. It wasn't as if I could confront him about what I'd seen. I would basically be throwing myself under the bus, and I needed to get back into his computer. Tossing my covers off, I sat up on the side of my bed, rubbing my sleep-deprived eyes.

Surely, Adam could explain why he had pictures of Kyler, too. They weren't just any images, either. Once I'd figured out who Drew, Wynter's father was, I realized he was the other man in the photos. Then I stumbled on the one with Drew, Adam, and Kyler laughing. What had really freaked me out though were the pictures of Kyler and Bell. I had no fucking clue they knew each other. Granted, Bell and I ran in different circles, but we were close. She confided in me, and I made sure no motherfuckers touched her if she didn't want it.

I sighed and walked to the bathroom. Maybe a shower would clear my mind enough to talk to Adam. I had to tiptoe around the conversation. No way could I tip him off that I was snooping, or he would change his laptop password. I pondered what to say to him that wouldn't shine light on the fact that I'd been in his office.

After drying off and dressing in jeans and a basic T-shirt, I slipped on my tennis shoes and made my way downstairs.

The smell of eggs and bacon teased my nose and my stomach growled in agreement.

Entering the kitchen, I spotted Adam at the table drinking his coffee.

"Hey, Lena. It smells really good."

She offered me a sweet smile. "I can't send you boys off to school without a proper breakfast."

Footsteps alerted me to Brody's presence, and I turned as he joined us. He scooped up a bagel from the plate that Lena had for us on the island.

"Fancy seeing you here." Brody took a bite of his food, then shoved the piece into his cheek so he could talk. "You're always gone when I'm home." A hint of bitterness clung to his words.

"Let's grab something to eat after practice, then let's catch up over the weekend."

"Yeah, sure. Time and place?"

I mentally ran through my schedule for the day. "Four-thirty. I'll text you the place later."

"Here, Quinn, Brody." Lena held up two plates full of food.

I gave her a kiss on the side of her head and took my plate from her.

"I've gotta take mine to go," Brody said. "Early football practice."

Brody had followed in my footsteps and was the star running back at his high school. It had given him a way to expel the hate and anger about Adam using him as a punching bag when he was young. Not to mention, the loss of Bell had left Brody bitter and broken. As she got older, she was the glue that held us all together. Mom's death had devastated the family, but we kids had actually lost both parents because Adam turned into an abusive bastard.

I pulled the chair back, then sat at the table. "Adam." I shoved a piece of bacon into my mouth before I grabbed my fork and dove in.

"Quinn." His tone was sharp, warning me to tread lightly.

"Rough night? You seem a bit cranky." I smirked.

Lena placed a glass of fresh-squeezed orange juice in front of me, and I took a sip while I waited for Adam's response.

Adam folded the newspaper he had his nose in, then set it next to his plate. "What can I do for you?" His voice was matter of fact, lacking any compassion for me. It wasn't anything unusual, but every once in a while, it still unnerved me.

I reminded myself that I had dirt on him and could probably put the fucker in prison, but I needed him first. Deciding to cut to the chase, I leaned in and propped my elbow on the table. "Where did you get all of the details on Wynter?" I asked in a hushed voice so Lena wouldn't over hear me.

Irritation flickered across his face. "It doesn't matter."

"It does."

Pans clanged behind me, reminding me that Lena was still there. "I'm happy to eat my breakfast in your office." I held his gaze and stared a hole through the soulless son of a bitch.

He huffed but picked up his plate. "Ten minutes is all you have."

I quirked a brow at him, then gathered my food. Without a word, we left the kitchen and walked down the hall to his office. To my surprise, the door was open. He always locked it even when he was gone for only a short amount of time. I waltzed into the room as if I owned the house and everything he touched. If I didn't, he'd look for my weak spot and catch me off guard.

He already knows your weak spot. It's Wynter. Nearly tripping over my feet as the words whispered through my mind, I righted myself before my food went flying. *Where the hell did that come from?*

Adam settled into his executive chair and steepled his fingers together, staring at me.

I chomped on another piece of bacon, trying to shake the voice in my head as I sat in one of the black leather chairs in front of him.

"I gathered the information from different places. The police report I was able to get because of Bell. The pictures are all over the internet. She's a whore." Adam leaned forward and tapped his fingers against his desk.

The little hairs rose on the back of my neck and my entire body bristled at his words. *She's not a whore. At least not yours.* Adam had no idea I'd already claimed her at the society.

"And the letters?"

A wicked smile curved his lips. "A nice touch, huh?"

"Where did you get them?"

"Can I trust you to keep your fucking mouth shut?" He took a bite of his food, waiting for me to answer.

"Of course." *Not.*

"I knew Drew Baldwin. We worked together. After ..." Dad took a deep breath, tears welling in his eyes. "He got fired. His last day at work, he left his personal belongings. Once he was gone, I searched his office and located a box filled with some of Kyler's belongings. It was too difficult to look at the contents then. That was almost five years ago. When Wynter showed up at Whitmore, I decided to look through the box. That's when I saw the letters."

"Why weren't they opened?" I rested my plate in my lap, watching him intently.

"I opened them very carefully, then made copies and resealed the envelopes. At the time I wasn't sure if I was going to give them to you. They're pretty revealing, but then they just stop without the rest of what happened."

After years of studying Adam, I knew the clench of his jaw, the fidget of his hands, and every other telltale sign that he was hiding something. I saw nothing. He was being honest.

"I've not finished them."

"You should. It shows that Wynter and Kyler were close. She could have changed the course of what happened."

I shook my head. "After five years, we still can't say it out loud." My attention dropped to my shoes, a knife piercing my heart and twisting. Soon, Wynter would have her wish and I would bleed out on the floor because the memories and her presence would fucking kill me.

Adam released a heavy sigh. "The sooner Wynter is gone from Whitmore, the sooner we can move on with our lives. That's the only job you have other than going pro."

"I'm working on both of those."

"Work faster." He looked at his watch. "I have a meeting."

"Okay." I stood and left, ready to dig into the rest of those letters. I needed to know what Adam meant by Kyler's notes just stopping. What had changed?

A niggling feeling crept down my spine as I hurried to my room. Fuck class. I had to find out what happened. But before I lost myself in a dark world of memories, I decided I couldn't wait any longer. Removing my phone from my back pocket, I pulled up Gabby's number.

Hey, do you have Wynter's number? I want to ask her out.

Within seconds, the grey dots began to bounce with Gabby's reply.

Oh, that's exciting! Let me ask her if it's okay to share. And yeah, I be like that. LOL.

I groaned. Why did Gabby have to be one of those people that asked someone's permission first. What if Wynter said no? If I was going to bring Wynter down, then I had to spend time with her and fast, which meant texting often. I had a feeling Adam's patience would run out soon too.

I flopped onto my bed and grabbed the file from the nightstand drawer, opening it as another message came through.

That text had the phone number and a typical Gabby threat:

You better be good to her, or I'll kick your ass. 509-555-2050.

Grinning, I saved the information as a new contact. Even though I would appear desperate, I messaged Wynter right away. Maybe she would think it was a good look on me.

Hey, it's Quinn. Willing to let me make up for the fact that my asshole father barged into my room and interrupted our fun?

I stared at the screen waiting impatiently. After almost ten minutes, her response came through.

What do you have in mind?

My fingers flew across the keyboard. *Dinner, then whatever else you're up for.*

My nerves tingled as I waited. What if she didn't want to hang out? Then what would I do? Stalk her?

When?

I was tired of wasting time. Plus, if I was able to encourage her to talk about her past, I could use it against her. I glanced at the clock on my phone and mentally reviewed my schedule.

7:30 tonight. I'll pick you up. I know you live with Gabby and the girls. At least my plans with Brody were early enough I could see both of them.

A half an hour ticked by slowly before she replied.

Dress code?

Holy shit, what was up with her? She got right to the point without any chitchat. I wasn't used to a chick being a word minimalist.

Casual. I'll be in jeans and a button down.

I barked out a laugh. I hadn't ever told a girl what I was wearing for a date, but Wynter wasn't just any girl.

My phone vibrated with another message.

See you at 7:30.

Satisfied that I was kicking my plan into action, I tossed my cell on my bed and returned my attention to the next letter.

Chapter 18

Wynter

"Oxytocin" by Chandler Leighton played in the background on my small Bluetooth speaker. It was one of the few splurges I'd made other than clothes, and it fit perfectly on my bedroom desk.

"Girl, I want all the deets when you get home tonight. Although, I should say when you come back." Everlee fake-coughed into her hand and sat on the edge of my bed. "Notice I said *come*." Her giggle was infectious, and I couldn't help but laugh.

Gabby flipped her long, straight hair behind her shoulder as she circled me and assessed the outfit the girls had helped me choose. My black skinny jeans showcased my figure, and the bright blue top brightened my eyes. Everlee had loaned me her Tory Burch belt and ballet flats for the evening, which surprised me—those didn't come cheap. But apparently loaning out your clothes was pretty common. I just hadn't had friends in high school after …

I cleared my throat, shoving the memories into the darkest part of my soul. *Not tonight, Ky.*

"You look absolutely magnificent." Gabby clapped as if she had painted a masterpiece.

A blush crept over my pale skin. "Thanks for your help. For everything. The makeup, clothes, and support." I couldn't stop myself from fidgeting. "Shit, why am I so nervous?"

"Because you're going out with a football god." Everlee blew me a kiss, mischief flaring in her hazel gaze.

"Stop, Everlee. Poor Wynter is going to need a Xanax by the time Quinn picks her up."

Everlee's shoulders slumped. "Sorry. I just want you to know that Q never dates anyone. He's been a straight up player. When you said he asked you out, I nearly dropped to the floor."

Gabby tilted her head toward her friend. "She's right. There's a long line of hopeful girls and guys wishing they had even one night with him."

My forehead scrunched in confusion. "Why me, though? I don't understand. I danced with him at the party, but that's about it."

"And the sexual tension with you two was insane!" Everlee smacked her palms on my bed and wiggled her brows.

"Yeah, we had fun. He probably just wants to hook up." *Maybe we won't get interrupted this time.*

"Hey, I'd take that pony for a ride." Gabby winked at me.

The room filled with our laughter. "It wouldn't hurt my feelings. I'm totally down for an occasional rail and bail."

"Girl power." Everlee held her hand out, and we gave each other a high five.

"I hate that women are put down for having a sex drive. I've never shied away from mine. I know what I like, and if the guy isn't getting it right, I have no problem guiding him." Not that I had to do that very often working for Dimitri, but on occasion I took the lead.

"Hell, yes," Gabby said. "Why are we slut-shamed when the guys can act like total fuckboys? Screw them if they think we're witches because we know what we want. Apparently, they don't understand that W.I.T.C.H. stands for wisdom, integrity, truth, courage, and honor." Gabby snapped her fingers, her tone sassy and fun.

Hanging out with the girls had eased my nerves while waiting for

Quinn to arrive, but a twinge of sadness pulled at my heartstrings. This was what I'd been missing in my life—hanging out with friends, laughing, dating. I swallowed over the lump in my throat, steadying myself, then squared my shoulders. It was almost certain that my friends would discover my secret eventually, so I needed to make the most of the time I had with them. "Hate It/Fight It" started to play, and I tapped my foot to the beat. There were days I really missed being on a cheer and dance team. Teams worked hard, but I loved dancing, and I was good.

Everlee pointed to her Apple watch. "He has two more minutes to get here." She wagged her finger. "That's a first strike if he's late. The guy plays football, he knows how to be on time, so show up for the lady, dammit."

I snickered, loving how protective the girls were over me.

The sound of the doorbell chimed. I froze as my stomach flip-flopped, then dropped to my toes as if I were on a crazy rollercoaster ride. Gabby gently squeezed my shoulders. "He's just a boy. Make sure he actually deserves you instead of trying to convince everyone you deserve him. You have nothing to prove, girl."

Tears welled in my eyes, and I blinked several times, forcing them away. "Thanks." For the first time in years, I hugged someone other than my sister. I grabbed my handbag from the back of my desk chair and gave myself a pep talk.

"Go, go, go." Everlee slid off my bed and ushered us all out of my bedroom. "We'll stay at the top of the stairs in case you need us."

I nodded, more grateful to them than they would ever understand. I sucked in a lungful of air, then descended the stairs. Wiping my clammy palms on my jeans, I hesitated briefly before I peeked through the peephole. It was Quinn. Butterflies scattered in my chest, leaving me lightheaded. Maybe a drink would help calm my nerves. I'd had no problem sucking his dick at the party, but here I was all sweaty and unsure of myself.

"Open the door!" the girls whisper-yelled from above.

I glanced over my shoulder, wishing they were going with me. A triple date sounded nice right about now. Before I chickened out, I flung the door open and plastered a smile on.

"Hey." Nice opening, Wyn.

Quinn's hazel eyes lit up, then took a slow hike up and down my body. "You look gorgeous."

Do not melt on the fucking floor right now. Say thank you.

Quinn might not have realized it, but he had just handed me control for the evening. Dimitri had taught me that if a guy made it clear he was attracted to me, and I played my cards right, I could manage a situation. I was going to wear that power like armor to protect my fragile heart.

"Thanks. You don't look too bad yourself." Still a bit nervous, I closed the door behind me and stepped onto the porch, my pulse beating faster with each step. My gaze seemed to be magnetically pulled towards Quinn, as though my eyes had a will of their own. I couldn't tear them away. Quinn's broad shoulders and bulging biceps were on full display in his burgundy button down that was tucked into dark-wash jeans clinging to his muscular thighs.

He looked good enough to eat. Right here. On the fucking porch in front of the entire world. *Slow down, girl. Remember the rules of Hormones 101. Don't act desperate.*

Quinn placed a warm palm against the small of my back. "I made reservations for us at a restaurant on the river."

"Really?"

"Personally, I'm ready to sink my teeth into some meat." He flashed me a silly grin. "Steak."

Quinn was flirting with me already, and I craved his attention. "You're a beef man, huh?" I cringed as the words slipped from my lips.

Quinn didn't miss a beat. "Nah, dudes don't do shit for me, but I've seen plenty of dick in the locker room."

My body shook with laughter as he opened the passenger door for me.

"At least I've started the evening off right ... with my foot in my mouth. Maybe I got the awkward moment over with." I climbed in, sinking into the plush grey seat. While he hurried to the driver's side, I discreetly ran my fingers over the soft leather of the dashboard. My broke ass had never sat in a luxury sports car before, and I wanted to touch it all.

Quinn settled in and the engine purred to life. "Drinking With Cupid" by Voila blared through the speakers, nearly blasting me through the roof.

"Sorry!" Quinn turned down the volume from a button on his steering wheel. "Guess we're even on the awkward shit now." He offered me a sweet smile.

"The night is young, Quinn. We'll see what the tally is at the end of the evening." I tucked my hair behind my ear as he backed the car out of the driveway.

"Is Wynter Baldwin a bit competitive?"

"Sometimes. I used to be in cheer and on the dance team in high school. I know it's not viewed as a sport by some, but it is. Not to mention the competition level is nuts."

"That explains the dance moves at the party." Quinn kept his eyes on the road ahead. Soft raindrops landed on the windshield, and his wipers automatically turned on. He tapped his fingers on the steering wheel. "I've been meaning to apologize to you about when we were in my bedroom."

Turning my head fast, I nearly gave myself whiplash. "I think that awkward moment is at the top of our list so far."

"No shit. I was so pissed my father came home."

I could have sworn that Quinn cringed as he said father.

"So that *was* your dad." I pursed my lips together. "I've done a lot of things, but being caught by someone's dad while I had his son's dick in my mouth was a first. Hopefully a last." A flush swept up my neck and cheeks, and I turned away, hiding how much that situation had embarrassed me.

"I felt bad, and I didn't have your number to call you afterward to see if you were okay. I couldn't have cared less what he thought, but I'm sure you didn't feel the same way."

I scrunched my nose. "Nope. It was bad."

To my utter and complete shock, Quinn reached over for my hand and gave it a gentle squeeze. "You've been on my mind a lot since then. Honestly, I didn't know if you were just down for a hookup, or if you were interested in going out."

My throat suddenly grew dry. Quinn hadn't released me, so I threaded my fingers through his. Although I'd worked for Dimitri, Quinn touching me was more intimate than having sex with those guys.

"I'm sitting in your car, so I guess you got your answer."

He offered me a wide smile. "Glad I bugged Gabby for your number."

"Me too."

A beat of silence hung in the air, and I reveled in the sweet moment of our hands joined. I'd missed so much over the last several years while I was forced to hide at home and avoid public events. A wave of hope washed over me. Maybe, just maybe, I could have all those things now. I stared out the window and listened to "The Devil I Know" by Allie X. Moving my body to the beat, I snapped my fingers. "Good tune. You might have decent taste in music."

"The tunes depend on my mood. I love rap, pop, and indie. Hell, if I need to study for a game or big test, I listen to classical focus music."

"No shit? I would have never pegged you for classical."

He gave me a half-shrug. "I don't attend the symphony, but it has its purpose." He paused, his attention cutting over to me. "We should go clubbing."

My eyes widened. "Yeah? There's one around?"

"A few. We could get a group of us and go for the night. There's a good one within walking distance of a nice hotel, so we could get smashed and not worry about driving. The club is about an hour from here."

"That sounds fun. I haven't gone clubbing before."

Shock registered on Quinn's gorgeous face. "Seriously?"

"Very."

"Can I ask why?" He slowed the car, then turned into a parking lot.

"My family went through some shit, and instead of having a normal life and going out, I had to take care of my younger sister. I worked and took care of Janine while I attended online college classes." Sadness weighed on my words.

Quinn pulled the Mercedes into a parking slot, then turned off the car. His gaze was full of kindness when he faced me. "That sounds like a lot of responsibility."

I nodded. "It is sometimes."

"Well, let me take you on some of your firsts, then. We can do anything you want. Dancing, karaoke, dinner, picnics. Whatever makes you happy."

My eyes narrowed suspiciously. "Why me?"

Fuck, what is wrong with me, blurting shit like that out?

Quinn's smile lit up his face. "Because you, Wynter Baldwin, are a mystery. You seem to know exactly what you want in life, but I can't help wanting to know more. I like that. A lot."

Instead of replying to him, my stomach growled in response.

Quinn chuckled. "Let's get some food. I'm starving."

Chapter 19

Quinn

I laced my fingers with Wynter's as I led her to the building. Her skin was smooth and warm, and the tenderness of her touch surprised me.

I glanced at her face, and what I saw—a hint of sadness that seemed permanently etched into her features—gave me pause. According to the file, she had spent her last two-and-a-half years of high school hiding from the world. I didn't blame her. I suspected everyone in her life had turned on her. At least I had football and Brody after losing Bell. Wynter had kept to herself and seemed to have no friends.

Taking a deep breath, I pushed open the restaurant door and led Wynter inside. I could feel my chest constricting with sympathy for her, though I tried to push it away. I had a job to do, and it didn't include getting too close to Wynter. After the hostess seated us in a corner booth, I ordered a soda while Wynter asked for a water.

"Are you a nibbler?" I asked, looking over the food options.

"Huh?" Wynter peeked over the top of her menu, her blue eyes sparkling even with the low light of the restaurant.

Shit, she's beautiful. My dick woke the hell up and I shifted in my seat, trying to ease the discomfort. She didn't know I'd already fucked her as the Red Dragon, but I planned on fucking her senseless as Quinn when I got the chance.

"Are you one of those people that orders dinner, then eats two bites, takes it home, then devours it? Or do you dig in, even in front of a guy? I've never understood it. I'll eat everything in front of me."

She leaned back in her seat, smiling. "If I'm hungry, I eat. I don't care who is staring at me." The corner of her mouth curled up.

My heart—the bastard organ—betrayed me, skipping a beat at the sight of her beautiful smile.

She's the enemy, don't forget what she's done. A steely resolve swept over me.

"Excellent. Order whatever makes you happy."

"Anything?" She stared at me and licked her bottom lip.

I met her smoldering gaze with mine. "Anything." I wanted to jerk her up, take her to the bathroom where I could bend her over a sink, and fuck her until she was screaming my name. But I would have to wait.

The server interrupted our banter, and we placed our order. To my surprise, Wynter ordered a smaller New York steak, potato, and broccoli. I was impressed. If she ate most of it, I might have to reward her for good behavior and give her dessert.

She took a drink of water, then set her glass on the table. "Can I ask about your family?"

That was strange. Most people didn't want permission, they just asked. But I assumed Wynter had a view from a different window than most, which probably made her more sensitive about the topic. She wanted to hide who she and her family were. Surprisingly, I understood since I felt the same about Bell and Adam.

I stretched my legs beneath the table, brushing her calf with mine.

"I live with Adam, my father who you had the unfortunate pleasure of meeting, along with my younger brother, Brody."

"I would have preferred to meet—Adam?—another way."

What I wouldn't tell her was that he probably jerked off that night to the mental image of her on her knees with my cock stuffed in her hot little mouth. A shiver of disgust skated down my spine.

"You didn't mention your mom. Is she an off-limits topic?"

"Not really. She died when I was young, and my brother was just a baby. Car accident."

"Oh, Quinn ..."

Goose bumps broke out over my arms at the gentleness of her voice. She sounded almost as heartbroken as I was when Mom passed away.

"I was young. Lena, our housekeeper and chef, became mine and Brody's mother figure. It wasn't as though we were left to our own devices."

Liar. Adam beat your ass almost daily, and no one was there to protect you.

"I know it's not the same, but when my father took off, my mother fell apart. I lost both parents the same day. It might sound cold, but I love and hate both of them."

My head buzzed with her words. I had never considered what had happened to her after that terrible day. I had lost Bell, but had she suffered far worse?

I ground my molars, struggling to stay focused on my original mission and why I was here instead of being taken by surprise by her pitiful little story. She wasn't the only one who had grieved. I had lost my twin, and nothing could ever replace the damage that had been done. Nothing.

"Sorry, that was probably too much information. I just understand what losing a parent is like." She picked at the edge of her rolled cloth napkin. "Seems like we did a deep dive on the conversation front."

"It's all right. I expect people to want to hear more when I tell them about Mom."

"Well, I don't feel like being sad tonight. Not tonight. Tell me about football. I'm not a big fan, but I can follow the game."

I slapped my hand over my heart and gave her puppy-dog eyes, pretending that her words had hurt my soul.

Her laugh reached my ears, and my dick waved at her. I would be the first to admit I loved sex, but that wasn't what was happening. I was responding to her because there was something different about Wynter, and it was rattling my cage.

"Do you want to go pro?"

I shifted in my seat, rubbing her leg with mine again. "That's the plan. Kane and I both registered for the draft and completed all the requirements. Now, I play my ass off and hope I'm selected."

"That sounds intense."

The server interrupted and set our plates on the table. "Thank you," I said. "This looks great." I glanced at Wynter, laughing while she cut into her steak and shoved a piece in her mouth. Her eyes rolled in the back of her head.

The server stared at her, his hard-on obvious through his black slacks as he watched her.

Wynter chewed slowly, appearing to savor every moment. "My God, that's the best steak I've ever had." She peeked at the server's name tag. "Mic, thank you."

Shit, she used his name. The guy would be rubbing one out in the fucking bathroom as soon as he got a break. My red-hot anger simmered below the surface as he smiled at her. "If there's *anything* else I can do for you, don't hesitate to ask."

What the fuck? The asshole was hitting on her right in front of me.

"She doesn't need anything else. We're good, man." There was no room in my tone for him to misunderstand that he'd been dismissed.

To my dismay, he winked at Wynter before he turned and walked away.

"Quinn? Are you okay? Is something wrong?"

Shit. Apparently, I hadn't hid my feelings very well.

I leaned into the table and said, "Mic was hitting on you." I paused to see if what I'd said registered with her. "In front of me. Your *date*."

Confusion flashed in her eyes. "He probably thought you were my brother." As soon as the words spilled off her pretty lips, her entire body stiffened and pain flashed across her expression, but she recovered quickly.

"I mean, we look alike, right?"

Fuck. Me. No, Bell and I didn't even look alike, and we were twins.

She dug into her potato, concentrating on her food instead of me. I needed a second anyway. My head was about to explode. One minute I wanted to ruin Wynter, the next I was jealous as hell. I never got possessive over pussy. It was all just a hot cunt for me to fuck.

"Do you have a team that you want to play for?" she asked between bites.

At least she dropped the Mic conversation.

"Awkward moment four?" I responded, attempting to smooth out the tense air between us.

She arched a brow in my direction. "Three, but I feel like we might set a new record if we keep going at this rate."

I couldn't help but chuckle. One thing I would give Wynter was the fact that she knew how to redirect conversation. Then again, she'd probably had plenty of experience.

"Is that a dare?"

She pretended to think about it. "Nope. If I was going to dare you to do something, it wouldn't be about awkward moments. But you still didn't tell me what team you want to play for."

I reached for my napkin and wiped my mouth. "I have a few. My first pick would be the Dallas Cowboys, second would be the Seattle Seahawks. I seriously doubt I'm good enough on the field to have multiple offers, so we'll see how it turns out."

She set her knife on the edge of her plate. "I hope you get everything you've dreamed about."

I set my fork down, wondering why she would want that for me. She didn't even know me.

"Why?"

She hesitated, then grabbed the white napkin in her lap. She swallowed, then took a drink of her water before she spoke. "Because you work your ass off for it. Plus, you've already had enough disappointment in your life with your mom. You should get to have good things, Quinn. Believe in yourself."

A jolt of electricity burned through my chest. She had no idea how much disappointment I'd really had, but she would find out soon enough.

Chapter 20

Wynter

The evening sky was filled with twinkling stars as Quinn and I silently walked towards my new home. I wasn't sure if he would kiss me goodnight or not, but I'd excused myself to visit the ladies' room before we left the restaurant to brush my teeth with the toothbrush and a travel-size toothpaste I'd hidden in my purse. Just in case. I wasn't about to deny myself garlic on my potato when a bit of prep made everything fine.

I tried to hide my nerves when Quinn escorted me to my front door. We had stayed at the restaurant until it closed, and the staff asked us to leave, but the conversation had been so captivating that neither of us wanted to end the date. While our discussion had started off deep and serious, it slowly turned into an easy back and forth as we settled into each other's company. It was a strange feeling, the comfort of being with someone I didn't know very well. Oddly, I felt as though I'd known him for years.

"It was a great night," Quinn said, his voice full of sincerity.

"Yes, it was. Thank you for dinner."

The electricity in the air ignited my body, sending shivers of desire through my veins. Quinn looked at me and my heart skipped a beat when I saw longing fill his hazel eyes. I was lost in the moment, rendered motionless by the intensity of what was happening between us. Nerves twisted in my belly and his fingertips grazed gently along the side of my waist. His lips were soft and inviting as he kissed me. But while our kiss deepened, I became aware of the fear that had been lurking in the background of my mind—fear of losing control and being vulnerable to another person. Fear of what might happen if I gave in to the feelings and let it consume me. Yet despite my concerns, I couldn't pull away from him—not yet.

Quinn broke our kiss. "Are you busy tomorrow night?"

I couldn't stop the silly grin that eased across my face. "I'll have to check my schedule. Can I text you?"

Quinn pressed his lips to mine, his tongue dipping inside my mouth one last time before he stepped away. "Yeah. And if you are, then look at Thursday." His smile was infectious as he gave me a little wave before walking back to his car.

Lightheaded and deliriously happy, I unlocked the front door and walked inside. I pressed my body against the wall, attempting to catch my breath. How had I worked for Dimitri and rarely been nervous, but a date with Quinn had me giddy like a schoolgirl waiting for her first kiss?

I laughed at myself, then turned around.

A scream escaped me and within seconds the doorbell was incessantly ringing.

"Shit!" Three eager faces stared at me from the living room window, spotlighted by the single lamp. "Spy much?"

I flung open the door, staring at a distraught Quinn.

"Are you okay? Are you safe? I heard a scream."

Before I could respond, he stepped past me and into the entryway. He looked around before his attention landed on the girls.

Heat feathered my cheeks. "I'm so sorry. I didn't realize we had an audience. When I saw them, they scared the shit out of me, and I screamed."

Quinn's shoulders relaxed and he massaged his forehead. "I

thought someone was in the house, trying to hurt you." He took my hand and squeezed it.

"Ladies, try to not to scare the hell out of us next time, okay?" Irritation dotted his tone, but he chuckled as he rubbed the back of his head.

"Sorry," Leighton said, scrunching her lightly freckled nose. "We were just watching out for her. Ya know, making sure you weren't stepping out of line on a first date." She crossed her arms over her chest and shot him a syrupy sweet smile.

I muffled my snort with my arm.

"Noted." Quinn bent down, his breath tickling my ear as he spoke. "Can I talk to you on the porch for a sec?"

Anxiety infiltrated my veins and slithered into every part of me. "Sure," I whispered, my voice cracking with nerves. *Is he pissed that I screamed?*

"I'll be back in a minute." I gave my roomies a pointed look before we slipped outside, and I once again closed the door. I looked up at him and saw concern still etched into his handsome features. "I *am* really sorry. I didn't mean to freak you out."

Quinn's eyes burned into mine as he cupped my chin. I shivered beneath his touch, barely able to withstand the fury that vibrated from him. "I swear on my life, if anyone ever lays a hand on you, I'll fucking kill them. No matter what time it is, promise that you'll call me if you need me," he growled.

My throat tightened with the realization that he wasn't upset with me at all. Quinn wanted to protect me and make sure I was safe.

I took a shaky breath before responding softly, "Promise."

The warmth of his lips grazed my forehead before he turned and walked to his car.

Tears trickled down my face. I quickly brushed my wet cheeks, mortified that his words had pierced through my hardened armor and rekindled a piece of my fractured heart. But after years of drowning in shame and loneliness, Quinn had left me standing in an emotional whirlwind, desperately attempting to protect myself.

I clenched my teeth together, refusing to let him in.

Good luck with that. Too late.

A cold reality seeped into my bones. No way in hell could I allow him to get closer to me. My nostrils flared that I'd let my guard down with him, I spun on my heel and marched back into the house.

"Uh-oh," Gabby said from the couch. "We're sorry. We didn't mean to scare you."

I blew out a sigh. "It's okay. I appreciate that you all waited up for me."

Everlee jumped out of the recliner she had taken over and gave me a quick hug. "Did he say something to make you cry?"

My stupid heart melted all over again. "No, I'm okay."

"I say we make some drinks and Wynter can give us all the deets of her date." Without waiting for agreement, Leighton hopped off the couch and walked to the kitchen.

Everlee arched her brow and searched my face. "You don't have to."

"The night was amazing. That's the problem," I said to her and Gabby.

"Make it a double, Lei! We might have a crash and burn on our hands," Gabby yelled.

Leighton popped her head around the corner. "Oh. Shit. That good, huh?"

I nodded and giggled through more tears.

Everlee placed her hand on my back and led me to her favorite seat, the recliner. "Just chill. I'll grab snacks. We'll be tired tomorrow, but you may need an intervention." She winked at me before she joined Leighton.

"It's scary when you connect with a guy like that. Especially when its brand fucking new. We've all been there." Gabby shifted on the couch and tucked her legs beneath her. "Just remember, babe. If he's the one or if shit goes sideways to hell, we'll be there for you."

I choked on my sob, overwhelmed with her words. "I'm sorry. It's just been a crazy ... life."

Everlee and Leighton returned with four glasses of coke. "Girl, I want to reach inside you and make all of that pain go away." Everlee handed me a drink. "Rum and Coke."

"It's hard watching a friend hurt," Leighton added as she joined Gabby and Everlee on the couch. "So start from the beginning."

I took a gulp, hoping the alcohol would soothe my frazzled nerves, then proceeded to tell them every amazing and wonderful thing about my night with Quinn. Each word that poured from my lips, I sealed into my heart. Even as I did, if Quinn and I had anything special, it would burn to the ground when he found out the truth.

Chapter 21

Quinn

Tossing my cell phone onto my bed with a thud, I closed the door as a wide range of conflicting emotions crashed into me.

What the hell had just happened?

Scrubbing my face with my hands, I seriously wondered if I needed therapy for multiple personalities. I'd flipped from hating Wynter for what had happened to Bell to falling for her within a few stupid hours. Everything I had thought I knew about her had been proven all wrong—she wasn't cold or ruthless, but instead a kind and gentle person. I couldn't help but admire her resilience and strength. I would swear that girl didn't have a vindictive cell in her beautiful body. But could I trust her? Maybe she had mad acting skills.

To add to my constant flip-flop of feelings toward her, I'd about come unglued at her scream when she entered her house. The moment I heard the shrill cry, I was ready to kill some motherfucker for hurting her. Fear had me twisted up like a damn pretzel.

"Fuck! Fuck! Fuck!"

A soft knock on my door caused me to groan. "What?"

"Dude, you sound like you're fucking having a breakdown in there. Do I need to call 9-1-1?" Brody asked.

"Don't be a smartass." I rushed over and jerked the door open. "I don't need any help."

Brody skirted around me, proud of himself for getting past me and into my room. "Who is she?" He jumped into the air and flopped onto my bed, landing on his back. Brody tucked his hands behind his head and crossed his legs at the ankles.

"You're not staying," I barked. My heart raced as I looked into Brody's eyes, images of Bell swimming through my mind. I never had the courage to tell Brody, but with every glance at him, I was reminded of Bell. Fucking loved and hated him for that, just like what Wynter said about her parents. When I heard her words, I could have sworn that she saw right through me and recognized what I really was—a fraud. I didn't have feelings like most people. After losing Bell, I'd had a massive hole inside me. I wasn't capable of feeling anything, but I was smart and learned to mimic those around me. Until recently, I wasn't sure I would ever have real, honest emotions again. Now, the sleeping dragon was stirring, and I was scared shitless of what would happen if it woke.

"Tell me who she is." Brody shot me a cocky smile, and I resisted the urge to wipe it off his face.

"Don't worry your pretty little head about it." I slapped at his shoe, knocking his foot off my bed. "Besides, don't you have girl problems of your own?"

"Nope. I'm all good. Just fucked her tonight, actually."

I tipped my chin at him. It was weird to think of him old enough to have a girlfriend and get laid. "Have I met her yet?"

"Nah. I really like this one, so we're keeping it on the down-low for a bit. We just want to be left alone without the entire senior class sticking their nose into our business."

Realizing that he wasn't leaving my room anytime soon, I plopped down in my desk chair. Maybe it was a good thing, though. Brody was a good distraction. I needed to clear my head after spending the evening with Wynter before I figured out what the hell to do about her.

"You love her?" I grabbed the football off the floor and tossed it into the air. It would help ease my anxiety about Wynter if I kept my hands busy.

Brody rolled over on my bed, facing me. "I think so."

I lowered the ball and looked at him. "Could you still love her if her brother or sister did some fucked-up shit like kill someone?"

Brody flinched. "What the fuck kind of question is that, bitch?"

"Just answer me, asshole." I leaned forward, eager to hear his answer.

He massaged his temple, clearly perplexed. "If I got to know a chick and she didn't have some crazy-ass shit going on in her brain, and she was a good person ... I don't think I could hold the sins of her sibling against her. Hell, out of both of us, you would be more likely to kill someone than I would." He gave me a half-shrug. "Maybe I'll be in those shoes one day and a girl will have to decide if I'm mean or crazy enough to murder someone, too." He chuckled.

"You're not funny, Brody. I'm being serious."

He pulled on a loose thread on my comforter.

"As I said, if she didn't have anything off-kilter and didn't want to become the next Lizzie Borden, then I wouldn't hold her family's shit against her."

"Who the hell is Lizzie Borden?"

"Q, man, she chopped up her mother and stepfather in 1892. She's one of the most notorious female serial killers. We're studying all about the ladies in psychology." He snorted. "Did you ever pay attention in class?"

"You know I was more into math. Numbers don't fuck people over." I tossed the football at him. "You seem way too excited about Lizzie. Maybe you need *your* head examined."

He reached out and single-handedly caught the ball.

"Really? Because you're the one who started this bizarre conversation in the first place."

I leaned back and folded my arms across my chest. "I was just curious." A heavy sigh escaped me as I began to unravel what he'd said, my thoughts plunging into a full-on tug of war about Wynter. She was responsible for Bell's death ... wasn't she? My brain said yes, but my heart was telling me a different story. I just wasn't sure what the truth was anymore.

But I have facts. Facts speak louder than possible pretend actions.

"When you're ready, I want to meet this girl with no name. I gotta make sure she's good enough for you."

Brody stared at me quizzically. "Don't you mean that I'm good enough for her?"

I shook my head. "Don't care about her, only you. And before you get all mushy on me, get out of my room. I have shit to do."

Brody climbed off my bed, then strolled over to me. "Thanks." He squeezed my shoulder before he left, leaving me alone with my fucked-up whirlwind of thoughts.

I locked my door so I wouldn't be interrupted again. Then I unlocked my desk and removed Wynter's file. It was time to finish Kyler's letters.

Chapter 22

Quinn

y eyes burned like a son of a bitch, and they felt as if they'd been doused in salt water. I rubbed them in an attempt to clear my hazy vision, but it was no use. I threw off the heavy comforter and placed my feet against the cold, hardwood floor.

For some reason, I'd hoped reading Kyler's letters to Wynter last night would answer my questions, but I was wrong. Kyler hadn't gone into detail about what drove him over the edge, which was frustrating as fuck. He hadn't provided any of the insight I was searching for. Now, I was more confused about Wynter than ever before. The girl he portrayed wasn't the same one Adam talked about, but I was also biased toward Bell and Brody. I suspected Kyler was the same about Wynter.

The lack of sleep weighed on me like a ton of bricks, and even though I had probably dozed off for a few hours, it wasn't enough to give me the energy I needed to be successful on the field during practice. Coach had radar like a bat, and he would zone in on the fact that I was exhausted.

I stretched, then made my way to the bathroom to take a piss. My mind began to spin again, and I released a frustrated groan. From the letters, Kyler and Wynter had been super close. If that was the case, why had he written instead of talked to her? What had happened for him to pull away? The last note only hinted at what was going on, but there were no clear details. Did that mean he finally spoke to her, or did his secret die with him?

I slapped my palm against the wall, then finished my business. A niggling thought tugged at the corner of my mind. Before I made it to class, I had a call to make. Tonight, I would spend more time with Wynter, take Brody's lead, and watch for any signs that she was like her brother.

After I showered and dressed in clean jeans and a Whitmore University hoodie, I scooped up my phone from the nightstand. Maybe it had been intuition, or maybe just stupid luck, but a while ago Kane had confided in me that he and Brie had needed security. I didn't need a bodyguard, but he mentioned he would bet a lot of money that Sutton Westbrook was better than any PI. I wasn't sure why I asked for the phone number, but I had, and now I had a use for it. Reaching out to her for help was worth a shot.

Locating Westbrook Securities contact information, I tapped the green icon on my screen before I held the phone to my ear. My heart jackhammered against my ribs as if this was the worst idea I'd ever had. Maybe it was.

"Westbrook Security, this is Sutton Westbrook."

I cleared my throat. "Mrs. Westbrook, my name is Quinn. Kane Cooper gave me your number. I'm on the Whitmore University football team with him."

"Hi, Quinn. What can I do for you?"

I liked her immediately. She neither confirmed nor denied that Kane had been a client. Pacing the room, I told her about the file Adam had given me and about the letters. She remained silent until I was finished.

"Just to confirm, you need to know if the information is legit?"

"From what I have found on the internet, it is. But the letters ..." I shoved a hand through my damp hair. "Would you think I was weird if I told you something didn't feel right?"

"Not at all. I trust my gut all the time. If yours is saying something is off, always follow that nudge."

She'd just confirmed what I thought. "Okay. What's next?"

"I have a friend who's a specialist in handwriting. I'm currently in Portland, so how about we meet, then you can give me the letters. Make copies to keep, though. Actually, copy the file. If you don't mind, I'd like to take a look at everything that you have."

"Sure, and if you see anything that's off, please tell me. How much do you charge?"

"I tell you what. I'll be driving through the area on my way back to Spokane, so let's meet on the outskirts of town where you won't run into anyone you know. I don't want to cause problems if a parent or friend sees us having a meal together. Let me look over the info you've got, then I'll give you a price before we get started." She paused for a moment. "Wait, you're a college student, aren't you?"

"Yeah, but if you're concerned about money, it isn't an issue. I can pay you."

I could almost hear her smile through the line. "Okay. How about lunch around one today?"

"I can make it work. Tell me where and I'll be there."

Sutton gave me the name of a café before she described herself with long blonde hair, average height, and blue eyes. I told her what I looked like, then we disconnected the call.

The cafe was a cozy space with green-and white-striped wallpaper. I took a deep breath, glancing around, searching for Sutton. Nervous energy bubbled in my chest as I squeezed between tables and chairs. A booth in the corner caught my attention. I hoped it would be free, so I could have a private conversation with Sutton. Reaching the vacant seat, I slid in, my heart pounding faster with each passing second.

I nervously bit my cheek, considering the worst-case scenarios and all the moments I had thought about skipping this meeting over the last few hours. Sutton would either confirm that Adam was being honest about Wynter or prove once and for all that I couldn't believe a word out of the bastard's mouth. Even though I hated Adam, I still had a need to trust him. If he was feeding me shit, it would fuck with me since about the only thing I could count on was that he'd always been straight with me in the past.

From what you can tell.

I stared at the folder in my lap while I waited, fiddling with the corner of the manila file. I had left home early to meet Sutton so I could first stop at the local library to make copies of the documents.

The bell on the entrance jingled and a woman in her late twenties sauntered in, a picture of confidence in her tailored navy suit and high heels. Her honey-blonde hair was pulled back into a neat bun, and she wore an expression of determination. She strolled toward me with purpose, her presence commanding the room.

"Quinn?"

I rose and extended my hand. "Nice to meet you, Mrs. Westbrook. Thanks for meeting me."

"Please, call me Sutton." She set her purse on the seat and slid into the booth to sit across from me. She shucked off her black overcoat, smiling warmly at me. "It sounds like you've been through a lot. I'm really sorry about your sister."

My jaw clenched. I hated it when people apologized. It wasn't their fault. I nodded, then laid the file on the table.

She placed her palm on the manila folder and dragged it toward her. "Have you eaten? I'm starving."

"I could eat, but maybe we can look everything over while we wait for our food?"

"Of course. I have a long drive ahead of me, so I just want to get my order in now."

"Spokane, right?" I folded my hands in my lap, appearing calmer than I was.

"Yeah. My husband Pierce and I live there. We have several locations for Westbrook Security, but we're pretty happy splitting our time between Washington and Oregon."

An older waitress brought us waters, then took our order. I hadn't realized the menu was written in chalk on a blackboard, but it was easy enough to grab a late breakfast packed with protein with a stack of pancakes on the side.

Once the waitress left us alone, Sutton opened the file. After her first pass through the documents, she lifted her head, her blue eyes widening as they stared at me. "Quinn, I remember when all of this happened. Nothing I can say will help, but I would like to look into what you need at no charge. What I may discover could not only affect you and your family, but so many others' lives too."

Sutton's compassion caught me off guard, and I struggled to swallow around the ball of emotions that lodged in my throat.

"I need to know about the letters, but if you want to dig into the police report and Wynter's background, it might help. I'm trying to figure out what's true and what isn't. I've researched as much as I can. I need a professional."

Sutton nodded and closed the folder.

"I ... uh, Wynter worked for Dimitri Photography. I took out the images from the file, but she did porn in order to pay bills and support her sister after her father split and her mom began to drink all the time. I realize you'll need that information, but if you go to the website, just understand what you're about to walk into."

Sutton removed a pen from her purse, then scribbled the details on the inside of the file. "Got it. Any detail you have is important. Also, any conversations we have are confidential. I don't want you to worry that I'll talk to anyone other than my team."

"That helps, thanks. I really appreciate you looking into Wynter's background. There are unanswered questions, and for a while I thought it didn't matter, but then I met her. She attends Whitmore

University now. I've talked to her a few times, and the way the article reads, it sounds like she was questioned as a person of interest. But ..." I took a drink of my water, needing to tell Sutton the shit that was spinning around in my brain. "That's not the girl I've spent time with. Not at all."

The waitress brought our food and set it in front of us.

"Thank you," Sutton said, giving her a warm smile.

My stomach reminded me I was hungry, and I dove into my pancakes.

"Is that why you're wanting to look into the letters? You feel like something isn't adding up? Not to mention that the media spins stories all the time."

I speared my scrambled eggs with my fork, then popped a bite into my mouth. Surprisingly, they were really good. I hadn't eaten at any cafés, since we ordered delivery or Adam took us to an upscale restaurant when Lena didn't cook, but I liked this place.

"Honestly, I feel like I have two personalities. One hates her and one ... doesn't. I lost my sister because of her."

"How was Wynter responsible?" Sutton took a bite of her bacon as she waited for me to respond.

"It's clear from the letters that Kyler and Wynter were close. She could have talked to him. Stopped it all." My fists clenched. "My father also said he and Drew Baldwin worked together, and Kyler and Bell met when they were younger. Maybe they were still friends. Hell, maybe not. Bell and I ran in different crowds. Maybe that they were dating and keeping it quiet so my father wouldn't blow a fuse."

"Anything is possible, but I understand your need to find answers. I would too." Sutton wrote another note on the inside of the file, then continued to eat. "Can I ask you something?"

I shrugged. "Sure."

"Do you have any other brothers or sisters?"

"Yeah, a younger brother. Brody."

"Are you two close?"

A smile eased across my face. "Yeah. I'm the only one he really has. He's a good kid. After all the shit he's gone through, I'm surprised he's turned out so well."

"I'm glad he has you. It's important. Does he tell you every detail about his life? My sister does. My best friend is her fiancé, and he talks to me too. Sometimes I wish they didn't." A soft laugh escaped her.

I chuckled. "Nah, he doesn't tell me everything. Honestly, I don't want to know. He's been through enough without having an over-bearing asshole looking over his shoulder. That's Adam's job."

"Adam?"

"Our father." Cleaning my plate, I leaned back in my seat. "He's a real dad of the year, if you catch my meaning."

Sutton wiped her mouth with her napkin. "I do."

"So, no. I don't know what Brody is into most of the time. He plays football, his grades are excellent, and he stays out of trouble. I don't worry about him too much."

"I see."

My brow quirked at her, waiting for her to explain her simple comment. She remained silent, so I spoke first. "And?"

"You mentioned that Kyler and Wynter were close. What if they had the same kind of relationship you and Brody do, and she didn't know anything until after the fact? Is that possible?"

I gulped, feeling like a kid caught red-handed looking at his dad's porn mags. "I hadn't thought about it." Embarrassed, I stared at my empty plate.

"Quinn, it's hard to put ourselves in someone else's shoes when we're grieving. Maybe enough time has passed that you can look at the situation with a more open mind. It might bring you the answers you're looking for. It might not. Sometimes it takes a stranger to say the right words to make a difference. Plus, I butted in where I shouldn't have."

Now it made sense why she wanted to know how close Brody and I were. I tapped my fingers on the table. "No one's asked me that before."

"I hope I didn't cross a line." She folded her hands in her lap.

"You didn't. I would rather you be up-front and talk rather than speculate and judge me." I glanced at the clock on the wall and realized I had football practice in a few hours. My stomach flipped at the thought of seeing Wynter again that night. With Sutton's words ringing in my brain, I wondered if I would look at Wynter differently.

"Okay, then as we learn more, I might ask you some questions that could help you see the situation differently. It often brings up bits of memories or information that you've forgotten. However, I need to get on the road now. I'll be in touch as soon as I know something."

We stood, and I pulled out my wallet. "Lunch is on me."

"Thanks. That's sweet of you. Just go up to the counter and they'll have the bill there. I'll talk to you later."

"Have a safe trip." I gave her a small wave before I found the server and paid for our food.

Sutton's conversation fucked with my head for the rest of the day, and all I could think about was seeing Wynter again.

Shit. I was royally screwed. Wynter was getting to me. One date and a few fucks at the society had me dropping my guard, and no way in hell could that happen. Falling for her wasn't in the damn cards. I imagined Bell telling me not to be an idiot and reminding me who Wynter was. The thought of Bell slammed into me like a rhino on speed.

I refused to let Wynter derail my plan. I would take her down for Bell.

After football practice that afternoon, I read the files and searched for Bell's obituary and police report online. I stared at it, unblinking. I hadn't heard her voice in years. She should have grown up next to me, attended law school, gotten married, and had babies. It was all in black and white in front of me. There was no denying that Wynter had been involved.

My twin was gone. Stolen from my family and ripped from this world too soon. She had an entire life ahead of her. She was beautiful and smart with a bright future until ... I sucked in a sharp breath, my emotions on overdrive and kicking me out of the driver's seat.

Regardless of Sutton's valid points, Wynter had all but confessed to the cops. She was guilty and Bell's blood was on her hands. Agony and anger returned with a vengeance, and once again I promised Bell that I would avenge her death.

Chapter 23

Wynter

I stood in the middle of my room and took a last look around, making sure I hadn't forgotten anything for my date with Quinn. I had my trusty toothbrush and toothpaste in my purse. This time the girls had talked me into wearing my denim miniskirt paired with a long-sleeved lace shirt over a white tank with spaghetti straps. Everlee did my makeup and Gabby curled my long hair. The girls had a cheerleading meeting, so after they'd finished helping me, I was left alone for my doubts and jitters to ravage me quicker than a pack of monkeys devouring a banana.

My phone vibrated and I glanced over to where it lay on my bed. It was Janine on FaceTime. I scooped it up off my mattress and tapped the screen.

"Hey. Everything okay?" I asked, my nerves standing on tiptoes. She never called unexpectedly.

"Yeah. I was just missing you." Janine jutted her lower lip out as she walked around her bedroom, then crawled onto her bed.

"I miss you, too. How's your week been?" I sat down on my desk chair, giving her my undivided attention.

Janine's eyes narrowed as she looked at me suspiciously. "You look awfully hot for a night at home. Your hair is even curled. Are you holding out on me?"

A giggle escaped me. "I wasn't going to say a word until I figured out if it was anything or not."

"Oh? Do tell." Janine flopped over on her stomach and propped her chin on her hand, eagerly waiting for me to share with her.

"There's not much to say. We had our first date last night, and he's picking me up again in a few minutes." As hard as I tried, I couldn't stop the huge grin that split my face.

"Well, fuck me." Janine sat up, grinning. "Wynter, I've not seen you genuinely happy since ..." Her smile faltered, shadows of the past ghosting across her expression. She slammed her eyes closed, then opened them. "I'm tired of the past dictating our futures. I can't tell you how proud I am of you. Two whole dates." She held up her fingers.

"Me too. The past sucks, and there's nothing I can do to change it. Just build a new future, right?"

Janine nodded so hard I thought she might give herself whiplash.

"Is he hot?"

I fanned myself, heat consuming me, my body remembering his kiss last night. "I'll see if I can get a picture of him while we're out. He plays football, and according to the roomies, he never dates. He's a straight up player."

Janine's nose scrunched in distaste. "I don't like him already."

"Janine, you've not even met him. And who cares if he's a player? I can handle him. The point is that I'm making friends and going out. That's all that's important." *Unless the Red Dragon tells the world the truth.* Internally groaning, I slammed the mental gateway on the ugly possibility. I was bound and determined that I was going to have a fun evening.

The doorbell chimed. "That should be him. I love you." I blew Janine a kiss.

"Love you, too. I want all the details tomorrow." She gave me a stern look before she laughed and disconnected the video call.

Grabbing my purse from my desk, I closed the door behind me before I hurried down the stairs. I peered through the peephole and confirmed it was Quinn before I answered.

"Hi," I said, smiling so hard my cheeks hurt.

"Hey, beautiful." Quinn's arm moved from behind his back, and he presented a dozen gorgeous red roses.

My hand flew to my mouth as I stared at them. No one had ever given me flowers before. It seemed Quinn was going to check off a lot of my firsts, but if the evening went well, I would be okay with it. If not, I had fun while it lasted.

Keep telling yourself that. You're falling for him fast and hard.

"Oh, thank you. Come on in. I'll need to put these in water before we leave." I hurried into the kitchen as Quinn stepped into the house. A gust of wind followed him, and I shuddered.

"How was practice?" I called while I snipped the end of the stems and grabbed a vase from the counter. Quickly, I filled the container with water, then arranged the roses and set them in the middle of the dining table. I washed and dried my hands before I returned to Quinn.

"It was good." He rubbed his chin, giving me a wistful expression. "Well, I fucked up a little, actually. I couldn't get this gorgeous, smart girl out of my head."

I folded my arms across my chest. "Who is she? I'm going to kick her fucking ass. You're supposed to be focused on your career, not some chick." I tapped my black flat against the wood floors, pretending to be pissed.

A laugh bellowed from him. "I have to admit, I like it when you're feisty." He walked forward and slipped his arm around my waist, then pulled me against his muscular body. He reached up and gently dragged his knuckles down my cheek. "I've been thinking all day about this." He dipped his head, his warm mouth melding to my lips.

I moaned softly, arching against him as his tongue danced with mine. My core throbbed, eager for him to touch me. To my surprise, he drew back, then took my hand.

"More of that later." He led me out of the house, and I locked up behind us.

We laughed as we made a mad dash through the rain to his car. Once again, he opened the passenger door for me, and I climbed in quickly, hoping the downpour didn't ruin my curls.

Quinn hopped in and started the Mercedes. The engine purred to life and before he put his seatbelt on, he leaned over and kissed me again. "You taste so sweet you're probably toxic."

He buckled up, then backed out of the driveway and made a left down our street.

"Hmm." I tapped my chin. "Are you saying I'm toxic?"

Quinn glanced at me and took my hand in his. "If you are, I would never see it coming."

"Guess you better keep your guard up then," I said playfully.

"Too late."

His words were so soft, I thought I might have misunderstood what Quinn had said, but the expression on his face clued me in. He liked me as much as I liked him.

Shit. This can't happen. If Quinn really knew me, he'd learn quick how toxic I was. I promised myself this would be our last date. My future was at risk if I allowed him to get too close.

"Where are we going?" I asked, changing the topic.

There was that gorgeous smile I loved to see.

"You said you were competitive, so I guess we're about to see just how much." He shot me an ornery look, then focused on the road.

"Well, that could be anywhere."

"Just sit back and chill. You'll need your energy." Quinn turned on the stereo, then tapped his fingers on the steering wheel as "Call it Love" by Felix Jaehn and Ray Dalton thumped through the speakers.

"Hey, that's the song we danced to at your party." I moved my arms to the beat, dancing in my seat.

"I wondered if you'd remember."

"How could I forget? It was the night your father caught me on my knees." I barked out a laugh.

Quinn shifted in his seat, appearing uncomfortable. My gaze dropped lower, and I saw the telltale signs of arousal pressing against his jeans. A sudden heat rushed through me from head to toe and I felt a familiar stirring between my legs. I thought back to the evening of the party, when we'd danced together in his crowded living room, our bodies pressed against each other in near-perfect harmony. We had been so close to taking it further when Quinn's father had ruined everything. Yet Quinn had only kissed me goodbye last night. What was so different now?

Ten minutes later, Quinn pulled into a parking lot, the gravel crunching beneath his tires as he searched for a spot to park. I peered at the dark building with no windows and wondered where the hell he'd brought me.

To my surprise, Quinn grabbed his jacket from the backseat before he climbed out of the car and hurried around to my side. He opened the door, then held the clothing over me as I got out. My heart fucking melted on the spot. I pushed up on my tiptoes and kissed him before we made a mad dash through the pouring rain and to the entrance of the building.

I cringed when the door closed behind us. Quinn laughed while he took my hand and led me to a table in the back of the room. I slid into the booth large enough for two, glued to the pretty girl on stage belting out the lyrics to "You Should See Me in A Crown" by Billie Eilish ... completely and horrendously off-key. Karaoke wasn't for everyone, but from the way she was dancing and singing her heart out, she had no clue it wasn't her gig.

Quinn leaned over, his lips brushing my earlobe. I shivered as he wrapped his arm around my shoulders.

"No lip-syncing this time, babe. Just your own voice."

Finally realizing what his challenge was, I glowered at him. "What if I can't sing any better than she can?"

Quinn placed his thumb on my lower lip, gently pulling it down. He leaned in again. "If you lose and can't give a stellar performance that brings the crowd to its feet, then *I* win."

My chest heaved, his touch sending delightful chills through my body. Liquid heat pooled deep in my belly, and my pussy throbbed. I wanted to part my legs and slide his hand beneath my miniskirt until he touched my most sensitive place.

"What happens if you win?" I asked, breathless.

"Then I get to decide where I eat you out. The hood of my car, in the hall here at the club, definitely somewhere in public." The corner of his mouth kicked up. "Maybe I'll even tie you to my bed. There are so many good choices."

Jesus Christ. I was going to come with him just talking to me. "Guess I'd better lose then."

"But what if you impress the hell out of me yet again and I lose?" His heated gaze collided with mine.

I really wanted to tell him he could fuck me until I couldn't walk, but that would be too easy. When I was in a good place and happy, I was highly competitive, and I wouldn't just roll over for him because my panties were soaking wet from a little dirty talk.

Licking my lips, I squeezed his thigh. "Then you have to sneak me into your bedroom and spend the night with me ... *without* touching me."

Quinn gaped at me, then he laughed. "Game on, beautiful."

A half-hearted applause filled the air as the off-key girl hopped down from the stage, beaming as if she'd just won a Grammy for best song of the year. He nodded toward the front of the room. "Looks like you're up. Good luck."

My stomach dropped to my toes, then I remembered what I got out of the deal. An entire night to torture Quinn. It was interesting what you could learn about someone when they were horny and exhausted. Before I lost my nerve, I rushed to the stage.

I looked through the song options, selecting one that would match my voice. I grabbed the cordless mike and pinned it to my shirt, then waited for "I'm Not Sorry" by Neoni to start. Remembering the dance routine Janine and I had put together before I moved to Oregon, I started to move as the music played and belted out the lyrics without even needing the prompter. Pulling from my performance days on the dance team, I squared my shoulders and danced in between the tables, turning on the charm. Skipping down the aisle, I headed toward Quinn who was sitting there with his mouth hanging open. The crowd began to clap as I continued, and whistles filled the air.

I winked at my competition then swayed my hips as I marched back to the stage and finished the song. Everyone in the place was on their feet, cheering and clapping when I was done.

I took a bow, laughing my ass off. I hadn't had this much fun since before I'd lost Kyler. And for the first time, my heart didn't split into pieces when I thought about him. It felt damned good.

Quinn met me at the stage, slipped his arm around my waist, and dipped me backward.

"Not bad, gorgeous. Looks like you might be going home with me tonight."

He shocked the hell out of me when he laid a searing kiss on my lips in front of the audience. More whistles and catcalls filled the lounge, and I giggled against Quinn's mouth.

He righted me before he searched for a song while I made my way back to our booth to watch. I'd seen some of his dance moves at the party, but I was curious to see if he had anything more.

Quinn waited, then the first few beats of the song filled the air. He pointed in my direction as he began. His deep, strong tenor nearly made me pant as he sang "Love on the Brain" by Rihanna.

Every girl and a few of the guys in the room cheered and clapped as Quinn worked in some sexy hip moves while he performed. I was pretty sure I could watch him all night. I bit my lower lip while I listened to him, my body becoming more willing for him to tie me up and fuck me with each lyric.

Quinn ran and slid down the aisle, then jumped up on the table and held his hand out to me. He hoisted me up and we fell into a sexy rhythm just like we had the first time we'd danced together while he finished.

The girls were louder with their cheers and whistles. Scanning the room, I realized no one was on their feet though.

I pushed my mouth into a pout before I said, "Looks like you lose." I playfully batted my eyelashes at him.

"But did I?" He kissed me, then hopped off the table and helped me down.

Shit. I was just trying to mess with him when we'd made the bet —do the unexpected. It took me a minute to realize I'd fucked myself right along with him when I said we would spend the night together without touching.

Chapter 24

Quinn

It was after midnight when I snuck Wynter into my house. If we were quiet, I doubted Adam would even know we were there. One thing was for sure, Adam needed to stay the hell out of my plan. If he messed it up this time, I would be ready for him.

I held my finger up to my mouth, then leaned near her ear. "My room is up the stairs, last door on the right. Brody's is on the left, so don't go in his on accident." I flashed her a grin. "I'll meet you up there."

Wynter nodded then tiptoed away. My attention glued to her, my dick hard as hell while I watched her hips sway. Visions of her at the society, sprawled out for my pleasure, danced through my head while she disappeared down the dark hall.

I wished I had time to rub one out before I joined her, but I wanted to see how long she could hold out without touching me. Sneaking into the kitchen, I used my phone's flashlight and grabbed a bottle of Adam's vodka and two glasses. If we couldn't fuck, then I would get her relaxed enough to talk freely. Maybe she would divulge her secrets without me pushing the conversation.

I hurried to my room, then closed the door with my foot. Tucking the alcohol under my arm, I locked the doorknob. "We're safe this time." I set the bottle and glasses on top of my dresser and opened the mini fridge next to my desk before collecting a soda and making us a few drinks. "Here."

"You have a fridge in your bedroom?" she asked, disbelief in her tone.

"Yup. Brody does too. There are nights we don't want to see Adam, so we keep snacks and sodas up here."

Wynter's brows furrowed. "He seemed like he had a ... very big personality." She took a sip, then sank onto the edge of my bed. Her eyes darted around my room. The last time she was here, she hadn't been focused on seeing what my bedroom looked like.

"That's a nice way to say it." I sat in the chair at my desk, downing half of my drink before I set it down. "So, tell me why." I leaned back and stretched my legs in front of me.

"Why what?" She pressed the glass to her full lips, peaking at me over the rim.

"Why did you want to spend the night?"

She crossed her long legs, and I swallowed. If I had it my way, her creamy thighs would be pressed to my cheeks, and I would be tongue deep in her pussy. Not touching her would be tough as hell while she was in my room, but I had let her think that she could trust me. If she believed I was capable of talking with her until the wee hours of the morning, it would be front-door access to her heart. Girls loved that shit.

"I mean, you knew you would win tonight." My pulse stuttered as she gave me a mischievous smile.

"I thought I would, but I wasn't positive. At first it felt like cheating, but you never asked if I could sing." She tilted her head and batted her eyelashes at me, all innocent. Even though I knew she wasn't innocent at all, I couldn't help but laugh. She sighed while she pointed at my pillows. "Can I?"

"Of course, make yourself comfortable."

She placed her drink on my nightstand, then crawled onto the bed and fluffed the pillows. Wynter leaned against them and crossed her legs at the ankles.

I stood before strolling over to my closet, where I grabbed my Seahawks blanket. "You look cold." My eyes never left hers as I covered her up. I wondered what Bell would think if she knew that Wynter was at the house and in my bed.

Stay focused. You're after the truth so you can squash the ridiculous feelings you have for this girl.

"Thanks." Her cheeks pinked as she placed her arms over the blanket. "There are multiple answers to your question."

"Oh?" I returned to my chair and sat down again. My cock told me it wasn't safe to sit on the bed with her. "Please share." I took another drink, watching her expression and body language. I'd had years of practice observing and figuring out what someone was going to do. Adam had given me plenty of lessons. This time I was failing miserably; —I couldn't read her at all.

"I wanted to see if you were just being nice or if you wanted to fuck me," she said, her tone matter of fact.

"Fair enough." I couldn't tell her my real plan, so I kept my mouth closed to let her draw her own conclusions. "And?"

She picked up her glass and took a long drink before she spoke again. "I *wanted* to spend the night with you."

I couldn't help that I loved how blunt she was. "Are you always this up-front?"

"I try. Not always. Sometimes circumstances dictate answers for me." Her gaze drifted away from me and onto the blanket.

I understood that too well. The shit with Adam and Bell had me avoiding some topics altogether. Since I knew Wynter's secrets, I understood why she would skirt certain conversations as well.

"Tell me something I don't already know about you." I propped my feet on my desk and leaned back in the chair.

"You don't know a lot about me, actually." A hint of a smile shadowed her beautiful, full mouth.

"Why Whitmore?"

"It's an excellent college, and the fact that I'll graduate from here will open doors for me. I need a good job. I'm still taking care of my sister."

Guilt punched me in the gut, but just as quickly I remembered that Wynter had cost me *my* sister. Fury roared to life inside me, and I smashed it into a box, compartmentalizing it while she was here. I wished the guilt was as easy to shed, but it even haunted me in my dreams.

"You?"

"Football. My chances of being drafted are thirty percent higher if I play at Whitmore. Scouts fucking love the university."

Wynter stifled a yawn and took a deep breath. "Quinn?"

"Yeah?"

"I think I like you, and I'm not sure how I feel about that."

Son of a bitch. This girl was catching me off guard every time I turned around.

I placed my feet on the floor and ignored my instincts when I sat on the edge of my bed. "Why are you confused?" I wanted to touch her, but a deal was a deal, so I grabbed the stress ball off the night-stand in order to keep my hands busy. My gut clenched when I saw the pain in her blue eyes. A pain I knew all too well.

"I don't know that confused is the right word. The man I've seen so far, I like a lot. But ... I have a past, and I'm terrified when you find out about said past, you'll never want to talk to me again. I'm not sure I can handle that. If I walk away now right now, it ends, but it doesn't end with you hating me."

I sighed. I was playing with fire and about to get scorched. Suddenly, I wanted to absorb her hurt and reassure her that I already knew her worst, yet here I was, falling for her. *How can I fall for the girl who was responsible for my sister's death?*

"What if we make the best out of our night together, then tomorrow you can decide if you want to walk away?" I reached over and set my glass next to hers on the nightstand. "You have to say it, though. You have to tell me that I can touch you and call off our bet."

"The bet's off." Tears filled her eyes, and she blinked them away. "One." Her voice was soft, vulnerable. "I can give you one last night."

A part of me realized that I could crush and ruin her right now, but my offer wasn't just for her. Sometimes a lie is easier to digest than the truth.

One night. Then ...

Chapter 25

Wynter

Sexual tension swirled, igniting the air between us, and my senses heightened while my pussy begged for Quinn to touch me.

With a heated gaze, he peeled the blanket away, and I shivered under his intense stare. His eyes moved over my curves, my heart thrumming in anticipation. Every inch of me craved him, yet I knew that if I gave myself to him there was a chance I wouldn't be able to walk away.

One night, then it's goodbye. Little liar!

I reached up and pulled Quinn down to me, our mouths meeting and our bodies colliding. His fingers slowly trailed up my side, and I sighed when he broke our kiss to nip at the sensitive skin on my lower belly.

"Lift your hips." He pushed my miniskirt up, then moved the damp fabric of my G-string aside. Our gazes locked for a moment before his tongue explored my most intimate place, sending waves of pleasure rushing through me. I gasped while he ravished me, worshipping me as if he knew it was our last night together.

It is.

I writhed beneath his mouth and dug my fingernails into his shoulders while my world exploded, losing myself in the euphoria.

"I need to see you." Quinn's voice was hoarse as he pulled off my panties and tossed them onto the floor. With skilled fingers, he flipped open the snap on my skirt and tugged it down until it was at my ankles. I kicked it off, unconcerned about where it landed.

"Sit up."

Apparently, Quinn was a man of few words in the bedroom. He grabbed the hem of my lace shirt and lifted it over my head, then he removed my tank top. My nipples hardened against the chill in the air. His mouth lowered, teasing one taut bud between his teeth as he moved me to the mattress.

"You're beautiful." His pupils darkened while he paused, his eyes roaming up and down.

There were no longer any clothes to protect me from his powerful gaze, and I felt exposed and ... timid.

Our lips met once more, and his tongue eased into my mouth as his finger slid into my slick center. My hips rocked against his hand, echoing the building pressure in my body. His tempo increased, and my breath caught in my throat.

"Oh my God, Quinn," I moaned. "Please, don't stop."

To my surprise, he removed his fingers and eased them into his mouth. I watched while he licked and sucked my arousal off. A teasing smile tugged at his lips as he stood and reached into his back pocket, producing a condom. Tossing it on the bed, he made quick work of removing his shirt, then his jeans. His cock bobbed free before it rested against his toned abs. The muscles in his shoulders and chest rippled as he tore open the condom wrapper and rolled it over his thick erection.

Quinn kissed his way back up my stomach, and I wrapped my legs around his waist, whimpering as he positioned himself between my thighs. He lifted my hips, and I spread my thighs, granting him full access. The head of his cock slipped up and down between my pussy lips, and his growl of desire sent a delicious shiver straight through me.

He positioned himself at my entrance and pushed inside, watching my face. I closed my eyes and lost myself in his touch.

"Open your eyes, Wynter." His voice was low and dominating. My lashes fluttered open, focusing on him.

Quinn pressed his mouth to mine and his searing kiss blazed through me as he moved, our skin growing slick with sweat. Our bodies clung together, and our fingers were intertwined, desperate to hold onto the moment. My muscles coiled as resounding waves of ecstasy radiated throughout me. My pussy clenched around his dick in intense rhythmic pulses, so powerful I struggled to breathe.

An uncomfortable mix of vulnerability, fear, and hope ricocheted through me like a bright burst of light. Quinn's expression shifted, pleasure washing over his face, consuming him with his release, even as he never broke our gaze.

Quinn stilled, then pressed a gentle kiss to my mouth. "One night." He nuzzled my ear. "I won't lie, though. I hope we will have more."

I looked up at him, tracing my fingertips along his strong jawline. "Maybe friends with benefits." I cracked a grin in an attempt to ease my panic.

The guys I'd been with at Dimitri's knew how to get me off and have fun for hours, but what had just happened between Quinn and me was different—somehow my emotions had snuck up on me, slapping me silly. Before I fell down the rabbit hole, losing myself in my feelings for him, I gave his ass a playful smack.

Quinn chuckled and rolled off me, lying on his side. He traced a little circle around my nipple before his fingertips danced between my breasts and down my stomach. Quinn swallowed hard, then looked into my eyes. "I think that might have been more intense than I'd expected."

Unable to hide my surprise, I frowned and wondered what he meant by his comment. "I'm not sure if that's a good or bad thing."

"Definitely a good thing." He rolled over onto his back and motioned for me to snuggle up to him. In all of my twenty years, I had never snuggled after sex. Hell, I hadn't ever dated either, but here I was. I'd done both in less than twenty-four hours.

Quinn wrapped his arm around me as I placed my head against his chest, listening to the beat of his heart. The sound of his soft breathing soothed my anxiety, and my eyelids fluttered closed as I gave into sleep.

"Wynter." Quinn's voice reached my ears.

"Yeah?" I attempted to move my neck and winced, realizing I was still plastered against Quinn in his bed.

"I need to sneak you out of the house before Adam finds out you're here."

I jolted upright, hitting him in the jaw with my elbow. "Oh shit! Are you okay?"

He smirked. "I've been hit a lot harder on the field."

Rubbing the haze from my gaze, I squinted until the red numbers on his digital clock came into focus. "It's seven? I guess we got a few hours of sleep." I crawled off the mattress in search of my clothes.

Quinn stretched, his naked, muscular body catching my attention. "You shouldn't do that unless you want to give me a ride before I leave."

His chuckle filled the room and I stepped into my G-string. Quinn stared at me as I dressed, watching my every move while his dick lengthened. "I wish we could, but I can't risk Adam's temper this morning." He wrapped his fingers around his shaft. "I'll obviously be thinking about you today." His focus remained on me.

Feeling silly from lack of sleep and giddy from our evening together, I cleared my throat and said, "As the wounded zebra attempts to hobble away, she's unaware of the crouching lion in the thick of the grass," I narrated in my best National Geographic voice.

The color drained from Quinn's cheeks, and I hesitated as I hiked my skirt up my legs and over my hips. What had I said to upset him? "Did I get the lion part wrong?"

He stood and shot me a half-hearted smile. "Nah, it was pretty good, but I think I'm more of a panther."

"Noted." After losing Ky, I learned really fast to read people and Quinn wasn't being honest with me. Something else had bothered him about what I said, I just had no idea what.

"We need to be quiet leaving the house. I'll drop you off at your place."

"Thanks. It would be a long walk from here," I joked, trying to lighten the mood.

Maybe Quinn wasn't a morning person. If we hooked up again, I would have to remember that tidbit about him. *One night.* My heart sank at the reminder of our one-night agreement, but I needed to walk away if I knew what was best for my fragile soul.

Dressed in jeans that clung to his muscular body like a second skin and a black T-shirt that showed off his broad chest, Quinn entered the bathroom. I seized the moment to frantically rummage through my purse for my tube of toothpaste. I twisted off the cap, squeezing out a minuscule amount and smearing it over my teeth in hopes it would freshen my breath in case Quinn kissed me. Struggling to hide the nervous anticipation coursing through my veins, I gave myself a pep talk and firm reminder that I needed to walk away from him. He had the potential to destroy what little life I'd managed to piece back together.

My pulse pounded against my wrist as I tried to make sense of my feelings for him. He was everything I had feared and more. He was kind and gentle, he listened and made me feel valued. The fact that he was unbelievably gorgeous made him irresistible—like an ice cream sundae smothered with whipped cream that I wanted to savor every last drop of.

"Are you ready?" He grabbed his keys, wallet, and phone before he took my hand and led me downstairs.

I suppressed a giggle, feeling a little silly about sneaking out, but from what Quinn had said, Adam wasn't the best father, and I didn't want to get him into trouble.

Minutes later, we were in Quinn's car and on the way to my house.

"Bury a Friend," by Billie Eilish played softly as he focused on the road.

I didn't know how to read the silence between us, but I had been the one to say I wasn't sure how to process our evening together. We'd talked, laughed, and the sex had been mind-blowing. In my gut, I knew it would be disastrous if he knew who I really was. Yet for the first time in my life, I wanted to be with a guy. It didn't matter, though. When Quinn found out the truth, he would run and leave me shattered again. If I left before he did, the aftermath wouldn't be as damaging.

Glancing over at him, I sighed, my heart and mind in a full-on war about Quinn.

"I had a good night with you." He offered me a tired smile.

"I'm sorry I kept you up late. Hopefully you don't have a big test or anything this morning." Guilt nudged me, but he was grown and responsible for his own choices just like I was.

"It was worth it."

And I just melted into a gooey puddle in my seat.

Doing a quick pros and cons list to make sure I really wanted to spend more time with him, I finally reached over and placed my hand on his. I held my breath as I waited for a sign that we were on the same page. Even though Quinn had said he wanted to be with me, that was before we slept together, and I had to make sure. My heart nearly jumped out of my chest as he threaded his fingers through mine and stroked my knuckles with the pad of his thumb.

"Does this mean you'll give me one more night?" Hope flickered in his hazel eyes as he briefly took his attention off the road and placed it on me.

"One more." I leaned my head back and looked over at him, smiling.

"One more." His lips curled up before he placed a kiss to my fingers.

Quinn parked near the curb since the girls had their vehicles in the driveway. Before I could object, he turned off the engine, hopped out and hurried around to open my door for me.

He gave me a small bow. "My queen."

My hand fluttered to my chest. "My king."

We laughed softly as I climbed out and he slid his arm around my waist.

"What's your class schedule like today?" Quinn led me to the front door and turned toward me, tipping my chin up.

"Classes are from ten until three."

"I have football practice this afternoon, but I'll text you afterward." He leaned down and brushed his lips against mine. "Have a good day."

"You, too." I remained rooted in place as I watched him stroll to his car, his strides long and powerful.

He waved before he drove away, leaving me with my whirlwind thoughts. I quietly let myself in the house and locked up behind me.

"Morning," Everlee said from the couch, blowing on a steaming cup of coffee.

"Hey." I couldn't wipe the silly smile off my face.

"So, are you in love with Quinn?"

Chapter 26

Quinn

With one hand on the steering wheel, I rubbed my shoulder with the other in a vain attempt to ease the tension from my muscles. Last night with Wynter had gone off the rails, and I wasn't sure how to fix it. My palms grew sweaty, and I wiped it on my jeans before I pulled away from her house.

"This is ridiculous. No girl has ever made you nervous." I continued to remind myself that she was Kyler's sister and responsible for the world losing Bell. But the girl I'd spent time with over the last few days wasn't mean or vindictive. She wasn't out to hurt anyone. My thoughts drifted to the file. In fact, I wasn't sure she was the same girl the media and cops had portrayed her to be.

I white-knuckled the steering wheel while I recalled my meeting with Sutton yesterday, desperate for answers. Hopefully I would have the truth soon.

You already have it in the police report, asshole. The truth is right in front of you, so stop making excuses. It's time to make her pay. I growled at that stupid inner voice. *You've only known her a few days. She's playing you like a fucking fiddle. You're losing control!*

I really had to quit talking to myself, but sometimes it was the best way for me to put crap into perspective and shut down all of the questions swirling around in my mind. "Focus on the plan. Fact, Bell is gone. Fact, Wynter could have stopped everything. Fact, she was close to Kyler and should have talked to him before my world turned to shit."

Conjuring up my hatred for her again, I pulled into my driveway. I wondered if Adam was up yet, but it wouldn't matter if he saw me waltz into the house early in the morning. I did it all the time. If he'd caught Wynter here though, all hell would have broken out. It was simple; I refused to give Adam the privilege of scaring the crap out of her. That was my job, and I couldn't allow him to upset my plan.

After locking my car, I strolled through the front door and slipped into the entryway. I wanted to shower before I headed to an early class, but first I needed a gallon of coffee to keep me going.

I shoved my key fob into the front pocket of my jeans, then reset the alarm before I made my way to the kitchen. The closer I got, the more a hint of freshly brewed coffee hung in the air. *Adam.* Squaring my shoulders, I spotted him at the table reading his newspaper.

A quizzical expression crossed his face as he eyed me. "Morning."

I tipped my chin at him in acknowledgment while I made myself a double espresso.

"I was hoping to catch you before classes." He glanced at me briefly.

I grabbed a coffee cup from the cabinet, still ignoring him.

"Quinn." His tone was stern.

I turned slowly and looked at him. "Yeah? Can't I wake up before you start with your shit?" Until I was strong enough to defend myself, I never talked crap to Adam. Times had changed, and I no longer had to offer him respect that he didn't deserve.

"Not today." He glowered at me, his fingers balling into a fist, then relaxing.

Whatever was going on had Adam in a fucking tizzy.

"How can I help you?" Sarcasm dripped from my question. I hid my smirk behind my cup before I took a drink, willing the caffeine to kick in fast.

"I wanted an update on Wynter." He removed his black reading glasses and set them on the table.

"What about her?"

Adam leaned back in his seat and adjusted his navy jacket. When Adam worked at the office, he always looked sharp as hell in his tailored suits and expensive shirts. At least when I was younger, he made a big impression on the ladies. Too bad he didn't make a good impression on his family.

His lips pursed, and he nodded slowly. "She's getting to you. You fucked her, didn't you?"

A couple times, twice at the society and once in your own house.

"That's none of your business, but no. I'm stringing her along." I should have felt guilty for flat-out lying to him, but I didn't give a shit. The asshole would probably imagine us fucking and get off on it. He was clearly obsessed with her online pictures.

"I was hoping I wouldn't have to do this, but you've left me no choice."

My pulse skyrocketed. When Adam was up to something, it was rarely good. I just had no idea what that something was.

"Sit down." He wasn't asking.

Since I needed to hear what he had to say, I kept my mouth shut and joined him at the table. Once I was in my chair, he cleared his throat.

"Quinn, I mentioned to you that I worked with Drew, Wynter and Kyler's father."

"Yeah, and?"

"There were several times when we lived in Washington that Drew and I would meet for business. You were knee-deep in football. It was when you were taking private coaching lessons. You and Bell were about thirteen. Anyway, you weren't home that day and Bell didn't want to watch Brody on her own, so I took him and Bell with me. It wasn't a big deal to take them with me since Drew also had kids."

I didn't miss the sadness in his expression when he mentioned my sister's name.

"Drew and I thought the kids would occupy each other. They did. Wynter was at cheer practice, but Kyler and Bell hit it off right away. For a while, we would meet at his house, and I would take Bell so she could visit Kyler. At first, I thought it was innocent, but as they got older, it was clear there were feelings between them."

I leaned forward in my seat. The fucker had my attention now.

"I wasn't crazy about Bell getting involved with any boy at fifteen and sixteen years old, but I later learned that she and Kyler saw each other every day at school. Plus, when both kids are driving, it's hard to track where they go and spend their time."

I wanted to tell him to hurry up and get to the point, but he would have to leave for work in a few minutes, so I kept my mouth shut.

"After we lost Bell ... Drew pulled me into a conference room one day. At first, I didn't think much about it because we always talked business. But the moment he closed the door behind us, I knew it was bad."

I drained my espresso and loudly set the cup on the table, growing more impatient. Adam ignored me and took a drink of his coffee, glaring at me.

"This is difficult for me to talk about. I never told anyone."

I caught myself before I rolled my eyes, not appreciating his drama. "I have class soon, so if this is as important as you say it is, spit it out."

The vein in Adam's neck pulsed. He was getting pissed, and I was enjoying every second.

"One of these days you'll have sons of your own, and I hope they're pieces of shit just like you are."

Red hot anger lit me up like the fourth of July, but I remained in my seat and mentally beat the hell out of him instead. "The point of the conversation with Drew?" Surprisingly, my voice held steady.

"This information goes nowhere, do you understand? It's private, and the only reason I'm letting you know is to help you stay focused on the plan—getting rid of Wynter. We can't live with a constant reminder of what she did right in our fucking faces." Adam's cheeks burned red with his anger.

"Okay."

Adam swallowed several times, and a sheen of perspiration broke out over his forehead. *Holy shit. This is big.*

"I was afraid for Drew's safety if I ever told you. It's a moot point now. He took off a few days after our conversation, and I haven't heard from him since. I kept thinking he would reach out to me at any time. Apparently, I was wrong, and I feel as though I can share this with you."

I leaned over the table, my eyes narrowing on him. "What did he say, Adam?"

"Quinn, Bell ..."

Chapter 27

Quinn

The silence in the room was deafening. All I could hear was my ragged breath, each inhale like a razor slicing through my throat, each exhale a plea for control. The second hand on the wall clock hammered against my skull as Adam and I faced off, the dark storm of anger between us looming.

"Your sister was pregnant with Kyler's baby."

My vision blurred as Adam's sentence hit me like a tidal wave, drowning my awareness of anything else except those four words. "What?" My voice sounded strangled and ragged. "Why didn't she tell me?"

Adam shook his head, his expression growing darker. "The only reason Drew found out about the pregnancy was because Kyler asked him for money to help with an abortion. When Bell learned she was pregnant, it was too late for the abortion pill."

My shoulders slumped as I collapsed in my chair, struggling to process that not only had Bell been pregnant, but I hadn't been there for her. She had to have been terrified of what Adam would do if he'd learned the truth.

Adam shifted in his chair. "Kyler said that Wynter also knew, and she pushed Bell to have the baby, upsetting her even more. When Bell refused and insisted on an abortion, Wynter shamed her and called her a baby killer. Bell was distraught, pleading with Kyler to help her. That same day, Kyler went to Drew."

I grabbed my head as fury whipped around my throat and strangled me. The pain of losing my twin and how I'd failed her dug its claws into me. The guilt crushed my chest, asphyxiating me. I blinked several times and breathed in, hoping to fill my lungs with much-needed air.

Adam slapped his palm against the table. "Snap out of it! Get your shit together and concentrate. Wynter is vicious. She's just as responsible as Kyler is for Bell's death. Wynter bullied her and pushed her over the edge without an ounce of remorse. Wynter is a master manipulator and skilled at hiding who she really is. Evil." He leaned forward, my guilt captive under his gaze. "And where were you when she needed you most?"

That feeling of suffocation turned to full-blown pain as his words slashed me open, cutting and tearing at my already broken soul. *Bell! I'm so sorry!* I gripped the ends of my hair, trying not to completely lose my shit in front of Adam.

"I won't tell you again. Finish. Wynter. Baldwin. Or I will." The sound of his chair scooting across the tile floor reached my ears, his footsteps slapping against the tiles as he walked away.

I shuddered with rage, unable to control the emotions that crashed down on me. My sobs filled the room as my tears mingled with my fury. Wynter had broken through my defenses, leaving me exposed and vulnerable.

Rage constricted my throat and clawed its way through my veins as I renewed my vow of vengeance against Wynter. I was done making excuses. It was time to make her pay for destroying Bell.

I regained my composure and stood up, the reminder of my plan jolting my mind back into action. I didn't care if Adam was in town or not—I was going to throw the biggest party Whitmore had ever seen, and I knew just who to call in order to make it happen. With my hands shaking, I pulled out my phone and dialed the number of the one person who could give me what I needed.

An hour later, Remington Barlow, a football teammate and member of the same exclusive society, sat across the room from me in the society's dimly lit office. I tried to appear nonchalant as I propped my legs up on the mahogany table, but a trickle of sweat ran down my back. Remington crossed his legs at the ankles and leaned forward, elbows resting on the armrests of his chair as he studied me intently. I told him about the file and my plan as he listened without interrupting.

"Can you do that for me?" I fidgeted in my seat, ready to get to practice and pound motherfuckers on the field. It was the best place to take out my aggression.

"I can do it, but ... Dude, are you sure? There's no going back after that shit's out."

No. I gave the thought a big *fuck you*, my mind returning to the conversation with Adam earlier that day. "Yes. I'm positive. She has to pay."

Remington nodded. "All right. Whatever you need, man. You know that. We're brothers."

I ground my teeth and my jaw clenched tight with anticipation while I rubbed my hands over the smooth planes of my freshly shaven face. All the pieces of the plan had been set in motion and now I only had to endure the agonizing wait until Saturday night. If all went accordingly, Wynter Baldwin would be gone for good.

Chapter 28

Quinn

In order to keep up appearances over the last three days, I texted Wynter pretty regularly, despite a raging fire in my gut that churned at the thought of her. Every time I conjured up the image of what she had done to Bell, my stomach rolled with disgust. But even as I had typed the hollow words that explained my need to "rest up for the game on Saturday and catch up on some assignments," I hoped she felt the sting of rejection.

A sharp rap on my bedroom door as I yanked on a crisp new sports jersey momentarily pulled me away from my thoughts. Whitmore had won again that afternoon, and I was now ready to put my plan into motion and watch Wynter crash and burn in front of everyone.

"It's open!" I called out, knowing it wasn't Adam or Brody since they weren't home. Neither of them would return until tomorrow night, so I didn't have to deal with any interference from either of them.

Remington strolled in with his hands in his jean pockets.

"What are you down about? We won the game, man. It's time to party." I grinned as I shoved my cell in the back pocket of my jeans.

My stomach churned with nerves. The plan had to play out the way we'd wanted it to.

"I'm stoked we won, Q. I just have to ask if you still want to go through with what you have laid out for Wynter."

I rubbed an imaginary itch on my nose. "Are you having second thoughts? If so, you should have fucking told me that before now." My lips pressed into a thin line. "Are you bailing on me?"

"Nah. Never. But this is going to do a lot of damage. *A lot.* I'm down with revenge, but this is pretty intense ... even under the circumstances."

I fucking snapped and barreled across the room, my nose a mere inch from his while I fought to contain my anger. "You weren't the one who lost your twin sister. Keep your judgment to yourself and do what you fucking said you would."

Remington held his hands up in the air, surrendering. "You're right, man. I haven't lost a member of my family. For the record, I wasn't backing out, Q. Just wanted to make sure you were ready for the aftermath."

I released my hold on him and backed away, my emotions clouding my thoughts. "Sorry." Shoving my fingers through my hair, I blew out a heavy sigh. "It's been a lot. All the memories have fucked with my head."

"I can't even begin to imagine. I'm not sure how you kept it under wraps at Whitmore for as long as you have. That's a lot to live with."

I nodded and checked the time on my clock. "People will start showing up any minute. I have no clue about how many will fit in the house, but we're about to find out."

"Everything is set up outside, too. All systems are a go," Remington assured me.

"Thanks, man. I'll feel better once she's gone for good. Then, I'll be able to concentrate on football again." Maybe my anger would fuel my focus.

The doorbell chimed, and I pasted a grin on my face. "Let's have some fun. After the shit goes down, I'll be fucking some chick's brains out at the society."

"Same. My dick and I are both seriously happy about that part too."

I slapped Remington on the back as I led him to the hall and closed my bedroom door behind me.

Excitement swirled in my chest. I couldn't believe I was only hours away from avenging Bell's death. I wished she could watch the show from up above. Hell, maybe she would. One thing I wouldn't do again? Let her down.

Remington and I parked ourselves at the top of the stairs where we had a good view of the activity on the main floor.

The moment Kane opened the front door, people flooded the mansion. Remington had made sure they knew it would be a party above any other, and the crowd was the biggest I'd seen yet.

I leaned against the wall, watching Wynter, Gabby, Everlee, and Leighton stroll into the entryway. Wynter's gaze bounced around the groups, a slight frown marring her beautiful features. I figured she was searching for me, but I wanted to wait for a while before I announced my presence.

The girls weaved through the crowd to the kitchen and fifteen minutes later worked their way through the crowd to the living room with drinks in both hands. That's how it went at my parties. The lines were long to the alcohol, so normally people would make two beverages at a time.

Wynter downed a shot, then tossed the plastic cup in the garbage. "Butterfingers" by Oli Fox shook the walls. One thing I could say about Adam, his taste in state-of-the-art stereo equipment was off the hook.

Gabby grabbed Leighton's and Wynter's wrists, coaxing them to the makeshift dance floor. Everlee danced behind them, laughing.

"Wynter and her friends are having a good time." Remington folded his arms, his gaze trained on the group.

I wondered how fast Gabby, Everlee, and Leighton would pack

Wynter's belongings and toss her out of their house once they'd heard the big reveal. If I gambled at all, I would have bet Remington that Wynter was back on the road to Washington by Monday morning. Imagining the horror go down, I couldn't wait to see her drive away, defeated. Her leaving was a good enough reward for me. I squared my shoulders and stood up straight. I was about to test my acting skills with Wynter one last time.

"Good luck. Text if you need me." I slapped Remington on the back as I descended the stairs and elbowed my way over to where I'd last seen Wynter. "Different Man" by Kane Brown and Blake Shelton drifted from the speakers as bodies gyrated.

Finally reaching Wynter, I placed my finger over my lips as Everlee and Gabby spotted me walking up behind their roomie. I snuck up to Wynter and slid my arms around her waist. Her coconut-scented shampoo tickled my nose as I pulled her to me, my cock waking up the moment the back of her pressed against me.

"Hey, beautiful. I've missed you," I said against her ear.

She spun around, a huge smile on her face. "Hey." She placed her palms on my chest and looked up at me. "I've missed you too."

I leaned down and kissed her slowly, her body falling into mine as I continued. "We should dance."

Wynter eagerly nodded and I clutched her hand, dragging her to the center of the room. A fierce and powerful beat blared through the speakers as Corvyx's "Burn it All Down" played. Our bodies moved in perfect sync, melding against each other, and we swayed to the song. I ran my fingertips up her back, giving her my undivided attention as we kissed during the song. Her deep blue eyes met mine, and for a second, I felt torn between Remington's warnings, Kane's and Sutton's words, and my plan. But when Adam had spoken of Wynter's betrayal, a blind rage consumed me like a wildfire, blazing uncontrollably until I realized it could only be extinguished by Wynter's tears tonight. The music shifted to a more upbeat tune as we separated, leaving me with a darkness I couldn't shake.

My cell vibrated in my back pocket and my entire body tensed. I glanced at the grandfather clock in my living room. We were only five minutes away from showtime. Hopefully Remington wasn't having a hiccup with the setup.

"I'll be right back, beautiful." I kissed Wynter, realizing it would be our last, but I was good with that.

Reaching for my phone, I excused myself to move where I could hear. Frowning at the unknown number, I answered.

"Hello?" I plugged my other ear with my finger as I made my way through the crowd and outside.

"Quinn, it's Sutton. Did I catch you at a bad time?"

Shocked to receive a call from her so late in the day, I assured her it was as good as any and shared that we were celebrating another victory on the field.

"Congrats on the win. It sounds like you have a great team again this year." Her tone shifted as she continued. "I'm sorry that I didn't get to you sooner with this information, but considering the allegations, it was important to make sure our research was spot on. As it is, we have only scratched the surface, but I felt it was imperative to tell you this right away. Quinn, the letters from Kyler to Wynter aren't real. Some of the words are original and were used to engineer the rest of the handwriting."

I rubbed at my chest where my heart hurled itself against my ribs. The palpitations were full of shock. "Why would anyone do that?"

"In my experience, it's because they're usually trying to hide something, but I don't know if that's the case here yet. The documents that you gave me in the file are real, but the letters were fabricated. From what the specialist said, the letters were original notes from some English homework, then the rest of it was generated and spun to appear that Kyler wrote them to Wynter. Since the police report was real but incomplete it probably was done to make you think your source was trustworthy."

I groaned. "What the hell. This is nuts." My pulse stuttered and a wave of dread crash over me. If Adam had deceived me about the letters, then what else had he lied to me about? The rest of the information about Wynter had proven to be true, so how much of this new reality could I actually believe? With my hands shaking, I shut my eyes and tried to keep my composure as I wondered how deep this rabbit hole would go.

"Quinn, with your permission, I would like to continue this work. I have a feeling there's a lot more to this."

I stared out over my yard littered with people and empty cups. "Me too. Let's find out anything else we can." I looked around as it dawned on me what time it was. "Sutton, I don't mean to be rude, but I need to call you later." A sudden panic struck me in the temples, making me wince as I hurried back into the house. I had to find Remington and stop the reveal before it was too late. Fuck!

What have I done?

Chapter 29

Wynter

I gritted my teeth, willing my bladder not to burst when I spotted the lines to the bathrooms on the main floor. I was desperate not to piss myself, so I gave up and made a beeline for Quinn's bedroom. I was pretty sure it was off-limits, but when I peered up the stairs, I couldn't see anyone around, and no one had seemed to notice me slip away. I ran up the steps, each one creaking beneath my feet, and looked around before I finally snuck inside his room, then bolted to the bathroom.

After hastily closing Quinn's bedroom door when I was done, I started down the hall, only to be stopped dead in my tracks by ear-splitting screams echoing through the house. Out of nowhere, a massive screen dropped from the ceiling and blocked the entrance. I stood rooted to my spot at the top of the stairs, my eyes widened in alarm as I observed the multiple television sets placed around the main floor all playing the same video. Chills shot down my spine as I recognized the halls of my high school. A disguised voice bellowed out of the speakers as the TVs projected films of students running in all directions, their faces frozen in terror.

"Welcome to Timber Creek High, home of Kyler and Wynter

Baldwin. Most know Kyler as the school shooter who murdered thirteen people before taking his own life." The narrator paused as the sound of bullets firing in the background held the audience captive.

Acidic bile surged in my throat as I plastered my body into the wall, praying that no one would see me while the video replayed my brother's heinous acts, naming every innocent victim he had taken. My pulse pounded, and I tried to breathe through the sheer panic as I was forced to witness the tragedy again. Every cell inside me bent with terror as I watched the horror wash over the crowd below me. Salty tears burned my cheeks as I relived the worst day of my life, the massacre that left me broken. My heart twisted, then crumpled in on itself as each name uttered from the speakers sent a fresh wave of anguish crashing into me, leaving me with nothing but a hollow void in my chest.

"Kyler's heinous acts of evil should have been squashed long before this tragedy happened. Lives were taken and families destroyed. Wynter Baldwin, Kyler's own sister, was well aware of his plans yet chose to remain silent and disregard the atrocities that were happening around her. She was just as responsible as Kyler and doesn't deserve a place at Whitmore University. We as a community have the right to deny her attendance and ensure she's held accountable for her brother's actions."

I clamped my hand over my mouth, trying to strangle the revulsion that clawed its way up my throat. People would be searching for me at any moment and leaving a telltale trail of vomit would only make it easier for them to find me. I had to get the fuck away, but I was stuck upstairs with no way out. Desperately, I searched for a place to hide and wait out the storm. This party had just turned into a fucking witch hunt—for me.

Tears prickled my hazy stare. My knees quaked and nausea bubbled in my belly as I stumbled down the hall and into Quinn's room. I locked the door behind me and plastered my body against the wall as sobs overtook me. Angry voices floated upstairs, and I slammed my eyes closed, trying to force my fear down long enough to think. As I ticked off the names of the victims—names that deserved my acknowledgment every day but that I had been afraid to remember—the truth bitch slapped me hard enough to draw blood.

Bellamy Astor. Shit! I had been so fucked up with the fact that the video was on display in front of hundreds of people, I'd missed the connection. Quinn had lost his sister that day. When he'd learned who I was, he set me up, playing me the entire time.

I hiccupped, my fear slowly turning to anger as I started to put two and two together. Our high school was huge. Three separate middle schools were funneled to our high school, so there was no way to even know everyone's name. Plus, I was a basketball cheerleader, and I never paid attention to the football players. The year we attended school together, we ran in completely different circles.

Pacing the room, I was grateful his lamp was on so I didn't have to go looking for light. The last thing I needed right now was to trip over my two feet and land on the floor with a huge thud, giving away where I was.

"Think, goddammit." My nostrils flared as the Red Dragon's words raced through my mind about Kyler and declaring me a liar. "Son of a bitch!" I fisted my hands—it had been Quinn all along. Every fuck, every kind and vicious word ... it was all a setup to tell the world who I was. I felt myself snap inside, and my blood boiled. I was sick and tired of running. I was sick and tired of people believing lies about what had happened. If I had to leave Whitmore, then I was going down in flames and Quinn Astor was going down with me.

I bit my lip, forcing myself to carefully plan my next move. Scanning his room, my attention landed on a dagger sitting on top of his dresser. My eyes narrowed as I approached. I picked it up, admiring the red dragon etched into the white marble handle. The knife cemented my suspicions that Quinn was also the Red Dragon. The motherfucker had held this to my throat, then whoever the other guy had been had taken over.

It was proof that Quinn was in the secret society. With enough backing, that tidbit might be enough to ruin his shot at going pro. "Payback is a bitch, isn't it, Quinn?"

I clenched my fists and forced myself to stay focused, remembering the lessons I'd learned. It had been almost five years since the basketball cheerleaders back home had blamed me for not stopping Kyler and used that as an excuse to attack me. That was when I knew I needed to learn to protect myself. Too ashamed to show my face out in public, I had called a Krav Maga dojo. The martial art was known for its extreme brutality and strength, but I was desperate. I had to ensure my safety at all costs—even to the extent of hurting another person if it meant saving my life or Janine's. The sensei agreed to train me after hearing my story, and I remained under his private instruction until finally coming to Whitmore.

Noticing that cars were driving away from the house and the voices downstairs had quieted, I unlocked the door and hid behind it, waiting patiently for Quinn to return. After all the shit I'd lived through, I'd grown quite good at being patient.

My muscles burned from standing in the same spot, but I couldn't afford to fuck up. Two hours later, the doorknob turned, and I held my breath. Waiting.

Chapter 30

Wynter

My heart raced as I waited for confirmation that the person in front of me was Quinn. The sight of his distinctive Nike shoes told me it was him, so I slammed the door shut once he was fully through the threshold, the thunderous sound echoing throughout the room. Quinn spun around in surprise, but I didn't give him time to react. I lunged at him, kicking him in the groin. He doubled over, and I grabbed his neck to hit a pressure point and control his movements.

I forced his back against the wall, then let him go. Before he could blink, I brought his dagger between his legs and nudged his dick through his jeans. His face turned white with fear as I gave him a cold, threatening stare.

"Hello, Quinn. Miss me?" A maniacal laugh escaped me. "I would think twice about moving if I were you. I hear the dick bleeds like a motherfucker when it's cut off."

I actually had no idea if that were true, but I was pissed as hell that he had played me and turned the entire school against me. The sorry son of a bitch was going to listen to what I had to say, or bleed to death in his own bedroom.

He slammed his eyes closed as I moved the blade against his junk. "How does it feel, Quinn? Do you like seeing your entire life flash before you?"

"Wynter, wait. Let me explain." He attempted to touch my shoulder, and I shrugged out of his reach.

I ran the tip of the knife up his stomach, then placed it against the side of his throat. "One wrong nick and I'll hit your jugular so watch those hands. I may get ... twitchy."

Quinn swallowed, his body trembling. "I'm sorry, Wynter. Please let me explain."

My nostrils flared. "I'm tired of listening to the entire world as they continue to judge me. You're going to fucking listen for a goddamn change." A quick nick to Quinn's neck and a drop of blood bloomed from the small cut.

Quinn's fear was palpable, and I fed off it, a sickening satisfaction coursing through my veins. In that moment, I realized what a monster I'd become. Was I no better than Kyler? A wave of guilt swirled inside me at the thought. All I wanted was to scare the shit out of him, then force him to listen.

"The sad part, Quinn? I liked you. I really liked you. I thought what we had was special and it meant something to you. It certainly meant something to me. After what Kyler did, I missed dating and the prom, school events, friends. Not only did he steal lives from other families, he stole mine too. Drew, my father, left us with an alcoholic mother who curled up in a ball and is drinking herself to death while I work my ass off to take care of my younger sister and pay the mortgage. At seventeen, I was forced to keep a roof over our heads and food on the table. Nobody bothered to ask me how I was. All along, people assumed I knew the truth, wanted to believe I could have stopped it. And that was the biggest lie of all. But they bought it hook line and sinker because they needed somebody alive to blame." My heart thundered in my ears so loudly I couldn't hear myself think.

"Wynter, then tell me. I'm listening." His voice was soft and for a brief moment I thought Quinn might be sincere, then I remembered how he shared my past a few hours ago. There was no way I could trust him. He was just trying to manipulate me again, talk his way out of a knife to his neck.

I watched the small trickle of blood make its way down toward the hollow in his throat.

"Do you know what hurt the most? That nobody—not my teachers, not my parents, not my so-called friends—ever checked in on me after what happened. Nobody asked me if I knew anything, they just started making shit up. And for the record, I had no idea what Kyler was planning. We had been close at one time, but about six months before all hell broke loose, he stopped talking to me. He was moody and sullen, and I begged and pleaded with him to talk to me, but he refused. I tried to tell Mom. I tried to tell my dad. I went to a school counselor, telling them that something was terribly wrong, but I had no idea what it was. Do you know what they did? Of course you don't because you never asked me either. You believed all of the lies too. You're just as bad as all of the others."

I mentally swore, angry at myself because I had done the exact same thing that I'd just accused Quinn of. I'd swallowed his lies, believing them as truth. I had stupidly allowed my loneliness to dictate who I trusted.

"Wynter. I'm so sorry. I won't lie. After losing Bell, I didn't give a fuck about you and how you felt. I lost my twin." He gritted the last sentence out.

I blinked rapidly, wondering if I had heard Quinn correctly. "Your twin?" My hold on the knife eased up a tad.

"Yeah, Bell was and always will be my twin. When I lost her, not only did I lose my sister, but she was also the only human being that truly understood me. We had that twin bond. All the shit people say about twins is true. The day I lost her was the day I lost everything."

A part of me wanted Quinn to suffer, but he already had. It didn't slap a lid on my box of anger, though. My brain slogged down memory lane, reminding myself of all the evil things I'd wanted to do to people that hadn't listened to me. I understood Quinn more than

I'd realized. We were both angry at a situation that had stolen our lives, and if I'd had the chance to strike back, I know damn well I would have. In some ways, Quinn and I were a lot alike. My heart softened at the realization, but I wasn't ready to forgive him yet.

"I'm sorry. I had no idea she was your twin." The warmth of my apology filled the room like smoke, masking the pain that still lingered between us.

The air was thick with tension and my thoughts raced, smothered in panic and regret. My chest heaved with empathy for the pain he must feel. I had experienced the same for the loss of my brother. Kyler hadn't always been broken.

"I lost my brother even before he ruined so many lives. And I wonder sometimes ... I wonder how it would have turned out if one adult had listened to me and not blamed Kyler's moods on puberty. One evening when he wasn't home, I remember sneaking into his room and searching for anything he could hurt himself with. I was that afraid for him, but I had thought he would commit suicide before he hurt other people." My gaze fell to the floor, then back to Quinn's. "Even the police report and media didn't mention how hard I tried to get help."

Quinn swallowed, eyeing the knife still at his throat. "It was because the full police report was buried, and the cops needed someone to blame for Kyler's actions."

I stared at him in disbelief. "How do you know that? My parents and I are the only people aware of that fact. Maybe there were others, but nobody ever spoke out. Nobody ever stood up for me and realized that I am *not* my brother. I am Wynter Baldwin, a completely different person than my brother was the last six months of his life."

My forehead creased, the memories rushing at me full speed ahead and threatening to drag me into a sea of despair all over again.

"After everyone's world was turned inside out, I was beaten, chastised, and asked to leave school because I was a *distraction*." Tears pricked my eyes, but I refused to let them fall in front of him. Quinn was now a pawn in the game called my life, and I was determined to tell somebody the truth even if it meant I was briefly holding them against their will.

He gulped as his gaze cut to the knife. "Wynter, I have a lot to tell you if you'll listen. I ended up hiring a professional to help me dig into what happened. When you arrived at Whitmore, someone gave me some information about you, including pictures of your work with Dimitri, your home, who lived there, and more. It brought back losing Bell all over again and I hated you. I swore I would avenge Bell's death. I couldn't get to Kyler, but *you* were in front of me." His expression filled with regret and compassion.

I could see straight into his tortured soul for the first time, and for a second it felt good to see him hurt after what he'd just done to me.

"Right before the video was set to play tonight, I received a phone call."

I tilted my head and smirked. "I know. We were dancing, remember?" My tone was sarcastic, unfriendly, but I didn't care. All I wanted was to be heard.

"Yeah, so I went outside to take the call. It was the person I hired to look into you and the shooting. Something in the back of my mind kept poking at me, probably because of who my original source was. I questioned if they were feeding me bullshit, if I could trust them. My own initial research proved that the documents in the file, including the police report, the information on the school shooting, and the media articles were accurate. By that time, I didn't have any reason to not trust what I was being told." He cleared his throat and pressed his body against the wall as much as he could to avoid the dagger at his neck.

"When I started hanging out with you, I began to question who you were, the smart, beautiful girl I was falling for or the person the media portrayed to the public." His voice cracked and he blinked rapidly. "Right now, I see the girl the police forced into hiding when they buried the fact you tried to get Kyler help."

I searched his face, wondering if he was being honest or filling my head with more lies so that he could hurt me even more. What he had done with the video had burned me, but I'd been hurt so much worse. My logical side said run, but my heart said something else. Oddly enough, my pulse had settled down and my breathing was normal as I processed what he'd told me. Quinn's actions had been born from anger and the horrific pain of losing his sister. My brother had taken her from him, then took his own life. I was well aware of the need to lash out at people, force them to feel my agony and darkness with me. As fucked up as it was, I understood why Quinn played the video. Not only had he been manipulated, but someone had pinpointed his weakness and exploited it. My anger began to shift from Quinn to whoever had fed him lies and hate about me.

"Were you really falling for me, or are you just feeding me more bullshit?" I lowered the dagger to my side but kept it in my hand. I had never intended to hurt Quinn, I just wanted to scare the crap out of him, but that didn't mean I fully trusted him yet. Now it was time to see if he would turn on me without a knife to his neck.

"Her name is Sutton."

My defenses slammed into place, realizing that I'd misunderstood him. "Oh nice. You fuck me in your bed last night and now you're gonna tell me about some girl you're serious about and most likely met at the Viper Secret Society. Make up your mind, Quinn. You're giving me whiplash."

Quinn frowned before he continued. "Sutton's the person I hired to help me find out the truth. She called me right before the video started and told me the documents I'd been given had some accuracy to it. However, there was another police file that included the real story that the media never shared. I practically hung up on her and tried to stop the video, but I was too late. By the time I was able to get through all the people to turn it off, it had played in its entirety." He shoved his fingers through his hair, his eyes pleading with me. "Wynter, please understand that I did try to stop this, to make a different choice. I've been lying to myself, and I do have feelings for you. I want to protect you but at the same time, I'm still angry about losing

Bell. I've been confused, but after I talked to Sutton this evening, I'm clear about a few things."

I knew firsthand about confusing feelings. "And those are?"

"I fucked up, and I can no longer deny that I'm falling for you. I also realize it might be too late. I know I can't take back what I did." His gaze traveled to the floor and his shoulders slumped from the weight of his words.

I waved my free hand as if I was swatting away his confession. "You now have proof that supports what I just told you? And you know that I'm not lying when I say I tried to help Kyler?"

Quinn reached up and his fingertips trailed down my cheek to wipe away the tear that had slipped free. No one had believed me before, and that single moment had stitched a part of me back together.

"Yeah." His tone was gentle as moisture welled in his eyes.

Relief washed over me, and I sank down onto the foot of his bed. "I thought using your dagger against you was the only way to make you listen." I set the knife on the mattress, still testing him. *Does he really care about me, or is he trying to talk his way out of danger?*

Quinn walked toward me and knelt in front of me. He placed each of his palms on my knees. "Nothing I can say could make up for what I just did tonight, but I can talk to people, and we can turn this around together. We can start spreading the truth. Let me help make things right, Wynter. I realize there's probably no way you want to give me another chance, and I don't blame you one fucking bit. I'm sorry I hurt you."

Everything inside of me wanted to believe Quinn. I wasn't in love with him, but I probably had been on my way before he fucked me over with this evening's stunt. "What you did was horrible. You literally turned the college against me." I pursed my lips and glanced away from him. "But if you hadn't, I would have never been able to speak my truth to someone who knew what my brother had done." I took a deep breath to steady my nerves.

"I can't imagine how hard it was for you to see me when you realized who I was. My life changed so much after what Kyler did. I often wished I had died that day too. It was Janine, my younger sister, who kept me going. I was all that she had left, and no way in hell would I let her down the way I'd been let down. As crazy as it sounds, somewhere inside me, even after how I've been treated, I still believe that one person speaking out can make a difference. And if only one person listens and takes action, then lives might be saved."

"I do too. Will you let me help? I think people will listen to me since I lost Bell and I'm trying to clear the air to help you, Kyler's sister. We will use my voice to speak the truth until people will listen to *yours*."

I wanted to believe him, but he had betrayed me in a split second. However, the only way I could find out if he was serious was to let him help me. With each promise he kept, maybe my heart would finally be able to heal, and I could build a future, once and for all. Only time would tell if he was really the guy I had fallen for or if it was all one big show. But the big question? Was I willing to risk everything and take one last chance on Quinn Astor?

Chapter 31

Quinn

I cursed myself for not trusting Remington's warning, and now I had to face the consequences. My desperate need for revenge had cost me any chance of a future with Wynter. Even though Sutton's report proved Wynter's innocence for me, it was too late.

The fear and vulnerability in Wynter's expression clawed at my chest. I wanted nothing more than to take away her pain and protect her, even if that meant I had to take on all the suffering myself. It had taken Sutton's call to make me realize that Wynter had nothing to do with Kyler's actions, and I hated myself for believing lies instead of asking her like I should have in the first damn place.

"How can I trust you, Quinn?"

"Unfortunately, you're going to have to take my word and let me prove it to you. After talking with Sutton and you tonight, I know I was wrong. Just one more chance, that's all I ask." I pressed my lips into a thin line. I doubted I would if I were in her shoes, but she was a better person than I was.

Her gaze narrowed on me and her forehead creased. "Quinn Astor, you have one more chance. But if you fuck up this time and screw me over, a little nick on the neck will look like child's play when I'm finished with you. Something inside me broke tonight when that video played. I'm tired of hiding to stay safe, so if you mess up again, you should know that I've trained for the last four years in Krav Maga. I could kill you with my bare hands if I wanted to. Although I'm not the violent type, I have had to learn to protect myself, and if someone puts me in harm's way, I have no qualms about putting them in their place."

Was it wrong that I was turned on right now? As she spoke and promised to put me in my place physically, I admired her even more because she wanted to take a stand for herself after all the shit she'd been through.

"I understand."

A shoulder slumped, and I could see some of the tension ease from her neck and shoulders. I hated that I had caused it. Wynter gave me a quizzical look. "I won't tell anyone that you're the Red Dragon at the secret society, but I'm glad I now know it was you. I wish we could start off under different circumstances, but maybe something good will come out of this horrible mess."

Wynter stood and waited for me to do the same.

It would be a waste of time to deny that I was the Red Dragon. The same knife I'd used on her was in my room. It was hard proof. Maybe being honest with her was a foot in the right direction.

"I appreciate that you won't say anything. I'm actually the leader of the society."

Wynter gawked. "Wow. I wouldn't have ever guessed, but again, no matter what happens, I won't say anything. If I did, others would be hurt too."

Although Wynter didn't trust me, I finally felt as though I could trust her, thanks to Sutton. When Wynter unloaded about Kyler and that she'd tried to make someone listen, it smashed into me like a freight train. Although Sutton had told me what she'd learned, it was the anguish in Wynter's eyes ... she wasn't lying. She'd tried so fucking hard to save her brother. Not only did I find myself wanting to protect her, but more than ever, I needed to know what pushed Kyler over the edge.

"I have no right to ask that of you after what I did tonight, but thanks." I rubbed my jawline, wondering how I was going to make things okay with Wynter, or if I even had another chance.

"I should go home. With what you shared with me about Bell, I can understand why you snuck me out of the house yesterday morning before your father woke up. I'm probably not his favorite person, and I get that. Losing a daughter..." She shook her head, grief consuming her beautiful features. "All I can do is tell both of you how horribly sorry I am."

"I know, but Adam." My face twisted in disgust. "Adam doesn't deserve your apologies." After Sutton's call, there was no doubt in my mind that Wynter had always been honest with me about who she was. It was me that had been the fucking dumbass.

"Now I have to see how much damage was done. It's time to see if the girls will hear my side of the story." She nibbled on her lower lip before she spoke again. "Or if they already packed my shit and it's waiting for me on the front porch. If they want me out of the house, I have no other choice but to go back to Washington. I don't have another place to live, and I'm not sure Whitmore will allow me to continue to attend. I might be a liability and distraction for other students." Her head bowed, then she straightened and braced herself.

Even though she probably didn't want me to touch her, I took her hand in mine anyway. "Then let me start fixing shit right now. I'll take you home and walk you inside. I'll talk to the girls with you, and make sure they listen to what you have to say. If they still want you gone after that, and you want to continue to attend Whitmore, I'll make sure you have a safe place to live. But Wynter, I've known Everlee, Leighton, and Gabby for a few years, and I'll say that I would be surprised if they didn't at least hear you out."

Her body relaxed enough for me to catch it. "You'll do that for me? You'll go with me and talk to the girls?" Her forehead creased.

I squeezed her hand. "Wynter, I'm learning there's a lot that I'm willing to do for you. I know we have a ton to figure out. I have things to tell you, and I assume you have things to share with me about Kyler and Bell. I don't see my feelings for you changing." I pressed a kiss to her temple, unwilling to let her walk out of my life. If I stopped and listened, I suspected I would hear Bell whisper in my ear, telling me to ask Wynter to forgive me and make up for what I'd done to her.

She stifled a yawn, clearly exhausted. "I doubt we're going to get any sleep tonight, but I can buy you some coffee on the way to your place."

"I'll be okay. Caffeine will just make my anxiety worse."

"If you change your mind, let me know." I scooped up my dagger from the mattress and hid it in my top dresser drawer. "Let's go." Gathering my keys from my desk, I gripped them hard. It had been a fucked-up night and it wasn't over.

Twenty minutes later, we entered her house. All three girls were sitting on the couch with drinks, and their attention landed on Wynter first, then glowered at me.

"Quinn, you're the last person I expected to see standing next to Wynter," Everlee said, her eyes rimmed with red.

"Same," Gabby said.

Leighton nodded in agreement.

Wynter cleared her throat and stood tall. "I would like an opportunity to share my side of what happened, then you three can decide if you still want me as a roommate."

Everlee snorted. She wiped her runny nose and stared at Wynter for a minute. I knew Everlee well enough to realize she was processing.

"I definitely want to hear your side, but I already know who you are, Wynter Baldwin." Everlee took a sip of her drink and smacked her lips. I suspected that she was tipsy.

"And who is that?" My question held a protective and cautious tone. I wasn't clear on Everlee's intent.

Everlee tucked her leg beneath her, and everyone's attention landed on her. "Kind, you care about other people, your past has shredded you to pieces, and you're trying to find your way. You are *not* your brother. *You* Wynter, are your own person. No matter what has happened in the past, I am proud to call you my friend."

A squeak escaped Wynter, and her body trembled as a sob broke free. It was then that I realized how much she'd missed, including good friends. I mentally shamed myself from almost taking that from her too when I played the video.

"Thank you, Everlee." Her words cracked with emotion. "I just wanted the chance to tell you all what the media and police never told the world."

"I'm all ears. And if we're the first to give you an opportunity to speak up, then that's fucked up," Leighton chimed in.

Wynter glanced at me, and I placed the palm of my hand on her lower back, reminding her that even though I'd caused the shitstorm, I would now protect her from the monster I'd released.

"Before we dive in, I have a question." Gabby glowered at me. "Quinn, why the fuck are you here with her? I mean, I assume you were behind the video. When I saw it along with Bellamy's name ... I had no idea you had a sister until that moment. I swear to God, my blood chilled in my damned veins. Not only did it break my heart for you, but I was scared for Wynter. The girl I knew wouldn't hurt a fly unless she was cornered. Revenge is a messy bitch. So, why are you in my house standing next to the girl you just tried to destroy? More than that, tell us why we shouldn't beat your damn ass."

Without any hesitation, I said, "Because I fucked up. I tried to stop the video when I learned that I'd been given inaccurate information about Wynter. I was told that she knew what Kyler was going to do, and she didn't try to stop him."

A gasp slipped from Wynter, and I looked at her. "As I said, we have a lot to talk about."

"That's *not* what happened." Her voice was strong. She wasn't going to hide anymore. *Good.* At least my fucked-up actions hadn't destroyed her, but that had nothing to do with me. Wynter was strong and determined to get her life back.

"Hang on. We can get to all the details in a minute. Quinn, from what I can tell, you really, really fucked up. That was low. Like, starting a rumor or some shit is bad enough, but a replay of the actual event with Wynter's name all over the video? That's some PTSD right there, but I doubt that ever crossed your mind." Gabby grimaced, then stared a hole through Wynter. "And you just up and forgave him?"

The corner of Wynter's lips kicked up. "No. But he apologized profusely, then offered to help make it right. Only time will tell if he's really sorry. If he helps me fix the part he broke ... then I'll believe him."

Gabby folded her arms over her chest and harrumphed.

"What she said." Leighton tipped her head in Gabby's direction.

"I'm open to giving Quinn an opportunity to help me fix this mess. I don't want to be physically attacked or kicked out of Whitmore, but no one will listen to me now."

"We are." Everlee glowered at me, her words heavy with more sass than I'd heard from her before.

"Maybe it's because we've lived together for almost six weeks. You've seen who I am ... not the girl that was talked about at the party tonight."

"Well, Quinn, it sounds like not only do you have to make it right with our girl, Wynter ... You have to make it right with me, too." Gabby glowered at him.

"And me," Everlee added.

"And me," Leighton said.

My heart fucking soared. I was fine proving to them that I was on Wynter's side, but Wynter needed to hear them fight for her. The only person that had fought for her was Janine. Wynter deserved more.

Wynter hiccupped, and I pulled her against my side, letting her cry. I was surprised that she allowed me to hold her. I rubbed her back, absorbing her pain. It was so strong, I could taste it on the tip of my tongue. *What the hell did I do? Why had I listened to Adam?*

Instead of wasting my energy trying to figure out why I had trusted Adam, I reminded myself to focus on making shit right. Once Wynter and the girls were on the same page, and I knew she had a safe place to sleep, I had some calls to make.

Wynter pulled away from me, then Everlee hopped off the couch and grabbed the tissues on the coffee table. "Here, hon."

Wynter peeked at her, then removed a Kleenex from the box. "Come on. Get comfy in the recliner." She slipped an arm around Wynter and led her to the chair. "Quinn, you can sit on the floor."

If the situation weren't so damned serious, I would have chuckled. At least the girls hadn't kicked me out of the house. It was most likely because we'd been friends for a while. I'd even bailed Leighton out of a bad evening with a drunk asshole at a party. Maybe that would help them not hate me for the rest of my life. Maybe. I had a feeling there would be more surprises along the road Wynter and I were on. Not only would I have to tell her about the file and where I got it, but I also needed to talk to her about Bell's pregnancy. At this rate, I no longer believed a fucking word that came out of Adam's mouth, but I had to be careful not to let him know.

Dread twisted my gut. What was Adam afraid I would learn if Wynter didn't leave Whitmore? A more accurate question ... what was he hiding? For now, I needed to help Wynter explain what happened that day, then hope by the end of the conversation, the girls still welcomed her with open arms.

Chapter 32

Quinn

I arrived home around four in the morning. Once the girls had listened to Wynter's side of the story, they all cried and hugged. I finally felt it was okay to leave Wynter alone even though I didn't want to.

I hadn't escaped their questions about how I planned to fix what I'd done to Wynter, though. The three of them could start their own law firm after college the way they had interrogated me. Honestly, I wasn't sure how to make it better, but I shared where I would start. I was almost positive they were mentally taking notes, so they could follow up and make sure I was doing what I promised. They weren't the only ones. I was well aware that Wynter would watch my every move. This time, I refused to let her down.

After I snatched a few hours of sleep, several cups of coffee, and a shower, I was ready to face the world. Anxiety pulled and tugged at my insides, but I knew what I had to do.

For Wynter. For Bell.

Fifteen minutes later, I arrived at Coach's house. I'd asked if he and Kane could meet with me. I had to get ahead of the shit show that I anticipated would go down on Monday. If it got bad enough, I would hire a bodyguard for Wynter. No way would I allow her to be beaten down again. Hell, I'd done enough damage. It was time that I grew the fuck up.

Kane parked his car next to mine in Coach's driveway, then hopped out. I approached him with my hands shoved in the front pockets of my jeans.

The early fall day was dry, which was rare for mid-October, but cooler than what we'd had so far that football season. I knew the storm was coming.

"Hey." Kane slapped me on the back. "I'm guessing we're here about the video last night?"

Shame twisted my gut into knots. "Yeah. Figured I better start making things right by talking to Coach before Monday." I winced. "I'm pretty sure he'll kick me off the team." At the time, my anger had been in the driver's seat, and all I could see ahead of me was the road to revenge. I hadn't been able to think through the consequences and how it would drag me to hell too.

Kane rubbed his jaw. "I can't say, but ..." He glanced at the mansion, then back to me. "I've done some stupid and mean shit, too. I hurt Brie, a lot, but she still found a way to forgive me. Hopefully it will work out for you and Wynter. I mean, if you still want her."

I hated how well this motherfucker saw right through me. "I do." I blew out a heavy sigh. "I just realized how much I cared about her too late. There were other factors involved, too. I'll have to catch you up after I talk to Coach. I wanted you here since you're the QB ... and hopefully not furious with me. Remington wasn't happy about the video, but he helped me splice it together. I won't tell Coach that, though. As far as he's concerned, I did it all. No one else was involved. Back me on that, please."

"As I said, I did some mean shit to Brie. I can't throw a rock at a glass house I lived in first. If I'd known, I would have tried to stop you, but we've all fucked up. It's what we do after the fact that defines us."

"Hopefully it doesn't cost me a spot on the team. I've allowed my hatred and anger to drive my choices ... just like Adam." The realization punched me in the chest, leaving an even bigger hole inside me. "I can't end up like that sorry son of a bitch. I have to get my shit together. If I lost my chance at pro ball, then I'm the only one to blame. I was too fucked up about Bell to have thought the consequences of the video all the way through."

"Adam got in your head, huh?"

At least he hadn't said *I told you so.* "I let him." This time my hatred was directed at myself. "I need to get this conversation over with. My entire career is hanging in the balance until I know what Coach is going to decide."

"Have you considered that Adam has fed you lies since you were little? He's brainwashed you, man. That shit is hard to break out of. Maybe the fact that Wynter got hurt in all of this will help you see Adam for who he really is. A piece of shit." Kane paused. "As for Coach, I'll do what I can, Q." Kane's expression grew more serious.

Kane's words about Adam hit me like an eighteen wheeler moving at a hundred miles an hour. It hadn't ever occurred to me until he'd said something. "Thanks."

Kane texted Coach that we were there and together we walked to the entrance in silence and waited for someone to answer.

The door swung open, and Coach's wife said, "Hi, boys."

"Mrs. Cooper." I offered her the best smile I could conjure up, then followed Kane into the house.

"Coach is waiting for you both in his office."

"Thanks."

Kane shot me a look, probably wondering if I was keeping my shit together or about to lose it all over Coach's marble floors.

"And Quinn?"

I faced her. "Ma'am?"

"No matter what happens today, the fact that you're here to talk about the video will go a long way with him."

Inwardly, I cringed. I wished she hadn't found out, but I figured Coach would talk to her.

"I hope so. Um, how did he find out?"

"Social media. Someone used their phone to capture it all the moment it started to happen."

I rubbed the back of my neck, trying to ease the tension, but it was no use.

Kane and I walked down the hall and past the kitchen to Coach's office. I'd been here several times before, but this one was different. My palms grew sweaty, and I wiped them on my jeans. Kane knocked on the partially open door, then I heard Coach's voice tell us to come in.

My heart nearly jackhammered out of my chest as I walked in, tension snaking down my neck and spine.

"Quinn." Coach nodded to one of the two chairs in front of his desk.

I sat down and Kane settled into the chair beside me.

"I know you explained a little bit about the video when you called, but I would like the rest of the story. At this point, your actions were despicable, but I'll try to hold judgment until I understand the entire situation."

I stared at my shoes, wishing the floor would swallow me whole. Coach had been a father figure to me since I'd landed a spot on his team, and I felt like shit for letting him down. I straightened in my seat and began to tell him about Bell and how Kyler had killed her in a school shooting.

The color drained from Coach's face, his jaw tensing. "I had no idea you lost your twin. I can't imagine what that did to you and your family. I wish you'd told me this when you had arrived at Whitmore. Maybe I could have helped when you needed it most."

My soul soaked in his words. Here I was judging Wynter because I thought she hadn't told anyone about Kyler, but I was just as guilty of not confiding in the people who gave a crap about me. "No one knew. I had convinced myself that I was leaving my past behind if I never talked about it again."

"I can speak firsthand when I say that shit doesn't play out like that," Kane added.

When I explained that Wynter was Kyler's sister, Coach blanched. "I didn't realize they were related. I've not seen the video. I hope it's been destroyed, but I would assume kids at the party probably recorded it on their phones. It's most likely all over campus ... or even viral by now."

"That was my stupid plan." My fingers drummed restlessly on my jean-clad thigh. "After the video, Wynter was waiting for me." I explained what she had told me, leaving out the part that she was hiding in my room and held a dagger to my throat. At least I'd had the presence of mind to clean the small cut and blood off my neck before I'd taken Wynter to her house. It was barely visible now, which supported my theory that Wynter wasn't a violent person unless she was backed into a corner.

"Well, since it didn't happen on school grounds, I don't think the university can take action against you. As far as keeping you on the team ..." Coach leaned back, his brown eyes focused on me and his poker face in place. "You're a hell of a player and a good kid, Quinn. You made some bad choices." He scrubbed his jaw with his hand and stared at the floor for what felt like an eternity. Slowly, he looked at me again. "What are you going to do to make this right?"

"I might need your help with Wynter, if you're open to that?"

"In what way?" He studied me, waiting for me to reply.

"If Whitmore feels Wynter shouldn't attend anymore, can you help me fight for her to stay?"

Coach looked at me as if I had three tits. "Quinn, a school shooting is a difficult topic. People are going to be furious. Some will understand that she's not the same as her brother, but as history has already proved to her, that's not always the case. Plus, have you considered that she might be in physical danger if she stays? What if it's safer for her to leave?"

No! She can't leave. I just found her.

"Yeah. I'm already working with Sutton Westbrook. Kane

referred her to me. If I need to, I'm prepared to hire a bodyguard for Wynter. Sutton's helping me dig into the shooting. Some information never came to light ..." I bowed my head, the truth weighing on me. "The media never mentioned Wynter's efforts to talk to Kyler, her parents, the school—anything to stop the shooting. I want to help Wynter bring her story to light. Maybe ..." My fists clenched, Bell's smiling face flickering through my mind's eye. "Maybe we can make a difference together. I want to try. She lost her brother, and I lost Bell. I think I can be Wynter's voice until others listen to hers."

Coach's brows rose. "That's a big commitment when you're not even sure what Monday will look like."

"I'll help, too." Kane said. "It's a worthy cause and could also help families heal over what happened. Shit, Coach, you know what I lived through. My past affected everyone around me."

Coach's attention bounced between us, and I could almost see the wheels turning in his head. "Okay. I don't know Wynter, but if both of you vouch for her, I'll do what I can. I agree, her story could be powerful. I say let's help her shine."

A huge wave of gratitude flooded my system. I fisted my hand over my heart, showing my appreciation since I couldn't seem to get the words out.

Coach cleared his throat. "I'm not kicking you off the team."

I blew out a breath. I grinned and stared up at the ceiling afraid that I would tear up with relief in front of the two men I respected.

"Holy hell, that was intense." Kane laughed and slapped me on the back. "Glad you're not going anywhere."

"Same, man." I glanced at Coach, resisting the urge to hug him. "Thanks, Coach."

"Quinn, keep your shit together or you're off the team. Don't fuck up like this again. Learn from your mistakes and realize how your rash decisions not only impacted you, but Wynter and everyone on the team."

"Yes, sir. Thanks for meeting me on a Sunday."

"I appreciate that you owned up to what you did and wanted to get ahead of the situation. Keep me posted." Coach stood. "I'll walk you two out."

As my feet slapped against the marble floors of Coach's home, I desperately searched for a solution to the nightmare I'd created. Fifteen hours ago, I'd had one of my closest friends play a video that had now spiraled out of control. Despite my plans to fix it, I wasn't sure if any of it would work. But there was one thing I knew with absolute certainty—I couldn't let Wynter go. We had forged a unique bond that seemed almost impossible given our traumatic pasts. Yet in a single night, we had shared everything—the good, the bad, Bell and Kyler. Somehow, fate had found a way to bring us together. Our trauma had tied us together in a strange environment of distrust and vulnerability, yet we'd prevailed.

I told Kane and Coach goodbye and stepped outside into the warmth of the sunshine. Soaking it up, I took a moment to breathe the crisp autumn air and looked at my Apple Watch. Adam and Brody weren't due home until later that evening, which gave me an opportunity to take care of one more thing on my fix shit list.

Chapter 33

Quinn

After I left Coach's house, I sent Wynter a message and she replied almost immediately. When I arrived, she was even more beautiful than the last time I saw her. Wynter's long strawberry-blonde hair was tied up in an effortless bun that was just begging to be unraveled. She was wearing an oversized grey hoodie and black yoga pants that displayed her gorgeous curves. The sight of her sent my blood simmering and my cock standing to attention, yet I reminded myself that a relationship with Wynter wasn't meant to be.

Maybe she can forgive me. Maybe she will be mine soon. Regardless, I have to set things right.

"What was so important that you interrupted my sleep?" Wynter yawned as I led her through the front door of my place. To my surprise, the football team had cleaned up the house after the party ended on a quick note. I owed them big time.

"If I'm going to learn the truth, I need to show you what was in the file before Adam and Brody come home."

Her nose twitched, and I resisted the urge to kiss the perky tip of it.

"Are you hungry?" I wasn't sure if she'd eaten with all of the excitement.

"No. Just tired, but if you have a soda, that would be nice."

"Yup. Come on." I took her hand and showed her to the kitchen. Her eyes widened as I opened what appeared to be a lower cabinet.

"The cabinet is a fridge for drinks?" She peered over me, perusing the selection. "Dr. Pepper, please."

"You have excellent taste." I grabbed two of them. "Glass or can?"

"Can is fine." She folded her arms across her chest as if it would protect her from allowing me in.

"We don't have a lot of time, so we should dive in." I led her down the hall to Adam's office. When we reached it, I tested the doorknob. As I suspected, it was locked. "Can you hold these for me?"

"Sure." Wynter held her hands out for the cans.

I dug into my front pocket, locating the lockpicks I'd started carrying with me for when opportunities to snoop in Adam's office presented themselves. In seconds, the lock popped. I pushed the door open, motioning for Wynter to go in, then turned on the overhead light, flooding the dark room with brightness.

She watched me as I walked around to Adam's desk and flipped open his laptop. He had one for work and one for the house, which ended up being a blessing in disguise because Adam rarely took his personal computer on business trips. I wouldn't either considering the websites he frequented.

"What are we looking for?" Wynter whispered.

"No one's here. We don't have to whisper." The machine whirred to life, and I typed in the password. "Adam was the one who gave me the file on you. I'll show it to you, but I wanted to check his search history. Then ... then you should know something else."

She set the sodas on his desk before she popped hers open. The crack of the tab and hissing of the soda filled the room. From the desktop, I clicked on the path to the hidden files on Wynter. "I'm sorry. Adam has been following you on Dimitri's website for a long time."

Wynter's face turned ashen as I began showing her a few of the images that Adam had saved.

She visibly swallowed, her entire body rigid. "How long has he known about my work?"

"I don't know. But he has pictures from before you were eighteen."

Wynter pressed her fist against her mouth. "I couldn't pay the bills. I tried a part-time job while I worked to finish high school, but a mortgage payment is no small feat at seventeen. I did what I had to do to take care of Janine and secure a future for us." Her voice was tight, anxiety hanging off her words.

"Wynter, don't misunderstand. Yeah, I enjoyed the hell out of the pictures, but I'm not sharing this because I judged you. I want you to know part of what we're dealing with. Adam filled my head with a lot of lies about you. I need to understand why."

Her eyes narrowed on me. "The website ..." She barked out a laugh. "It's how you knew I would be a good fit for the society."

Wynter was sexy as hell, but I was falling in love with her intelligence first. "Yeah. It was the fastest way to get to you. I want you to know, I regret the shit I said to you as the Red Dragon."

The color returned to Wynter's cheeks, but she ignored my last comment.

I showed Wynter the pictures of Adam and Drew with Kyler, and explained that Adam had taken Bell and Brody to her house when they were younger.

"Holy shit. That's why Adam looked familiar the night he barged in on us." Her lips pursed, anger flashing in her gaze. "I must have only seen Adam briefly, but Bell looks more like him than you." Her hand trembled. "Can you go back to the one with my dad?"

I did as she asked, watching her as she stared at the image. "I don't know whether to love or hate him."

Her voice hovered above a whisper, her confession hitting me hard. "What happened after the sh—situation with Kyler?" I almost said "shooting," but it sounded insensitive at the moment.

Wynter paced the small area behind Adam's desk. "It all turned to shit so fast. Dad was getting death threats, and bricks were thrown through the windows of our home. At first the cops protected us, but they didn't have the staff to continue to keep us safe. After a few weeks, we hoped that the public blame and outrage had calmed down, but then Dad showed up after work one day broken and defeated. He'd been fired from his job. It was too much for him and the next day ... he was gone. No note, no phone calls, just gone." Wynter placed her hands on her slender hips and tilted her head back, looking at the ceiling. "A part of me doesn't blame him for taking off, but why wouldn't he take us too?"

"I wish I had the answer for you. Adam said they worked together for years and were friends. I don't trust the bastard, but maybe he knows why Drew left. Do you want me to ask him?"

"No. He'll just fill you with a shit ton of lies again." She picked up her soda and took another drink. "What did he tell you about me, Quinn?"

I leaned back in Adam's chair, checking his browser history to see if there was anything new before I closed the laptop down. "I would feel better if we took the conversation elsewhere. Adam isn't supposed to be home until later, but I want to make sure we're not in his office in case he surprises us again."

A heavy silence hung over us as I locked Adam's office and led Wynter to my bedroom.

"Really, Quinn? You destroyed my life last night and now you're taking me to your room?" She stood in the hall, refusing to enter.

"It's not like that. If the alarm beeps because someone came inside, I can hide you here, then I can safely sneak you out. We've done it before, so you know I'm not bullshitting you."

She shot me a look of disapproval but walked in.

"I'll leave the door open." I approached my dresser and set the drinks down before I located my desk key, then opened the drawer where I kept the file. Removing the folder, I gave it to her. "This is what Adam put together. I even did my own research, and it was all true as far as anyone can tell."

She took it and sank onto the end of my bed, then began flipping through the pages silently. Every once in a while, she would peek up at me, then return to read the so-called evidence that Adam had on her.

"He's good. Really good." She huffed as she closed the folder and tossed it back on the mattress. "The police report didn't tell the entire story, the rest is crap, but I've already told you that the media spun shit. I'm not sure about the letters from ... Ky." She wrung her hands in her lap. I understood how hard it was to talk about Bell and Kyler, but I had to keep going.

"Sutton said they're fabricated. I'm sorry I gave the first one to you. I didn't know the truth until seconds before the video played." I sank into my chair near my desk and propped my elbows on my knees.

Tears welled in her eyes, and she turned away as if ashamed. A soft sniffle filled the room before she trained her attention on me again. "If you were having it all investigated, why didn't you wait before setting that up?"

"Pressure from Adam and my own unresolved anger at losing Bell."

Wynter pressed her lips into a thin line. "I can see that. But Adam gave you the correct police report with the facts, so I can understand why it took you a beat to question the letters. I'm sorry if this upsets you, but he doesn't sound like a good person." She glanced at me apologetically.

"He's not even close, and it was a friend who urged me to look past my hatred and see if Adam was fucking with me. I'm sure it was hard for you to see the articles and police report again."

Wynter stood. "Quinn, it's nothing I haven't seen or heard before. The media spun it to make me look almost as guilty as Kyler. It was a fucking disaster. I *never* told the cops or anyone else that I knew what Kyler had planned. Ever. Why? Because I had no fucking clue."

"I believe you, Wynter. I need to ask you something, though. Please, just be honest with me."

Fear flashed through her eyes, but I couldn't soothe it this time. "Did you know that Bell was pregnant with Kyler's baby?"

Chapter 34

Wynter

I was clearly too exhausted to have that conversation. A soft giggle escaped me, and instead of stuffing it down, it grew into a full-on belly laugh. Tears flowed down my cheeks as I doubled over and sank to the floor, unable to get a hold of myself. Gasping for air, I finally managed to control my crazy outburst. I peeked at Quinn who looked like he wanted to toss me out of his window for laughing about something so serious.

"Is that what Adam told you?"

"A few days before I played the video at the party, Adam told me that Drew had confided in him. Apparently, Kyler went to Drew for help with an abortion for Bell. Adam said when you learned about the baby you shamed and bullied Bell for wanting an abortion."

I snorted. "I'm sorry. I giggle uncontrollably when I'm exhausted. None of this is funny ... well, except the shit pie you ate off Adam's plate."

Quinn glowered at me. "Could you please try to get a handle on yourself and answer me? Did you know? Did you say those things to Bell?"

My giggles abruptly stopped with the rage that flared to life in his eyes. I held up my hands in surrender. "First of all, you need to understand that Adam flat-out lied to you. If Bell was pregnant, I knew nothing about it. I talked to her at school a few times. Hell, I didn't even know that you and Brody existed." I paused, wondering if I'd just deflated his ego a little. I hoped so.

"Likewise," he grumbled.

"Second of all, there's no way in hell Kyler got Bell pregnant. Zero. Zilch. Didn't happen."

Quinn frowned. "There's always a chance, even with birth control."

I picked myself up off the floor and walked over to Quinn. Cupping his chin, I forced him to look at me so he would understand that what I was about to tell him was the honest fucking truth. "Dude, Kyler was gay. He came out to me when he was eleven. Kyler even admitted his junk didn't even work when a pretty girl was around."

Quinn gripped my wrist, an abundance of emotions flickering across his face. "You're positive?"

"Ab-so-fucking-lutely."

Confusion creased his forehead. "Then what's Adam's motive?"

I leaned down, my mouth close to his ear before I whispered, "Why does anyone lie? To hide something." I backed away and waited to see if Quinn would confess to knowing anything else, but the questions that radiated off him gave me his answer. He was as clueless as I was.

Quinn dropped his hold on me. "At times I wonder if it's personal or business, but sometimes your personal lies cover illegal company activity. Do you think that Drew and Adam were committing tax fraud or scamming clients?"

For some stupid reason, I wanted to crawl onto Quinn's lap and bury my head against his warm neck. Even though he was responsible for the video, I still found myself drawn to him. The need to stand together, united, was powerful. I'd argued with myself the entire night and most of the day that he didn't deserve my forgiveness. There was more to it, though. I'd spent time with him in and out of the society. I saw his cruelty and anger, but I'd also seen his heart. The good parts of him that were broken from losing Bell, the parts of him that were fighting the current, and how he was pulling himself to safety.

He hadn't fucked me the other night, either. He'd taken his time, touching and taking care of me even while his heated gaze revealed his feelings. Quinn was falling for me, and I knew it then. I was falling for him, too despite his betrayal—I had been treated worse by others, after all.

What kind of woman was I for being willing to try again with him? I demanded a shift in his beliefs about me, but did my unwillingness to grant him the same make me a hypocrite? All he'd known about me were half-truths. We were both fucked up by situations completely out of our control.

"The more we talk, the more I think something bad was going on way before Kyler snapped." My stomach plummeted to my toes as another piece of reality penetrated my exhausted brain. "I'm scared," I said, my pitch climbing. Flashes of the cheer team beating me bombarded my brain. "I have classes tomorrow. What if people gang up on me again?"

"Again?" A hint of anger peppered his word.

I told Quinn about the cheerleaders and how Everlee was the only person who knew about it.

He shot out of his chair. "Jesus Christ, what is wrong with people?"

My muscles tensed, like a cornered animal, when I heard Quinn's voice. My heart raced and my body burned with rage as the echo of his words brought my dark past back to life with a deep, burning anger coursing through my veins. What Quinn had broadcast all over the party had called up memories I had shoved into the pits of hell. A stone-cold fury bubbled up inside of me, and I stomped over to him. I raised my arm, balled my fist, then released the angry, hurt beast and punched him square in the nose.

He staggered backward, covering his face as blood streamed down his mouth and chin.

"I don't know, Quinn. What *is* wrong with people?" Reminding myself that my martial arts training was viewed as a weapon in the state of Oregon, and I could serve time in prison for fucking Quinn up, I opted for low blows. I stomped on his foot and landed a square kick to his shin. "Seriously? You're getting pissed at others for doing exactly what you just did to me? Blasting me without ever finding out my side? That makes you a hell of a man, doesn't it!"

Blood seeped into Quinn's dark T-shirt, and I laughed as I swept his foot out from under him. He landed with a thud. "Seems like you wouldn't fall for that move, but here you are. On your back for me." My fists clenched and unclenched. "Guess we both have tempers, huh?" I straddled him, but before I could drop on him with my full weight, he grabbed my knees and forced them to buckle.

His eyes darkened and narrowed before he spoke. "Get mad, Wynter. Get really fucking pissed. I fucked you over good. Everyone hates you now. No one wants you here," he spat.

A million little knives sliced through my heart. "I hate you! I fucking hate you!" I screamed, pummeling his chest with my fists.

"You could have stopped Kyler, and you know it. You didn't even try hard," he seethed.

"I did! I tried everything, and nobody believed me." I clawed at his hands as he tried to block my punches, tears streaming down my cheeks with his brutal words. "You're a liar just like the rest of them. None of you care! I fucking hate every goddamn person who judged me for Kyler's choices." I hiccupped, my fight with Quinn slowing.

Finally, my fists dropped to my sides as my body shook with my sobs. "I trusted you. I trusted you, Quinn. You were the first guy that's ever taken me on a date and kissed me goodnight. I wanted there to be an us. The other night in your bed, it was different. You were attentive and kind, and I really thought you had feelings for me." I scoffed at my stupidity. "I wanted you to fall for me. I needed to be fucking normal again." I covered my face with my hands, crying so hard I couldn't talk anymore.

I gasped for air as Quinn wrapped his arms around me and pulled me down against him. He stroked my hair, "I know, beautiful. Get it out, baby." He kissed the top of my head. "All that shit people said to you, all the judgments, just let it go. I'm right here, and I'll make sure you're safe. I swear on Bell's grave to protect you, even if it means I follow you to every class, every stop. No one will hurt you again. No one."

My sobs quieted as I realized what Quinn had done. He'd baited me until I could no longer deny the rage and pain, then he let me take it out on him. He had just laid still, taken my wrath and absorbed my agony. For the first time since that horrifying day at school, I'd released a bit of the toxic emotions I'd shoved down for the last five years. I relaxed against his warm body, allowing myself to be held by one of the few people that understood my world—understood the horror of losing a sibling and any semblance of a life we'd once had. The grief of not being able to stop any of it.

I sat up slowly, my attention landing on his nose. "You should have that reset." Staring at his bloodied shirt, I glanced down at mine. My top was covered in my hate and need to make Quinn pay.

"I might look sexy with a bump in my nose."

I rolled my eyes, cracking a smile. "I should be sorry that I hit you, but I'm not. I *am* sorry that every time you look in a mirror and see a crooked nose, you'll think about me."

"You say that as if it's a bad thing." Quinn tucked my hair behind an ear. "I should get cleaned up."

Slowly, I crawled off him. "I have your blood all over me." I held up my palms, still slick with the sticky substance.

"At least it's no longer Bell's or Kyler's."

I stared at him as if he'd just handed me a check for two million dollars. "You no longer blame me?" My chest tightened, desperate to hear at least one person say they didn't hold me accountable for what happened.

"I no longer blame you, beautiful. I never should have." Quinn pressed a gentle kiss to my temple before he disappeared into the bathroom. If I was this emotional now, what would tomorrow look like when I returned to classes and waited to see if the dean wanted to talk to me.

Shit. I needed a plan of my own that didn't involve Quinn swooping in to rescue me. At least I wouldn't let myself down.

Chapter 35

Wynter

As expected, I received a call that the dean of Whitmore University wanted to see me bright and early Monday morning. I'd hardly slept a wink, anticipating that I would be sitting in front of him explaining the video Quinn had released to the world.

My hands trembled as I waited to meet with him. I was too fucking nervous to wait in the lobby and chose to pace in the hall, wearing grooves in the ugly brown carpet.

I'd decided not to text Quinn and instead speak to the dean myself. I didn't want to rely on anyone. Plus, if I gave Quinn the appointment time and he had an excuse not to attend ... I rubbed my temples at the thought of being disappointed by him yet again. I wished there was a way to turn back the clock so that Kyler had never hurt anyone and I wouldn't be facing the collapse of my future now. No use harping on it, though. I just had to take hold of my life and make it what I wanted.

The door to the Dean's office creaked open slowly.

"Ms. Baldwin, Dean Holcomb will see you now," the pretty blonde said, ushering me inside.

"Thank you." I smoothed my green blouse and black slacks. This meeting called for nicer clothes, and I was determined to make a good impression.

My leather purse was slung over my shoulder, and I gripped the strap, hanging onto it for dear life. At least the sweat from my palm had a place to transfer to other than my top.

The dean's assistant seemed pleasant enough and offered me a warm smile as I passed her and entered his office.

"Ms. Baldwin." Dean Holcomb removed his glasses and motioned for me to have a seat in front of his desk.

Slipping into the black chair, I clutched my bag to my stomach and glanced around the room. To my surprise, the dean was older, probably in his sixties, with light brown hair and streaks of grey. His stern gaze landed on me, making me squirm in my seat.

"It's come to my attention that there's a video circulating about a very serious incident at a high school in Washington State."

I gulped as sweat beaded across my forehead. Reminding myself not to rush into the conversation, I bit my tongue and forced myself to remain quiet. I had to see where the dean was going first.

"Once the video landed in my email, I did some research and found that the information is true."

"Yes, sir." Pain stabbed me in the stomach and I stared at the floor, wondering if I would ever be free of the ridicule from my brother's horrible choices.

"Due to the scholarship, I also looked into your Whitmore application. It was flagged in admissions and landed on my desk. I knew who you were before you stepped foot on campus." He folded his hands in front of him.

Blanching, I blinked furiously. Had I misunderstood him? I had been accepted even with my connection to the school shooting?

"And you accepted me anyway?" Clearly he had, or I wouldn't be sitting in his office right now, but I was nervous as hell and not thinking his words all the way through.

He offered me a kind smile. "Your grades and determination to move forward after a"— Dean Holcomb cleared his throat—"a situation like that is remarkable. I'm not sure many people would have the resolve to create a better future for themselves. I'm impressed."

Tension eased from my body, then returned tenfold. "Did you call me here to ask that I leave Whitmore?"

He leaned back and tapped his fingers on the top of his closed laptop. "No. The only reason I'd ask you to leave is to suggest taking online courses in case you're in danger. Honestly, that's my biggest concern."

I'm not being kicked out! Tears filled my eyes, and my hands fidgeted in my lap while I tried to get a hold of myself.

"You can't go in there! He's in a meeting, young man," a female voice yelled from the other side of the wall.

Startled, I turned in my seat and looked over my shoulder.

"What in the world?" Dean Holcomb hurried to his door and flung it open.

"Dean Holcomb, I have to see you ASAP. It can't wait. I did something really stupid, and I need to make sure that my actions don't affect a student on campus. Her name is Wynter Baldwin. Please, give me ten minutes. I have a plan to fix it and hopefully help her and others in the future."

I shot out of my chair, recognizing Quinn's voice.

"Hey," I said from behind the dean. "I had no idea that you were going to talk to Dean Holcomb."

The dean's attention bounced between Quinn and me.

"Morning." Quinn looked at the Dean again. "I'm the one who made and played the video. Since Wynter is here, would the both of you be okay if I join the meeting?"

A heavy silence loomed over us like a storm cloud refusing to move on.

"I'm fine with him being here," I said to the dean, "but it's your choice."

"Okay, then." Dean Holcomb moved aside, allowing Quinn into his office and motioning to the chair next to the one I had used.

"Mr. Astor, what do you have to say for yourself?" Dean Holcomb glowered at Quinn.

"First of all, I've apologized to Wynter, and I'm hoping to undo the damage, but I know it will take work. I'm willing to put that time in. But I need to ask Wynter something first."

Dean Holcomb's dark brows rose slightly as Quinn leaned over to me.

"Did he kick you out of Whitmore?" he asked so softly I almost didn't hear him.

"No. He knew about my past before he accepted me as a student here," I explained out loud, giving the dean a grateful smile.

Quinn's hazel eyes landed on me, sparkling. "Then I won't spend our time trying to keep you in school. I'll get right to the point."

Hmm. I wasn't sure what to expect next. Quinn hadn't talked to me about it.

"Sir, I met with Coach and our quarterback yesterday. Coach and Kane are both willing to publicly speak at events on campus along with me. Since the weather is cooling off and the rain has moved in, it will be difficult to set up places outside. We will need your permission to set up in the cafeteria or other public places with large numbers of students. It will be the fastest way to spread the truth." Quinn glanced over at me. "To explain that Wynter had nothing to do with the shooting. We want to clear her name as quickly as possible. Also, I'm guessing that most of the football team will be willing to help once I talk to them."

An audible gasp escaped me. Quinn had not only talked to Coach and Kane, but he had a plan in place. A lump formed in my throat, overwhelmed with what Quinn had already put together ... for me.

"I can help make that happen, but are you sure you're ready to step into that kind of spotlight? It might not be as forgiving as you hope." Dean frowned as he directed his question at Quinn.

Quinn focused on me. He didn't smile. He didn't respond. He

simply stared right into my eyes. Without breaking our gaze, he nodded. "I can handle it."

The raw determination in Quinn's voice sent shivers down my spine.

"Wynter? This isn't a decision without you. You've had a lot happen, and if you would like to drop out of Whitmore and start fresh somewhere else, I'll write you a letter of recommendation. You have my support either way, but this needs to be your choice, not anyone else's. Take a minute to decide what's right for *you*."

His support nearly tipped me over backward. No one had ever told me to make the right choice for me. I had always taken care of Janine, and I thought I'd lost the right to choose for me. Working for Dimitri wouldn't have ever happened for starters. *Although it was great stress relief.* I caught myself before I smiled.

"I'm in with one exception. If we can't turn around popular opinion, can I take you up on the letter of recommendation at a later date?"

"Absolutely. I admire your desire to stay, but if you're in danger and need to transfer, I'll be happy to help."

Relief saturated the room.

"Looks like we have some work to do," Quinn said to me.

I peered at him, wondering if he really needed my help or if he was just trying to spend time alone with me.

I stood. "I should get to class." My overworked nerves shot tingles through my fingers and toes.

Quinn stood. "Sir, thank you for your time. I'll be in touch after I talk to the team today."

"Let me know what else I can do." Dean Holcomb shook Quinn's hand, then smoothed his suit jacket. "And Quinn?"

"Yes, sir?"

"No more malicious actions or you're out of Whitmore."

I watched the blood drain from Quinn's cheeks and his Adam's apple bob. "Understood."

Damn. If he got kicked out it would screw up graduation, which would mess up any plans if he didn't go pro. I wasn't sure if the video would mess up his chance to play pro football, but probably not. Regardless, he would have to figure that out. I wasn't the one who blasted the video in order to destroy another person. He was. Now he had to pay the consequences.

Struggling to control the ebb and flow of my anger toward Quinn, I politely excused myself and collected my jacket from the coat rack near the door. I needed to put some space between Quinn and me, fast. The moment I stepped into the dean's waiting room, Quinn grabbed my arm. My body briefly stiffened at his touch.

"About class." He led me to the corner and spoke in a hushed tone. "Until we know the climate of the other students ..." Quinn shoved his fingers through his hair, his expression sheepish.

"Tell me outside. This is weird, whispering when the dean is around."

Quinn nodded, then opened the door for me and escorted me to the hall. I spotted a guy in black clothes near the wall but kept walking. The last thing I needed was to slip into class late and be called out by the professor.

"Wynter," Quinn called from behind me.

I spun on my heel, glowering at him as the guy in black moved to stand next to him.

"Wynter, this is Vaughn Reddington, your new bodyguard."

My gaze took a slow hike up and down Vaughn—short blonde hair, broad shoulders, bulges in all the right places. His black slacks molded to his muscular thighs but holy shit. Those eyes. I hadn't ever seen someone with one blue and one brown. A flush crawled up my neck, my hormones charging full speed ahead.

Finally realizing what Quinn had said—that this guy was my bodyguard—I barked out a laugh.

"No."

Chapter 36

Quinn

Wynter stomped off, clearly pissed at me. I wasn't sure how she'd snuck into the dean's office and escaped the crowd, but I was pretty sure she hadn't seen what was waiting for her outside. Luckily, Vaughn had just ended a quick assignment in Portland and Sutton sent him my way.

"Shit." I chased after her, my long strides easily closing the distance between us, and I stepped in front of the door that led outside and to the lion's den. "You can go out there, but Vaughn and I are going with you. This isn't up for negotiation. In fact, I think it's also our first opportunity."

Confusion clouded her beautiful features.

"How did you get to the dean's office?"

"Gabby dropped me off. It was pouring rain and she loaned me her jacket with a hood." She tugged on the black coat hanging over her arm. I hadn't noticed it until then, but it explained how she wasn't spotted.

"Move, please. If I'm late, the professor will call me out, and everyone will be staring." Fear flickered in her gaze. "I'm trying to stay under the radar, Quinn." Impatient, she tapped her foot.

I looked over her shoulder. Vaughn was a few steps behind her and quietly closed the gap, ready to face what was beyond this wall.

"Quinn. *Move.* I'm not in the mood for your shit today." Her blue eyes blazed with anger.

I figured Wynter would hate me even more by the time she went back to classes. If she were pissed now just fuck my life, she was going to tear me a new one when she saw what was waiting for her outside.

I pushed on the metal handle, then cracked the door open. "Shit." Allowing it to close, I stared at Wynter, remorse driving my next action. "I'm sorry." I pulled her against me and placed a kiss on the top of her head. I wasn't sure I would have the opportunity to do that again, and I needed her ... was desperate for her to understand how sorry I was that I played the video.

I released her and she took a step away. Fear flickered to life in her expression, and she shrank back, closer to Vaughn.

"I saw people out there. Are they waiting for me?" She clutched her bag until her knuckles turned white.

"There are students, adults, and reporters waiting for you," Vaughn said. "They're all here to see what the dean had to say, and I think you being inside was a bonus."

"Fuck!" She gritted her teeth. "Do you know what you've done? I won't be safe. I worked so fucking hard to have just a little normalcy in my life, then you ..." She fisted her hands, then looked at Vaughn again. Realization dawned over her face. "This is why he's here, Quinn? You already knew there were vultures circling?"

"Yeah. I had a bad feeling Monday would be chaos and called Sutton, Vaughn's boss, last night. Wynter, I couldn't take a chance of someone attacking you."

Tears brimmed in her eyes, her body trembling.

"Wynter, I'm armed, and I'm also trained in Krav Maga. You have my word that I will keep you safe. Let's see what it looks like out there, then determine what to do next." Vaughn's soothing tone seemed to help, and I was glad as hell that I hired him. "Here's what I propose ..." Vaughn rattled off a plan and we all agreed.

It was time to face the damage. Although I'd held out hope that it wouldn't explode to this proportion it had, but that was social media at its finest.

Per Vaughn's suggestion, I slipped my arm around her waist to show the world we were a united front. Opening the door, I walked outside first, Wynter slightly behind me, and Vaughn to the side of her.

Reporters bolted toward us, and I gave Wynter a reassuring squeeze. I held up my hand in an attempt to quiet the barrage of questions. The rain had stopped, and a large group of students had popped up all over the lawn, holding signs to either support Wynter or run her out of town.

"I would like to say a few words, if everyone will calm down." Wynter trembled against me, and I wished like hell I could make it better. I cleared my throat, then began to speak. "My name is Quinn Astor, and I'm responsible for the viral video concerning the shooting and loss of ten students and three teachers at Timber Creek High School in Forest Dale, Washington."

The chanting quieted as people started to listen.

"Over the last few days, additional information has come to my attention, shedding light on Wynter's actions. I was wrong. I was wrong to air the video. I was a hundred percent wrong in assuming that Wynter knew about Kyler Baldwin's plans."

Rude comments came from the group, but I ignored them and continued. "With some help of friends, I have obtained the accurate report that Wynter provided to the police. For whatever reason, the report with full details of how Wynter tried to get Kyler help had been buried. She reached out to her parents and a teacher, and when that didn't work, one of her school counselors. The report also documents that Wynter searched Kyler's room in fear that he might have been suicidal. There were no guns or harmful weapons found at that time."

The crowd grew quiet again.

"My twin sister was one of the people lost that day, and I've spent the last several years angry and grieving. When I learned that Wynter was attending Whitmore, I took it upon myself to make her life miserable without learning the facts." I glanced at Wynter. "It's my responsibility to right my wrong and prove to the public that Wynter isn't the criminal. The police interview and documents will be available at noon today on multiple news outlets. I recommend that you start there to get answers to your questions."

"Quinn, are you saying that you no longer hold Wynter Baldwin responsible for Bellamy's death?"

Inwardly, I cringed. Of course, the reporters had done their research, but to hear Bell's full name was a slap in the face. Another reminder I'd lost her.

"That's correct. She had no proof of Kyler's plans. What was presented to the world was misleading, and we were all lied to."

"Wynter, who did you talk to about your brother, and what made you worried in the first place?" A reporter held out a microphone.

"I will be happy to provide interviews at a later date. A lot of your questions will be answered at noon today." She peeked at her watch. "In two more hours. Now, if you'll kindly excuse me, I have a class to attend."

Vaughn stepped up to her right side while I remained at Wynter's left, ensuring her protection. To my surprise, the crowd parted without a fight. Only a few hecklers popped off with nasty threats, but that was to be expected. Assholes were everywhere, and no matter what Wynter or I said, some people always focused on hate. Unfortunately, I'd been one of those assholes, and it was time to change.

I finally had a reason to become a better man. That reason was Wynter Baldwin.

Chapter 37

Quinn

The day stretched on like the last few drops of honey dripping out from the bottom of the jar. I attended my own classes, weighed down with worry for Wynter. A deep sense of guilt lay heavy on my chest. Vaughn had promised to call if any issues occurred that he couldn't handle, but that did little to console me.

I slammed my football locker shut, ready to take out my aggressions on the field. Before practice, Coach had called a team meeting concerning Wynter and revealed she had been wrongfully accused. He provided the websites where the news had aired the full report and updates of the interview Wynter had with the police after the shooting. Then Coach asked for volunteers to spread the word around campus that Wynter was innocent. He asked if they were willing to share the video to every friend and family member they had. The plan was to have the buried, real police interview video go viral by the end of the following day. As much as we were all on social media, it shouldn't be difficult, but it would take everyone's best effort.

To my surprise, every member of the team volunteered to help.

My heart filled with gratitude as I stood before my brothers, and I was humbled by their selflessness to support me even when I'd been a fucking prick. More than that, only a few of them knew Wynter, and they were taking me at my word that she was a good person.

"Great practice today," Kane said, joining me at the lockers.

"It felt good to get out there and clear my head."

"I saw you and Wynter on the news before Wynter's interview with the cop aired. You did right by her this time." He removed his phone and keys from his locker and shoved them into his jeans pocket.

"I'm trying." I finished pulling on a clean shirt, then collected my cell. I checked the messages, but there weren't any texts or calls from Vaughn or Wynter.

Kane faced me, leaning his shoulder against the locker door. "I was going to ask if you were going to the society later, but my guess is no."

"No. I'm meeting Wynter. We have some shit to go over. From what we can tell, there's a lot of unanswered questions on both sides. Maybe we can fill in some of the blanks for each other."

"Good. I hope you both find some peace, man." Kane smirked. "How long have you been in love with her?"

I chuckled, having wondered when he was going to ask me that. Closing my locker, I turned to him. "Honestly? No idea, but I figured it out right after I played that fucking video. A few hours later, I saw her, and that's when I knew. I also realized I lost her." I kicked the locker below, frustrated.

"Chin up. You keep taking care of her and showing up when you say you will, and she'll forgive you."

"Let's hope so because I can't fucking let her go." Gutted all over again that I might not win her back, my shoulders sagged.

"Go see her, then let me know if you need anything." Kane straightened and gave me a little wave before he strode off.

Realizing that I'd admitted I was in love to one of my best friends had me smiling. I never thought I would want to settle down. But my smile faded as quickly as it had appeared. If I was going to win Wynter over, I still had a lot of work to do.

"Is your dad here?" Wynter asked, tiptoeing into my house with Vaughn right on her heels.

"No. He's out of town again. Brody will be here later, but we have a few hours before he gets home. Lena, our chef and housekeeper, should be around somewhere."

"I'll stay out of sight but watch the property. If I see anything suspicious, I'll let you know." Vaughn nodded at us before he stepped back outside.

As soon as the door closed, Wynter blew out a sigh. "All of a sudden every girl and guy on campus wants to be my friend." She rolled her eyes. "First, they ask who Vaughn is, then they ask me about the video. It's been a crazy day."

When I met Vaughn, I knew Wynter might act like she didn't want him around, but she would cave the second she saw him. Jealousy roared to life inside me. The motherfucker was a chick magnet.

"Come here." She relaxed as I palmed her head and pulled her against me. Holding her in my arms felt so right.

"Quinn?" She peered up at me, gentleness in her beautiful features.

"Yeah?" I smoothed her hair, not wanting to let her go.

"Will you tell me about Bell? I mean, can you talk about her? I want to know her through your eyes."

Startled, I paused. I hated the conflicting feelings churning inside me whenever we were in the same room. I wanted to share my life with Wynter, but she was also connected to what nearly destroyed me. Maybe being able to talk about Bell with her would ease the pain.

"I have pictures and our yearbooks on my bookshelf."

A peculiar expression crossed over her face, her lips pressing into a firm line. "Okay."

Once I gathered snacks and drinks, we headed upstairs to my bedroom.

"Open or closed?" I asked Wynter, pointing at the door.

"Cracked. That way we can hear the alarm if someone comes home. I'm pretty sure I can fit under your bed or in the closet if Adam surprises us again."

"Vaughn knows to call if anyone shows up, too."

Setting the paper plate and snacks down on my desk, I grabbed Bell's high school yearbooks off my shelf, then collected several photo albums she'd put together over the years. After the shooting, I'd taken her yearbooks since she'd had nearly the entire school sign them. The books were filled with why people loved her so much, and I wanted to remember her that way, too. Wynter sat on the floor with her back against my bedframe. I joined her, then set the plate between us and dumped some chips onto it. I opened the sodas I'd brought and handed one to her. She must have been hungry because she popped a chip into her mouth. Her tongue darted over her lower lip and my dick throbbed, wishing it was between those pretty lips instead.

She halted mid-chew, her cheeks turning pink. "What? I'm starving."

"Nothing. I'm happy to make sandwiches if you want, but Lena should be cooking soon. I can bring our dinner up here." I hadn't asked her if she wanted to stay and eat, but with Adam gone, there wasn't any reason for her not to.

"We'll see." She motioned at the pile of books and pictures waiting to be opened. "You and Bell were obviously fraternal twins. She looks more like your dad than you."

"She and Brody look alike too," I confessed, opening her freshman yearbook.

"Shit."

I glanced at her, curious why she'd said shit.

"It's hard for you to look at Brody and not see Bell, isn't it?"

"Yeah. Some days are really hard." I leaned against the bedframe and shared the book with her. Wynter reached out to turn a page when I asked, "What about you? Who looked like Kyler?"

She froze, her attention traveling from a picture of Bell to me. "Are you just trying to be nice? Because that's kind of a fucked-up question to ask about the guy who killed your sister."

I heaved a sigh. "Wynter, I'm trying to understand what it was like for you. Yeah, Kyler killed my sister, and I'm determined to find out why ... but you said he was a good guy until six months before shit went south. Regardless, I understand how painful it is to see someone every day that looks like the person you lost."

She nodded. "I don't want to hurt you anymore since it stirs up your awful memories, too." She looked away from me. "I'm afraid to talk about him. People might think I'm sick if I admit how much I miss him. Miss the Kyler I knew before he changed."

Empathy had never been one of my strengths. I didn't give a fuck about anyone other than a few friends in the society and on the football team. Spending time with Wynter and learning her story, I was growing a little more open-minded. I wanted to understand who he was to her, and maybe someday I could even forgive him.

"Tell you what. I'll share with you about Bell first, then maybe I'll be ready to hear about your Kyler."

Her chin wobbled. "Okay, but not until you're ready."

Before I could stop myself, I pressed a gentle kiss to her mouth, but she didn't resist or push me away. Pretending I hadn't just done that, I focused on the yearbook.

"Bell and I ran in different crowds, but we were both popular." I pointed to a silly image of her in drama club with her friends. "She was so full of life, always laughing at school. The second she set foot in our house, her mood plummeted. She stayed gone as much as she could, but when Adam wasn't traveling, he insisted she be home to spend time with the family. She hated him as much as I did."

"Why?" Wynter asked, softly.

My jaw tensed, anger simmering beneath my calm exterior.

"What is it, Quinn?"

"What I'm going to share with you, promise me it stays between us." I pinned her with an intense stare. I wasn't fucking around. Other than Brody and Bell, only one person knew what went down behind closed doors. I was about to make it a second.

"You have my word." Wynter wrapped her arms around herself, bracing for what I was about to tell her.

"Adam beat my ass almost daily after my mother died. Bell saw a lot of it, and she would scream and kick Adam, trying to help me. One day when we were thirteen, Adam went after her. He'd never laid a hand on her before, and I stood there in shock as he slapped her. It was then that I swore I would get strong enough to beat him to a fucking bloody pulp. I'll never forget the look of horror on Bell's face." My fist clenched. "I didn't protect her. The son of a bitch tripped me up, and I stood there like a fucking dumbass." I closed my eyes as memories punctured me.

"Quinn." She placed her warm palm over my fist.

I couldn't look at her. The guilt was twisting me into a million relentless knots, and I couldn't lose my shit in front of her.

"That night, I grabbed a butcher knife and snuck into his room. I woke him and pressed the blade against his throat. His eyes flew open and he stared into mine. In that moment, I knew he would make me pay for that, and he did. But I told the bastard that if he ever laid a hand on Bell again, I would slowly poison him to death. He would get sicker and sicker, then die a painful death while I watched from the sidelines."

I wondered if Wynter was scared of me now. I'd just admitted to threatening to kill my father, but she didn't pull away.

"Did it work?"

"Yeah. He left Bell alone. He was able to kick my ass for another year, though. It took working out hard and building my confidence for me to finally put him in his place." I rubbed the back of my neck, the tension tightening my muscles. "The night before the shooting, though, he'd turned on Brody. Bell had run up the stairs to my room, tears streaming down her face, telling me that Brody needed my help.

That was our last night ... taking care of our little brother together." I choked on my words, unprepared for the level of grief that still plagued me. "The next day at school we were supposed to meet in the library to come up with a game plan on how to take care of Brody, but she never showed up. I went looking for her. That's when I heard the gunshots." I leaned against the edge of my mattress and closed my eyes, fighting tears. "I should have been with her that day, Wynter. I should have been there to protect her."

The book clattered to the floor, and I felt her crawl into my lap. Silently, she wrapped her arms around me and laid her head against my chest, soaking up my agony. Wynter trembled against me, struggling to contain her silent sobs. We were in our own little bubble of pain, cut off from everyone else. Our twisted worlds had collided, pulling the rug out from under us and forcing us to stare into our darkest hours.

Finally, I wrapped my arms around Wynter, holding her in return. "You probably have a crick in your neck."

Wynter straightened, anguish and adoration battling on her face. "I'm okay. I understand this is difficult and it takes a lot for you to open up. It's hard for me too. We don't need to talk about her anymore." She crawled off me and stood.

"It's all right. Strangely enough, the fact that you're here with me as I look through her life is making it bearable. It would be nice to remember all the good she did, the lives she touched."

"Are you sure?" she asked, concern bleeding through her question.

"Yeah." I patted the floor next to me, grinning. "Bell was the class clown and the life of the party." My chest warmed while I shared stories about my twin with one of the few women I'd loved in my lifetime. I could count them on one hand—Mom, Bell, and now Wynter.

Chapter 38

Wynter

Fate had thrown two people full of hate and anger together, then watched as the shit show unfolded. I wondered if Fate realized that Quinn and I were stronger than our pasts and that maybe, just maybe, we could heal together.

Over the last five weeks, Quinn and I had continued to share my story to the people who were interested in the truth and not a media frenzy. Quinn and I were both stunned as invitations to speak at high schools and colleges began trickling in. First it was an interview here and there, then speaking engagements with rooms full of hundreds at a time. We made sure that all correspondence went directly to me through my email or to my mailing address, so Adam wouldn't find out. It worked in our favor that Adam was out of the country for several weeks, and never used YouTube, Instagram, or TikTok. Luck had kept him busy and out of our business. Quinn still hadn't figured out what his endgame was.

I tossed the letters on my bed. "Three more emails and two invites by snail mail today." Sinking onto my mattress, I studied Quinn.

"We're becoming quite the speaking duo. How do you feel about that?" He sat in the chair at my desk and waited for my response.

"I'm grateful that we're helping other people by sharing our stories." I laid on my side and propped my head on my fist. Quinn had consistently moved forward with his promises after he'd released the video. He'd been kind, patient, and attentive to my every need. His words and actions lined up. Day by day, I forgave him a little more for what he'd done and realized that I could count on him. Grief had a fucked-up way of showing itself, and every person was different in how they managed it. Having his father, the one who should have helped him through it, spoon-feed him lies and misinformation, had to have destroyed him even further.

"Me too. I just didn't realize it would get this big."

"Same. But here we are, on our way to stardom." I grinned, trying to assess where his mood was. Something was different today, and I wasn't sure if I liked it. "Are you still on board? I can speak by myself. Maybe Vaughn could go with me, so I'd stay safe."

Quinn's jaw clenched. "No. I'll go with you."

I swallowed my giggle. It wasn't the first time I'd caught Quinn jealous over Vaughn.

I sat up, deciding to get to the point. "So what's wrong then?"

He straightened his long legs in front of him, and the urge to straddle him hit me fast and hard.

"Next week is Thanksgiving. Are you going home to visit?" His voice was low, haunted.

I slid off the bed, my feet silently landing on the hardwood floor. Over the last few weeks, I forgave him. Quinn had earned my trust back, and that paved the way for my heart to fully embrace what it wanted to feel. Not only had I forgiven Quinn, but I'd also fallen head over heels for him. The more he shared with me, the more I saw that Quinn had been as broken and tortured over his past as I was.

I stood in front of him, searching his eyes for a clue of what he hadn't said. "Do you want me to?"

A muscle in his jaw jumped, and he inhaled a slow breath. "No."

My pulse surged, my mind racing a million miles an hour at his answer. Quinn and I had seen each other every day for the last month, and I wasn't sure that I wanted to be away from him anyway. "I can stay if you want."

He reached for me, his strong hands wrapping around my hips. "As long as I'm with you, I don't care where we are." Quinn stared at me with such unwavering intensity, I had no choice but to believe him.

The second his fingers grazed my skin, my spine tingled with anticipation, and a surge of electricity ran through my veins. I willed his hands to drift lower. It had been too long since we'd slept together, and now that I was clear on my feelings for him, I craved him.

Quinn's eyes darkened with desire before he released me, and I took a step back. Maybe I had misread his intentions. Maybe Thanksgiving was a hard day at his house, and he wanted to spend it with a friend who understood his past.

I folded my arms across my chest and chose my next words carefully, ensuring my tone was even. "I haven't decided if I'm going home or not. I'm guessing that Janine will want to see me, though. We'll probably order pizza and watch movies, catch up."

Quinn stood, towering over me. "Wynter ... I think you're misunderstanding my intentions."

I swallowed. "Guess you need to explain it."

"I expect nothing from you. This last month with you has been more than I could have hoped for." He leaned down, his mouth brushed against my ear. "But I want more. I want all of you." Quinn straightened. "Not for a night or a few days. I want to hold and kiss you. Take you to dinners, spend nights with you, fuck until we're delirious every single day."

Delicious goose bumps dotted my skin as his gaze slowly swept up my body.

"Tell me you feel the same. If not, then I'll walk out the door and leave you alone."

No, no, and no. At the same time, was I ready to commit to him?

Have a relationship? I almost laughed. We were already seeing each other every day. He hugged and kissed my forehead daily, and even though I was angry with him, I wanted him to touch me. We held each other when the pain of our past was too much. Every waking second we could, Quinn and I were together. We talked about Bell and our individual futures. If we weren't in the mood to talk, we watched movies or studied in the same room.

I'd already forgiven him for the video. He'd worked his ass off to undo the damage and had more public speaking events scheduled. We were spreading hope, forgiveness, and that there was always more happening behind closed doors than the public realized. We were a powerful team together, but even more than that, Quinn had followed through with everything he said he would ... and more.

"Are you asking me to exclusively be yours, Quinn Astor?" I'd learned a long time ago not to assume anything, so I tried to ask for clarification.

Quinn's hazel eyes burned through me, setting me on fire. "Yes. That's what I'm asking. I'm in love with you, Wynter Baldwin."

Holy. Fucking. Shit. Didn't see that coming. "You are?" I croaked.

"I have been since before the night the video played. It just took Sutton's call to wake me up."

"What if I'm not there yet? What if I have deep feelings for you, but I don't know what to call it right now?"

"You don't have to. Just say you're mine."

My heart thumped as his low, raspy voice sent me into a spiral. I hadn't ever had a boyfriend before, and how would Janine handle it when she met him? Not to mention my brother killed his twin sister. That made for real daytime drama. When I'd told Janine about the video, she threatened to chop off both of his heads until I explained what he was doing to make up for it. She said she might give him a chance if he followed through, but she doubted it.

Breathe. What did the dean ask you to do? Make a decision for me. No one else. Just me. One that would make me happy. Wynter Bald-

win, what do you want? After everything that's happened, do you trust him?

I already knew the answers to my questions. It was just taking the time to put myself first for a change. It was a foreign and scary concept.

"Yeah. I'm yours, Quinn."

His smile lit up his face. "Yeah?"

"Yup." I popped the p and grinned.

Instead of Quinn kissing me, he backed away and sat in my office chair again. That was *not* the reaction I expected.

"Undress for me."

Oh. Yes. I grabbed my phone from my back pocket and turned on some music. I wasn't sure if the girls were home or not, and if Quinn and I got loud, I needed something to muffle the noise. "Fangs" by Neoni played through my Bluetooth speaker.

I placed my cell on the nightstand, then turned my attention to Quinn. Slowly, I unbuttoned my shirt, allowing it to fall open just enough to reveal the swell of my breasts in my pink lace bra. His gaze darkened while he watched me slide the shirt over my shoulders, letting it drop to the floor. My fingertips trailed down my stomach and dipped into the waist of my jeans. Unfastening the button, I lowered the zipper and dragged the fabric down my hips and legs. I stepped out and moved them to the side with my foot, then removed my bra and G-string and stood in front of him naked.

"Lay back on the bed and spread your legs."

I faced the bed and crawled on top of the mattress, my ass sticking up in the air. I glanced over my shoulder. Quinn's erection pressed against his jeans, and I licked my lips. Once I was settled, I turned to him and propped up on my elbows as I slowly parted my thighs, allowing him a full view of what was waiting for him.

He stood and walked toward me, focusing on my pussy. "Do you want me to touch you, Wynter?"

"Yes." My reply came out breathy, needy.

"Do you know what I want?"

"Tell me." My lips parted in anticipation.

"I want to run my finger down that sweet cunt and see how wet you are for me. Then I want to spread your lips apart as I kneel between your thighs, eager to taste you. The tip of my tongue would swirl around your clit before I licked your slit, your juices dripping down your ass cheeks and coating my chin."

I whimpered, mentally pleading with Quinn to follow through.

"Will you cry out when I ease my tongue into your slick walls, licking and sucking what's mine?"

I moaned, loving what he was doing to my body without even touching me. "God, yes."

"While I'm bringing you to the brink of coming with my mouth, I would slide a finger into that tight asshole of yours. Watching you writhe, knowing it's for me."

My ragged breathing filled the room, my chest visibly rising and falling the longer he talked.

Quinn crawled onto the bed, his eyes never leaving mine as he whispered, "Make no mistake that, when I come inside you, I'm marking you as mine. Do you understand?"

Unable to speak, I nodded in response.

"Roll over." He got off the mattress.

I propped up on all fours, waiting for him to put me out of my misery and make me come.

"The Art of Survival" by Ramsey streamed through my speaker, covering my loud moan as Quinn spread my pussy apart, then flicked my clit with his tongue. I rocked back, wanting him to dive in and take me.

He grabbed my outer thighs, digging in as he licked and sucked me. I moved against him, desperate and needy for my orgasm.

I gripped the comforter between my fingers, bunching up the soft fabric as Quinn continued. Teetering on the edge of a mind-blowing release, I groaned in frustration when Quinn moved away.

Irritated, I shot him a nasty look over my shoulder. I waited while he shed his clothes and rolled a condom over his thick cock.

He lined up at my entrance, running the tip of his dick along my soaking wet slit, teasing me even more.

With a hard thrust, he slid inside me, moved out slowly, then shoved inside me again. Every nerve ending in me responded to his rhythm of hard pushes and slow pulls.

His soft moan reached my ears, and I closed my eyes. Quinn ran a finger around my clit, sending me to the edge of a cliff again. Removing his hand from between my legs, he pushed against my puckered hole, easing a finger inside me as his cock continued to plow into my pussy.

"That's my beautiful girl. Will you take it this well when I fuck your tight ass with my dick? Can you take me all in?"

"Oh God, Quinn."

"That's it, say my name as I claim you." He grunted. "Who do you belong to?"

"You. Only you."

He pumped into me hard, our bodies slapping together in a heated frenzy. With his free hand, he fisted my hair and jerked it back. "Come for me, Wynter. Come all over my cock."

As if on cue, my inner walls clenched his shaft as a soul-obliterating orgasm ripped through me, stealing my breath.

Quinn's body jerked and tensed, bucking against mine as he came. Once he stilled, he gently pulled out of me and removed the used condom.

I collapsed onto my stomach, then rolled over, grinning like an idiot. "There's a trashcan in the bathroom." I pointed to the closed door.

He chuckled. "I thought that was a closet. I had no idea it was a bathroom." He disappeared, then I heard the water running.

I took a minute to revel in the moment, basking in the afterglow. Life had been crap for a long time, but with Quinn by my side, surely it could only get better from here.

Chapter 39

Quinn

I stared at myself in Wynter's bathroom mirror, wondering if I'd lost my damn mind. Only minutes ago, I told her I loved her. How in the hell would she take what I was about to ask? I washed my face, then I used the bottle of minty mouthwash that was on the edge of her sink.

Finding my courage, I joined her again. I couldn't help but smile at her naked on the bed, looking thoroughly fucked. I climbed onto the mattress next to her and smoothed her hair. "I love you." I kissed the tip of her nose. "No need to say anything, it just feels so good to tell you."

She gave me a sad smile. "I'm almost twenty-one, and you're so many of my firsts, Quinn. I know we've both had sex with other people, but ..." She traced my jaw with her fingertips. "Have you been in love before?" She slapped her palms over her eyes. "Don't answer that. I don't want to know. I just want to be a first for you, too."

I gently grabbed her wrist and pried one hand away. She peeked at me with one blue eye. "I've never been in love before. I've never spent the night with a girl. I've never been jealous over a girl before either."

"Really?"

"Yeah. Really."

Her other hand slipped away from her face. "When were you jealous over me?"

I pressed my lips into a thin line. "Several times. When I saw the way you looked at Vaughn, when I realized Adam had seen you on Dimitri's website, when I shared you at the society."

Wynter just blinked at me with an astonished expression. "I didn't realize that you hadn't been in love before. For some reason, I just assumed you had."

"Nope. You're the first, and if I have my way about it, the last."

Wynter grinned. "I might like the sound of that."

I wrapped a strand of her strawberry-blonde hair around my finger. "I do want a future with you, but I also know that we have to figure out what happened with Kyler."

That was the first time I spoke his name without cringing. Maybe it was the way Wynter talked about him. They seemed similar in a lot of areas before all hell broke out. In some ways, I felt as if the good parts of him were still with her, but maybe I was just talking myself into that idea to ease the pain.

"Babe?"

"Yeah?" She placed her palm against my bare chest, sending warmth radiating through me.

"Tell me about Kyler. Better yet, what do you think about taking me home with you for Thanksgiving? I have to be back Friday though, since we have a game on Saturday. Maybe we could drive up Thursday morning and back on Friday afternoon."

If the music hadn't still been playing, I'm pretty sure I could have heard a pin drop. I released Wynter's hair, focused on the many emotions that flashed across her face. She gulped, then sat up slowly. "You know it's the same house that we lived in with Kyler, right?" She tucked her legs beneath her, staring at me as if I had a hole in my head. Hell, I probably did. My idea was fucking crazy, but something was pulling me in that direction. I had to trust my gut.

"I do. I want to see his room and find out if anyone else close to him will talk to me about who he was." I tapped my temple. "I need to try to make sense of what happened. In no way will I excuse what he did, but maybe understanding why I lost Bell ..." I dropped my hand to the mattress. "I know it's crazy, but if I can't handle it, I'll drive back, and you can stay with Janine until you come back after break."

"What about Vaughn?"

I sighed, taking a minute to think that through. "I think you're safe now, but I wanted to make sure you felt you were."

She gave me a half-shrug. "I'm not sure about at Whitmore, but I'll be fine in my hometown. I never had a bodyguard there and survived, so I think we should give him some time off to be with his fiancée and family."

"Fiancée, huh?" I rubbed my neck, giving her a sheepish look. "How did you find that out?"

A wicked little smile eased across her face, and I wanted to kiss it off.

"I asked. He's a dad. Just thought I'd let you know that you have nothing to be jealous about." She leaned over and pressed her soft mouth to mine. "Quinn, my house doesn't look anything like yours. It needs paint and new wood floors, repairs. I've done the best I could with keeping a roof over our head, but I couldn't afford to keep our home looking nice too."

I placed my palm on her knee. "I don't care, Wynter. I want to spend the holiday with you. I also want to meet Janine and get to know her. The fact that Kyler lived there too, if there's anything we can look through or ..." My voice trailed off, and I shoved my hand through my hair. "If we don't find answers, maybe Sutton will have some soon. She's still digging."

Fear and concern warred in Wynter's expression. "What if it's too much? I could visit alone and search his room, then bring back whatever I may find."

"Please. Let me meet Janine and spend the holiday with you." I'd probably fucked up this conversation by putting too much emphasis on Kyler. That was only a small part of why I wanted to go. I couldn't stand the thought of being away from Wynter for four days.

"Are you sure that's the biggest reason?"

"If I could, I would have you over at my house, but not with Adam in town. I still don't trust him. We can either stay here, or I'd like to take you to visit your sister." Hopefully my explanation helped.

"I hadn't thought about not being able to go to your place." She briefly closed her eyes. "Let me talk to Janine and see how she feels about you visiting. It's a big step for all of us. I need to include her on the decision. My vote is yes, though. I would love to spend the holiday break with you. But, Quinn, what about Brody? Will he be safe alone with Adam? As soon as you get home on Friday, you turn around and leave for your football game."

"I've thought about that, but he's ready. He can protect himself. And he has a lot of friends he can stay with if shit gets out of hand, friends I trust too." I smiled at her. "That's another thing I love about you, you know."

"What's that?"

"You care about other people and what's best for them." I cupped the back of her neck and kissed her forehead.

"I try. I've gotten used to taking care of Janine, so thinking about Brody is second nature, I guess." Wynter hopped off the bed, then strolled to her bathroom and closed the door. It opened again and she poked her head back into the room. "I'll FaceTime Janine after I get cleaned up." She bit her lip, her gaze narrowing as if she were thinking. "I actually need to shower if you want to take one with me."

"Love on the Brain" by Rihanna filtered through the speakers.

"I added it to my playlist." She winked at me, then crooked her finger, motioning for me to join her.

A shower with a girl I was in love with? Hell, who was I to say no?

Chapter 40

Wynter

Time seemed to stand still as Quinn and I locked eyes on the porch of my Forest Dale home. My pulse raced so hard I could feel it in my throat. I realized what awaited me on the other side of the door. Not only was I about to waltz in with the guy of my dreams and introduce him to Janine, but Kyler's and Bell's histories had the power to overshadow our visit. With each step forward, I understood that everything could unravel in an instant.

No. It's going to be okay.

Quinn took my hand in his, confidence in his posture. "If we need to bail early, we can, but I'm ready to do this."

"Yup. Okay." I texted Janine that we had arrived and the front door flew open seconds later.

"Wyn!" Janine nearly knocked me over with her hug. "I've missed you."

I wrapped my arms around her, embracing her. "Same." Tears gathered in my eyes and spilled down my cheeks, and I took a slow, deep breath.

When we released each other, I couldn't help but laugh as Janine and I wiped the moisture from our faces. At least they were happy tears.

I turned my attention to Quinn, his expression unreadable as he watched us. I wondered if he remembered that Janine and Ky looked alike, or if he just thought we were weird. Most likely the latter. "Janine, this is Quinn Astor, my boyfriend."

"It's about fucking time I met him." Her nostrils flared.

Quinn's gaze widened as he towered over her. Janine was an inch shorter than me, so she was probably hurting her neck glaring up at him.

Janine stepped toe-to-toe to him and placed her hands on her slender waist. "Fuck her over and they will never find your body."

"Janine!" Good God. Well, we were definitely related. I had threatened to kill Quinn myself just weeks ago, but I hadn't meant it. And under the circumstances, I'm not sure it was the right thing to say.

She backed away. "Happy Thanksgiving and welcome to our humble home." She cracked a grin, then gave me one of her sassy "don't screw with me" looks. Apparently, Janine had grown up while I was gone, learning to stand her ground when she needed to.

She spun on her heel and shivered. It was then that I realized she was in a hoodie, shorts, and socks with little turkeys all over them.

Janine kicked her feet up, showing me the grippers on the bottom.

"Good. Glad you listened to me before I left."

Janine grabbed my wrist, her attention bouncing between Quinn and me. "I have a surprise."

I cringed. "Janine, you know I hate surprises."

"You're going to love this one. Trust me on this." She pushed open the door and led us inside.

The sound of the lock clicking into place reached my ears and I held out my hand for Quinn. Visiting the house was hard enough for me, so I had no idea what it would be like for him. I glanced over my shoulder and he gave me a little nod, reassuring me that he was doing okay.

The heavenly smell of turkey wafted through the air. "You cooked! Oh my gosh. You didn't need to. I would have been happy with pizza." I gave her a quick hug.

"You're welcome, but it wasn't me, Wyn."

My forehead creased in confusion. "Oh, one of your friends is here, too? That's great." I couldn't remember the last time Janine had a good friend to invite over, so I was genuinely excited for her. I tugged on Quinn, pulling him to the side of me.

Footsteps sounded, then the mystery chef appeared. "She helped, but I enjoyed cooking for everyone. It's been a fucking minute, huh?" My mother wiped her palms on a beige dish towel before she flung it over her shoulder.

My mouth hit the damn floor as I fixated on a woman I thought was my mother, but it had been so long since I'd seen her looking like a human being, I wasn't sure.

"Mom?" I looked at Janine for an explanation. "What's happening? And you really shouldn't be cooking. You're going to hurt yourself and burn our home down the second your alcohol lights up."

Quinn placed his hand on my lower back, offering me support. I'd told him all about my mother on the drive, so he had an inkling of how shocked I was.

Mom gave me a sad smile. "I've been sober for five weeks. Not long after you left, I went to my first AA meeting."

"You're serious? *Now* you're sober?"

"She is. I was afraid to tell you," Janine admitted, grinning. "I'm so proud of her. She's taking care of the house again and looking for work. Wyn, we have our mom back."

My heart fucking broke, the pieces of it falling at mine and Quinn's feet.

"Janine, take Quinn to my bedroom."

"But—"

I spun on her so fast, I almost lost my balance. "Now." I said through clenched teeth.

Quinn kissed my cheek before he followed Janine up the stairs. The moment they were out of earshot, I stomped over to my mother. "Two months does not make you a fucking mother. What you did to us is unforgivable. We needed you, and you hid in a goddamn bottle. Now I come home a few months later, and everything is fucking roses? *No.* And Janine thinks you've won the battle. You and I both know alcoholism is a lifelong fight. Don't you dare jerk her around like that, you selfish—" I caught myself before I called her a bitch.

She wore the guilt like a weight on her shoulders, aging her beyond what time could ever do. Her face was a mask of sorrow and rage, her inner turmoil seeping through her pores like acid as it slowly dissolved her from the inside out until there was nothing left but a shell of the woman she'd once been.

"I know, Wyn. I'm so sorry. Losing Ky and your father destroyed me, but I'm really trying to get myself back together. For you. For Janine. For me. I understand that you won't forgive me, but I hope with each passing day, we can find some common ground to meet on. I love you, Wyn, and I'm so happy you're here for a few days."

She hugged me but my arms remained at my side, my body stiff with tension and fury. "If you hurt her again, you'll never see either of us," I said quietly. "That's a promise you can take to your grave with you ... the one right next to your son."

Breaking free from her, I rushed to the front door, desperate to have a minute alone to pull myself together.

A gust of wind whipped around me, blowing my hair into my face as soon as I stepped onto the porch. The tightness in my chest almost made it impossible to breathe. I shivered, grateful I hadn't taken off my coat yet. Listening to the soft pitter-patter of rain falling, I wondered if I would be able to walk back into that house.

How could Mom just get out of bed not long after I left and put her life together? A tear snuck down my cheek, and I angrily wiped it away. Crying wouldn't solve anything. Feeling childish for wanting to grab my boyfriend and leave, I remembered that I was here for Janine. She would need my help and support if Mom returned to drinking.

I heard the door open behind me, but I didn't turn to see who it was.

"I'm so sorry," Janine said. "I thought you would be happy."

My stomach twisted with regret and sadness. "I know, but there's just too much bad shit with her." I choked on my words, my shoulders shaking with my sob.

Janine wrapped her arms around me, and we clung to each other. I wasn't sure how long we stood there, but my cries finally ran dry.

"Are you and Quinn leaving?" Janine released me, worry flickering in her expression.

"No. I came here to see you. I wanted you and Quinn to get to know each other."

"Yeah, when you told me about Quinn? That was a whole lot of crazy-in-a-handbasket conversation."

I twisted the corner of my mouth. "Guess we both took each other off guard."

"Well, he's hot as sin, so I can understand why you fell for him, but why did you have to fall for Bell's brother?" She let out a low whistle. "That's some intense shit."

I nodded. "I know. But it's working, and he ..." I looked at her. "He told me he loved me a few days ago."

Janine's face lit up. "Wyn! That's amazing." Her excitement faded, and she quirked a brow at me. "Do you not feel the same?"

I shrugged, staring out across the street to our neighbor's muddy yard. "I care about him, but I'm scared."

"Oh. Hell. No."

Oh goody. Sassy Janine is making an appearance again.

"What now?" I leaned against one of the dirty white columns that supported our porch.

"You're not going to admit how much you love this guy because you're *scared*?"

"Janine, it's not like that."

But isn't it?

"From where I sit, it's exactly that. But,"—she raised her hands, halting the conversation—"the food is done. If you don't want to eat with Mom at the table, then I'll meet you in your room later."

"I'll do it. For you."

Janine grabbed my arm. "This is the first Thanksgiving together since Ky ..." Her shoulders slumped. "I need you there."

"I'm here, sis. I'm here." I gave her a quick hug, then sucked it up. My feelings about my shitty mother could wait.

Silently, I followed my sister back into the house, my stomach growling. Voices came from the kitchen, then Mom appeared with a casserole dish in her hand. She placed it on the dining room table. Quinn was behind her, carrying the platter with the turkey. He set it down and looked at Mom. "What else can I help with?" He offered her a warm smile.

"You're company, Quinn. Sit down ..." She caught sight of Janine and me, standing in the entryway. "Well, there is one thing." She cleared her throat and nervously wiped her palms on her apron. "Maybe you could carve the turkey for us."

Quinn's gaze landed on me, understanding in his eyes. "I would be honored."

And in that split second, I fell in love with the man who was brave enough to walk into the home of his sister's killer and have dinner with my family.

Chapter 41

Wynter

"In my opinion, it went well, babe." Quinn said, tossing our overnight bag on my full-size bed.

"Never in a million years did I think my mother would join us, Quinn," I said, keeping my voice down in order not to be overheard by Janine or my mother. The walls were thin, and I didn't want to upset my sister.

My room hadn't changed in the last few months, but I hadn't expected it to. The same beige paint covered the walls, brightening the small space. I only had one window, and it faced the neighboring home, so I rarely opened the brown blackout curtains. Some days, it felt as if I lived in a little box with a peephole to the outside world. At the time, it had kept me safe. Maybe my room hadn't changed, but I had. Even after the video, I'd had the strength to take a stand with the people I loved and talk to them instead of running.

Quinn sat on the edge of my bed, staring at the floor. I wedged my legs between his and wrapped my arms around his neck. "This has to be even harder for you. I've had my head up my ass instead of supporting you."

"No. Your pain isn't worse or easier than mine. It's been hard as hell walking into this house—for both of us."

I smoothed his dark hair. "How can I make it better, Quinn? How can I make up for what Ky did to you?" Tears slipped down my cheeks. "I'm sorry. You're right. This is way harder than I thought it would be."

"Beautiful, you can't make things right. Stop trying to fix what's out of your control. Shit, I'm taking my own advice, too."

I looked at Quinn, unashamed that I was crying in front of him. A slew of emotions twisted my gut, but the one I felt the strongest was for him. Janine was right, I could no longer deny my feelings. Quinn was my future, and I knew it. "I love you, Quinn."

His eyes widened. "Wynter, you don't have to tell me that to try to make me feel better."

"I'm not. I really love you. Janine was the one that made me stop hiding from the truth." I smiled at him, sniffling. I wiped my face with the sleeves of my shirt.

"Then if that's the only good thing that came out of this trip, I'll take it." He grabbed my waist and ensured I didn't fall over as he stood.

I placed my hands against his chest, his heart beating beneath my palm.

He cupped my chin in his hand. "I love you, too, Wynter Baldwin. All of you. All of the tormented, beautiful soul that you are."

A soft laugh escaped me. "I know exactly when I realized that I was in love with you."

"Yeah?"

"When Janine and I walked back into the house, and you were helping Mom." I pressed my forehead against his shoulder, hiding the fact that my tears were falling faster. "That you had the ability to love me enough to have Thanksgiving with my fucked-up family ..." I peeked up at him. "I saw the amazing man you are, and I turned into a puddle of goo right there on the spot."

"If I'd known that was the way to make you fall in love with me, I would have carried food around for your mom a long time ago."

His beautiful smile radiated warmth and safety, something I'd craved for way too long. Quinn smoothed my hair and kissed me gently. I savored the taste of him and wished that moment would last forever.

"As soon as everyone is asleep, we can go into Ky's room. I mean, if you're ready." I gulped. Hell, I wasn't sure I was ready, but maybe it would be easier if we looked around together. Suddenly needing a minute, I said, "I'm going to see if there's something to drink. Do you want a soda?"

"That or water is great."

"Okay. I'll be right back." I left, then my breath stuttered in my throat as I focused on Ky's door. A fiery heat spread across my chest. I tried to suppress the hatred that was boiling over inside me, but it was useless. I shook my head in disbelief, wondering how Ky could have been so foolish to throw away the life he'd had and take so many others with it. We'd all had a good life. He was well-liked by people at school and a star on the soccer field. From what I saw, Ky was happy.

I rubbed my neck. It had been five years, and although I would never get over the harm Ky caused, maybe after this visit I could mentally move on more than I had in the past.

I crept down the stairs and made my way to the kitchen. To my surprise, Mom was sitting at the dining room table. She looked up from her book and gave me a sad smile.

"There are leftovers in the fridge if you're hungry."

I took a moment to really look at her. Streaks of grey threaded her dark hair, and fine lines were visible around her mouth and the corners of her eyes. She seemed exhausted and worn out. *Welcome to the club*. But I hadn't given up on my kids like she had.

"Thanks. Dinner was good," I muttered.

Mom closed the book she was reading, then set it down. "How is Quinn? I can't imagine how hard it is for him to see Ky's home."

My entire body bristled. Not once had she asked me how I was doing after Ky took so many lives and then his own.

"He's hanging in there."

Mom glanced down, then returned her attention to me. "Ky had a journal, Wynter. If you can find it, you might learn why he changed so fast and ... and why he ..." She grimaced.

"You don't have to say that your son and my brother shot up a fucking high school, killing fourteen people, including himself. I've had plenty of practice saying it loud, so I'll do it for you." Anger brewed in the pit of my stomach, and my hands itched with the urge to slap her. In my opinion, Mom was weak. I'd carried the family after Ky snapped us in two like we were dried-up brittle twigs.

"I know what happened. I remember getting the call from the police. The only reason I mentioned the journal is because I'm assuming you and Quinn will go into Kyler's room to see if there are any clues. I can tell you there's not. The cops went through his room a few times, and took his computer, notebooks, phone, anything that might have shed light on what he did. But ... they never found his journal, Wynter. I'm guessing it's hidden in the house somewhere. Try to find it."

"Why are you telling me this? It's been years, Mom. Why now?"

Her brown eyes misted over. "Because I should have been there for you and Janine. I should have tried to help you girls make sense of how Ky changed. I was a horrible mother, and if I can help you find peace now, I will. Regardless of whether you believe it or not, I love you and Janine more than anything else in this world."

I stared at her, wondering if she had taken a few nips from a bottle of gin stashed somewhere. When she started drinking, she was full of sweet words and promises. After that, it was a slippery slope into darkness and screaming before she finally curled up in bed and hid from reality.

"Okay. If I can look for it while I'm here, that would be great. Quinn needs to understand what happened between Ky and Bell.

Maybe it won't ever make sense to us, but maybe Ky told us all along what was happening, and we didn't know how to listen."

Mom wiped the tears from her cheeks. "If you find that he put his thoughts on paper, would you mind letting me know?"

A flicker of compassion welled in my chest. "I understand how horrific it was to learn that my brother, the one I adored since I was little, murdered people. But ... I can't imagine what it feels like to have lost a son, and in such a violent way. I wish it had never happened."

Mom's shoulders shook with her muffled sobs. I headed to the living room and retrieved a box of tissues. Placing them on the table, I sank into the chair across from her.

"I should have listened to you, Wynter. You tried. None of what Ky did was your fault, but I know you paid dearly. I'm so sorry."

A painful lump swelled in my throat. Not once had Mom said any of those words to me after Ky left us. Not. One. Fucking. Time. I slammed my eyes closed, holding my anguish at bay, and trying to carefully choose what came out of my mouth next.

I waited until her cries subsided. "If Quinn can look past what Ky did to his sister, then maybe there's a chance for us. I won't lie, though. It all depends on if you stay sober or not. If you relapse, I'm taking Janine with me, and you can rot and die alone in this fucking house."

A heavy, heartbroken silence hung in the air. "I'll take it. At least it gives me some hope and very clear boundaries with you. I need those."

Ugh. She was getting to me. I stood. "I'm going to grab something to drink, then see if Quinn is ready to visit Ky's room. If you hear crying or yelling, please just let us have some space to process."

"Okay. Try not to scare your sister. She's been through enough."

Why was she concerned about everyone except me? I shook it off, reminding myself I didn't need her in my life at all. It was a constant roller coaster of drama, and I was ready to hop off that ride. How she chose to show up moving forward was her choice, and I refused to coddle her. I had other things to focus on, like finding Ky's journal in the next twelve hours.

Chapter 42

Quinn

I knew I'd lost my mind when I'd asked Wynter if I could spend Thanksgiving with her in Washington. A part of me was desperate not to sit at a table with Adam and Brody and the constant reminder that Bell and Mom were gone. At the time, it seemed easier to visit the house of Bell's killer instead. How fucked up was that?

I rubbed the back of my neck, waiting for Wynter to open Kyler's door. My heart slammed against my ribs, and I struggled to breathe.

"Ready?" She looked up at me, a combination of fear and courage dancing across her face.

"Yeah." I wasn't, but I knew there might be answers inside those walls.

The door creaked open and a strong, musty scent nearly knocked me backward. Wynter fanned her hand in front of her nose. "Ugh. I'm going to have to crack a window in here." She flipped on the light, and for the first time I saw Kyler's bedroom.

I walked in slowly, searching the posters on his wall—Metallica, Portugal the Man, Twenty-One Pilots. Then, I came to an abrupt stop, my vision tunneling in on the area before me. I was in the same space where Kyler Baldwin had plotted the violent act that had taken my sister's life. The room began to spin wildly, the walls closing in on me like a vacuum, terror and rage bubbling up through my chest until it seemed as if I couldn't contain it any longer. I gasped for air, desperately trying not to let out the anguished cry that was screaming to get free.

"Quinn! Quinn!" Wynter gripped my bicep and shook me gently. "Talk to me. Are you okay?"

I blinked rapidly, and mentally cleared the darkness that threatened to overtake me. "Let's do what we need to and jet."

"Okay. You can wait in the hall or downstairs if you need to."

No way in hell would I let her face Kyler's memories on her own. Her parents had already done that, and I was determined not to do the same.

Wynter walked across to the window and unlocked it. She groaned in an attempt to lift it, but it didn't budge. I hurried over to give her a hand. Together, we forced it open after years of being closed, and a rush of cold air blasted in.

"Maybe grab your coat if you get too cold." She shivered, then lowered the window until it was only open an inch. Her expression clouded as her attention scanned the area. "We used to sit on his bed and listen to music together." Her voice sounded hollow. She pinched the bridge of her nose and placed the other hand on her hip.

"Wynter, if this is too much for you. We don't have to stay." I hoped she would want to leave, but instead she waved me away as if I were a pesky fly on a hot summer day.

"I'm thinking." She tapped her foot against the wood floor. "Mom and I talked a few minutes ago."

"Oh?" Maybe focusing on Wynter would help me manage the suffocating feeling that was pushing on my chest.

"She said that the cops searched the house and his room. They took his cell, laptop, notebooks ... everything that might be used for evidence." She bit her lip before she continued. "Mom said Ky had a journal, but it wasn't ever found." Wynter looked at me. "When we were young, we played all kinds of games together. Hide and seek, tag, you know the usual stuff, but we took it a step farther and instead of hiding *ourselves*, we would sometimes decide on an object. Normally it was a stuffed animal and completely harmless." A soft laugh escaped her. "Ky always cheated and eventually confessed."

It was strange to watch my girlfriend have a good memory about the same guy that killed innocent people. *She knew a different person.* If I was going to survive the visit to Ky's world, I had to keep in mind that she probably knew him better than anyone else had. According to her, he'd been a kind, good person. I wasn't sure I would ever be able to believe that, but I knew Wynter wanted to learn the truth as much as I did.

"He finally showed me the hiding places." Her eyes narrowed as if she were reliving the memory. "I need your help." Wynter walked to Kyler's closet and flung the door open so hard I thought she might rip it off the hinges. She hesitated when she saw his clothes hanging up. Her hand trembled as she reached out and touched one of his T-shirts. "Mom used to hang up all of his clean laundry because he would throw them on the floor, and she hated to see wrinkles. It was like she was allergic to them."

Wynter knelt and moved his shoes out of her way. She crawled to the back corner, but I couldn't see what she was doing.

Completely distracted from my surroundings, I crouched down. "Wynter?"

"Yeah?" Her response was muffled. "Dammit." She backed out, her perky ass appearing first. It took everything inside me not to rip off her clothes and fuck her until she was senseless. I'm sure that would piss Ky off to no end. My dick agreed as it hardened and pressed against my jeans. But I understood that wanting to have sex with her at the moment was a way to escape the tumultuous feelings that were spinning out of control inside me.

"Someone fixed the damn closet." She dusted her hands off, frustrated. "There used to be a gap in the corner, like whoever built the house was in a hurry and the walls didn't quite meet. Ky had cut out a small piece of the paneling and made a hiding place. But it's sealed up now. Maybe Dad found it after the cops searched the room." She rubbed her forehead. "It just doesn't seem real, but at the same time, I'm afraid the memories might destroy me where I stand."

I took her hand and kissed her knuckles. "I think both of us have been in here long enough. You knew Ky better than anyone, so I'll let you search the house for the journal." That was the best I could do. The walls had begun to spin like a vortex, threatening to drag me under a sea of my grief.

"Good idea." She hurried to the window, closed and locked it before we hightailed it out of there.

We stood in the hallway, staring at each other. Wynter grabbed my wrist and dragged me back to her room, then secured the door before she forcefully unbuttoned my jeans. She dropped to her knees and shoved my hard cock in her mouth. Wynter sucked and licked me like her life depended on it. Maybe it did.

I threaded my fingers through her hair, rocking my hips to the same rhythm that her hand was pumping me. She dug her nails in my ass cheeks, taking my entire length in until the head of my dick hit the back of her throat.

"Good. God," I muttered, trying to stay quiet. The last thing we needed was for Wynter's mom or sister to barge in.

I focused on Wynter's hot mouth, forgetting about Kyler and Bell for just a few minutes. Apparently, Wynter had needed a distraction as much as I had.

A low growl rumbled through my chest. I was going to come, and I wasn't ready to yet. Pulling her up by her arm, I jerked up my pants but left my cock out.

"Bend over the bed."

She hurriedly shed her jeans and panties and stepped out of them. "No condom. I want to feel all of you. I'm on the pill and have been for years. I also got tested regularly while working for Dimitri. If you've been tested recently and are clean, forget the rubber. Just fuck me."

"I always use a condom, but I've been tested too. I'm clean." I lined up at her soaking wet entrance and pushed inside her, overwhelmed by how amazing she felt.

I dug my fingers into her hips and slammed into her. The fact that her mom and sister were in the house should have tamped my desire down, but it didn't.

"Touch yourself, Wynter. Stroke your clit until you're coming all over my cock."

She gasped and slid her hand between her thighs. "Harder. Jesus, Quinn, fuck me, baby."

The bed squeaked, and we both stilled.

She glanced over her shoulder at me. "Dammit."

I eased out, then nodded at the corner. "Brace yourself against the wall by your desk."

As soon as she was ready, I moved inside her again. One of my hands trailed beneath her shirt, and I played with her nipple through the lace of her bra. Cupping her breast, I moved the fabric and freed her tit.

She massaged her bundle of nerves as I fucked her hard. Every damn emotion I'd felt in Kyler's room, I turned it toward Wynter.

I removed her hand from between her legs and pinched her clit. She gasped as I continued to stroke her. "Come for me, baby."

With a few more deep thrusts, her fingers curled against the wall and her mouth parted in a silent scream. Her pussy throbbed around my shaft, clenching. My body jerked as I came inside her, gritting my teeth in order not to yell her name. I shuddered again before I pulled out.

Wynter straightened and gave me a weary smile as she tugged her panties and jeans on. "Thank you. I'll be right back." She pushed up on her tiptoes and kissed me before she disappeared into the hall. A few minutes later she returned with a damp washcloth. "You're welcome to shower, but I figured this would clean you up for now."

"Thanks. And you're welcome. And thank you." I chuckled while I cleaned myself. "Where should I put this?"

"I'll take it." Wynter held out her hand, and I gave her the damp wash rag. She opened her closet door and tossed it into an empty hamper.

Wynter climbed on the bed and patted the empty space beside her. "It's only ten, but I'm so tired."

"It was probably all the turkey we ate." I snuggled next to her and pressed a kiss to her temple. "Maybe we should try to get some sleep before the drive home tomorrow."

"Are you sure?" She peeked up while she traced little circles on my chest.

"Yeah. It's been a long day."

"I agree. I'm going to change into my pajamas and brush my teeth. I want to tell Janine goodnight and check on her. I'll be right back."

"I'll be waiting." I gave her a goofy grin, finally feeling the tension ease from me. Mix turkey in with traumatic memories, and it apparently made me tired. I yawned, then my eyelids fluttered closed.

Chapter 43

Wynter

I hadn't meant to leave Quinn alone for as long as I did, but I wanted to check on Janine. It had been a big day for her, too. Once we'd caught up, and I was positive that she didn't need to talk to me about Mom or Ky, I returned to my room.

I laughed as Quinn snored softly. He was still on top of the covers and sprawled out in the middle of the bed. Quietly, I set my clothes on the floor, but grabbed my phone out of the back pocket of my jeans. Staring at him, my heart pitter-pattered in my chest. I had no idea how he'd walked into Ky's room with me, but he had. One step into that cold, lifeless space sent Quinn into overdrive. Every muscle in his body tensed so hard, I was worried they might snap in two. I couldn't do that to him. Maybe I'd made the decision for him, but I couldn't handle both his emotions and mine. It was too much, and I was clawing my way out of a deep, dark pit of despair all over again.

Realizing this was my chance, I snuck out of my room and tiptoed down the hall to Ky's. I cracked open the door enough for me to slip through, then closed it behind me.

I bit my lower lip, guilt washing over me for lying to Quinn, but I had to get him out of Ky's space. It was going to consume him, chew him up, and spit him all over the floor. Ky had done enough. I wasn't going to stand by and not protect Quinn this time.

I tapped the screen of my phone and flipped the flashlight on. The bright light broke through the darkness and an eerie feeling descended on me. Hurrying to the closet, I crawled to the corner again. A black, leatherbound book was wedged in between the cracks in the wall. No one would have known to search here, but there was also a shelf blocking most of the view. It's why I never found it when Ky and I played. I wanted to tell Quinn, but I needed to look through it first.

I reached up beneath the shelf, still filled with more of Ky's shoes, and wedged the book free. Dust flew up my nose, and I covered my mouth in time to muffle my sneeze. An idea popped into my head, and I shook one of Ky's shirts off a hanger and used it to wipe off the leather. My heart skipped a beat, then broke into a full-on gallop as I cracked the book open. I ran my fingertips down the paper, over his thin, messy handwriting that filled the page.

"Ky," I whispered. "I miss you so bad." Tears streamed down my face, landing on my chest. "Why did you take innocent lives? What happened?" I inhaled a shaky breath, my attention focusing on the words he'd left behind.

Nothing
Nothing, nothing, nothing
It echoes from my soul
And screams right back to me
Nothing, nothing, nothing
It lives in my head
And shows me agony
Nothing, nothing, nothing
It's the numbness
And the silence
Nothing, nothing, nothing
It's the peace that isn't peace

And the silence that screams
Nothing, nothing, nothing
It's the quiet that is loud
And the success that is defeat
Nothing, nothing, nothing
It's the end
And the beginning
Nothing

I clutched Ky's shirt, my tears falling like plump drops of rain. Turning the page, I read the next poem.

Don't Let Go
I cry in the silence where no one will know
I cry by myself cuz I can't let it show
The crushing depression and crippling despair
The pain of nothingness so hard to share
I can't let it out, can't let you know
I can't stand this nothing, can't take the low
I smile pretty and play make believe
I cross my fingers and pray you won't leave
When the cycle makes me bitter and angry
I pray you'll see through it and still love me
Can you see me through it and still hold fast
Can we build a love that will last
Please, oh please, don't let me go
Show me love like I've never known

Ky had never mentioned he wrote poetry. Blowing out a shaky breath, I tried to inhale past the crushing agony in the center of my chest, but I couldn't. Ky's truth was on these pages, and I had no fucking clue what had happened to him.

I turned page after page, spotting poem after poem. After about a third of the way through the book, there was a full page of his handwriting. Before I read it, I wanted to see how many more entries there were. I thumbed through the last part, catching snippets of what he'd written, until I reached the last page, which contained another poem. I hiccupped through my tears as I read.

Abyss
The dark abyss welcomes me
Like an old friend
Arms open wide to pull me in
Sinking into her cool embrace
I give in with simple grace
There's comfort in the quiet dark
She's forever left her indelible mark

Swallowing painfully over the anguished lump in my throat, I hid my face in his shirt, allowing my sobs to break free. How did I not know that he was in so much pain? *You did, and you asked for help.* I leaned my head against the wall, reminding myself of everything I'd done to try and save him. After a few minutes, the hollowness in my soul spread, leaving me numb after my cries have stopped.

Curled into the corner of my brother's closet, I stared at the black book of horror. I flipped the pages to the beginning and read under the light of the cell phone. I checked to see if a date was on the page, then realized he had started writing a year before the shooting.

September 14th, 2018

I thought I was going to fucking puke, but I did it. I finally told one of my closest friends that I was gay. I figured she would yell and scream at me, but instead, she kissed my cheek and told me she was proud of me. I hadn't shared that with anyone other than my best friend, Wyn. My sister is the only person I really trust in this world.

I bit my lip, willing myself not to cry anymore. My head was already pounding from the barrage of emotions and sobbing.

What surprised me was that Bell burst into giggles once she'd assured me that she still loved me. I was completely confused why she thought me being gay was funny. It wasn't. It was terrifying. Last soccer season, some of the guys were walking around naked in the locker room with their dicks swinging, and Lance Rutledge saw me looking. He popped me with his shower towel and called me a faggot. Of course, the other jocks jumped in and before I knew it, I was covered in red and purple welts all over my body. I fucking hate them. It took me a few days to realize that Lance had never covered himself after he caught me. He strutted. Guess I hold someone else's secret, too.

Anyway, I'm getting sidetracked. From that experience, I had no idea how Bell would react, but I'd hoped she would still be my friend. She said her giggles were because she'd had the biggest crush on me since she was fourteen. It made me feel good, and if I'd been able to fall in love with a girl, it would be Bell, but my brain and body just aren't wired that way. I do love her, though. I would do anything for that girl, too. After I told her I was gay, and that night, she messaged me and for the first time in my life, we talked about cute boys. She made my fear disappear like a puff of smoke. But I wish she could make me disappear too.

· · ·

I sat frozen in place. Ky and Bell were friends at that point. Good friends. "He loved her" kind of friends. So what went so wrong that he took her life? Shifting to get more comfortable, I continued to read.

Fully entranced with Ky's journal, I lost track of time. It was nearly four in the morning before I came out of my reading daze, and I had no idea if Quinn had woken up and started looking for me or not. I scrambled to my feet, swearing as sharp pinpricks shot through my legs. I shook them out, then wrapped the book in Ky's shirt and tiptoed out of his room.

Thank God, Quinn was still asleep when I returned. The journal was the last piece of Ky I had, and I needed to process my emotions before I talked to Quinn. I couldn't handle both of us falling apart. I heaved a sigh and tucked the book under the jeans I'd tossed on the floor. I had every intention of telling Quinn about the journal, but I wanted to read it first. I decided to tell him I found it after we got up and showered in the morning.

Chapter 44

Quinn

When I woke the next morning, I was still in my jeans and long-sleeved shirt from the night before. I reached for Wynter, but she was nowhere to be found. Her side of the bed was wrinkled and the blankets had been kicked to the foot.

I sat up, wincing from the crick in my neck. Yawning, I placed my feet on the floor, and looked around at Wynter's childhood room. When Janine had shown me around the day before she had asked me a million questions about my intentions with her sister, and I hadn't had a chance to look around much. After being in Kyler's room, I'd been too fucked up in the head to notice who she'd been before we met. Part of it I knew. Wynter had been lonely and angry, just like me. It's probably the reason we found each other.

Walking to the large bulletin board on her wall, I looked at the images she had pinned to the cork. I smiled at a much younger Wynter holding a baby in her arms. Her mom was on one side of her, helping Wynter support the baby's neck. I was guessing that little bundle wrapped in a pink blanket was Janine. Each one depicted a happy Wynter with a ton of friends. My pulse stuttered when I saw the pictures of her and Kyler. He had his arm flung around her shoulders and she was rolling her eyes as the camera snapped the moment. Several more of her and Kyler cluttered the board, but the one tucked into the corner grabbed my attention.

I snatched it up, making sure I was seeing it right. It was Kyler and Bell, laughing as she kissed him on his cheek. From the look in their expressions, they cared about each other. A lot. Confused, I tucked the picture back where I'd found it.

Wynter had shared that Kyler was gay, and that there was nothing going on between him and Bell. But was it possible he was bisexual and Wynter didn't know? There was no denying the feelings between Bell and Kyler. And, even if they were just good friends, what the fuck happened to make him turn against her and kill her?

I rubbed my eyes, willing the flashes of memories to fucking leave. The door opened and I focused on a dressed and showered Wynter. That girl could even make baggy jeans and a black hoodie look sexy.

"Hey, you're awake."

"Yeah. Sorry for bailing on you last night." I gathered her in my arms and gave her a quick peck. "I need to brush my teeth before I really kiss you."

Wynter smiled. "The bathroom is all yours. I even saved some hot water so you could shower."

"You're the best." I turned to the duffle bag that we'd packed and rifled through it until I found a pair of clean jeans and long-sleeved T-shirt. Hesitating, I glanced at Wynter who was busy picking up her clothes off the floor from last night. She seemed preoccupied, and I suspected it was due to the nature of our trip. "Hey, beautiful?"

"Yeah?" Her lips tipped up in a smile.

I cleared my throat. "I know we were going to look for the journal. At this point, I'm not even sure I want to know what he might have said. This is a lot. Are you okay if we leave earlier than planned?"

Wynter approached me and placed her hand on my cheek. The warmth of her touch sent my cock into overdrive.

Her mouth closed and opened as if she were about to say something, but then she stopped. "Yeah. I think we should leave as soon as we're ready. It's been a bitch of a few days, and I want to get back to Whitmore. If you don't want to see Adam, you're welcome to stay with me. The girls are gone for the long weekend, and I'm sure they won't mind anyway."

I tossed my clothes onto the mattress and pulled her against me. "I love you. Thanks for the offer. After I spend some time with Brody, I'll probably take you up on that and sleep at your place. Hopefully Adam will be gone soon, and you can sneak back into my bed, but at some point, Brody is going to discover you."

Her body shook with her laugh. "Sorry, it makes me nervous just thinking about it."

I rubbed her back, soothing her the best I could. "I think Brody will be pretty open about who you are."

Wynter looked up at me, our gazes colliding. "I hope so. He sounds like a great kid. He and Janine are the same age, right?"

"Oh shit. I hadn't even thought about that, but yeah. Seventeen."

She rolled her eyes. "We probably shouldn't introduce them then. They might get along too well."

I chuckled. "He has a girlfriend. I think it would be okay." Eager to leave as soon as possible, I released Wynter and scooped up my clean clothes. "I'll make it quick."

"Okay. I'll find my sister and talk to her while you're getting cleaned up. She'll understand about us leaving earlier than planned."

I didn't miss the sadness in Wynter's expression, but I suspected that she was ready to leave, too. The shit with her mom had slapped her in the face the second she entered the house.

At around two that afternoon, I pulled into Wynter's driveway but left the car running. "Thanks for taking me home with you. I wouldn't have wanted to spend the day with anyone else." I leaned over and pressed my mouth to hers, denying myself the opportunity to throw her over my shoulder and march into her house, then to her bedroom, where I would ravish every beautiful inch of her.

"Will I see you later?"

"Let me see how it goes. If Adam is still in town, then definitely expect me. I feel a little bad for ducking out on Brody, so he might want to hang and play video games."

"Quinn, one day he'll be grown, and you'll have wished you'd had hung out more with him before he was working and married. Life changes too fast to ever take it for granted. I wished I'd done that with Ky, and I'm guessing you would have wanted more time with Bell." She kissed me before she let herself out of the car and grabbed the duffle bag from the back seat. She bent over, poking her head back in. "I'm assuming you have plenty of clothes at home?"

"Yeah, maybe just wash those with yours and I'll keep them here?" I flashed her a big grin, knowing what I'd just said to her.

Her eyes widened. "You want to keep some of your things here?"

"If you're cool with that, I would."

Wynter nodded enthusiastically. "I would love that." She patted the bag before she blew me a kiss and closed the door.

I watched her approach the house, then hopped out of my vehicle.

"Wait!" I jogged to her and kissed her. "Let me go in first. Vaughn isn't with you, and the house has been empty ..."

"I hadn't even thought about that." She used the key to unlock the door, then stepped aside as I went in and searched the house. If anything ever happened to her, I would never forgive myself. I'd already lost Bell. I couldn't stand the thought of losing Wynter too.

A few minutes later, I'd checked every room and closet. The coast was clear.

"It's good to go. I just needed to make sure."

"Thanks, babe." She pushed up on her tiptoes and kissed me. "Talk to you later."

She slipped inside, and I headed to the car. Backing out of the driveway, I was relieved to be back in town, even if that meant I had to see that sorry son of a bitch, Adam.

My phone buzzed from the center console, then the message was announced through my car system.

I love you. Wynter's name flashed on the screen. Warmth flowed through me as I pushed the button on my steering wheel to reply.

Love you too, beautiful. I'll call you later.

A growing sense of apprehension nagged at me as I drove home. Brody and I had texted a bit yesterday, then again this morning. He knew I was coming back early. Brody promised that he was fine, so I wasn't worried about him. Worst case scenario, he could take Adam in a fight. But old habits died hard. I'd spent so many years looking over my shoulder, I was tripping over leaving my brother alone with our piece of shit father. I tried to shrug it off, then pressed the accelerator a little harder.

Ten minutes later, I pulled into my driveway and parked in front of the garage.

My footsteps slapped against the sidewalk as I hurried to the front door, then let myself into the house. My gut twisted with the silence. Something was off.

"Brody!" I yelled. "I'm here."

The mansion was big enough that he might not have heard me, so I headed to the kitchen, searching the living and dining area as I passed them. Not seeing anyone, I picked up my pace and checked Adam's office, but it was locked.

With my heart in my throat, I ran to the other side of the house, to where mine and Brody's rooms were located. I hightailed it up the stairs and came to a screeching halt as I noticed no one was in Brody's room. I knocked, waiting to hear him respond.

"Brody!" I called out.

Nothing. I rushed to mine and turned the doorknob. It was locked. I pounded my fist on the door. "Brody! I'm home, let me in."

"Quinn?" Brody's voice shook as he answered me.

"Open up, bro."

The door cracked open, and I pushed through, only to once again stop in my tracks.

"What the fuck?"

Chapter 45

Quinn

Astonished wasn't even the word for the emotion that twisted inside me. I stood rooted to the floor, unable to move as my attention swept my room, then landed on Brody again. "What the hell is going on?"

He paced in front of me, grabbing the sides of his head. He hadn't looked at me yet, and I didn't like it one bit.

"What is it? Tell me?"

Brody slowly turned toward me, and rage tore through my body. His eye was black and his nostrils were crusted with blood.

"Don't worry, Adam looks worse," Brody said with a smug smirk on his lips, but the look on his face told me a different story.

"Like that makes me feel better. What the fuck happened? I've left you alone with him before and he didn't pull anything. I'm going to bury the motherfucker when I see his punk ass."

"He left. I figured since you had a lock on your room that it would be the safest place to wait for you. Otherwise, after I see him again, we'll be planning his funeral and you'll be bringing me fucking cookies in prison."

"Won't happen." I winced. "How did it start?" I walked over to

271

my desk and sat down, propping my elbows on my knees. A thick, heavy tension snaked between my shoulder blades, and I was ready to pounce if my bedroom door opened. Recalling that I hadn't locked it behind me, I fixed that situation.

Brody massaged his forehead and looked at the ceiling. "Q, you've been a good brother to me, and I appreciate it, but I need to know the truth."

The tiny hairs on the back of my neck stood on end. "Okay." I sounded calmer than my churning gut made me think I could.

"Dad said that you're responsible for Bell's death. You and Wynter."

"That motherfucker." I leaned back, my pissed-off gaze landing on my brother. "Tell me what he said." It was one thing for Adam to mess with my head, but another to screw with Brody's. He would pay for what he did to my brother.

"Dad said that Wynter, your new girlfriend, is Kyler's sister. *The* Kyler, the one who killed all those people at the high school, including our Bell."

"I'm aware who Wynter and Kyler are. Remember I asked if you would give someone a chance if a person in their family had killed people?"

Brody nodded, eyeing me. "Yeah, but you didn't say killed our sister. You fucking left that important detail out. And you're fucking her?" Brody's face turned beet red and he pinned me with a venomous glare.

I stood, slowly. "Asshole, you're about to cross a line with me, so I highly recommend that you simmer down and keep talking. Tell me what he said, then I'll fill you in about what's been happening. I've not told you because I didn't want to upset you until I knew what was going on myself. There are two versions—Adam's and then the truth."

Brody shot me a skeptical look and remained standing. "He said that you were fucking some chick in the janitor's closet instead of meeting Bell at the library like you two had agreed on. When I asked him how he knew that, he said you texted him and bragged about it before we found out about Bell."

I detected vulnerability in Brody's tone. Somewhere inside of himself, he was questioning what Adam had told him, which was a good thing. "First, I would never tell Adam about who I fucked. Plus, I had no idea there was a janitor's closet." I blew out a sigh. "Brody, I wasn't fucking anyone. Bell didn't show up at the library, so I went looking for her. If Bell and I had a test, we always met there and reviewed our notes together. It wasn't like her to skip out on study time. I waited for ten minutes and was on my way to the cafeteria to look for her when I heard gunshots. Adam's filling your head with bullshit just like he's been doing mine." I clenched my fingers into a ball, imagining I was driving them into Adam's nose.

"Why would he do that? He's our father. Dad has no reason to lie." His voice bounced, indicating his anxiety.

I barked out a laugh. "Have you met Adam? The guy that picked a fight with you while I was gone. The same bastard that beat my ass until I was fourteen and could hold my own? Why would you ever trust a man ..."

I held up my hand to stop myself. I had trusted Adam when he shoveled shit down my throat about Wynter, the last thing I could do was blame Brody for wanting to see the best in his father. I was guilty of the same, but those days were over. I sat down, not wanting to fight with my little brother. Enough of that had already happened in our house.

"I don't know why. Yet. When Wynter arrived at Whitmore, Adam pulled me aside and told me to ruin her. He handed me a file with the police report, background check, and other information on Wynter. I tried to verify the info, thinking he was lying to me, but it all matched up."

"Then you're fucking Wynter as a way to get revenge?"

When I heard it from his mouth, I felt like a fucking douchebag. "At first, but then I hired my own PI to dig into Wynter. Some of the truth was hidden and covered up by the police and the media, and it put her in a bad light. Wynter tried to stop Kyler."

"She tried to stop him?" Brody's tone softened and he sank onto the edge of my bed.

"There's a lot you don't know. When I have more information and can share it with you, I will. Wynter and I are working together to learn more. But yeah, I'm in love with her. I won't bring her here, though. I respect that you might not be willing to give her a chance after what her brother did."

Brody's eyes misted over. "Goddammit, I miss Bell every fucking day."

"Me too."

Brody focused on me. "Has it been hard looking into the shooting?" His shoulders tensed beneath the weight of his words.

"You have no idea." I pondered if I should tell Brody about my trip to Wynter's house and meeting Janine, but I decided to keep my mouth shut. All I'd told him was I was heading to Washington with some friends.

I rubbed my jaw. "Here's the deal. You'll be eighteen in a few months, and you can choose to live here or elsewhere. Go to college, play ball, and live on campus. Get the fuck out of here."

"I want to apply at Whitmore University. Coach reached out to me about playing there already."

"Is this a for sure deal?" I wanted Brody to have the best, but staying in the same town as Adam wasn't safe for him.

"No. Coach and I have only talked."

"Okay. Keep me posted and apply to other colleges out of state, ones where he can't get to you on a daily basis."

Brody's expression fell. "I only want to play for Whitmore."

"Bro, there are other colleges out there that are just as good as Whitmore. Plus, if I get on with the NFL, it won't matter where you play. You'll have eyes on you if you want to go pro."

"You'd do that for me?"

Why did Brody sound so shocked? Had I been that much of an

asshole to him over the years? We had certainly had our fights like most brothers I knew, but I loved him. God knows I'd fucked up a ton, but I protected him the best I could. "You're a hell of player, and yeah, I'll support you any way I can."

The corner of his mouth kicked up. "Maybe we'll play against each other in the pros like the Manning brothers."

"Who knows? But for now, leave Wynter alone and stay off Adam's radar. You're going to have to explain your face to your coach, too. We should come up with a game plan. Right now, we need Adam's money and a roof over our head, so we can't tell anyone what's happening."

Brody's eyes widened. "I hadn't thought about that. I was going to tell Coach the truth."

"You can't. If I'm drafted and you get a scholarship, I'll take care of anything else you need for college. Just hang on until then. We don't have much longer to get the hell out of here."

"All right."

"Give me your word, Brody. I know that means something to you."

Our gazes connected. "I swear that I won't throw Dad under the bus ... yet."

That was good enough for me.

Chapter 46

Wynter

I was a brat. After a week of having Ky's journal, I'd sworn a million times to tell Quinn and hadn't. It wasn't that I had anything to hide from him, but Ky was my brother and I needed to read all of what was inside before I shared it with Quinn. Oddly enough, as much as I hated Ky for what he did, I still wanted to protect the good parts of him. But his journal was anything but good. It was dark and tormented, and I suspected that I was seeing Ky's internal descent to hell.

I tugged the blankets up to my chin and snuggled farther into my bed. Quinn was gone at an away game for the weekend and so were the girls, which gave me the house to myself and time to process before I had to face another human being. I opened Ky's book of secrets and located where I left off. There weren't many more entries and I hoped to finish reading over the next two days and sift through my emotions before I told Quinn what I had discovered. My stomach rolled. I hoped like hell Quinn would understand, but it was a sensitive topic for both of us, and I needed to give him room to be pissed.

I fluffed my pillows behind my head and began to read.

.   .   .

September 20th, 2018

Today fucking sucked. Lance and his asshole jock friends ganged up on me today, but instead of using towels to leave marks, they used their fists. Who knew looking at some guy's junk would land me in a bad situation over and over? Hell, I'd seen the entire team's dicks at some point. We showered and changed in front of each other like it was no big deal. I honestly thought that Lance would move on to someone else because that's how he does, but he's hyper-focused on me. My guess is that he's gay and in the closet, too, but that's not my fucking problem.

I finally went to the school counselor, Myra Smith. I showed her the bruises, but she dismissed the bullying as guys accidently getting too rough. How the hell could she dismiss it as horseplay when my entire side was purple? It was a fucking miracle I didn't have a cracked rib, but maybe that would have gotten her attention.

An idea just occurred to me. Maybe she's fucking Lance's father and is protecting Lance. That's some bullshit. All the parents say, talk, tell us what's happening so we can protect you. Fuck that, I'm trying but no one is doing shit.

It was blind luck that I met Dr. Metcalf while working at the coffee shop. He came in for a chai tea and noticed that I was limping. I was trying to hide it, but he spotted it. Shit, he was the first adult to call me over and ask if I was okay. Not even Mom and Dad noticed, but it was easy to hide from them. They thought my injuries were from soccer. Plus, after school and work, I almost immediately went to my bedroom with an excuse to do my homework. The only pitstops I made were to the kitchen and bathroom.

Dr. Metcalf began visiting the coffee shop daily, checking in on me. It's been a few months now that I've talked to him, but I was afraid to put it on paper. I didn't want to jinx it. He's really been helping me, and I think things are looking up. He's given me some good tools to use against Lance and the fuckers who can't keep their hands off me. The bag of my shit I put in Lance's locker on a Friday after practice had plenty of time to stink up the school hallways over the weekend. Since I worked in the office during fifth period, finding Lance's locker combo had been easy.

What's even funnier? Dr. Metcalf gave me the idea. Kind of hilarious that a psychiatrist is telling me to get revenge, but he said enough was enough. It was time to take things into my own hands, and the only way to get a bully's attention was to bully them right back.

What the hell? Ky had gone to Mrs. Smith, and she hadn't done a fucking thing? *Fuck.* It took me a minute to put the pieces together. Mrs. Smith was one of the people who had died that day.

Lance's family had a ton of money, so maybe Mrs. Smith had sucked up to them, but that was complete negligence on her part.

A white-hot fury shot through me, sending my pulse into overdrive. I took a picture of Ky's journal entry with my phone to investigate farther. Maybe Quinn could ask his PI to help, too. If so, I would need to turn over the journal, so I wanted to keep proof of the incriminating evidence on my cell.

Once I calmed down a little, I grabbed my phone and Googled Dr. Metcalf in Washington. His face popped up immediately. I glared at his image, his beady brown eyes peering at me through round glasses. His smile was friendly enough, but something about him didn't sit right with me. I noted the date of the journal entry. It was five months before the shooting. I set my cell down, my mind spinning out.

Was Dr. Metcalf a good guy? From what Ky had said, he seemed to care about him. But who recommend putting shit in a locker? I chuckled, cheering Ky on for standing up for himself. I would have done much worse to Lance and his fucking goons if I'd known. Hell, Ky and I would have both been expelled from school for putting those assholes in their place ... but at least people would still be alive.

I focused on Ky's entries again.

September 24th, 2018

It was an okay day. Lance was absent from school, which was a relief. The other guys left me alone in the locker room today, so my bruises had an extra day to heal.

I called in sick to work, but I felt fine. No one knows, but I met Dr. Metcalf at his office. He said he wanted to work with me where we could talk more openly and not be spotted at the coffee shop. It made sense, plus he's not charging me for sessions. At least I'm getting some help, right? He's a great guy. The doctor could have asked Mom and Dad for money, but he's never told them he's helping me. I guess he thought I might be a good pro bono case. I hear lawyers, doctors, and psychiatrists take on cases for free sometimes.

But I have huge news! Even though Dr. Metcalf suspected, I confessed that I was gay. I guess the safety of an office made all the difference because I told him the rest of the shit that Lance and his friends had been doing to me all year. I even told him I'd tried to go to the school counselor, but that my plea for help had fallen on deaf ears.

Dr. Metcalf was furious and scribbled Mrs. Smith's name down. It felt good that he was angry and wanted to stand up for me. He said I reminded him of himself at that age.

I've been talking to him for a few months now, and this was the best I'd felt about opening up. For a change, I have a bit of hope.

I flipped the page to the next entry that was written a few days later.

September 30th, 2018

It finally happened. I'm no longer a virgin. I can't wait to tell Bell, but she has to swear she won't tell a soul.

I frowned, searching on the following page for a name, but he'd written another poem. A love poem. Tears welled in my eyes. I would have cherished that moment with Ky. Good for him! My excitement took a quick turn as I read the next entry a few days later.

. . .

October 5th, 2018

Dr. Metcalf looked hot as fuck on his knees sucking my cock. I came in record time. It was incredible. He reminded me not to tell anyone about our relationship, and I promised I wouldn't, but I really want to talk to Bell. She's the most nonjudgmental person I know, and I think she'd be excited for me. Yeah, Dr. Metcalf is older, but it's nice to be seen and heard. Plus, he's an expert in bed. I can't wait until he thinks I'm ready for him to bend me over his desk and fuck me. I'm terrified and eager to take our relationship to the next step. I've never been so happy before.

I slammed my eyes closed, tears silently streaming down my face. Dr. Metcalf took advantage of Ky, played him. At the time this was all written, Ky was sixteen. A minor. A scared, underaged kid. That sick son of a bitch played Ky like a fucking fiddle. Even though it made me ill, I had to read on. I had to find enough evidence to ruin that fucker's career.

October 10th, 2018

I think I upset Dr. Metcalf today. I asked if I could call him by his first name, Richard, and he snorted, reminding me that we were patient and client, not friends. That was news to me since we've been fucking each other for a few weeks now. Maybe he'd just had a bad day, but him scrambling backward on me messed with my head. What if he left me? He's my confidant and the only person in the entire world I feel safe with. I'm going to puke just thinking about it.

I turned the page, devouring the words as fast as I could.

. . .

October 12th, 2018

Well, I did it. I stood up to Lance and the second he tried to come at me, I punched the fucker in the face. I wouldn't have ever had the guts to do it on my own, but Dr. Metcalf has helped me so much. I can't wait to tell the good Dr. how much progress I've made with his help. Hopefully, he'll be proud of me and stop treating me like someone he hardly knows. It's been three days since he objected to being called Richard and he's been giving me the cold shoulder. Normally he messages me at night from a burner phone, but I haven't heard shit from him. Tonight, I'll message him with the good news.

I scowled. Ky was trying to please the *good* doctor. My jaw clenched so hard, pain ricocheted through my head.

October 14th, 2018

Dr. Metcalf rewarded me for standing up to Lance. Goddamn that man can do wicked things with his tongue and mouth. If this is how I'm rewarded, then I'll have to make sure I keep him happy. I won't tell him, but I think I'm in love. I really need to talk to Bell about this.

Speaking of Bell, she's been super sad the last week, but she won't tell me what's happening. I know her father is a piece of shit because she told me how Adam beat Quinn. She was terrified that he would turn on Brody someday. I have to find a way to help her. She's my best friend, and I want to protect her.

Hope flickered to life inside me. Maybe he would say what happened for him to turn on Bell. They were so close. Closer than Ky and I had been.

October 22nd, 2018

Lance is a god damn piece of shit. He released a video of me on my knees sucking someone's cock. It was all cartoon form, but my name was plastered all over it. He made me a target to every person that saw it. Maybe being gay is more acceptable these days, but the hate outweighs the acceptance. Now, my hate is outweighing my need to do the right thing. Lance isn't playing fair, so it's time that I stoop to his level and make him pay. Dr. Metcalf has had some good ideas, and whenever I make a step in the right direction, Dr. Metcalf hangs out with me. I think I'm addicted to him. His praise or disappointment sends me on a crazy roller-coaster ride, and all I want is to make him proud of me. I can't wait to see what he thinks I should do about Lance this time.

I had to take a break. Reading Ky's words were destroying me all over again. If I'd known! God if I'd only known, I could have done something—convinced him that Dr. Metcalf was a sick fuck that was apparently super good with manipulative control and mind suggestions. I wondered how many Ky had carried out when they hadn't been his idea to begin with.

"Dammit." I scooped up the journal again, craving the truth as much as Ky had craved Dr. Metcalf.

Chapter 47

Wynter

November 1st, 2018

Holy shit! Dr. Metcalf brought his business partner into my session, and what a mind-blowing session it was! So much cock, I wasn't sure what to do with it. Dr. Metcalf has opened a whole new world to me. Not only have we come up with a plan to retaliate against Lance, but the doctor has upped the rewards for my good behavior. Hell, I never thought I would get laid, much less with two men at a time. What they didn't know was that I recorded the whole thing. I had to download it to my backup laptop so it wouldn't ever be found, but I'm going to watch it over and over. Just thinking about today makes my dick hard as a rock.

Tomorrow, Dr. Metcalf said that he wants to talk to me. I have no idea about what, but the longer I work with him, the better I feel. Anger and rage are a powerful tool and he's promised to help me redirect my emotions and take control of my life. I'm fucking ready to take the world by storm.

November 2nd, 2018

Sometimes I feel like Dr. Metcalf's monkey. If I don't like his suggestions of how to stand up to Lance, he berates me ... tells me I'm useless, a sorry excuse for a man, and a fucking pussy, then gives me the cold shoulder for days. It fucks me up, and in a week, I come crawling back with evidence that I've done what he's told me to, begging for him to love me again. I just thought a razor blade in Lance's jock strap was a bit extreme. Yet I do exactly what I'm told. I'm his puppet. Just a slave to Dr. Metcalf's suggestions, but I want his approval and the sex even more. I'm in way too deep, and I can't seem to stop spinning.

I have to talk to Bell no matter what, but every time I open my mouth, no words come out.

Bell is still moody as hell, so it's probably not best to talk to her yet anyway. I think she's stressed over midterms. It stresses everyone out. I'll call her and try to make her laugh. It might do me some good too.

November 13th, 2018

I'm not writing as much these days. Between school, work, and Dr. Metcalf, my schedule is full. Being with Dr. Metcalf consumes me. The sex with him and Dr. Craig is off the charts, and I've continued to record our secret sessions. If he knew, he'd fucking kill me, but I need to always have him with me. I'm his dirty little puppet and he's my dirty little secret, but by the time I realized he was filling my head with shit, it was too late. I don't think I could get free of him even if I wanted to.

December 18th, 2018

My mind is getting darker, and Dr. Metcalf is fucking toxic. How do I break free from the only man who's loved me like he has? I know what he's telling me to do is wrong, but I can't stop. Thankfully, he gave me a meditation to listen to every night when I go to sleep. His voice is so soothing, and I'm sleeping my ass off. But my moods are

*fucked, and the horrible shit going through my head would send me to
hell if anyone knew.*

December 26th, 2018

*Bell called me last night and she needs to see me. She sounds as
bad as I fucking feel. The more time I've spent with Dr. Metcalf, the
more I've pulled away from Bell. She thinks I'm mad at her. She has no
idea that I'm trying to protect her from the goddamn devil.*

December 30th, 2018

*It's almost 2019 and after meeting Bell, I was afraid to put this on
paper in case anyone ever found it. Bell told me what's wrong.*

*Wynter is the only person who knows about my hiding place, but
she doesn't realize the hole in the wall is bigger. My second laptop is
hidden there too. Now, Bell's secrets are hidden with mine.*

I sat up in my bed and stared at the entry. If I turned the page, would
I finally learn what happened? If Ky was willing to hide Bell's secrets,
then he still cared about her. I pulled my knees to my chest, ready to
continue. Or I thought I was. Dr. Metcalf was already on my shit list
and so was his business partner. What they did was despicable. But
what if it was all in Ky's head and these pages were his fantasies
about this psychiatrist? Fuck, I needed that laptop, but how? I had a
driver's license, but I always drove mom's Sentra when I was living at
home. Gabby had left her car for me in case I needed anything, but a
three-hour drive without her permission wasn't cool. And an Uber
would be way too expensive. It was time I asked for Gabby's help.

I grabbed my phone and texted her even though I knew she was
getting ready for the game. Without giving her all of the details, I told
her I needed to take a trip to Washington on an urgent matter and
would replace the gas if she was comfortable with me taking her car.

To my surprise, she messaged almost immediately.

Yes! I have full coverage insurance, but don't crash my baby, please. Just park her at the parking lot where our buses will unload. I have a key with me. Love ya, bitch. Fill me in when I get there.

A cry of relief filled my room. Thank God we were close friends. I would have to find some way to pay her back for putting up with me. I returned to the journal, ready to finish Ky's story before I made the trip home.

January 3rd, 2019

I feel sick all the time, unable to break free from the evil Dr. Metcalf. Last night, he introduced me to another of his clients, then charged him to have sex with me. The man I thought loved me fucking sold me for sex. He said that if I didn't cooperate, he would report me as psychotic and have me locked away in a mental institution for the rest of my life. I puked on his fucking shoes, then took my clothes off for his client. My body was used and abused, ripping out my heart in the process. Betrayal doesn't even begin to describe how I felt.

January 11th, 2019

I've been sold eight times now, and I can't seem to claw my way out of hell. If I report Dr. Metcalf to the cops, he'll have me institutionalized. I was so fucking stupid to think he ever loved me. He's been my master, pulling the strings and dictating every evil thing I've done. I'm going to hell, but it would be better than what I'm living in now. Soon. Soon I will find a way out of this. I have to for Bell. She needs me.

January 25th, 2019

This will be my last entry. The last few will be on my laptop in case anyone gives a shit. It's almost over, and if there's peace on the other side, I doubt I'll find it there either.

Fuck off, world. Fuck off, Mom and Dad, for not seeing signs that were under your fucking nose. Fuck off, Mrs. Smith, for not listening to me. Fuck off, Dr. Metcalf, Dr. Craig, and all the men you sold me to. Fuck off, Lance and all your bastard followers, for beating me nearly every day for almost six months. Fuck off, world.

There are only three people I love and care about. Bell, Janine, and Wynter. My sister knew something was wrong, she begged me to talk to her, and even tattled to dear ol' Mom and Dad. I treated Wyn like shit, but I love that girl so much.

Bell, we've got this.

I turned the page, but it was blank, as were the last fifteen or twenty pages.

"Dammit!" I tossed off the covers, gathered my phone and the journal, and stuffed them into my purse. In half an hour I was showered, had packed an overnight bag, and was behind the wheel of Gabby's Lexus Coupe. Rummaging through my purse, I located my cell and texted Quinn. He probably wouldn't see the message until after the game, but that was okay. I wanted him to focus on his career. I could take care of myself. I'd done it for years.

Kick their ass today, baby. I love you with all my heart. I'm off to see Janine, but I'll be back by the time you get home from your trip. Tell Kane good luck for me, too.

My hands shook as I started the engine, then tested the touchiness of the accelerator and brake. I squared my shoulders, then turned the car toward Washington.

Chapter 48

Wynter

I slowed Gabby's car, then pulled into the driveway behind Mom's silver Sentra. Janine had mentioned in an earlier text message that she would be out grocery shopping, which allowed me to see if Mom was drinking while no one was around. Plus, Mom wasn't expecting me.

My sister had given me updates over the last few weeks and swore Mom was doing great, but I was about to find out for myself.

If learning about Ky's abuse and how Dr. Metcalf had fed him lies and talked Ky into getting revenge on Lance wasn't bad enough, I had to sneak around to see if my mother was lying about staying sober too.

I hopped out of the car and ran up the steps to the front door. Instead of knocking, I used my key to let myself in. To my surprise, the house was clean, and the heavenly smell of cookies filled the air.

"Hello!" The last thing I wanted was to scare someone and get hit over the head with a cast iron skillet.

Mom hurried out of the kitchen, wiping her hands on an apron covered in apples. Maybe cooking was her new therapy. "Wynter?"

Her voice was full of surprise. "What are you doing here? Are you okay?"

She approached me slowly, then gave me a hug. I discreetly sniffed her breath and searched for any sign that she'd been drinking. I found none.

"You're just in time for fresh-baked chocolate chip and macadamia nut cookies. I got a part-time job baking for a local shop. They let me cook at home and inspect the kitchen once a week to make sure I'm keeping a clean environment." She grinned at me.

"Wow, that's amazing. You make the best muffins and cookies." I swallowed, searching the house for my sister. "Is Janine still running errands and grocery shopping?"

"Yeah, for another four hours. She has hockey practice after school."

"What? Hockey? That's amazing!" I frowned. "I wonder why she hadn't told me." With all the chaos, I realized we hadn't chatted as much and that was my fault.

"This is her first practice. She's just trying it out. You know how she's always been good on the ice."

"Yeah. I'm glad that after Ky ... after the shooting I was able to keep her skating lessons going. She has a lot of potential."

Mom's lips pursed. "I'm really curious how you managed to pay the bills, Wynter, but something tells me that I probably don't want to know."

I nodded. "What you don't know can't hurt you." I looked away, not wanting to get too cozy with her. "Um, I need to get in Ky's room."

Mom's brows dipped low. "You found something when you and Quinn were here, didn't you?"

My chin trembled as tears pricked my eyes. "Maybe, but I need into his room again. Once I figure everything out, I'll let you know. Otherwise, as far as Janine is concerned, I'm visiting while Quinn is gone for the weekend. He has a football game in Arizona."

Mom's gaze grew glassy with moisture. "Let me send you up with some cookies and milk at least. I'm sure you're hungry."

The only reason I agreed to the sugar was because I knew I might need something to stuff in my face and muffle my cries if I found anything more Ky wrote. I'd had to distract myself on the way up in order not to drive over to Dr. Metcalf's office and beat him until his life was hanging by a thread. But unlike Ky, I was going to be a hell of a lot sneakier. There was a list of names in my head that would meet my darkness soon enough. It had been five years since the shooting, and revenge was a dish best served cold.

Mom returned with a plate full of cookies and a glass of milk. My pulse stuttered against my wrist. I couldn't remember the last time she'd baked, but it warmed my heart.

"Thanks," I muttered, then made a mad dash up the stairs and to Ky's room. I flipped on the light, then set my overnight bag on his bed and my snacks on his desk. Unzipping the duffle, I pulled out my coat and hat before I opened the window to air out the musty smell. This time, I was prepared.

I grabbed the screwdriver I'd found in the tool drawer at my house in Oregon and made my way to the closet with my phone in my hand. Even though Ky's closet had an overhead light, it was still too dim for me to see everywhere I needed to.

Staring at the corner where I'd removed the thin journal from the gap in the wall, I slipped the flathead in and gently attempted to pry a panel away. It took me a few minutes to find the right spot, but then a portion of the paneling popped open. Dust flew in my face, and I coughed as I swatted it away, trying to breathe.

I peered into the hole, my throat closing up. There it was, a black laptop and power cord. I used the light on my phone to make sure no rats had made a home in the wall before I reached in and pulled it out. From what I could tell, the cord was still in good shape. No critters had shown up unexpectedly and ate wires they shouldn't.

Tripping over a pair of Ky's shoes, I cursed under my breath as I made my way to his desk. I tossed my phone down and plugged the laptop into the outlet, praying it would power up. It had been a long fucking time since it had been used. Grabbing a cookie, I took a nibble and waited. I blew out a sigh of relief as it fired right up and displayed a desktop image with Ky and Bell.

It took me another hour to sift through the folders and files until I finally located what I hoped were additional journal entries.

I pushed play on the video and turned the volume up enough to hear what was being said, but not loud enough for Mom to overhear if she were upstairs.

Ky's voice reached me and I hit the pause button, overcome with too many emotions to process. Anger was front and center, but I hadn't allowed myself to really miss him. Hearing him speak again made the agony worse. I gave myself permission to cry. I couldn't carry the pain around any longer, it affected everything I touched, including Quinn.

My finger hovered over the keypad until I pushed play. Seconds later, my mouth gaped, and a blob of the cookie fell onto the floor. "Eww." I located a random tissue from my coat pocket and wiped it up.

Ky continued to talk but so did Dr. Metcalf. The camera seemed like it was on Ky's phone from the corner of the room.

"No!" Ky said.

"But you have to, Ky. What's been done to you is horrible, and Lance and his friends deserve to be treated worse than what they've done to you, be put in their places. Or are you such a despicable excuse for a human being that you won't stand up for yourself?"

Silence, then Dr. Metcalf strolled around his desk and produced a key. Ky watched as Dr. Metcalf walked to a tall cabinet and unlocked it. "You're ready, Ky. Don't let fear stand in your way. You're taking the world back on your terms. Those people don't deserve to get away with all the torture and physical abuse they've doled out to you. They're evil, Ky. Don't you understand?"

"Yeah." Ky's shoulders relaxed as if what Dr. Metcalf said made perfect sense to him.

"Do you know what you do to evil?"

Ky nodded. "Destroy it."

What the fuck? Ky's voice sounded different, detached and almost monotone, but he'd never been a violent guy. That's part of what had baffled me about the shooting.

Dr. Metcalf reached into the cabinet and produced a big gun and a box of ammo. "This is an automatic. You'll be able to destroy the evil, then protect yourself while you run. Are you clear on the plan?"

"You motherfucker," I spat. "The shooting wasn't even Ky's idea?"

The video stopped and as shocked shitless as I was, I had to keep watching. I could process and rewatch later.

The next one was dated February 13th, a day before the shooting. It was most likely the final entry. I closed my eyes, searching for the courage to hear what Ky couldn't tell me or anyone else.

I waited as the video cued up, then Ky's face filled the screen. I reached out to touch him, then pulled my hand away.

"I don't know if anyone will ever find this, but there's evidence in my journal and these videos that will hopefully put Dr. Metcalf in prison for life. I have to take advantage of the moments of clarity where I feel like myself and can think clearly, but those minutes are farther and farther apart. It's as if I'm two different people, trying to fight against what my brain is ordering me to do." Ky grabbed his head and winced. "I'm running out of time." He leaned forward.

"I finally confided in Bell about what Dr. Metcalf was doing. She said that we could both escape the hell we were living in, and we made a suicide pact for tomorrow, February 14th. If I'm going to die, then at least Bell and I will be together in the afterlife." Ky swallowed and the dark shadows beneath his eyes caught my attention. "A few days ago, Bell told me why she'd been so sad ..."

The world tilted on its axis as Ky's words bombarded me in slow motion. Seconds later, I puked all over the floor. My entire body shook as I clutched my stomach. There was no way I'd heard Ky right. No goddamn way. Cries escaped me as the truth sank in.

The truth had been so much worse than I could have ever imagined. So. Much. Worse.

Chapter 49

Quinn

There was no better sight than my girlfriend waiting for me at Whitmore University as I hopped off the bus along with the rest of my team.

Wynter shivered in the cold wind.

"Hey, beautiful." I wrapped her in my arms and kissed her senseless. "I missed you."

"I missed you too. Congrats on another win."

"Hey, Wynter," Kane said, walking past us.

"Congrats!" She waved at him, smiling.

Something was off about that gorgeous smile, but I didn't want to pressure her. I'd only been home for a few minutes. "Did you have a nice time with Janine?" I asked, leading us to my car.

"It was a quick trip, but it was good to see her."

I unlocked the car and we climbed in. Firing up the engine, I blasted the heat before my girlfriend froze to death.

"Quinn?"

The fear in her tone scraped across my skin. "Yeah, beautiful?" I reached out and touched her cheek.

"Please don't be mad at me, but we need to talk." She visibly gulped, obviously nervous.

My leg bounced, and I held my breath ready for her to tell me what she was so stressed out about. No matter what came out of her mouth, I refused to let her go. "Are you leaving me?"

Her blue eyes widened. "No! No. But you might leave me."

I stared at her, wondering what would be bad enough to leave her over. Hell, I knew her darkest secrets, and she knew mine. We'd climbed into hell and somehow found a light in each other.

"Did you mess around on me?"

"No. No, Quinn, I would never. But I lied to you when we were in Washington over Thanksgiving. I found Ky's journal, and I wanted ... *needed* to read it before I told you. I'm so sorry," she blurted.

God, this woman was even more beautiful than when I left a few days ago. "I know."

If the car door hadn't been closed, Wynter would have fallen to the ground. "What?"

"You were gone when I woke up to take a piss. I saw a light underneath Kyler's door, and I quietly peeked in. I saw you in the corner of the closet using your phone light. I knew you'd found it then, but I wanted to give you time to find out if there were any answers." I swallowed hard, fear grabbing my chest. "I also needed time to prepare to learn the truth. All these years I made up shit in my head about what happened, and what if I was wrong? How would I deal with that shit? I figured by the time you read it, if there was anything important you would let me know. I gave both of us the space we needed. Not to mention, if it were Bell's journal, I wouldn't tell anyone until I'd read it. She was *my* sister, and I would protect her last thoughts no matter what."

"Oh my God!" Her cry filled the car as she crawled over the console and onto my lap. "I'm so sorry, Quinn. It killed me, but I had to understand what happened with him."

I kissed her, wrapping my arms around her. My cock strained

against my jeans as she straddled me, stirring my need to connect with her on every level.

"I would have done the same, Wynter. Don't feel bad, beautiful."

She nuzzled my neck, her tears kissing my skin.

"That's why you needed to go home yesterday, isn't it?" I rubbed her back, trying to calm her.

She nodded. "I finished the journal, but it left me hanging. Ky mentioned in the last entry there was a laptop in the wall. I went back for it." She straightened, her eyes rimmed with red.

My fucking nerves were all over the place, but I had to know what she learned.

"Wynter," I whispered, "did you find out the truth? Do you know why he turned on Bell?"

Wynter covered her face, full-on crying again, but she managed a nod.

"He didn't kill her like we thought." Her voice cracked, her agony tugging at my heart.

"What?"

"Ky didn't kill Bell like we thought. It was a suicide pact, Quinn."

I shook my head, refusing to believe that my twin would take her own life. How would I not have known how devastated she was. For a moment, I understood how Wynter felt about Ky.

"When you're ready, I have the journal and laptop. Ky left videos. I can share with you what I know, but it will make more sense if you see it yourself."

A hunger for the truth shot through me. No matter how much it hurt, I had to learn what happened. I had to read Ky's words and watch the videos.

"Are we going to your place?" I asked. "Adam is still home, so my house isn't safe."

"Okay. I know the girls will be there, but we can keep the volume down while we watch Ky."

Fear ripped through me, but I'd waited five years to know the circumstances of why Bell left me. I sure as hell wouldn't stop now.

"Let's go."

Wynter crawled off my lap and as soon as we were buckled up, I pulled out of the university's parking lot.

The moment we arrived at her place, we bolted up the stairs to her bedroom and locked the door. I'm sure the girls thought I was about to fuck Wynter's brains out, but that would have to wait.

It took me less than an hour to catch up on the journal entries in the black notebook. To read Ky's words had me shifting in my seat, uncomfortable with the horror that was on the pages. I wasn't sure how Wynter hadn't gone after Dr. Metcalf when she visited Washington yesterday, but she hadn't. She was a better person than I was. What had fucked with me was that Dr. Metcalf seemed to have total control over Kyler. It was as if Dr. Metcalf had the entire thing planned. The bastard spotted Kyler's vulnerabilities and groomed him.

"Are you ready?" When I nodded, Wynter stood next to the desk and pushed play.

My leg bounced, waiting for the video to start. I sat in silence and watched as Dr. Metcalf handed Ky the gun and ammo that had been used in the school shooting according to the police report. I'm not sure where it had been stashed on campus for Ky to pick up, but I had a feeling Dr. Metcalf had figured all that out. I wondered if he felt like God as he witnessed his agenda unfold, taking innocent lives as he manipulated Ky to carry out his evil plan. It made me fucking sick. What still bothered me was that, other than the suicide pact, I still had no idea why Bell had decided to end her life with Ky's.

Ky's face came into focus, his voice filling Wynter's room. I grabbed her hand. If I'd seen Bell on a video again, it would fucking wreck me. I knew Wynter well enough now to realize she was just better at hiding it than I ever would be.

"I don't know if anyone will ever find this, but there's evidence in my journal and these videos that will hopefully put Dr. Metcalf in prison for life. I have to take advantage of the moments of clarity where I feel like myself and can think clearly, but those minutes are farther and farther apart. It's as if I'm two different people, trying to fight against what my brain is telling me to do." Ky grabbed his head and winced. "I'm running out of time." He leaned forward.

"I finally confided in Bell about what Dr. Metcalf was doing to me. She said that we could both escape the hell we were living in, and we made a suicide pact for tomorrow, February 14th. If I'm going to die, then at least Bell and I will be together in the afterlife." Ky swallowed. "A few days ago, Bell told me why she'd been so sad ..."

I stopped breathing. My mind had just played a dirty trick on me. There was no way I heard Kyler correctly. "What?" Dumbfounded, I looked at my girlfriend, who was chewing on her thumbnail. I backed up the video, Wynter's attention never leaving me as I replayed the clip a few more times. Ky's voice reached my ears again, but instead of turning it off, I let it finish playing.

"Bell had a doctor's appointment and learned that she was four months pregnant and too far along for the abortion pill. I wish it had been mine because it would have given me something to live for, but Bell and I never slept together. She had only been with one person. When I asked her who the father was, she sobbed uncontrollably, then finally uttered his name. Adam. Her father had been molesting her for years, and the sick son of a bitch got her pregnant. Bell can't stand to carry the baby to term, nor will Adam leave her alone. This is the only way for us to both break free."

Ky's image faded from the screen as the video ended.

My fists clenched and unclenched as I stared at the laptop, unmoving. In a split second, my switch flipped. Hatred ripped through me stronger than I'd ever experienced it before. I shot out of the chair, knocking it over.

"That goddamn son of a bitch!" I roared.

"Quinn." Wynter stepped away, fear written all over her face.

I stormed out of her room, nearly tearing the door off its hinges before I ran down the stairs.

"Quinn! Stop! Please."

Somehow, I had enough clarity to slow down and look at her. "I love you but stay away until this is over." I ran out of the house and to my car, Wynter screaming at me.

A sense of peace wrapped its arms around me as I started the car and peeled out of the driveway. Today, justice would finally be served.

Chapter 50

Wynter

G abby and Everlee flew out of the kitchen, wide-eyed at the commotion.

"What the hell is going on?" Everlee asked.

"Call Kane. Someone call Kane Cooper and tell him to get to Quinn's house now!" I ran back upstairs, trusting that one of the girls knew how to reach Kane. I had to call the cops and stop Quinn from making the biggest mistake of his life, but I'd left my phone in my room when I raced out, trying to stop him.

My legs shook so hard, I stumbled up the steps and into my bedroom. It took me a minute to find my cell in my handbag. I tapped out 9-1-1, my voice shaking as I provided Quinn's address. Hopefully it wouldn't be too late. When I hung up, all three of the girls were standing in my doorway, looking scared.

"Did someone talk to Kane?" I grabbed my purse. "I need a ride to Quinn's. Please."

"Kane is on his way to Quinn's, but he wants you to call him. Here's my cell." Gabby pulled up his number, then gave her cell to me.

"And we're all going with you," Everlee said.

"You can fill us in on the way," Leighton added, taking my hand.

I held up Gabby's phone to my ear as we rushed down the stairs and to Gabby's car.

"Gabby?" Kane asked.

"It's Wynter." I climbed into the front seat while Everlee and Leighton got into the back.

"What the hell is going on?"

"Kane, Quinn's going to do something horrible. We just found out that Adam was raping Bell. Kyler didn't kill her in the school shooting, they made a suicide pact because she was pregnant with her father's kid."

Audible gasps filled the car. Gabby shifted into reverse and burned rubber, realizing how screwed up the situation was and that Quinn was in trouble.

"I'm afraid he's going to kill him, Kane. Please tell me you're close." I choked on a sob, hoping someone could get there fast enough to stop Quinn from ruining his life.

"I'm pulling up to his house now. If no one answers, I'll break a fucking window. I can't let my boy go down like that."

A small flicker of relief blasted through me. "I'm on my way. I called the cops, too. Be careful, Kane."

We hung up, and my leg bounced like crazy as Gabby sped to Quinn's place. Minutes later, I jumped out of the car before Gabby had even fully stopped. The front door was open and I rushed through it, stopping long enough to try and track where the noise was coming from. Adam's office.

Sirens reached my ears as I bolted down the hall, slowing the last few feet to creep up to the office door. I wasn't sure who was in control at the moment, but I finally heard Kane's calm voice.

"Don't do it, Q. Give me the gun." I peeked into the room. Quinn was straddling Adam, pointing the weapon at his father's head. Adam was whiter than a ghost and frozen in terror. Served the motherfucker right.

Somehow having enough sense to not make a sudden move, I slowly joined Kane and Quinn.

"Quinn. I'm here. Baby, don't do it. The cops are on the way. Put the gun down."

Quinn's tear-stained cheeks were red and his eyes puffy.

"Babe, I need to tell you something else. While you were gone this weekend, I also gathered the evidence on Adam's computer that we had, then turned it over to the police. The police will arrest him as soon as they get here." I glanced at Kane. "For pedophilia. As soon as we can get the evidence to prove that Bell was pregnant with his kid, he'll be in prison for a long time. You and Brody are finally free."

Quinn stared at me, but I wasn't sure if he was comprehending what I was saying. His grip loosened on the firearm, and Kane grabbed Quinn's arm, aiming the barrel toward the celling before he wrestled it away from him.

Heavy footsteps approached, and Kane shoulder-checked Quinn, knocking him off Adam and onto the floor. Kane used his shirt to wipe the fingerprints from the gun, then stepped on Adam's chest and wrapped his hand around the weapon. Even though Adam could fight and rat Kane out in court, he was about to be a convicted felon, which meant his word didn't mean shit. Plus, there were three witnesses against one.

Shaking so hard that I could no longer stand, I sank to the floor and crawled over to Quinn.

"Let me do the talking," Kane said quietly before Adam's office was filled with the police.

I kissed Quinn's cheek. "Baby, are you okay?"

Quinn looked at me and wrapped his arm around my waist. "Thanks to you and Kane, I think I will be." He planted a kiss on my forehead, then whispered, "Thank you."

Chapter 51

Quinn

Oddly enough, I received a call from Sutton as the police were slapping handcuffs on Adam and arresting him. I updated her as quickly as I could. Sutton gasped when I told her about Bell's pregnancy, and she said she would find out if there was a way to get a DNA sample to prove Adam was the father. I wanted as much proof as possible to put the sorry bastard behind bars for a long-ass time.

The police confiscated Adam's laptop and searched the house, leaving it a fucking mess. By then, Gabby had called Brie, Kane's fiancée, and she'd joined us at my place.

The cops questioned Lena, who had almost slept through the entire thing. With her room on the other end of the mansion and away from ours, she was pretty much clueless about what happened since she wore earplugs. When they asked about Adam raping Bell, she nearly collapsed on the floor in tears, completely stunned.

It was almost one in the morning when the cops escorted Adam out of the house and into the back of a squad car. The police had grilled us hard about how Wynter learned about Bell, and she explained the videos to them. I was so fucking proud of her that I couldn't see straight. She was my hero. I just wish I could have been Bell's hero, too.

The rest of that evening was a blur. Brody came home from his friend's to a huge mess, and Wynter helped me fill him in on Ky's journal and the laptop. Wynter promised the police she would turn in the evidence against Dr. Metcalf the next day. I was guessing that we would make backups of the videos and take pics of the important journal entries in case they suddenly went missing. After the cops and media had covered up the first interview where Wynter went into depth about asking people to help Ky, I wasn't taking any more chances.

"Let's get the living room and kitchen cleaned up enough to have some food and a drink," Leighton said, glancing around. "Quinn, it's late, so how do you feel about having company for the night? I'm not sure leaving you and Brody alone is a good idea."

"I wouldn't leave him anyway," Wynter chimed in.

"Yeah, but as the dust settles, you're both going to need some friends to talk to," Brie said. "I've been there. What you learned over the last few days will sneak up and bitch-slap you into next month."

Wynter tilted her head, staring at Brie. I knew Brie spoke from experience because Kane had confided in me. Maybe one day the two girls could speak openly. Brie would probably make a great friend for Wynter.

As mentally and physically exhausted as I was, my mind still ran rampant. Wynter had uncovered the truth about Ky and why the shooting had happened. It would be interesting to see how the evidence played out against Dr. Metcalf and his business partner. Hell would be too good for them in my opinion. I suspected that, since Dr. Metcalf molested Ky and brainwashed him, he would find another kid to victimize if he hadn't already. The son of a bitch had to be stopped.

The girls took a shell-shocked Brody with them while they

cleaned up the kitchen and located some frozen pizzas. It would give him something else to think about surrounded by several gorgeous ladies. Gabby made drinks for everyone, too.

Kane sat next to me on the couch. "The house looks like it does after a party." He cracked a smile. "I won't ask if you're okay because I know better." He flexed his fingers, then tossed an imaginary football in the air. When Kane was stressed, he ran football plays in his head.

"I'm fucked up, man." I scrubbed my hands over my face, the girls' voices trickling in from the kitchen. I took a drink of my rum and Coke, hoping it would knock the edge off. "Adam knew how to play me, too. He used my hatred for Ky and Wynter against me and set it all up. It just took me forever to figure out his angle."

"I get it. I hated Brie, too. It's that blind anger that ruins us until we can see reality. But you did, man. You and Wynter figured shit out together. It should help now that you know what happened with Bell. In Ky's mind, he was protecting her and himself."

"That's what the entire thing was about, too. Adam wanted me to get rid of Wynter so I wouldn't learn what was happening ... that he was hurting Bell." Bile swam up my throat, and I forced it down. "It probably never crossed his mind that I would fall in love and Wynter would uncover the truth."

"A pretty fucked-up truth at that. Listen, be patient with yourself. Stay focused on all the good in your life—your potential career with the NFL, Wynter, your friends. That's what gets me through the hard days."

I looked at him, then took another drink. "You saved me from being arrested. Hell, you and Wynter saved my future. I can't ever repay you for that, but thanks."

Kane tipped his chin at me. "We're bros, Quinn. I've trusted you with some dark shit, too. We have each other's backs. If we make it to the NFL, we'll still have each other's backs."

"Always."

We sat in silence, listening to the girls' chatter in the kitchen. The oven timer dinged, then Kane and I joined them. It was nice to be surrounded by my people and not have to worry about Adam coming home.

Chapter 52

Quinn

I sat in the society's office, waiting. It was time to walk away, but I knew that Wynter and I could still use the rooms if we wanted. I was game if she was.

A lot had happened over the last two weeks, and Adam had been officially charged with child abuse and possession of child porn. He would be lucky if he got out of prison before he died on those counts alone.

The police had practically salivated over Ky's journal and laptop with the evidence against Dr. Metcalf and Dr. Craig. After both items had been reviewed and validated as authentic, the bastards were thrown behind bars and now waited for their trials.

I hoped that somewhere Ky and Bell were watching as the truth unfolded. Even though Ky had pulled the trigger and I still had a lot of anger toward him, I understood that he'd been strongly influenced by a sick man. At first, I wasn't too keen on the idea about brainwashing, but then they found recordings of Dr. Metcalf's meditative hypnosis music he'd given Ky. It was way more than just music and Dr. Metcalf telling him to take deep breaths and clear his mind. The doctor had filtered in a subliminal message that included plans to shoot up the high school. Ky had been listening to that every night for months. Metcalf's records were located in his home, and it came out that it had all been a game, an experiment to the doctor to see if he could truly control another human being. Ky had just been a pawn the entire time.

My phone buzzed, and I removed it from my back pocket to see Remington's text pop up.

She's here. I told her to strip and secure herself after I left.
Perfect.

That day, I didn't use the skull mask or dress in black. Wynter knew exactly who I was, and for the first time in my life, I no longer felt as if I had to hide it.

I pocketed my phone and left the office, strolling down the hall to the room where Wynter waited for me. Slipping inside, my eyes drank her in and my cock sprang to attention.

"Hi, beautiful." And that she was—naked with one wrist handcuffed to the bed, waiting for me to do as I wished with her body.

"Quinn." She smiled at me, melting away all the darkness that had surrounded me for too long.

I walked over to her and grinned. "Who do you serve?"

"The Red Dragon."

I loved that Wynter was down to try almost anything. Plus, she was mine.

I crawled on the bed and settled between her legs, kissing her inner thighs, I ran the tip of my nose over Wynter's slit. Her sweet scent filled my nose and my dick throbbed, begging to be deep inside her slick walls.

I had her completely at my mercy as I buried my tongue in her cunt, wanting to taste every inch of her.

My cock twitched in my boxer briefs while my chin brushed over her stomach. I pinned her with a heated stare, a look that said *you're mine.*

Wynter's face flushed, her nipples hard and pleading for my attention. I moved my hands up her sides and over her breasts, my thumbs pinching the rosy buds, before I slipped one into my mouth and sucked.

Her body writhed beneath me.

I hopped up. "Quinn! Don't leave me hanging." She tugged on the handcuffs, but she was tightly secured to the bed.

I peeled off my clothes before strolling over to the cabinet where the toys and lube were stored. After selecting what I wanted, I returned to her. Kneeling on the mattress, I settled between her legs, then eased the vibrator inside her slick walls. My tongue circled her clit, and she moaned as she bucked against me.

Her juices ran down her ass cheeks, leaving a wet spot on the blanket.

"More, baby. Please."

Her pleas were needy, and I fucking loved her begging for me. I brought her to the edge, then removed the toy from her pussy. "You're not allowed to come yet." A mischievous smile graced my lips as I crawled on the bed and hovered over Wynter, then forced my cock into her mouth.

"That's it, baby. Take it all the way in." My eyes fluttered closed while I focused on her sucking me like I was the best thing she'd ever tasted.

Wynter gently scraped her teeth over my shaft and I shivered, about to lose my shit. She felt way too good, and I wasn't ready for our fun to be over yet. I pulled out and kissed a trail between her tits and down her tummy.

I nipped the insides of her creamy thighs as I shoved a finger into her long enough for her desire to coat it, then I pressed it against her asshole. I couldn't wait to get my cock in her ass.

"Turn around and get that ass up in the air." I crawled off her, making sure that the swivel on the handcuffs allowed her to turn over. When she was situated, my gaze landed on her round butt cheeks.

Grabbing the vibrator, I slid it into her sweet cunt but didn't turn it on.

"Oh, God," she murmured.

I pumped her a few times with the toy, then I moved my cock to her puckered hole. Grabbing the lube, I slicked her up before I pressed against her, then pushed the tip in.

"More," Wynter pleaded.

"You're so tight, baby. That sweet little ass is all mine." I eased in some more, still fucking her with the vibrator at the same time. Finally, I removed the toy and tossed it on the mattress. Digging my fingers into her hips, I worked my dick inside her and currents of electricity surged through me.

Her whimpers and moans filled the room as I reached between her legs and pinched her clit.

"Do you like me in your ass?" I asked, smacking and then massaging her bundle of nerves.

"Yeah," Wynter answered breathlessly. "Fuck me, Quinn."

"Who do you belong to, Wynter?"

"You."

"No one else will ever touch you again. This is all mine. Say it." I leaned against her back and reached for her beautiful throat, squeezing.

"No one ever again," she agreed.

My fingers tightened around her neck as I thrust into her.

Wynter trembled from her release, triggering my own. Damn, she felt so good. My balls tightened, my orgasm building as her walls clenched my shaft. I let out a groan while my body stiffened, my fingers wrapped her hair even tighter.

I eased out of her, then hit the little button on her cuffs and set her free. We collapsed on the bed, grinning at each other.

"I love you." I kissed the tip of her nose.

"You too, baby." Wynter snuggled up to my side, right where she belonged.

Chapter 53

Wynter

Four Months Later

I stood in the hall with Mom and Janine. We stared at Ky's door, our hearts heavy with the loss and horror that he'd lived through. Although Mom's guilt had subsided a little, I knew Ky's past would always haunt all of us.

"Are you ready?" I asked, looking at my family.

"No, but it's time to do this." Mom squeezed my hand.

"Janine?" I glanced past Mom to my sister.

She took a deep breath before she spoke. "I'm ready."

I understood how hard it would be for Mom and Janine to walk into Ky's room for the first time since the shooting because I'd already done it. After the truth had come out, I talked to Janine about what to do with Ky's room. It was important to leave some space for him, but it was also imperative to heal as much as possible, and staring at his closed door every day wasn't the best way to do it.

I turned the doorknob and readied myself. *I love you, Ky.* The musty air tickled my nose, and I sneezed. Strolling over to the window, I opened it wide. It was a gorgeous spring day and his room desperately needed sunshine and fresh air.

A cry escaped Mom as she and Janine stood in the middle of the floor and looked around. I assumed they were overwhelmed with memories—good and bad.

"He'll always be with us. I have to believe that." At times, I felt Ky's presence so strongly, I thought he was physically next to me. The only person I'd told was Quinn in case he had felt Bell's presence too. He had, and it gave us something special to share that others wouldn't understand.

"What do you want to keep, Mom? I would love at least one of Ky's posters."

"I want one that you don't take. I don't care which one since I didn't like his music, but just something of his." She swiped at the tears running down her cheeks. "I've not allowed myself to admit how much I miss him until after the journal and videos were released to the world."

"Quinn and I worked hard to have his and Bell's story heard. I think it's helped some people heal, or at least start."

"You and Quinn make an amazing team, Wynter. I'm really proud of you both." Mom sorted through Ky's clothes in the closet, taking a few of his shirts and tennis shoes to keep. "Girls, take what you want, then I'll box the rest up to donate."

Since there wasn't much left after the police confiscated most of his belongings, it didn't take us long to pick out a few of our favorite things to keep.

The doorbell rang, and I smiled at Mom and Janine. "They're here."

Janine and I raced down the stairs, our giggles filling the house for the first time in years. I paused before I answered, then spun on my heel. "No drooling." I winked at her, then flung the door open. I gawked, unable to speak as my hand flew over my mouth.

"Quinn?"

"Hey, beautiful." He kissed me.

"Holy shit." Janine poked her head around me, taking in the sight on our porch.

"Kane? Remington? Anderson?" I asked in shock. "You came too?"

"Ladies." Remington bowed. "We're at your service."

Janine giggled, eyeing him. I discreetly nudged her in the side.

"I'm here!" Brody bounded up the stairs behind his brother and joined the other guys, giving Janine a lazy smile.

"And us, bitch!" Gabby waved at me from the drive, Everlee, Brie, and Leighton by her side.

A black construction truck pulled up and four big guys hopped out. "And us!"

"Quinn?" I choked on my sob.

A white van rolled up next with the name of a painting company on the side. Three men climbed out, smiling. "Howdy!"

"What in the world?" Mom said from behind me.

I moved out of the way. "Quinn is here, and he brought a few more people."

Mom gasped, taking in the amazing sight of everyone who had shown up to help work on our home. Her hands flew over her mouth as tears streamed down her cheeks. "How are we going to pay for all this help?"

"You don't have to," Quinn explained. "Everyone volunteered to help. If there are any additional costs, then we'll work it out later."

I nearly knocked my mom over as I barreled past her and into Quinn's arms.

"I love you. Thank you so much."

He wrapped his arms around me. "I'll give you the world, Wynter. You don't even have to ask, beautiful."

A huge-ass furniture truck pulled up, and all I could do was laugh through my tears.

I moved out of the doorway to let our house fill with more people than I'd seen in it in years. When I'd first talked to Quinn about wanting to turn my old room into an office for mom and take Ky's as mine, he objected loudly. He said there was no way in hell I was moving back there. Brody's best friend, Tyler, and his family took Brody in so he could easily stay in the same school district and graduate. For the time being, I had the place with the girls, and Quinn had been staying with me, but graduation was right around the corner, and we had to figure some things out and soon.

But for the next four days, we would focus on getting the home squeaky clean and moving furniture. Little did I know that Quinn had reached out to his football friends and several local companies about my story. Once Dr. Metcalf and Dr. Craig had been arrested, the full story had been aired on 20/20, 60 Minutes, and other huge shows. Quinn and I had been hammered for paid interviews, and we took as many as our schedules could handle.

"Okay, here's what we're doing. Ky's room will be the guest room, and my old room will be Mom's new office. She's officially doing well enough to open her own bakery for delivery orders!" I clapped, giving Mom a big hug. "And seven months sober. So proud of you," I whispered in her ear.

Over the next five minutes, I explained the plan to Quinn's friends, the painters, the furniture company, and the contractors who had shown up, then they told me theirs. I cried as they laid out the schedule to paint the house inside and out, buff and polish the wood floors, haul off old furniture, and replace almost everything we had. Mom would also have a bigger kitchen and a remodel so she could grow her business. For now, she wanted to keep it small so she didn't get overwhelmed and could focus on Janine and her sobriety.

A blubbering mess, I hid my face against Quinn's chest. Only nine months ago, I couldn't wait to leave this hell hole and never speak to my mom again. It was still going to be a journey, but I felt as if we were on the right track. Maybe someday, Dad would even reach out and we could heal the pain with him, too. Only time would tell.

Exhausted but ready for a break, Quinn and I climbed into his car. His smile lit up his hazel eyes, sending my heart soaring.

"You look amazing."

"Thanks. Gabby and Leighton brought some fun clothes for us to go clubbing in." I tugged the very short skirt down my thighs.

"They have excellent taste." He shifted into drive and pulled onto the street. Two other cars carrying the four girls and the rest of the football players followed us.

It was almost ten that night, but we'd agreed to have some fun. Quinn had booked a hotel room for us, the girls booked one together, and so did the guys. We would park our vehicles there, then Uber to the club so we could drink as much as we wanted. I wondered who might end up in a drunken hookup later. I asked Quinn who he thought would end up together, and we made a bet. Whoever won got to pick the next room at the society.

A few hours later, I was sweaty, tipsy, and having the time of my life with my best friends and boyfriend. Anderson tried to dance with me, but Quinn checked his ass fast. I almost felt sorry for Anderson. He didn't mean any harm, but I'd learned quickly that Quinn was a jealous, possessive asshole when it came to me. I was okay with that.

The music quieted, and we all made it to the table while Quinn and Remington grabbed us another round of drinks.

"Girl, my ass is having too much fun!" Everlee said, leaning back in the booth, her long, toned legs peeking out from beneath her hot pink dress. She looked as stunning as the other two girls did.

"I'm glad you're here. And thank you all again for helping my family," I yelled over the crowd noise.

"What happened to the music?" Gabby looked around as Remington brought a tray of drinks to our table.

"That is strange. I guess the DJ took a break." I glanced at our group. "Where's Quinn?" I asked Anderson.

He gave me a half-shrug as the music started playing, but this time I didn't recognize it.

"Look!" Leighton said, shaking my arm and pointing to one of the cages. The door was open, and Quinn was standing inside of it as it lowered. His low tenor voice sent goose bumps over my skin as our gazes connected.

"Holy hell. I had no idea he could sing!" Gabby elbowed me in the side.

I melted into my chair as I listened to the lyrics.

She comes to me like a fading dream
Beautiful but just out of reach
She calls to me like a whispered prayer
Always so close, but not quite there

At the tips of my fingers, the tip of my tongue
She's the one I crave, but she can't be the one
The echoes of the past grip me tight
Forever keeping me from her light

I watch from the dark, craving her touch
I'll take what I want, take too much
If I can't have her light, I'll give her the dark
Despite what she wants, I'll leave my mark

At the tips of my fingers, the tip of my tongue
She's the one I crave, but she can't be the one
The echoes of the past grip me tight
Forever keeping me from her light

. . .

I'll mark her even as she marks me,
Taking from her as she takes from me
I'll drag us both into the abyss
And seal our fates with a stolen kiss

At the tips of my fingers, the tip of my tongue
She's the one I crave, but she can't be the one
The echoes of the past grip me tight
Forever keeping me from her light

I bit my lip, almost drawing blood in order not to cry and ruin my makeup. Although the song was upbeat, the lyrics were full of pain. Our pain. The pain that ruined us but ultimately brought us together.

As Quinn continued to sing, he stepped out onto the dance floor. The crowd parted while he walked toward me. Quinn took my hand and led me back to the cage, then shut the door before he pinned me in the corner with his body, singing all the while. The cage slowly moved up, and we hovered above the audience.

Quinn finished the song and a roar of applause filled the club.

"Wynter," Quinn said, "I don't ever want to be kept from your light again. You're my present and my future. I want to spend the rest of my life with you, whether it's a life on the road with the NFL or speaking professionally about our story in hopes of helping others. As long as you're there, that's where I want to be."

I squealed as Quinn reached into the pocket of his jeans and dropped to one knee. He flipped the ring box open.

"I love you. Say you'll take the rest of this journey by my side. Let me give you the world, Wynter. Say you'll marry me."

The crowd went ballistic as I nodded and held out my trembling hand for Quinn to slip the one-carat princess-cut engagement ring on my finger. Quinn turned off the mic and set it on the floor of the cage, then laid a searing kiss on me while he dipped me backward.

I giggled against his lips. He righted me, grinning.

"You're mine, and I won't ever let you go, Wynter Baldwin."

I threw my arms around his neck as "Call it Love" by Felix Jaehen and Ray Dalton started to play. Quinn and I had our first dance to this song, and now our first as an engaged couple ... in a cage. I was never going to forget his unique proposal.

Glancing out across the crowd, my pulse spiked. It had been a fucked-up road to find happiness, but I was in Quinn's arms and my friends were dancing below us with the football players, laughing and having fun. At one time, I didn't think I deserved to be loved and happy, but the first step to healing over my past had been to realize that, even though Ky had been used by a madman for evil, his actions impacted all of us, I wanted something better than to be the shooter's sister. I wanted to be loved and valued.

My attention returned to my fiancé, and I pushed myself up on my tiptoes, kissing the man that had nearly broken me, then pieced my shattered heart back together again.

Don't Miss **Illicit Obsession, a dark, stepbrother, sports standalone!** **Turn the page for the Sample!**

Toxic Obsession had originally looked like a very different book! **Check out the deleted scenes for Quinn and Wynter**! Click here.

Illicit Obsession Sample

The day my stepsister died; she took my heart with her.

Now, I'm a shell of a man, a cold-hearted monster.

Imagine my surprise when the love of my life shows up at Whitmore University alive and well.

I'm ready to make her pay for destroying me.

This isn't a fairy tale, and I'm sure as hell no knight in shining armor.

I have no problem dragging her into my dark world along with me.
But when I dig for the truth of what happened that fateful day
I can no longer deny how I feel about the only girl I've ever loved.
Others see us as an abomination and will do anything to keep us
apart.
And just as I vowed to destroy her,
I vow to protect her even if it costs me my life.
She was once my target. Now she's my everything.

From the international bestselling author, J.A. Owenby, comes
a ***new dark, forbidden stepbrother, sports, secret society,
second chance standalone romance. Illicit Obsession*** features a hot, **possessive/jealous hero and a strong,
curvy heroine** who knows how to tame her twisted and morally
grey stepsibling. **No cheating, no cliffhanger**, and a **happily
ever after** guaranteed!

****This standalone is a BRAND-NEW story with Jagger and
Ariana** from the Whitmore Elite Series. If you have read Forbidden
Obsession, this book is completely different but with the same char-
acter names.

Download Illicit Obsession on Amazon or **FREE** in Kindle Unlimited! **Click Here!**

Turn the page for the Sample of Illicit Obsession.

Jagger

"What the hell is this?" I blinked rapidly, trying to clear the haze from my eyes. "Where am I?" Despite the struggle against my restraints, it took me a few seconds to realize that I wasn't going anywhere due to the tightness of the ropes. I frantically searched around the room in an attempt to figure out where I was.

A dark chuckle bounced off the cement floor and walls. "Don't worry, Jagger Whitlock, it's all a part of the plan," the disguised voice said. He peered at me through the holes in the skull mask as he paced a circle around my chair. I recognized him from the society invitation video. *Fuck, what the hell did I do?*

"What do you want?" Despite the chilly air against my bare chest, beads of sweat formed on my forehead. The bastards knocked me out, drug me out of the field house, and tied me to a chair. Apparently, it would have been too much for them to grab some sweatpants for me. Instead, I shivered in nothing more than my boxer briefs. I had no idea who I'd pissed off, but I mentally skipped down that long list.

"You're one of the chosen. Try to relax and enjoy the ride." The fucker laughed even more.

My blood boiled in my veins. The familiar feeling of fury and hatred reawakened the beast inside me.

The masked and cloaked person didn't speak, but I felt the power bubbling beneath his skin. He might be crazier than I was. I wasn't sure if it was a good or a bad thing.

I attempted to control my breathing, but I had no fucking clue who was behind the mask and had taken me prisoner. If I bargained for my freedom, it would tickle his ego, and I would leave wherever I was in one piece.

"A brotherhood will fight for each other, but only if they have something on the line. Something to lose. In your case, you want a pro football career. I can make that dream come true, but why should I if you have no skin in the game?"

I blanched at him. "You can get me a pro ball contract?" A sense of foreboding enveloped me. This wasn't good. Whoever was talking to me was fucking with my head, and I strongly suspected I knew who it was. *Shit. This is bad. Real bad.* Until I found his weak spot, I had to play his sick game.

"If you can get me a deal with the Eagles, I'll give you my damn soul." Even though I realized it wouldn't serve me well, I gave him a disbelieving snort. "What are you, the devil's right hand?" What he didn't know was that I was the devil's left hand. Maybe we could work together and solve a big problem I had that refused to leave me alone.

The figure stopped in front of me and bent over, the nose of his skull mask a mere inch from mine. "I can make it happen, Jagger Whitlock, but what will you give me in exchange? I have no use for a wasted, dark soul like yours." He straightened, staring a hole right through me.

"Name your price. Hell, I've done a lot of dark shit in my life. I'm pretty sure I can offer you something you'll find valuable."

I shivered, sweat drying against my skin and making me even colder. Minutes ticked by without another word from him.

"What should I call you? Skull? I mean, you know *my* name. That doesn't seem fair, does it?"

He folded his arms in front of his chest. "You can call me King Cobra. I am the leader of a secret society, and if you pass the test, you'll join us."

I barked out a laugh. "Sorry, man. You should have led with that. You're wasting your time. I pledge to no one. This shit show wasn't what I signed up for." If he wasn't lying, it wasn't who I thought it was, which meant this situation wasn't as bleak as I first assumed.

A spotlight blasted through the darkness and I shrank away, trying to shield my eyes until my vision adjusted.

"It's easy, really. I'll make sure you have everything you want in exchange for your deepest, darkest secret."

My heart skidded to a stop, and I reminded myself to breathe. "No fucking way," I said quietly.

"Are you sure? You're ready to walk away from all of your dreams?"

"I don't know you, asshole. How am I supposed to blindly trust you?" I tugged on my wrist restraints again, as if they had magically loosened.

The light dimmed and moved, illuminating the rest of the small area. Several people stood on the other side of glass walls, all of them wearing the same skull mask and robe as the King Cobra, arms crossed over their chests in what could only be called a power stance. They looked immovable.

A voice began to filter into the room.

"Jagger," a female said.

My throat constricted as she continued to talk. "I love you, baby. Promise me we'll never be apart."

"I'll never let that happen," I replied on the recording.

"What the fuck? How did you get that?" I yelled over the recorded conversation. Her voice sliced through me like hot knives carving out my heart and tossing it on the cold ground.

"If our parents find out, they'll separate us," she said.

As hard as I fought against it, tears pricked my eyes. It had been years since I'd heard her speak.

"Tell us your secret, Jagger, then all of this will disappear. You can finally move forward. I'm doing you a huge favor."

My body trembled as the recording continued, with the sounds of us kissing and moaning as we made out. I remembered every sound, every breath. Even though I'd promised her, it had been our last night together.

Agony twisted my stomach into a million knots as I was overcome with grief—the soft lilt of her tone wreaked havoc on me.

"What happened, Jagger? What did you do?" the King Cobra asked.

I sucked in a huge breath, trying to clear my head.

"If you tell us, then you'll have everything you've dreamed of: a family, a career, and more women than you could imagine at your fingertips. Most of all, I can grant you hope. All I ask is for your darkest secret in return. Pledge your loyalty to each man here and they will do the same."

Frowning, I looked around the room at each person staring at me. I could have sworn a few of them nodded. Had they already talked about their pasts?

"Who are they?" I gestured to the strangers on the other side of the glass.

"Members. Each have shared their secret and now have successful lives and careers. They will forever be a part of the brotherhood. You can have the same thing. Once you tell us yours, they will share with you as well."

I swallowed hard, wishing I had some water. Closing my eyes, I listened to the recording continue to play. She had sent me the video later that evening. It was still on my phone, but I couldn't bear to watch it. Now, I was listening to it and so were the people in this room.

"You're a perfect fit for the society, Jagger. Name your price. We need someone like you."

"I want the pro deal. Nothing else matters. I have nothing left except football."

Moans of her pleasure filtered through the speaker, and it took everything inside me not to break down and sob.

"Then you'll have it. Don't misunderstand my intentions. I've hand-picked every member. You have skills and value. Let the society give you the world. All I need is something that proves to us that you're all in. Betrayal of the members is punishable by death, so are you willing to pay the price to make all your dreams come true?"

The recording finally stopped, and a heavy silence hung in the room as the others patiently stood and waited for my answer. I had nothing to lose. Whoever the King Cobra was, he realized what I would say, or he wouldn't have the recording. He was one clever son of a bitch. I had to give him that. If he could deliver on the pro deal in exchange for dirt that he already knew, what the hell was I really losing? The others had to share too. We would all be on an equal footing. I was familiar with the pledge process since my uncle was the president of an MC, the Dirty Bastards. I understood how that loyalty worked—a secret for a secret.

Taking a deep breath, I realized that if this asshole knew, anyone could find out, and that knowledge left me vulnerable. Hell, I would need some friends to help me bury it. All this time, I thought I was protected. As soon as I was finished here, I would need to find a way to erase my past once and for all. Maybe the King Cobra had done me a favor and saved my ass.

I squared my shoulders, ready. "I . . ." My voice cracked. "My biggest secret is—"

Grab Illicit Obsession on Amazon or **FREE** in Kindle Unlimited! **Click Here!**

Download Your FREE BOOK!

SIGN UP FOR J.A. OWENBY'S NEWSLETTER and download your FREE book, Love & Sins. Stay up to date concerning exclusive bonus scenes, updates on upcoming releases, and more. https:// authorjaowenby.com/newsletter/

Also by J.A. Owenby

The Wicked Intentions Series

Dark Intentions

Fractured Intentions

The Torn Series, inspired by True Events

Fading into Her, a prequel novella

Torn

Captured

Freed

J.A. OWENBY

Copyright © 2023 by J.A. Owenby

All rights reserved. In accordance with the U.S. Copyright Act of 1976, the scanning, uploading, and electronic sharing of any part of this book without permission of the publisher constitutes unlawful piracy and theft of the author's intellectual property. If you would like to use material from the book (other than for review purposes), prior written permission must be obtained by contacting J.A. Owenby. Thank you for your support of the author's rights.

This book is a work of fiction. Names, characters, places, and incidents either are products of the author's imagination or are used fictitiously. Any resemblance to actual persons, living or dead, business establishments, events, or locales is entirely coincidental.

Edited by: PNWSandy Edits from KRS Author Services

First Edition ISBN: 978-1-949414-88-2

All poems and song lyrics are written by Jennifer Lee Watkins Copyright © 2023

A Note From The Author

This book may contain sensitive material for some readers. River and Holden's story is considered a dark romance with language, sex, and violence.

About the Author

International bestselling author J.A. Owenby grew up in a small backwoods town in Arkansas where she learned how to swear like a sailor and spot water moccasins skimming across the lake.

She finally ditched the south and headed to Oregon. The first winter there, she was literally blown away a few times by ninety mile an hour winds and storms that rolled in off the ocean.

Eventually, she longed for quiet and headed up to snowier pastures. She now resides in Washington state with her hot nerdy husband and three purebred Siberian cats who insist on using her computer as their napping spot. She spends her days coming up with ways to torture characters in a way that either makes you want to throw your book down a flight of stairs or sob hysterically into a pillow.

J.A. Owenby writes new adult and romantic thriller novels. Her books ooze with emotion, angst, and twists that will leave you breathless. Having battled her own demons, she's not afraid to tackle the secrets women are forced to hide. After all, the road to love is paved in the dark.

Her friends describe her as delightfully twisted. She loves fan mail and wine. Please send her all the wine.

You can follow the progress of her upcoming novel on Facebook at Author J.A. Owenby and on Twitter @jaowenby.

Sign up for J.A. Owenby's Newsletter:

https://authorjaowenby.com/newsletter/
Like J.A. Owenby's Facebook page:
https://www.facebook.com/profile.php?id=100064095791999
J.A. Owenby's One Page At A Time reader group:
https://www.facebook.com/groups/JAOwenby